IRL

E.A. FIELD

Text copyright © 2023 **E.A. Field**

All rights reserved. For information regarding reproduction in total or in part, contact Rising Action Publishing Co. at www. risingactionpublishingco.com

Cover Illustration © **Nat Mack**

Distributed by Blackstone Publishing.

ISBN: 978-1-990253-33-1
Ebook: 978-1-990253-48-5

FIC031070 FICTION / Thrillers / Supernatural
FIC009050 FICTION / Fantasy / Paranormal

#IRL

Follow Rising Action on our socials!
Twitter: @RAPubCollective
Instagram: @risingactionpublishingco
Tiktok: @risingactionpublishingco

To the readers and dreamers who live thousands of lives

IRL

CHAPTER ONE

NOREENA GRACE MOON WAS AFRAID OF THE DARK, loud noises, strangers, and confrontation. In fact, she was afraid of leaving her apartment most of the time. It had taken a year for her to venture out of the house after her parents' fatal accident six years ago. Now, she put on whatever face she had to and tried to embrace the world, even if it sometimes crippled her. Three weeks ago, she'd sat in her car for half an hour because she wasn't sure she could make a left turn out of the parking lot for fear of crashing into another car.

Shadows jumped at her, unlit corners whispered to her, and bad news always came at night. After her twenty-first birthday a week ago, she thought she might graduate from using nightlights, but that failed experiment ended only an hour into it. Nora faced the dark whenever she couldn't avoid it, like tonight after a study session at a local coffee shop, but as she hurried home, she tried to stay within the glow of the streetlights.

Whoops and laughter erupted behind her as she rushed

from the library to her apartment. The white-sided buildings with green roofs were located just off campus on well-lit streets filled with college revelers. The early spring air invigorated the Knox University students despite the ever-increasing news of bizarre violent acts around the rural towns in Bunker and as far as Chicago. The air was dewy with floral scents coated in the chill of winter's grip—a typical mid-west Illinois spring. A group of young men paraded past Nora, drinking from flasks and cat-calling girls on the sidewalk.

Nora ducked her head and didn't make eye contact. She stayed in the streetlamp pools of light as her boots thudded faster and faster. This was a reason she kept her gym membership—the need to be able to outrun threats if necessary. Her keys clinked in her left hand as she neared her building. A shout to her right made her cringe.

"Hey, girl, looking for a party?" a guy hollered, and his friends chuckled behind him.

"Asians need to represent!" an Asian guy said with a shout and clapped his friend on the shoulder. They didn't bother her any further as they made their way down the street toward the pubs.

There were quite a few students of Asian descent on campus. Nora was used to being a minority, but at Knox it was like a rite of passage to get in as an Asian. She was also in the minority of her chosen major of psychology and sociology. When she often had trouble facing her own issues, the irony of wanting to help others with their fears or trauma wasn't lost on her. She sometimes wondered if she took those classes to support herself as much as anyone else. Someday, she hoped to be a counselor or psychologist that worked with adoptees or potential adopters. Her uncle's voice again whispered to her, *you sure you don't want to do anthro? Follow in the ancient footsteps of man?*

Her archeologist uncle had been a second father to her after the car accident that killed both her parents. For a year after the accident, she'd lived with her uncle as the house was sold off and her parents' things were put away into storage or sold. She shuddered at the memory and shoved it deep down like she always did. There was no sense in dragging up the past when it already haunted her every day.

She ran up the one flight of stairs to her apartment and unlocked the door with a quick twist of the key. *Always practice something before it becomes an emergency*, the words of Uncle Emin floated through her mind. She slammed the door and locked the deadbolt. Her mother had always laughed off Emin's sense of danger and preparedness. Nora wished she had her mom's sense of adventure and whimsy; if her parents had been alive, perhaps she would have. She'd always feared the dark, but the car crash had set her fears spiraling out of control, like a deflated balloon flopping on the asphalt trying to get lift.

"Why does Jess have to leave all the lights off?" she whispered. The small two-bedroom apartment had large picture windows to let in natural light, but the sliver of moon wasn't illuminating anything to Nora's satisfaction.

As she went around the room, switching on lamp after lamp, she could hear the guys outside rambling off toward the downtown area. Jessica's jacket and several pairs of shoes were scattered all over the living room space, including the red leather sofa and lounge chair. Her roommate was a brief acquaintance that had become one of the most unusual friendships Nora had ever had. At first, Jess had seemed like a typical college girl, stressed out but living her best life.

After a few months, though, Nora had found herself missing pens and then shoes. When she confronted Jessica about it, the other girl apologized. She had kleptomania. She'd given back the shoes and said she was on medication, but sometimes she had the tendency to take things.

Nora figured it was too late to get a new roommate, and really, what were a few pairs of shoes and writing utensils? At least Jess wasn't a serial killer. Jess also paid half the rent on time and was out a lot, which meant she brought back food and necessary supplies like tampons and ice cream. Nora preferred to stay in the apartment for as long as she could, and Jess never judged her for that. She was careful where she put things now and kept track of them. And, selfishly, she thought living with Jess would help her understand kleptomania. That, in turn, could assist her in her chosen career path.

Nora flipped on the TV and sank into the plush couch. She glanced between the partially drawn curtains at a cloud-filled night sky and the artificial glow of bars still open in the distance. Clubs pulsed music until the early hours. She didn't mind the noise—it drowned out her thoughts so she could sleep most nights.

The screen showed a blonde news anchor with a frazzled expression and raised brows. "I'm not sure what I'm seeing. Five people, two men and three women, are confronting the Carlton police in a stand-off at the 7-Eleven. Shots have been fired ..." The woman was cut off as more gunshots cracked the static, and she backed up. The camera panned away from her to show the muzzle flashes of weapons.

Nora switched to the internet news app on the TV. The broadcasts wouldn't show what was happening, but the likelihood that a few people were recording with their phones was pretty high. She switched to a streaming news app. As expected, the slightly grainy footage popped up in real-time.

Nora was no expert on guns—she'd only ever shot her uncle's Remington 870 shotgun— but this standoff looked like it involved more than pistols. The cops shouted for a cease-fire, but the people didn't stop. She bit her lip, and her finger paused over the power button. She didn't want to end her night on a story like this. Yet she was mesmerized when the five perpetrators ran out of ammunition, left the cover of the store, and charged at the police officers.

"What the hell?" Nora grabbed a pillow and clutched it across her abdomen.

The officers hesitated until it was apparent the five were not surrendering or stopping. They ran at the officers with raised clubs, bats, and tire irons. In seconds, it was over. Five bodies lay prone on the pavement. They blurred together when the camera shifted quickly. Emergency vehicle lights made eerie shapes as they lit up the frightened faces of bystanders, the concerned expressions of police officers, and the dark shapes of the dead bodies.

The person's phone camera panned to the reporter standing near a news van. Despite her flawless makeup, she appeared shaken. The person inched closer, so the audio picked up.

"We're seeing several outbreaks of violence like this throughout the Chicago area. Gun incidents are higher than normal, and we're urging residents to stay indoors after dark and be vigilant. Police are on alert throughout the suburbs, and those further from Chicago are encouraged to report any unusual activity immediately."

Nora switched back to cable and another channel where

a Hallmark movie played. The soothing music and love-struck couple calmed her nervous brain. Bunker, Illinois, was about two hours from the city, and its residents were mainly cows and corn. *There's nothing to worry about.*

Nora got up to start her bedtime routine. Structure was imperative to her daily life, and years of therapy taught her that she felt more in command when she did little things she could control.

Her cell phone lit up, and Uncle Emin's ringtone played.

Nora grabbed it and slid the button to talk. "Uncle Emin?"

"... Nora? Can you ... me?"

"Barely! Are you okay?"

Her nerves tingled, and the darkness seemed to stretch around her.

"I've been detained, and I'm ... trouble. Don't worry, but do you have the gift I sent you last month?" Uncle Emin's voice was hoarse as if he'd been shouting too long, and his words rushed.

"Yes, I have it." Nora went to her room and retrieved the package that weighed about five pounds, still wrapped in protective cardboard and foam. She hadn't decided where to display the beautiful, ancient piece of rock with tribal hieroglyphics carved on the gray face.

"You need to keep it safe, all right? Don't let it out of your sight!" Uncle Emin's voice cracked, and he took deep breaths. "They're coming. I don't have time to explain."

"Are you in the city still? What's going on?" Nora's voice reached a higher pitch, and she clutched the phone tightly like it was a lifeline to her uncle. Her fingers traced the edge of the broken stone, and a chill went up her arm.

"Nora, just keep ... shit. They're here. I'm at the

university, but the CDC is coming for me. I'll ... get out."
Uncle Emin's voice hardened in anger as shouts erupted in
the background. The call disconnected.

Nora tried calling him back, but it went to voicemail.
She paced her room. She wanted to leave to find her uncle,
but what good would going to the city do? He would
probably be long gone, or would she find him in trouble?
She debated calling the police to help. But if it ended up
being something silly, like Emin overreacting or one of his
colleagues playing a prank on him, then she'd be the one to
look stupid. It wouldn't be the first time one of the
professors pulled a joke on the older man. But her uncle had
sounded serious ... Nora grumbled as she debated with
herself. All her classes on dealing with psychological trauma
didn't help now. Textbooks would only get her so far. Black
and white words didn't tell her how to deal with real pain
and stress in the moment except to breathe and focus on
what she *could* control.

She wrapped up the artifact. It was one of Uncle Emin's
personal finds. It should have been in a museum, but he'd
snuck it to her, saying they had other artifacts of higher
worth. This one wouldn't be missed as it was a small fraction
of stone, a fraction of history. He knew she loved ancient
history. Not enough to follow in his career footprints, but
enough to appreciate a piece of history on her bookshelf.
Was someone after it? She'd thought it was simply an
interesting artifact he'd brought back from a dig. Nora had
always appreciated rare pieces of history, as had her parents.
She recalled her dad saying Emin was like the cool brother he
never had. James Moon had been what he'd called a "boring
but reliable accountant." It paid the bills, and he was smart
with money. Nora never felt pressure from him to follow his

career path nor from her mom, who worked as a school counselor. However, she found she had a keen interest in psychology and social work, so perhaps she was destined to follow a little in her mom's wake.

She cradled the box in her lap and folded the cardboard edges down. She'd keep it safe.

Nora pinched her brows together as she ran through a preliminary plan to stay put. *I could go into the city just to check. No, I'll wait ...* Nora fought with herself and picked up her phone again. It was one of many times she wished her parents were still alive so she could call them for advice. She thumbed through to find the last text message from her gamer friend, Wesley. He could offer at least some insight, if not distraction.

The door to the apartment burst open.

CHAPTER TWO

NORA JUMPED AND ALMOST DROPPED HER PHONE.

"Nora? You must be home; you'll never guess what just happened!" Jessica called.

Her roomie always made dramatic entrances. Nora took several deep breaths to calm her heart palpitations. You'd think she'd be used to this by now. Yet a big part of her was relieved not to be alone anymore.

Jess' feet raced through the apartment, and she skidded to a stop in Nora's doorway. "Can I turn off, like, two of these lights?" The switches flicked and shadows filtered outside Nora's door.

Nora frowned. *Stop being a pussy who jumps at every loud noise.* But loud noises reminded her of the nightmares she kept having of what her parents might have gone through when the semi-truck had hit their Lexus. Her therapist said the night sweats and terrors were a form of post-traumatic stress disorder. Even though she hadn't been there when the accident occurred, her mind imagined her parents' last emotions and reactions. She conjured everything from their frightened expressions to the agonizing final breaths to their thoughts about what would happen to their only daughter.

She knew from her studies that the brain could not discern between reality and imagined events, so every time she thought about it, it would trigger a physical response in her body. The fight or flight. Certain parts of her brain would be oxygen-deprived and send her into a spiral.

"What happened?" she asked.

Jessica was the kind of girl who would get into a brawl for Nora but would also leave the bar with a new guy and leave her car behind. The klepto was something they'd both learned to live with. It was harmless, and Jess hadn't had an incident in at least a month. Jessica's tall, willowy frame swayed against the door jamb. She swept a manicured hand through her long, curled, brown hair.

"I was chased by a random guy. There's a full moon or something, chica, look!" Jessica pushed up her sleeve, and a giant red wound made a semi-circle on her right forearm.

"Is that a bite mark?" Nora rose to inspect her friend's injury. On her way, she couldn't resist the impulse to dash past her roommate and check that she'd locked the front door.

"I locked it, Tick-tock," Jess said, following after. Nora was satisfied that they were secure and turned to Jess with an apologetic face. She put up with Jess' idiosyncrasies, and her friend was willing to do the same for her. Nora had a habit of checking things like locks obsessively. As if they could keep the world out.

"I hate that nickname."

"I know, but it suits you."

Nora avoided arguments about her nickname when she

could. It wasn't worth the effort. She was more concerned about Jess' wound. "I think you should go to the hospital. Was it from a dog or something?"

"No, from a guy. What the fuck." Jessica chuckled and went to the bathroom to wash it and disinfect the wound. "I thought the guy was pranking me, but Matt had to step in when he started biting. It's fine, though. I don't need a doctor to tell me to wash it out and keep an eye on it for infection. Have you seen the news tonight too?"

Nora was used to Jess' nonchalant demeanor about nearly everything. Normally, it balanced Nora's out, but tonight she was on edge. She took several deep breaths. She was trying extremely hard these days to remain in control of her fear. *I cannot control anything but the space I'm in.* She reminded herself she was safe right now—she was in control of the apartment space. Lights were on. She could escape to her room if necessary.

"Yeah, I watched something on violent outbursts or whatever," Jess said as she peered at the bite mark with a grimace.

"Doesn't look too deep," Nora said as she looked at Jess's arm. The bite was shallow, but it had broken skin. Jess put a band-aid over it.

"I heard about those riots too!" Jess sighed. "Man, I've had my ass grabbed, but biting? What the hell is that? After I kicked him in the shin and Matt shoved him, he finally ran. How was studying?"

"I really think you should go to the emergency room!" Nora couldn't help the high pitch of her voice. She swallowed to make it go away.

"I'm fine, girl. Come on, how are you? How was study group? You're more on edge than me."

Nora sighed. She knew a lost battle when she saw one. Jessica wasn't going to any emergency room, and that was that. "Tea was good, but I hate study groups. I think I'm ready for Professor Hick's sociology test. Did you have fun with Matt?"

"You know it. He took me to Sully's, and then we had a few drinks at Downpour. Have you tried a watermelon tornado? It's gross." Jess droned on about how great her date was and how campus guys were dicks. "You should try a coffee sometime too. I still can't believe you don't like coffee."

Nora shrugged. She liked the smell of coffee, but the taste was too bitter for her. She'd tried it with cream, sugar, and flavor shots and still couldn't get used to it. There were other ways to get caffeine.

"We could go to Brewton again and troll the hot baristas," Jess said with a giggle.

"I'll pass." Nora pursed her lips. Every time they went out for drinks, it seemed the guys she was interested in were drawn only to Jess. Nora wasn't unrealistic—she knew she wasn't as bold as her friend. She didn't have her mother's flare for beauty and style. It was one of the areas Jess helped her. The vivacious brunette's big energy often rubbed off on everyone around her, which gave Nora the guts to strike up conversations, even if they ended up going nowhere. Part of it was that Nora was almost too focused on reading people. She enjoyed watching them, but sometimes she read into them too much, convincing herself a guy wasn't interested due to his body language. Yet, her intuitiveness to others was part of the reason she'd chosen psychology/sociology as her major and minor. She knew it was a little selfish to choose her major based on her past trauma, but she needed more tools than seeing a therapist to deal with her parents' deaths. She needed to be proactive and help other people, even if the motive was to make herself feel better sometimes.

She could almost hear her mother's voice in her head. *You're beautiful, sweetie; you need to own it. Look at those dark eyes, high cheekbones, and thick hair.* Even though she was a European mix with no Korean genes in sight, Diana had always made sure to keep up with Asian beauty trends. Nora didn't remember her adoption, as she'd come to the United States at two years old. Nora had no desire to track down her birth parents, not even after the car accident. What would be the point? It wouldn't change anything or give her the "answers" she had no desire to obtain. Her adoptive mom had stayed at home for the first eight years of Nora's life and then taken up a second career as a school counselor. Perhaps it was because of this that Nora wanted to work in psychology, to hang on to that part of her mom she could identify with.

Nora checked the front door lock again. Still bolted. Then she went to her room as Jess turned on the TV in the living room.

"You want to watch something?" Jess asked.

"Nah, thanks. I'm going to game."

"Nerd."

"You love me." Nora smiled as Jess waved a casual hand at her.

Nora passed her reflection in the mirror as she closed her door. Being petite and half-Korean meant most people were taller than her. She hadn't been told much about her birth parents, but her genealogy suggested Korean on her mother's side and a European mix on her father's. She brushed back long, dark hair that was freshly washed and still holding its curl. She might not have Jess' porcelain complexion and honey-highlighted brunette hair with hazel eyes, but she did have something many others liked online. She could be as bold and beautiful as she wanted on the internet.

Nora couldn't help the smile that crested her lips as she started up her laptop. The game icon loaded: *Pirate Scourge*. Her gamer tag, Hypernova, appeared with her picture. It was a real picture of her face, taken on a day leaden with clouds last fall when Jeremy had been the guy she'd thought would be her love forever; how things changed in a matter of months.

The game's adventure music piped through her headphones, and she relaxed a fraction. The online, first-person shooter cooperative game distracted her busy, anxious brain. Her friend list popped up, and she scanned it to see who was on.

BigCrusty22, Pyro50, Bear, Dr. Pho, Cupcake, Rimfire, AlphaSnake, Princess Xena, and Tango Strike.

Wesley, a.k.a. Tango Strike, was on. Nora swallowed as she started the game. Would he join? She knew all the guys quite well, but there was something different about Wesley. She'd first noticed it when they'd started gaming over three years ago—he'd stay by her side and watch her six. He'd offer advice only if asked and didn't make lewd comments.

Tango Strike's message box flashed on her screen, and Nora's heart leapt. She pursed her lips and shook her head. She really shouldn't care what some guy over the internet had to say. More often than not, they spoke online through the game even though she had his number. It wasn't like they texted all that often ... but he *had* given her his number. Did that mean something more?

He'd also texted her a picture of himself. He had dark hair, equally dark, hooded eyes, skin the shade of a perfect beach tan, a strong chin, and light stubble that defined his prominent cheekbones. His broad shoulders were covered in a navy, button-down shirt with a black tie, and his narrow waist was cinched with a silver-buckled belt and black slacks. He was business casual, but he looked like a guy who would also be at home lounging by a pool.

Jessica had forced Nora to send him a picture of herself from a Caribbean vacation a year ago, and to her surprise, he'd been very complimentary. Nora wasn't fooling herself that she could even pretend to be near beach model status, but she had a healthy body, and if she wasn't feeling brave enough for the gym, she'd do video workouts. But there was no way a guy who looked like Wesley would ever be into her in real life.

Hey, you gaming? Wesley.

Nora typed in the chat box. *Yeah, late-night studying and need to blow off steam.*

I'll join you if you want.

Yes!

If Bigtool joins I'm rage quitting.

Nora bobbed her head even though no one could see. *I'll quit with you.*

The game loaded, and pirates stalked about on the screen on their ships. Treasure maps marked different events they could play. It was a mix of modern weaponry and old-time guns and cannons. Nora picked her female avatar and armed her with a cutlass, sniper rifle, and pistol. The objective was to take as many enemy ships as possible and bury their treasure or use it to upgrade weapons. The enemy ranged from other pirates (players) to zombie-like creatures supposedly native to the Caribbean islands to the British East India Trading Company crews.

Nora slid her headphones on and adjusted the microphone.

"Hey, Moonbeam."

At the sound of Wesley's deep, raspy voice, all thoughts of her uncle's strange call and Jess' bite wound faded. His nickname for her was much less irritating than Jess's. He'd said it meant "flashlight" in Marine jargon, and Nora thought it was a funny coincidence as he didn't know her last name was Moon. He'd given her the name because she liked to turn on her flashlight all the time in the game, even when it was light out. Even in the game, her fear of the dark inserted itself.

"Hi." Nora couldn't keep the smile from her voice.

Wesley's low voice transmitted on the other end. "We ended in Mer-cove last time; let's raid that again to see if anything better drops." The music from the game swelled, and they loaded into the cove where their ship was beached on the sand. It was called 'careening,' and it was a necessary part of the game if they wanted to win. The mission was to repair it while fighting off the undead.

"Aye." Nora grinned as she slipped into her pirate persona. "You're not out on a date or having fun?" She couldn't help asking. They'd flirted around the relationship line for a while now, and she wasn't afraid to find out if he was dating anyone yet. He lived close by in the "suburbs of Chicago," but they'd never given out exact addresses. They'd also never crossed into the territory of meeting in person or "IRL." For Nora, it was too risky, and he'd never pushed her. She also didn't want to explain why she only left the house when she had to and how meeting at a coffee café was also a stretch for her. The more she invested in people, the more she had to reveal. Nora wasn't about to mess up a routine that worked and got her out of bed every day. School, working out, and home were pretty much all she could handle.

"I could be, but the city has a curfew now. Everyone in by nine," he said. "Why are you home on a Friday?"

"Oh, wow, I didn't realize it was that serious. I was studying for an exam on Monday. I wonder if the campus will have a curfew soon."

"I'd bet on it. Isn't it almost spring break there?" Wesley chuckled, but there was tension in his voice. He seemed distracted tonight—as was evidenced when he took a bullet to the shoulder in the game. "Got a lot of Mobs here."

Nora hurried to cover him. The Mobs—mobile object blockers to some or simply 'monsters' to others—ran at Wesley's avatar with swords slashing and pistols firing. His health dipped, but he patched his player with a quick rum potion. She returned fire at the barrage of undead that swarmed toward their beached ship.

"Yeah, but I'm not going anywhere. At least the weather's getting nicer for most people. I like the cold." Nora tapped keys and clicked her mouse furiously. Shot after shot felled body after body, Mob after Mob. The cerulean waters turned black with blood, and the crash of waves made it hard to see the oncoming enemy. They were blobs of vaguely human shapes with blackened, peeling flesh that wielded swords.

Wesley could stand, and he helped kill the herd of undead. "I like the cold too."

"So, you've seen the crazy violence in the city now, huh? It's like people are losing their minds," Nora said. She cursed as an undead swiped at her and took half her health. "Not unlike this game." She gritted her teeth as the zombie pirate tried to attack her. Wesley had her back and shoved two off, so she could shoot them. Her fingers clacked the keys even faster.

"Yup. I had two guys try to jump me last night."

"Whoa."

"It's fine. They weren't serious."

"How is being mugged not serious?" Nora shuddered at the thought. What if something had happened to him? What if she'd never spoken to him again and never known what happened? *See, this is why you don't want to get attached to people. Even online.*

"It wasn't serious because they didn't have weapons and ran the second after I threw a punch," Wesley replied in his calm baritone. She imagined him squaring up on two skinny punks, and it wasn't hard to imagine his broad shoulders and angled chin intimidating people.

"And what is it you do?" Nora teased. She'd been trying to get him to give her a straight answer for a year.

"I'm a pawnbroker." Wesley chuckled.

Nora snorted. "Okay. I at least am honest when I said I'm a college student."

"I was honest when I said I'm way older than you. Work is work. Nothing special," Wesley replied and let off a volley of shots that sent the last undead to its watery grave. The ocean turned back to brilliant blue, and the beach washed itself. Their ship listed to one side, needing repairs.

A ping sounded, and she saw *Cupcake* and *Rimfire*, also known as Elena and Kyle, join their game. Six people could join a campaign at a time, but they liked no more than four because it was often frustrating to get six people to go in the

same direction and agree on action. Elena had spoken with
Nora outside the game and liked getting to know her. They
didn't exchange intimate details, but Nora knew she lived
somewhere in Michigan and loved antiques and crocheting.

"Heya, anal bitches. Copy," Rimfire said over his mic,
and Nora greeted him with a cheerful hello. Sometimes he
could be too much, but she wanted to have fun tonight.

"What's up, y'all?" Cupcake answered, and her avatar
inspected the ship. "You destroyed the *Fancy*, guys?"

"Hey, guys. Yeah, we saved it from islanders, but it needs
help," Nora said.

"Copy that," Wesley said with a laugh.

"The fuck you do to it?" Rimfire guffawed and his
avatar, a highly overdressed pirate king, started to search for
materials to fix the ship.

"Undead, dude," Nora said. She scavenged around the
island for supplies and found pieces of driftwood. The game
wasn't exactly realistic, but no one played games for reality.
There was too much of that already.

"I found some barnacle remover. Come help me,"
Cupcake said, and her avatar beaconed.

"I'm on the other side of the island. It'll be a sec." Nora
hefted the wood and started to walk in the general direction
of Cupcake.

"I'll come with. I have a lot of wood," Rimfire said with
a short puff.

"I'm good with Tango, thanks." Nora rolled her eyes.

"Tango Strike? A little help?" Cupcake's voice took on a
decidedly flirty tone, and Nora chuckled to herself. They
might be friends, but Nora had a healthy understanding of
internet relationships. They didn't share too many intimate
details, yet there was a definite camaraderie built up over

years of gaming together. Cupcake flirted with every guy they gamed with and almost seemed to like the challenge of putting herself between Wesley and Nora. Yet her friends' familiar banter and voices helped her control what she could and forget about the things she couldn't.

"I'm with Hypernova," he answered, using Nora's gamer tag and not her name.

"It's not all about *her* all the time, Tango." Cupcake giggled lightly, but Nora heard the jealousy under it. She didn't let it bother her because there was nothing to be jealous of.

"It is."

Nora's breath hitched, and she licked her lips. How did she respond to that?

Rimfire saved her the answer. "Come on, penetrators, let's get out on the open water before we're attacked again. I want to do some plundering, and you know what I mean!"

Cupcake giggled and said he could plunder her as long as he gave her diamonds. They started to salvage materials, and the ship was ready to sail in a matter of minutes.

Nora stood at the ship's bow as her screen lit up with the open ocean and a red horizon. She gazed at the peaceful, endless possibilities in the game and wondered if life could be that way for her. She shook her head. With her OCD tics and careful way of living, there wasn't room for spontaneity or surprise. Nora glanced at her phone to see if her uncle had called back yet or texted. Nothing.

She needed to check the front door one more time to be sure it was locked.

CHAPTER THREE

WESLEY LOGGED OUT OF PIRATE SCOURGE AND SAT back in his chair. Two hours of sailing and commandeering ships were enough for him tonight, especially with Cupcake's high-pitched voice and attempts to flirt with him. Then her friend joined their party, and it escalated from there. There was only so much girl talk he could take while in game. Add in Rimfire's overtly sexual innuendos, and it was like he was back in high school.

He stretched and was delighted when Hypernova invited him to continue their conversation via video chat on Serma, the universal gaming chat and forum server. He accepted the request. He knew a lot more about Nora than she knew—or might want him to know. That was part of his nature. He had the resources to do a background search on her, but he didn't; he pieced together the information she gave him. He was good at stitching together data to form a bigger picture.

It wasn't hard with her phone number to figure out where she lived or more accurately, if she lied about where she lived. She hadn't. While she'd made no comment about attending university, she'd let slip the mascot of a charging horse. The only school around with that mascot was Knox.

His US marshal badge sat on his desk next to his computer. Wesley let out a breath. Was it his nature to be curious about everyone? Suspicious even? There was something about Nora that made him protective, and he couldn't understand it. He'd never been compelled to want a girlfriend or wife to protect because he'd seen too many abused women, too many abusive women. His abusive mother included. It wasn't that he didn't trust women. It was that he'd seen too much of humanity's wasted potential.

"You look zoned out. You tired?" Nora's sweet voice brought him back to reality. Her picture on the video chat was clear, if slightly grainy. Her long dark hair was down tonight. Her lightly freckled face smiled at him.

Wesley ensured she didn't see much past his wall with some metal art hanging on it. She did the same, he assumed. He couldn't see anything but a pale blue wall with a dog painting. They didn't video chat much, so he was pleasantly surprised she wanted to tonight.

"Yeah, sorry, got caught up in a work email." Wesley lied and wasn't surprised how easily it came to him.

"So, a pawnbroker must get a lot of emails at all hours of the night?" she said.

He didn't like lying, but the truth often caused a lot of tension. No one wanted to be friends with a marshal unless they needed help. And if they needed marshal help, it probably wasn't a great situation. The marshals didn't even have the stigma of friendly neighborhood cops because hardly anyone really knew what a US marshal did exactly— even if they had seen *The Fugitive*. Wesley had trained at Federal Enforcement Training Center in Glynco, Georgia.

Nineteen weeks of training in surveillance, use of force, high-threat trials, computer training, and several other fields. After working in all fields, he had chosen fugitive apprehension. But all his hard work had gone to shit when a situation pursuing a trafficker went terribly wrong.

And now he questioned whether he wanted to stay in the marshal service. Maybe it was *too* much of a fit for him; maybe he liked the violence and uncertainty more than he should.

"I do." Wesley kept the answer short to cover the unease at her question. He wished he could summon the courage to tell her the truth, but it wouldn't do any good. They weren't ever going to meet in person, even though they lived close to each other. It wasn't a good idea, and he got the impression Nora had a mistrust of people that he didn't fault her for. She was smart to not meet strange guys from online.

He tried to imagine what it was like being a woman and how much they had to protect themselves from guys. Not that he didn't get into trouble. But it was pretty universal that a girl in a dark alley was much more likely to meet an unpleasant end than a guy. Wesley trained hard never to be the guy who met an untimely end or the guy who was surprised by the callousness of humanity. He prepared for situations constantly until it was second nature. *'We don't rise to the level of our expectations; we fall to the level of our training'* was a quote by the Greek poet Archilochus and used by Chief Gibson to all the new trainees. It had stuck with Wesley.

"Are you sleeping any better?" she asked. Wesley's instinct was to dodge the question, but he'd been the one to confide that fact in her.

He didn't sleep much, and when he did, it was fractured

dreams of bullets and fire. Or his mother yelling at his father and throwing plates at his head. His father never fought back.

"Nah. The sleeping pills work for about five hours, and then I'm awake." Wesley checked the clock on his nightstand: 11:45. He was on leave and supposed to see a therapist the next day. He detested being made to speak with shrinks but hated the courts even more. Luckily, the therapy session was only one of two strongly encouraged, or mandated, by Chief Deputy Oliver Gibson. Wesley wasn't about to give his superior a reason to think pulling his gun was because of mental imbalance. The only thing bothering him was how a shoot-out with five fatalities would tie his job up for months as they investigated every corner of the situation.

"Didn't you wear that same shirt a few weeks ago when we chatted?" Nora asked. She tilted her head in a way that let him know she was teasing.

Wesley was surprised she noticed. It *was* the same shirt, a black T-shirt with a bulldog. He either slept or worked out in it. Then again, she'd said she was studying psych and sociology, so she might have been a stickler for details like him.

"You caught me. I only own five shirts." Wesley laughed with her.

"I'm sure that's not true." Nora yawned and stretched, showing a sliver of skin on her abdomen, and her breasts strained against the red patterned shirt. Wesley fought the urge to flirt harder—he didn't even know how if he were honest with himself. What would he say? Something stupid about how she should show him more of her shirts? Except lower cut? He shook his head at himself. That sounded super pervy.

"I should let you get some sleep. Any fun weekend plans?" Wesley asked to divert her asking further about him.

"No, not really. Just more studying. Although, my uncle called me tonight very upset. I should check on him." Nora sighed. "I hate going into the city, though. I can't drive worth a damn, and I'm going to get myself killed one day."

"What was wrong with your uncle?"

"Don't know. He asked if the gift he had given me a month ago was safe. He pulled a Gandalf on me," she said with a giggle and performed a bad impression of the wizard in the *Lord of the Rings*.

Wesley chuckled. "Well, I hope whatever it is, *is* safe. I bet he'll check in with you tomorrow. Let me know if you're still worried."

Nora's voice came over the mic. Her face loaded on the screen as the internet went in and out for a second. "Does that mean I should text you?" She asked it as a joke, but Wesley wanted exactly that.

He didn't know how to say that in a good way. "Uh, sure, yeah." He tried to paste a smile on his face that wasn't awkward. He didn't think he succeeded, judging from her lowered gaze and how she picked at her nails. He sounded like he was as interested in her as in watching paint dry.

Nora picked up on it. "Okay, well, have a good night, then."

"Thanks, you too."

The connection and video went silent, and Wesley cursed. *You can't even muster the will to try to flirt with her? You might as well be dead.*

The truth was worse. Wesley frowned and shut down his computer. Bourbon sat in a crystal glass in his small living room. He rarely drank because of what it had done to his dad; he'd coped with his abusive wife by using liquid courage. But sometimes, the tang and rich flavors of bourbon soothed his nerves. Wesley glanced around the two-bedroom condo that was spacious enough for more than one person and located near Lake Shore Drive. He'd worked hard for a place like this. A place his dad hadn't ever visited, and that was fine with Wesley. He didn't need his family to validate his life.

"Wesley, come on." His dad's soft whisper woke him, the whiskey on his breath a faint echo of the misery they lived in.

Wesley woke from sleep to see his dad and sister standing at the edge of his bed. His mother's crashing of plates and low moans told him she was in another one of her moods. His nine-year-old brain understood that she'd calm down in a few hours, but she was dangerous now. He dressed and followed his dad down the stairs. They crept over broken dishes, and a knife stuck out of the wall. They quietly made their way to the car.

His dad put a finger to his lips and unlocked the gray Honda. His sister's glassy, sleep-deprived eyes flicked to him for a second as she climbed into the back seat. His dad tucked a blanket over them as he started the engine. Oldies music softly crooned from the radio. It would forever remind Wesley of these night drives when they had a slight taste of freedom and fun.

"Where are we going?" Wesley rubbed his face, waking up fully.

"How about a milkshake?" His dad's voice was hoarse, as if he'd been yelling for hours.

"Okay. How long will we be gone?"

His dad shook his head.

"Why don't you call someone?" Wesley had often heard his dad threaten to call the cops or his mother's therapist. Wesley didn't have a high opinion of therapists even at a young age. His mother never seemed to get better.

"She's in a mood again. She needs to be alone for a little bit." His dad sped them down the black strip of backwoods road toward a midnight diner. This particular diner knew their family well, and Wesley had seen the pretty waitress slip whiskey into his dad's coffee before. It made his dad happy, and when he was happy, Becca was happy. When both his dad and sister were okay, Wesley was okay.

Wesley inhaled the earthy, woodsy smell of dewy trees and undergrowth. Their small town in Texas was hardly the place people wanted to stay. He sighed. He knew already that he wanted to live alone when he grew up. He wanted to get away from other people's judgmental stares and whispers.

Wesley resisted the temptation to drink more. Instead, he got his running gear on and headed out into the dark. Memories chased him like bodies that bloated and floated to the surface of the water. He had gotten out, but not without scars. Was it the reason he always had to have his place settings aligned? The reason he couldn't sit with his back to a door? And why he'd never had a steady partner because trusting people took too much from him? Still, he was luckier than Becca—her mind had deteriorated like his mother's from what they diagnosed now as bipolar disorder and schizophrenia.

The city's noise and violence didn't deter him as he started to jog toward the lake path. Screw the curfew seemed to be the mentality of hundreds of people, awake and alone like him. The black water shimmered with lamp post spillage, and a few late-night runners flitted in and out of the light like shadows. The city never quite slept, and Wesley liked it that way. There was always something going on to distract him from his mind.

CHAPTER FOUR

NORA WALKED TO CLASS WITH JESS IN THE COOL morning air. She still hesitated to go out, all the noise and people gave her pause, but she was determined not to let it stop her. Her black backpack, another gift from her adventuring uncle, was leaden with her laptop, a few textbooks since she liked actual pages to read, and notebooks. Her water bottle fit into a pocket on the side. It was similar to a tactical pack used in the military. Uncle Emin swore by them.

"I think something's wrong ..." Jess muttered.

"What's wrong?" Nora peered at her roommate.

Jess rubbed her hand against her forehead, and sweat beaded her upper lip. Her skin was pale and looked clammy. "I feel like ... I don't know. Weird."

"Do you want to go back and lie down?" Nora hefted her pack and turned.

"No, I can make it to the chem lab. Matt's going to explain it to me." Jess giggled as she talked about the dirty things they'd done instead of studying. Nora waved her off.

After last night's drama, she was proud of herself for going to class. Her mother would have wanted her to live a "normal" life, whatever that was, and being a hermit was not normal.

Nora shook her head. She was lucky she had Jess, even if they had opposite personalities. It almost made them better friends and roommates. The campus was unusually quiet, given that it was a Friday. A few students biked across the quad; others walked in groups. The air still had the tang of winter, and everyone wore down coats to keep the chill at bay. Nora liked that there were so few people. It made it easier to be out if she didn't have to run into anyone or pretend to wave or make small talk.

Her phone pinged, and Nora's heart sped up. She slid it from her pocket. The text was from her ex, Jeremy.

What's up, doll? I'm heading to Bluehouse if you wanted to join. Coffee's on me.

Nora scoffed. He still didn't remember she didn't drink coffee even after a year of tumultuous dating. And all the coffee or tea in the world wouldn't make up for him "accidentally" hitting her when he was drunk. Jeremy had been her one experiment living in the moment, attempting to be like her beautiful, spirited mother who was up for challenges. She tsked. There were some lines she knew even her mom wouldn't want her to cross. Dating an abusive loser was definitely one of them. Her counselor voice would sternly tell Nora to quit being naïve and that she deserved better.

No.

Short, simple, and hopefully a dagger in his side. Nora continued toward the library. Her sociology test loomed on Monday, and while she was marginally sure she was prepared, she also had nothing else to do except force herself to go about her rituals. Routine, keep it safe, no surprises.

Her phone pinged again. Nora glanced at the screen in annoyance. It was from Wesley. Her irritation melted.

Sorry if I was abrupt last night—not enough sleep.

Nora smiled; this text threatened to make her whole day better. She quelled the feeling. This wasn't the first time Wesley had apologized for being curt. That was the way he was. Nothing was happening between them. Further, did she want something to happen?

No worries. Hope you're feeling better. Nora bit her lip, trying to think of something witty to say. *Don't let any deals slip through today!*

She rolled her eyes at herself. So clever, so charming. Her mom would have known how to flirt back. Nora sniffed in the cold March air and walked faster to keep warm. She didn't like to dwell on an unfortunate life circumstance when she knew others had it worse, but her parents' deaths remained with her every day.

I won't. :) I hope you do something fun this weekend, explore those horizons.

If I go anywhere it'll be the library.

Wesley didn't respond, and Nora didn't expect him to.

"Did I lock the door?" She wondered out loud and thought about going back to check. No, she fought her OCD tendencies. How could she even think of a life with someone when she was "Miss Tick-tock," as Jess said.

Even if she did entertain a life with someone, it could all be taken away in a second. In a tenth of a second. The semi that had run a red light, all because he was taking a shortcut through a small town, ruined more than his own life. Nora shuddered as the memory of the accident scene unfolded in her mind. She'd been fifteen.

"We've come to deliver some bad news. Your parents, James and Evelyn Moon, were killed in a car accident tonight." The tone of the police officer, who explained he was the investigating officer, had been matter of fact, but his eyes had conveyed compassion that Nora hadn't been able to process. The man next to him explained he was also an officer and added a few details after Nora's initial shocked silence. Her parents were hit by a semi-truck, the driver believed to have fallen asleep at the wheel, but they'd know for sure when the toxicology screens came back.

"Is there a family member you can contact to stay with or anyone who needs to be informed right now?" the officer asked.

Nora was speechless. No, she was an only child. Her divorced uncle was away on a trip, and her father's family was insane, so there was no way she'd call them. The officers said they could not leave her alone until she found someone to stay with her. Nora called her neighbor who had a daughter her age whom she'd gotten a few rides to school or after-school activities with. Both the mom and her daughter came to stay with her. After two days, Nora visited the scene of the accident. It only made it worse. Following the funeral, she had a hard time leaving the comfort and safety of the house. It was as if she could insulate herself by controlling things in her immediate space.

Nora snapped out of her funk of memories and blinked rapidly. The cold stung her cheeks, and she was grateful for it. She jumped when a siren started up near her. Red and white lights flashed as an ambulance careened around the corner with two police cars behind it. They headed toward the west end of campus. The science buildings.

Nora's bad feeling intensified when her phone rang again.

"Nor?" Jess' voice, ecstatic and vibrant, blared over the line.

"Yeah, hey, are there police by you? I saw them ..." The sirens got louder on Jess' end.

"Oh. My. God. Yes! The police are here, babe!" Jess shouted, and Nora held the phone a few inches from her ear. "Nora, you gotta come try this with us. We're invincible! The chem building has this amazing rooftop."

Nora changed direction and started to jog toward the chemistry building. Her heart thudded faster than her feet.

"What are you guys doing on the roof?" She tried to keep her voice calm so as not to startle her friend. *See, this is why I stay inside, where it's safe.*

Matt's hollers and shouts drowned out the first bit of Jess' response. "... this is insane. You can see so much from here. I should have been an actress or some star shit, you know? This is what they must feel like—view from the top, and they've got it maaaade!"

"Jess, get off the roof."

"I wish you'd embrace life, Nora. I wish you could feel like we do! Don't be afraid to put yourself out there," Jess said, her voice breathless.

Nora sped up and reached the white brick building where the police had set up a perimeter. One had a bullhorn. They attempted to talk to Jess, but she continued talking over the phone.

"I know you're scared. I know you think you can control everything and nothing will hurt you, but truth is, you can't. I hate that your parents died like that. They'd want you to fly!" Jess shouted, and Nora's heart constricted.

Jess wasn't wrong, but her words stung like a rose thorn. Compulsively, Nora started to count her fingers. It was another tic she'd established after the accident. It helped her get out the door if she concentrated on something other than what was outside. And she needed soothing right now because she could now see Jessica on the ledge of the roof with her arms outstretched, phone clutched in one hand. Matt stood behind her with his head thrown back and his hair flying in the wind. Both of their jackets were missing.

"Can you get off the roof? What are you doing?" Nora shouted and skidded to a stop in front of the building, as far as the police barrier would let her. No one noticed her. Her limbs went numb.

"I'm living!" Jess spread her arms wide, and her breath misted in the air like dragon smoke. Her long dark hair streamed around her, and she was a shining star for a moment. A beacon of impenetrable greatness.

And then she jumped.

Bile burned Nora's esophagus, and she clutched her stomach in horror. Her mind reeled at the impossible sight of her friend dropping like an elegant diver. Screaming wasn't an adequate reaction.

Chapter Five

Wesley was frying eggs and drinking a protein shake when two things happened: his left wrist twinged, making him let go of the spatula, and a woman screamed down the hall. He cursed as eggs splattered the floor and cupboards. He let it lie, though, and went to peer out the keyhole in his door.

Flatlands Condos were usually peaceful, mainly housing older couples or young families. This wasn't the scream of a child at play. Wesley thought about the Glock 19 in his safe in the bedroom. His personal pistol, a non-issue marshal weapon. His other Glock, a 22 .40 S&W appointed by the US marshal's office, was under lock and key back at headquarters for forensics after the shoot-out. Had a twitchy nerve in his left hand caused the excessive three shots into the fugitive's chest? Or was it that the fugitive and trafficker, Juan Santana, had tortured and raped dozens of underage girls?

A woman in a robe ran out the door with jubilant wide eyes and screamed again. The commotion had people poking their heads out their doors. *Stay inside, don't open your door,* he thought with a sigh. Wesley had dealt with too many unstable people to trust people who appeared happy.

She shouted something about the "Materlus" coming and the end of days. Her skinny arms twitched, and her face contorted with frown lines etched like scars, elongated teeth bared, and lips frozen in a feral snarl.

Wesley was about to leave the shouting woman to whatever nonsense she was about, but a man entered the hallway. Mr. Abdul, in 325, had a son going through a divorce but was otherwise unattached. The older gentleman approached the woman with hands held out but a commanding expression.

"Ma'am, are you with one of the families in this building?" His voice was appropriately soft but firm.

The woman turned with bright, blazing blue eyes and a devil-can't-catch-me smile. Her curled blonde hair twirled in circles as she danced around.

"I followed a nice woman and her baby in. This building has always been on my wish list, but I could never afford it. Do you love living here above it all, with the homeless and dying streets away?" The woman giggled, and her robe fell to the ground.

Wesley's eyes narrowed. He'd seen a lot of decaying bodies, but her body looked as if it were rotting from the inside out. Bruises covered her abdomen, red scratches clawed down her breasts, her stomach sagged from plastic surgery that had lost its elasticity, and her arms sported track lines like a railroad map to hell.

It wasn't her body that spurred Wesley to action but the compact Ruger LCP she had pulled from the robe pocket as it fell.

"Ma'am, I don't want any trouble. Neither do you. Let me get you downstairs—do you want a coffee?" Mr. Abdul persuaded. Wesley knew that wasn't going to work. This woman was past reason. She was on drugs, perhaps.

Why had she entered a family building, though? Wesley's instincts were automatic as he used Mr. Abdul's distraction. He opened his door and flanked the woman before she knew he was there.

The woman's neck was slick with sweat when he wrapped an arm around it and yanked her right arm with the gun. She screamed and fought him with more strength than he could have imagined she possessed. She threw him back into the wall, and his breath hitched at the impact. She drove an elbow into his side. Wesley huffed but maintained a grip on her neck so he could steer her weight down to the floor.

The woman flipped as he got hold of the Ruger. It was a compact pistol, .380 caliber and a good choice at close range. She cackled and slid from his grasp like a fish. Wesley couldn't understand how until he locked eyes with her. They were an unnatural shade of milky pearl and shone with a maniacal light. He'd seen people strung out but never with this weird color to their eyes. She possessed an energy he'd never felt from someone before: dark, suffocating, and strong. The woman charged Mr. Abdul and her fingers grasped his throat. He rasped for help.

Wesley checked the pistol—no round in the chamber—but it had a full mag of six bullets. Yet, he hesitated. He charged the woman instead, knocked her on the head with the butt of the pistol, and yanked her off Mr. Abdul, who panted and scrambled back. Wesley laid the woman to the side and tossed the robe over her prone form.

"Why didn't you shoot?" Mr. Abdul shouted and

clutched his throat. He stood and pulled out his phone to call the police.

Wesley ignored the question. "Do you know who she is?"

"No. No, what is happening?" Mr. Abdul put the cell phone to his ear as other residents flooded the hall. They all speculated on who the woman was and what she wanted.

Wesley stood guard over her, ensuring she didn't regain consciousness and lash out again, as well as keeping people from touching her.

Why didn't you shoot? The question bounced around his head like an accusatory ball.

Because she might be mentally impaired, because she might be innocent, and because I like it too much. Wesley never pulled a gun on someone without the intent of using it. He'd trained with the marshals because his aptitudes were physical combat and marksmanship. He wanted a job that made a difference, that wouldn't have him sitting at a desk or stuck inside. Since he'd never planned on having a family, it was a good fit—benefits, no re-locations unless he wanted them, and every day could be different.

It wasn't killing the three men he'd been hunting that bothered him. It was sometimes hard to tell who was a monster and who wasn't.

CHAPTER SIX

DID MATT PUSH HER, OR DID SHE JUMP? IT WAS hard to focus amidst the screams and people shoving each other in a panic. Some held their phones up to record the event like they were ravers at a concert.

Nora's hand holding her phone fell limply to her side. Her body froze as if this were a movie screen, and Jess' body would get up any second now. She blinked. A cop rushed past her, shouting into his radio. She didn't have the tools to deal with the trauma as her brain whirred in panic. Only so much understanding of the prefrontal cortex, adrenaline response, oxygen displacement, and nervous system response could carry her through at the moment.

"Get someone up there, now!"

"Who's the guy?"

Nora took panicked breaths as she gazed up at Matt. He shouted jubilantly and disappeared back from the ledge. Ten seconds later, he, too, flew over the side of the roof and fell six stories. Any chance of survival was negated when Matt hit the large, decorative boulders in the rock garden below.

He lay sprawled at awkward angles a few feet from Jessica as if they were bound in insanity for eternity.

"He's her boyfriend," Nora whispered. Fear gripped her like a cold hand, making her voice unheard. Tears stung her eyes as her body's reactions caught up to reality.

"Wait, do you know them?" a girl next to her asked. She flagged down a cop. "This girl knows who they are."

A dark-haired cop with a short beard stopped and turned to Nora with raised brows and an open expression. "Any information would be pertinent right now."

Nora cleared her throat. She tried to keep a calm expression, but she was sure the panic in her eyes showed plainly. Cops would forever remind her of that night. But this wasn't like the policeman who'd come to tell her that her parents were dead. She shook her head. "Jessica Weiland is my roommate, and Matthew Jablonski was her boyfriend. I don't know anything about him. They've been dating for about six months."

The cop wrote it all down and hailed another officer over. They pulled her aside to a secluded spot away from the chaos. Ambulance lights and sirens threw the scene into a wash of red and blue. Paramedics covered the bodies.

The police took Nora's statement and Jessica's parents' number. She only had Jess' mom's number because last Christmas, Mrs. Weiland had wanted to surprise her daughter.

Her face was numb as she tried to process what the police said. Stay on campus. Don't talk to anyone yet. Was she sure she had no idea what prompted them to jump?

"No, she seemed okay to me. Nothing abnormal." Nora sighed and wiped at the tears pouring down her cheeks; they were so hot against her cold face that they felt like trails of lava. She tried not to hyperventilate as the policewoman asked questions. Surge after surge of nausea threatened to empty her stomach as her world was upheaved.

"No recent fights or enemies she might have made?" a female cop asked.

"Well, she did get bitten last night." Even as Nora said it, it sounded stupid. But it was the truth. She clenched her hands, touching each finger.

"Bitten? By an animal?" They exchanged furtive glances. They didn't have the usual bravado of police officers.

"No, a person. She and Matt were at a bar and said some guys harassed her. She was bitten." Nora shrugged. "It didn't look infected and hardly broke skin, so she didn't go to the emergency room."

"But the skin was broken?"

Nora sniffed. "Yeah." *One, two, three ...* she counted her fingers over and over in her head to keep calm. Subconsciously she played with each finger as she accounted for it.

The cops thanked her for her information and said they would be in touch. Nora swallowed panic. Now what? She could go back to her apartment, but she was fearful of the silence. She didn't have class. She couldn't leave campus. She counted her fingers over and over as the paramedics loaded Jess and Matt's bodies into the ambulance and left for the hospital. Her shoulders hunched as she struggled with the breakdown. She needed to hear someone's familiar voice.

Nora pulled out her phone and dialed her uncle. "Come on, Uncle Emin."

The line rang and rang until his voicemail picked up. She groaned in frustration, but at least that took the place of hyperventilating. In an effort not to break down completely in public, she focused on her uncle and not the fact her friend had died. Hadn't he said something about the CDC? What the hell would the Center for Disease Control want with an archeologist?

Keep the gift safe.

Nora turned on her heel and marched back to her apartment in a cold sweat. No one stopped her even as more people flooded the site. But she did notice a figure walking behind her. A middle-aged man in a black coat with thick, black boots. She made several left turns, and when the man stayed with her, Nora started to panic. She headed toward campus security. The large building housed the administration offices as well. Nora glanced in the glass door's reflection, and the man changed direction, disappearing around a corner.

She sat in the warm building for ten minutes, watching the windows. The man didn't reappear. Nora cautiously walked out and headed toward her apartment. She had to go home—the safety of her room beaconed her no matter what. She peered around at the few people milling around campus. Nothing suspicious. No one followed her this time. A lot of students headed toward the chemistry building, and from snippets of conversations she passed, rumors were already spreading.

Nora reached her apartment complex in record time. She raced up the stairs, unlocked the door, and slammed it shut. The lock was bolted into place—she checked it twice— before going to her room.

Jessica's Victoria's Secret perfume wafted in the air. It hit Nora like a punch. It hadn't quite set in that her friend was dead. She knew the five stages of grief. She knew what textbooks said on how to deal with loss and post-traumatic stress, but none of that helped her now. She sagged against the couch, washed in the scent of vanilla and honey, and let the tears fall. All the memories of Jess ran through her mind on a loop, with questions threaded through them like ghosts. Did the bite have something to do with Jess' suicide? What did that mean for Matt?

She wasn't sure how long she sat trying to gather herself. Helplessness was not an unfamiliar feeling, but it was one Nora tried to avoid so much that it was why she only left the house when she had to.

"Stop. There's nothing you can do sitting here freaking out. You've worked too hard to fall apart here," she whispered to herself. Nora knew this was it—this was the excuse she'd use for never leaving her apartment again. She could order pretty much everything she needed and hire someone else to do other errands. The school would have to accommodate her, or she'd find one that would. She'd vowed not to let her parents' accident leave her struggling for the rest of her life, and she'd worked hard to meet that goal. But now Jess' death would forever stain her conscience. She wiped her eyes again, looking at Jess' jacket still strewn across the couch. Her friend wouldn't want her to live like a hermit either. She'd yell at Nora to get out and figure out what the hell was going on. There was no good reason a life-loving girl like Jess would be so reckless and take her own life.

Nora needed to do something, not sit idly while more bad things happened.

She squeezed her eyes shut as she clung to the box her uncle had sent. The stone artifact sat like an anchor in her lap. She took the book-sized stone tablet out. Ancient writing was scratched into a gray surface that was at least five inches thick. It wasn't super heavy or flat like a true tablet.

The stick people depicted farming, animals pulled plows, a volcano erupted in one story, and birds scattered across the face of the artifact. The writing was foreign to her—some African tribal language, she guessed—even though it had been found in England.

Nora's eyes blurred with tears as she looked at her phone. Tears burned her eyes again, but she clamped her eyelids down on them. Emin and Jess were the only people to call her regularly. She'd spoken with her gamer friends before, but it wasn't their voices she wanted to hear. Perhaps one. Wesley didn't call her much, but his voice-over game chat was oddly soothing sometimes. Online gaming friends were the only people she spoke to on a regular basis.

Nora sat on her bed with her full pack on the floor. She didn't have a lot in her room: a few bookshelves, a desk, a bed, and a small dresser. She fidgeted with her mother's necklace. The white gold infinity charm inlaid with three diamonds on the left edge of the loop was the only thing of value she'd wanted from her parents. Her mom told her the three diamonds were their family, and they'd always have each other. Nora kept it as a reminder that her mother's promise was false. Only in death could they be together, and that was too morbid to dwell on today.

Thinking of parents, Nora swallowed hard at the thought of Jess'. She should wait for them to arrive. They were the nicest people, but would they understand when she told them their daughter became unhinged and killed herself? Nora took a breath that stuck in her lungs. She sputtered and sobbed.

She cursed her parents for dying and leaving her alone. She cursed Emin for being in whatever trouble he was in. She gathered the artifact into its protective cover and slipped it into her black pack. Through forced-back tears and waves of despair, she gathered her emergency kit to put in the pack. Uncle Emin's phone call and now Jess' death gave her the feeling something was very wrong. The man following her wasn't a fluke of her imagination either. The Boy Scout motto was "always be prepared," and Uncle Emin instilled that into her at a young age. But he also insisted she come with several plan b's and a gun.

Nora refused to let herself stay secluded in the apartment because her greatest fear was realized—doors didn't stop the world from coming in. Could she help herself or Emin?

Nora was not prepared for the next phone call.

CHAPTER SEVEN

WESLEY GOT THE CALL FROM THE CHIEF DEPUTY AS he expected. The older man of fifty was close to retiring. Oliver Gibson had served in the army before becoming a marshal, and Wesley owed all his military jargon habits to him.

"You didn't shoot," Gibson said to confirm.

"No, sir."

"Good. We're already tied up all these damn legal channels with the last shootout you were involved in." Gibson half-chuckled. Secretly, Wesley knew his superior agreed that he'd been in the right to take down the three gang bangers firing at him. But for appearances, Gibson couldn't pick sides or have too firm an opinion.

"Bet you wish I'd taken the wit sec job," Wesley said with a raised brow. He'd thought about working in the witness protection branch of the marshals, but it hadn't sat right. "Or quit while I was ahead."

"Stop that." Gibson's stern voice reprimanded him. "You'll quit the service only if I kick you out myself. You're the best kid I've come across in a long time, Soares. Keep your head down and stay out of trouble until this is closed. There's some nasty shit unrelated to the shooting, so keep your ears open." It was the second compliment Wesley had gotten in the five years he'd been in the marshal service.

"Will do, sir. Any news on the attacks in Wood Dale?" Wesley was resigned to keeping his job while he thought about what he wanted. He loved his work but wasn't sure he was stable enough to be of service. He refused to become anything like his parents: his mother, who was incapable of coherent thought without medication, or his dad, who lived like a hermit because he was afraid of dealing with people. A man who'd been cowed too many times by an abusive wife and couldn't find his way out of the self-deprecation.

Wesley peered out the window at the news vans still parked in front of the complex. People slowed as they walked by to determine what had happened. The still unidentified woman

had been taken to a psychiatric ward in the local hospital. Mr. Abdul had gone to the hospital to get checked out, and Chicago PD were all over the halls interviewing people and trying to piece it together.

Wesley didn't interfere, and they left him alone after taking the Ruger and his statement, though only after he flashed his badge.

"Night club went nuts last night in Wood Dale." Gibson paused, and Wesley could picture him shaking his head. "I don't really want to repeat it because it's ... stupid. But the bouncers apparently started attacking and biting the customers. Then when PD was doing body counts, some were missing, but they came back walking with bullet holes in them and all."

Wesley waited for the punchline. Nothing. His boss was serious, even if he sounded like he didn't take his own words seriously.

"What, like a hoax?" Wesley asked.

"That's my guess, but witnesses have started coming forward. There are plenty saying they saw these bodies walking around, and they became violent when approached. We've been called in to help the local PD there—panic is starting."

"Do you need me there?" Wesley shut the blinds on the window and sank down into his desk chair. His computer jolted from sleep to awake. Hypernova, Nora's tag, was idle. He wondered what she was doing. *Focus, dude.*

"Not sure yet. We don't even know what this is. But the police are getting slammed with calls of people rioting and claiming zombies are roaming the streets." Gibson snorted derisively. "I refuse to use the term "zombie," and some online streamers have started the term 'Mob.'"

"As in mobile object or monster or beast?" Wesley asked with a slight smirk. So, gamer nerds were naming the first zombie outbreak—awesome.

"Yeah." Gibson's tone was flat, but Wesley detected some amusement. The chief had been an avid gamer in his youth and still liked to break out the old PS5. Wesley had caught him playing *World of Scepters* on a late-night house call emergency and had never let him forget it.

Wesley couldn't hide his disbelief. "The first stage is always denial, right?"

"That's grief, son. No wonder you don't have a wife yet," Gibson said with a short laugh. "This is the first I've ever heard of anything like it. Insane. I'll keep you posted."

He ended the call, and Wesley did a news search. Sure

enough, the Wood Dale Police Department had a statement on their site urging people to stay inside after dark, report suspicious behavior, and not engage physically with anyone acting erratically. They didn't say "undead," but their suspects had pale skin, open wounds, and walked with a stiff gait.

The reporters, interviewees, and police used the gamer slang Mob like it belonged to them now. Many people didn't even understand where the term came from, but it was an apt description: a monster or A.I. enemy in a game whose job was to be aggressive and kill.

"That sounds like a ..." Wesley couldn't bring himself to say the unimaginable word. "Mob." It would all probably blow over in a week anyway. This had to be an elaborate prank of some sort ... but the woman in his hallway stuck in his mind like a splinter.

The knock on his door was more irritating than startling. Wesley peered through the keyhole to find two CDC officials on the other side. A man and woman both wore tailored suits and flashed credentials. Wesley opened the door.

"Can I help you?" He didn't show his star yet. Before offering any personal information, he liked to wait and see what the bottom line was. He figured it was a habit he developed when social services were called on his mother by some braver soul than his dad. The social workers never gave out information they didn't have to. They also never had enough grounds to remove the children, especially with both parents present and mostly accountable.

"Shana McCormick and Don Cooper," Shana introduced herself and her partner. She flashed a Public Health Investigator badge at him. It had the CDC logo in a smaller print under that. Her partner flashed a badge with FBI on it.

Huh, maybe the nerds are on to something for both the law and public health to be collaborating.

Wesley wasn't familiar with outbreak protocols, but he knew that when two institutions decided to work together, there was something worth looking into.

"We're going to need you to tell us if you received any injuries during the previous conflict, Mr. Soares. You were the one who tackled Ms. Janik?" Shana asked with a no-nonsense tone. Her stringy blond hair and no makeup made her appear much older than Wesley guessed. The man beside her shifted in an expensive suit, tailored to his slightly overweight physique.

Guess they ID'd the woman.

"I was."

"Was Ms. Janik extremely violent in the incident?" Don asked this time.

"Yes."

"Not a big talker, okay. We need details, Mr. Soares. How was Ms. Janik acting? Did she attack first?" Shana cocked her hip as if she were getting ready to beat it out of him.

Wesley smiled as if they were at a bar, and it had the effect he wanted—she wasn't sure what to do with it. "Better question, why is the CDC poking around something like this?"

They didn't look at each other but gave him hard stares. Wesley was good at the "don't blink" game. He wasn't put off by silence.

"We have an interest in this case. Do we need to do this

the hard way? You're obstructing national security if you don't cooperate," Don said, putting his hands on his hips.

Wesley quirked a brow and motioned for them to step inside. He was curious if they'd let any details slip. His US marshal T-shirt lay across the back of a kitchen chair. He didn't bother to move it but saw the man's eyes flit over it. It could be a T-shirt, or he could take it as a clue to who they were dealing with.

"Why don't you tell me something else," Wesley said. "Are the undead walking around Chicago?"

The CDC employee and the FBI agent exchanged looks, and their brows furrowed.

CHAPTER EIGHT

THE LOCKS WERE SECURE, BUT NORA CHECKED them again. She paced the apartment after a night of sleep that did little to assuage her nerves. The last phone call rattled her more than her uncle's.

"Miss Moon, did Miss Wieland attack you at all? Do you have any physical injuries sustained from her?" the coroner asked, a female with a suspicious tone as if she hoped Nora would say no.

"No."

"And the bite your friend had come from a boy the night before?"

"Yes, that's what she told me."

"We need you to be extra vigilant, Miss Moon. Any signs of behavior change, or if you feel unwell, go to the hospital. Wait for our autopsy results, and please don't venture out after dark."

It was an odd thing for a coroner to say. Nora hadn't had a chance to respond before the woman hung up. Now she knew for sure that something was up. She didn't intend to leave except that she wanted to find her uncle. Her new resolve to stop being a pussy vanished for a little while longer as she tried to decide what to do. Grief clung to her like secondhand smoke, weighing on her body and clouding her mind. She needed to do something to clear it.

She packed her bag with essentials and the artifact. She decided she needed to go into the city to find her uncle. Kick down doors, fly into action—all things that scared the shit out of her. The last thing to go in the pack would be her laptop. It sat staring at her, and the gamer friend's list blinked.

Nora saw all the guys were on and a few of the girls, including Elena. Tango Strike's name showed he was away. She debated calling him. But what could he do? This was her battle. However, since she didn't want to bother him over the phone, she typed a quick message that he could get whenever he was on again.

Going away for a few days. Things are getting crazy here, so won't be gaming for a bit. Nora bit her lip. Should she add anything else? There was no need to give more detail ... she wanted to, but she didn't want to border on being too overly familiar or as if she needed something from him.

You can do this. You must find Emin, and then you can hide in whatever room you want. It was a hollow lie to herself, but she gritted her teeth.

Nora packed her laptop and grabbed the keys to her Hyundai Sonata, purchased for her by her uncle. She was proud of the shiny black car because it resulted from years of work at a bank as a teller and paying her uncle back. She stepped outside, locked the apartment, and the twilight horizon almost made her turn back. She didn't like driving at night. But this was an emergency. She could do this ... she had to do this.

A few news vans were parked nearby, and students who knew Jessica were milling around the complex. Nora ducked her head as she slid into the driver's seat. The familiar smell of leather in the confined space was like a womb in its effect to calm her. In her car, which she'd named Patrice, she could go anywhere, escape everything. Did she drive like an old lady since her parents' accident? Yes. But Nora figured no one died from driving too cautiously, and tailgaters could suck it. It was a miracle she was even driving at all. It had taken several months of therapy and Emin's solid presence to get her into a vehicle. Nora understood her paranoia and fear were irrational on some level, but the trauma didn't leave her. She wasn't a fan of drugs, having tried several anti-depressants, but ultimately hating their side effects.

Her phone rang. Wesley's gamer tag flashed across the screen. She'd put him in her phone as Tango Strike.

"Hello?" Nora tried to keep the suspicion from her voice.

"Hey, it's Wesley. Is this a bad time?" His deep voice was clear over the line.

Nora swallowed. What could he be calling her about? "Uh, yeah, I'm about to leave, but I have a minute."

"I got your message on the game chat, and there's some shady shit going down. Where are you headed?" he asked. Something in his tone gave her a shiver.

"What's going on? You don't ever call me." Nora rested her head back on the headrest. She was getting tired of people's cryptic phone calls.

"A woman attacked someone in my building. CDC is sending FBI and Public health investigators to join forces, and police are starting to enforce curfews. Something's not right. Have you seen any unusual activity around you? I know I don't know where exactly you are, but we're both in the Chicago area, so I wanted to check." Wesley sounded like he wanted to know exactly where she was but was too polite to ask. "Are you safe?"

Tingles ran down her arms at his concern. "Yeah, I'm safe. You sound worried. I told you about my uncle's phone call a few days ago, and I haven't heard from him since. I need to find him."

Nora's voice trembled a little, and she swallowed. Before she could stop the words, she told him about Jess's weird suicide.

"Can you stay in your apartment, please? Where does your uncle live, if I may ask?" Wesley asked.

"That would tell you where I'm going," Nora said, only half-joking. She didn't see the harm in telling him, the city was pretty big, but she still hesitated. How well did she really know him? Wesley was an excellent shot in the game, he was a natural leader in their group, he liked peanut butter, and he would love to live on a ranch someday. None of this screamed serial killer, but hadn't Ted Bundy been a handsome, charming man?

"I realize that. You don't have to tell me, but I want to ask you to stay put for tonight. Things are starting to go sideways. Your roommate's behavior sounds a lot like the woman in my building. I don't know what's happening, but people are getting violent," Wesley said. She heard a barking dog in the background and music thumping.

"I really need to find my uncle. I appreciate your concern, but I can't stay in my place tonight. It's too ... creepy." As soon as she said it aloud, Nora realized how true it was. She didn't want to be alone, and it was enough to override her fear. Maybe that was why she wanted to go to the University of Chicago and find her uncle's small apartment around the campus. Despite her fear, anything was better than sitting and waiting.

"Maybe I can help find your uncle—I remember you told me he lives in the city. I know this is breaking internet stranger 101 ..." Wesley let the question hang in the air.

Nora warred with herself. She'd forgotten she'd told him Uncle Emin lived in Chicago. He wouldn't ask her to stay home unless he had a good reason.

"Fine, he lives in the Lakeside complexes, number 204. It's near the university campus. I'm sure I told you he teaches there sometimes. I'm assuming you're in the city or close to it if you can find him. Why are you helping me?" Nora couldn't help the accusatory question. She figured he wasn't worried she was going to race into the city to find and kill or abduct him. The problems girls had to worry about usually didn't cross guys' minds.

Wesley chuckled, but it was heavy with worry. "You mean none of the other guys have taken the time to check in on you? Just kidding. Listen, I meant it when I said I care even though we've never met. Something's going down, and I don't think it's a good idea to come into the city right now."

Nora smiled despite the situation. Her phone buzzed, and she took it away from her ear for a second. It was *Rimfire* and *Cupcake*. She'd given Kyle her number after a month of his pestering.

"Speak of the devil, Rim and Cupcake texted me. He says there's weird shit going on in his town—I think he's in Indiana, though. And Elena says something similar in

Michigan. So, there you go, I do have friends," Nora said with a small titter.

Wesley scoffed. "I'm glad Rim's so concerned he *texted*."

"How old are you? Texting is the only way to communicate—no one calls people," Nora teased. It felt like they were in a game, but the situation was much direr than a pirate ship raid. She could picture him as if they were video chatting like normal, giving her an odd sense of security. All her triggers should be telling her that this was too much. She needed to stick to her routine and find her uncle. But Wesley's voice melted a lot of her anxiety.

"I told you I *am* old," he said with a small chuckle. "Comparative to you."

"I'm twenty-one, dude, relax. A five-year age gap isn't that big." Nora was joking, but he might have lied about being twenty-six. She didn't care whether he knew how old she was. Rimfire, or Kyle, said he was twenty-four, working at a nursing home until he could afford the last year of nursing school. Elena was upfront about her twenty-three years of life, as she put it. It was hard not to get to know people when she talked with them almost every night for three years, but she'd made it a point to keep them at arm's length.

"I don't lie to you," Wesley said, and she believed him. "I know, I know, that's what every creeper you meet online would say."

Nora sputtered with laughter. "Exactly."

"Listen, are you staying put tonight? I'll call if I find your uncle. What's his name again?"

"Emin Moon. Doctor Emin. He teaches archeology."

Wesley's pause made Nora's pulse surge. She'd never told him her last name. For some reason, she didn't hesitate now.

She'd been willing to drive into the city for her uncle, but if Wesley could help, she would let him. She was determined not to let her fear override her. Not when she needed to stop being a coward and figure it out before something worse happened. She couldn't lose her uncle.

"Your last name is Moon?" Wesley's voice took on a husky quality.

"Yep."

There was a heavy pause, and Nora rubbed her cheeks as if that would help cool them. Her breath steamed up the car windows.

"All right, I'll be in touch, Moonbeam."

Wesley hung up, and Nora left her car. She headed to the safety of her apartment. Anxiety had coiled in her abdomen like a snake but subsided a little with Wesley's help. His use of her nickname sent warm shivers down her spine and boiled in a spot in her stomach.

It was a bad time for the morgue to call.

Chapter Nine

In the two days since Jess' death, Nora had kept music on in the apartment constantly to escape the nauseating quiet. Nora answered her phone as she went to the kitchen to find something to eat. She hadn't eaten much nor had an appetite, but her body needed sustenance. What did one eat after the death of a friend? Her stomach was in a perpetual state of tenseness.

"Miss Moon?" The unfamiliar voice on the other line sounded harried and upset.

"Yes."

"You're the roommate of a Miss Weiland, deceased two days ago?"

"Yeah." Nora rummaged around the pantry. Jessica's "diet" shelf made her tear up and cringe at the same time.

"Well, we've run into a problem ... Have you had any contact with Jessica's parents? We've been trying to reach them." The woman shouted something indistinct, and a clatter of instruments fell to the floor.

"No, I haven't seen them yet. Why?"

"Well, Jessica's body seems to be ..." The woman abruptly cut off as if someone were telling her to hang up. And then the line went dead.

Nora called back, but no one answered. As alarming as that was—what did the woman mean about Jess' body?— without anyone answering, there wasn't much she could do to get answers. The rumble in her stomach reminded her she needed to eat even if she didn't want to. She found popcorn kernels and got the popcorn machine out. Stove-top popcorn tasted so much better than microwave. She cranked the handle as the kernels began to pop, and her mind wandered to Wesley. She should take her laptop back out and maybe game tonight since she probably wouldn't be sleeping.

Why had he offered to try to find her uncle? They'd flirted for over a year, but he'd never crossed the line by asking to meet in person. She had grown to love their video chats and hoped for more of them, but his willingness to help her uncle shoved her comfort way ahead of what she was prepared for. Nora's phone went off again, this time the counselor for Knox, checking in on her. She appreciated the concern of people who otherwise wouldn't have known she existed. But she was also getting tired of having to explain the bizarre behavior she'd witnessed that made no sense.

Nora flipped through the TV stations and stopped on a news channel that was broadcasting people running around like rats trapped in a maze. They appeared to be very pale-skinned; some were downright blue and chasing residents.

"What the ..." She leaned forward and let popcorn spill on the couch. How did one analyze this? Psych majors believed in delving deep into the mind, but now seeing was believing. There was no way to talk to a living dead person and get them to change their behavior.

"We are not sure what's causing this outbreak of violent behavior. We can't make sense of this yet ... stay inside, do not confront anyone coming at you. It seems to be spreading like a virus, so keep contact to a minimum." The newscaster was at a loss for words, even when they were scripted. She kept opening and closing her mouth. Someone handed her a cloth mask to put over her face. "We encourage everyone to wear a mask if you have one. Do not let anyone get close enough to sneeze on you."

"You think sneezing is causing this?" Nora asked the TV news anchor. It wasn't like a new flu virus was causing violent outbursts.

"We don't have much information from the CDC. President Shoeman will address the country at nine tonight. We're told something in the air is causing people to lash out, and there are reports of people attacking and biting each other," she said with wide eyes. "Other reports are even more outrageous about these so-called 'Mobs', the gamer term that's been sweeping the nation. We will keep you informed."

Nora's breath caught. Mobs? She chuckled slightly hysterically. No one was going to say the word "zombie" with any degree of seriousness, yet this was pretty much the correct scenario. Was this what Wesley had referenced when he said the city was too dangerous? Dead people coming back to life? It was like a bad horror movie cliché.

She turned the channel to something less scary to try to fall asleep, but her brain wouldn't quit. Uncle Emin's voice rolled through her thoughts. Wesley's laugh-lined mouth and square jaw in their last video call. Her taking out rival pirates with single headshots.

Nora must have fallen asleep because the gunshots in her dreams woke her up. She bolted upright as the shots fired again. They were real and came from outside. A knock, or rather a pounding, exploded on her door a moment later. She raced to it and peered through the keyhole. A man stood on the welcome mat, anxious eyes glancing around, fist help up to bang again. Had he been the one following her before?

"Nora Moon? I'm a research associate with your Uncle Emin. I'm Jim Alvarado, and I teach at the university with him," Jim said in a loud voice. "There are gunshots out here. Please let me in if you're there. Riots outside the campus are spilling over into this neighborhood."

Nora glanced at her phone to check the time. 4:15 a.m. She'd been asleep for a good six hours. She resisted the urge to ask for more information. She had never seen this man in her life, but his name seemed a little familiar. Perhaps her uncle did work with him. Did that mean Uncle Emin had sent him? And what were people rioting about? She checked the lock and then bolted to her room. Her gut was telling her not to open the door.

Her black tactical pack sat on her bed, still ready to go. She would wait until he left and head into the city. Forget the promise she'd made to Wesley. If she ran into him and her uncle, all the better, but she couldn't hide in her apartment now. She'd go mad from wondering if someone was going to break in. The knocking quit, and Nora made sure all the blinds were drawn. She kept the lights on—he'd see if she turned anything on or off now. The paranoia in her also realized he might sit outside for a while and case the apartment.

She bit her lip. She could take her chances and run to her car. Then she could try to lose him if he tailed her. It would be pretty obvious if he did, right? Nora blinked away panicked tears. Or she could stay here and call the police.

First, the sane choice.

Nora dialed 911, but no one answered. She frowned. No one was answering a police line? She tried again.

"What's your emergency?"

Nora gulped. "A strange man is wanting to come into my apartment, and I need someone to help me." When she said it out loud, it scared her even more.

"Ma'am, we will try to get someone there to check it out, but there are emergencies all over Jackson County right now. Unless you're in a life-or-death situation, I'd stay put, and lock your doors. Someone will come by." The operator's stressed voice tried to reassure her, but Nora was less than confident a cop car would come even after she gave the woman her address.

She hung up and peeked out the window again. The man was gone, but a blue Ford sedan sat across the street. Nora knew most of the makes and models of cars of the people who lived in her complex. A few had blue Fords, but her instinct told her it was him.

Nora checked the front door lock. Secure. Her phone was fully charged, and her body hummed with unspent energy. Despite the fatigue from the past forty-eight hours, she couldn't fall back asleep. She wanted to wait the guy out or see if he had left. He had to pee eventually, right? Or maybe he had mason jars in his car. What did he want with her in relation to her uncle?

Her phone chimed, and she picked it up immediately. "Wesley?"

Garbled static for a moment.

"Nora? Are you there?"

"Yeah, did you find my uncle?" Nora bit her lip.

"Yes, but we're in a bit of jam. We're heading toward you, but can you meet us in Glenon? Your uncle said that's about a half hour from campus," he said.

"We? He's with you? Let me talk with him." Nora bolted upright and grabbed her pack. She shoved her charger in the front pocket as she ran to the front door.

"Uh, he's not conscious at the moment. Do you have a first aid kit you can bring?" Wesley mumbled something, and a groan followed.

Fear shot through Nora and paralyzed her for a moment. Uncle Emin was hurt? At least Wesley hadn't said he was bringing a body ... her uncle was strong. She had to get to them so she could help.

"Should you take him to a hospital first?"

"No, he insisted we meet you ASAP." Garbled road noise resounded in the background.

"All right, the first aid is in my pack. I'm on my way ... there's someone here who was looking for him, I think. They're still outside my apartment," Nora said and shifted the blinds slightly. The blue Ford still sat across the street with a lone figure leaning back against the seat.

"I'm going to assume this guy isn't looking out for your best interests. Your uncle, when he was conscious, told me people were coming for you. You're going to have to get yourself out of their sights." The sound of Wesley's engine thrummed as he accelerated.

"This is insane. I don't know how to do that." Nora's voice went an octave higher, desperately trying to calm herself down. She counted her fingers, but that didn't help this time.

Wesley cleared his throat. "There are many options, but I think your best bet is to get to your car. Try to find a lot of traffic and hide behind a large truck or another vehicle if you can. Weave in and out of traffic and see if you can lose him that way. If that doesn't work, get in the left turning lane, preferably on a yellow light, and gun it. He should be locked into traffic behind you. You'll only get one chance to do this, so make it count. If you lose him, head to an off-street or somewhere he won't guess where you're going."

Nora tried to concentrate on his words. *Was he for real?* She wasn't a spy with amazing skills. Her grandma-like driving gave the "bad Asian driver" stereotype credence.

"I can't do this. Can you meet me here?" she asked and hated the desperation in her voice.

"We don't have time, Nora. Things are getting worse, and people are panicking. You can do this. Remember the raid on Tortuga? Just like that—only easier because you don't have noobs slowing you down." He was so calm it helped her nerves.

Nora swallowed hard. Rimfire had been a bit of a jerk in that raid. She'd still managed to pull off stealing the treasure and killing the traitor with Wesley's help and instruction. He was speaking to her like they were in game: calm, focused, and with every faith she'd be able to pull her weight.

"How the hell do you know so much about losing a tail?" she asked as she readied herself. Nora didn't know when she'd be back at her place. She made sure everything was off and stepped outside to her car. She glanced at the Ford and saw the man straighten.

Her heart thudded in her ribs, and she cranked her engine.

"I'll tell you what my job is when we meet," Wesley said. "Once you've lost him, head to The Smokin' Patty. Do you know the place?"

"Yeah, Uncle Emin and I love that place. We go there whenever he comes to visit." Nora took a deep breath as she reversed the car. She froze for a minute. Her hands shook on the wheel and her vision blurred.

"If you need to, I can stay on the line."

Wesley must have read into her terrified silence.

"No, I can do this. Please, take care of my uncle until I get there."

"Copy that."

The confidence in his voice made her sit up straighter.

You've got this, sweetie. You need to get to my brother, and he'll protect you. Nora's mom's voice echoed in her head. It was time to put her latest resolve to the test.

Nora placed both hands on the wheel and sped out of her drive. The blue Ford followed a few seconds later.

CHAPTER TEN

WESLEY GROUND HIS TEETH AS HE PULLED INTO the Smokin' Patty. The restaurant-smokehouse was larger than he'd anticipated, with several cars parked in the lot. The smell of smoked meat wafted into the car as he tossed a glance at his back-seat passenger. *What are you doing, Wes?*

Emin Moon lay on several towels with his hands bandaged and ointment on the cuts on his face. He'd been running down the street with a newspaper hat, clearly trying not to be seen. Wesley had only recognized him from the database's pictures and the college website. Wesley had managed to coerce him into his silver Tundra while getting the story that Emin had been held by the FBI agents and Public Health investigators at a CDC facility for extensive testing. A few public health investigators had come and gone, but no one would give him answers.

Emin had escaped when they put him in a back room, thinking he was unconscious. He'd been trying to make it to Bunker. To Knox university. To a bus or train or his car, anything that would get him to his niece.

67

You don't get involved personally. This is a mistake. Wesley shut his inner voice up. This was Noreena Moon— she wasn't someone he would ignore. Even though they'd tried to keep it casual and friendly, she meant a lot more to him than he wanted to admit. She was a good distraction from his job, the trial, the travel, but more than that. She was someone he could help right now.

A thrill raced down his spine at the thought of seeing her in person. Would she be like her online persona? Would her voice sound the same? He'd seen pictures of her, and over the video feed, she was beautiful. A soft vulnerability when she spoke made him protective of her. He didn't want to delve too deeply into why. Wesley operated on the twenty-first-century principle that women didn't need white knights or a man to validate them. But the age-old instinct to protect others wasn't gender-specific.

He supposed it came from seeing his dad take abuse from his mom. A lot of the time Wesley had to shield his sister from both of them—his dad's inability to remove them from the situation and his mom's bipolar rages. He'd grown up with a strong sense of justice and a desire to protect those weaker than himself. He'd also been striving to be the strongest so he'd never be a victim. Perhaps he'd joined the marshals to prove he didn't deserve to be at the bottom of the pecking order. To prove his life wasn't worthless.

Wesley made sure the heat pointed toward Emin as the older man shivered. His eyes fluttered open. He parked far enough out in the lot so there were no other cars near them but not so far as to arouse suspicion.

"Where are we?" Emin croaked.

"Where you told me to go." Wesley turned in his seat but

kept an eye out for anyone coming toward them. He didn't know what was going on, but it wasn't heading in a good direction.

"Is she here yet?" Emin sat up with a grimace. He took the water bottle offered and drank. Deep cuts above his eye had turned the skin black and blue.

"No."

"I appreciate your help even if I didn't know that's what it was," Emin said in a hoarse voice. He wiped at his bloody knuckles with a rag. "You're a friend of Nora's?"

"In a sense."

"So, online friend?" Emin nodded. "I don't know much about computers, but she's told me about her games. I know I scared her, but I'm glad she's okay. I can explain when she gets here. No sense repeating myself."

When Emin had said he could explain what was happening, Wesley had tried harder to help him. First, it was just a favor to Nora. Now, it was curiosity. If they knew the enemy, he might have a chance to survive the increasing riots and chaos.

"Is that her?" Wesley jerked his head at a black sonata that sped into the lot. A harried female steered the car to a jerky stop in the row opposite theirs.

"Yeah, that's Patrice," Emin said with relief.

Wesley cocked a brow.

"She named her car Patrice," Emin responded, groaning as he opened the truck door. Wesley went around to the side to help him down.

Emin glanced at Wesley when he stood on the pavement, and though it appeared he wanted to run to his niece, he held back.

Emin cocked his head slightly. "I was thinking ... you

two haven't ever met until now, yes? Do you want to go first? The end of the world is only beginning—we've got some time."

Wesley chuckled, and the sound eased the tension. It was true, he wasn't sure what to expect, but it wouldn't be up to him since Nora was jogging toward them. Her black hair flew in long curls behind her, and a dark pack bounced on her back. He'd never imagined she would look as good offline.

Nora was even more attractive in person than in her photos. Her eyes, creased with worry, were framed by black lashes. Naturally tan skin complimented her white teeth, and her cheeks were rosy from the cold. Mostly, though, what Wesley noticed was her presence. She radiated a concern for her uncle that spoke volumes about who she was at heart.

"What happened? I can't believe I lost that guy! Are you hurt?" Nora cried as she skidded to a stop.

Emin reached out to comfort her and assure her he was fine. "I'm a little bruised, but I've had worse. I didn't think you'd call the literal cavalry out on me. I'm sorry I scared you with that phone call—they took my cell right in the middle of our conversation."

Nora paused her onslaught, and her eyes turned to Wesley's. He was prepared for a lot of scenarios but had never expected to meet someone he thought he'd only ever talk to online.

"Hi," she said with a shy glance, fully aware of him now that her panic for her uncle had subsided.

Wesley smiled. "Hi, Moonbeam."

Nora's cheeks flushed, and he couldn't say he didn't like the effect it had on her.

"So, cavalry?" she asked with a slight smirk. "Are you a Mountie? Is your secret job that you're Canadian?"

Wesley grinned. "Not exactly, but my line of work does hail from a great history of wild west lawmen who probably rode horses. I'm a US marshal." He extended his hand, and Nora took it with wide eyes.

"Wow, I did not guess US marshal." She tilted her head, and while her expression was still tinged with anxiety, it was clear she felt something other than panic now. Her skin warmed in his hand, and she didn't immediately let go.

"It's not something I like to tell people. I might have been in the middle of a career change when all this shit started going sideways. You care to explain this chaos?" Wesley addressed the latter to Emin.

He cleared his throat. "Let's get some barbeque first. I'm starving. There are idiots after me, and you have a lot more to worry about right now."

Nora walked between the two men even as her uncle waved her help off. He limped slightly. Wesley was a few inches taller than Emin, who stood around five-ten. Nora was as petite as he thought she'd be.

"You said you didn't think you lost the tail?" he asked in a low voice. No other cars had come screeching in after her. The restaurant was serving business as usual.

"I don't know." Nora blew out a breath. "I did what you said and gunned it at a yellow light. I took several back roads and almost got lost. What did we do without GPS?"

"I'm proud of you. Your mother would be, too," Emin said, and the wrinkles around his eyes creased.

"Thanks." Nora ducked her head, but Wesley could tell the statement meant a lot to her. He knew her adoptive

IRL

parents had died in a car accident, but they hadn't discussed it much.

The hostess seated them quickly at a table in a corner. Wesley took a chair to the side so he could see all exits, and his back wasn't exposed. Habit. He rearranged the silverware so it was straight and aligned the plate with the napkin and his water glass. He caught Nora watching, and she looked away. He was used to people wondering.

"It's a habit I can't break. I like things in a certain order," he said. He'd learned long ago that his quirks were best dealt with directly. Wesley didn't like to beat around bushes.

Nora lifted her shoulders. "I have to check the locks on all the doors a dozen times before I can 'relax.'" She used air quotes, and Wesley grinned.

Nora scooted slightly closer to him. Wesley had been down many black holes with women, but he had a feeling this was going to get him into the kind of trouble that he wanted. He turned to Emin.

"You were being held by the CDC for testing? You're an archeologist, right?" Wesley's question hung in the air.

Emin coughed. "Yes. I was on a dig in Gao, where the Mali empire expanded, and traveled to London with linked discoveries. The medieval warlords used enslaved people from Africa, and I happened upon ancient tablets—like the one I sent you." He nodded at Nora. "And they depicted tribal rituals. Ancient, real, black magic."

Wesley narrowed his eyes, and Nora scoffed. He hadn't been prepared for Emin to explain the undead with something even more implausible than a virus.

"Uncle Emin, we don't have time for this. Why do you need the artifact?" Nora asked and brushed the hair from her face. Up close, she had a few freckles across her cheeks and

72

nose. Her skin was smooth, and a faint scent of cherries and honey wafted his way. Wesley attempted to study the menu while Emin described what he thought was happening.

"Let me try to shorthand this. Count Ulrich, in the sixteenth century, used his enslaved people and even a few knights for experiments. The Mali empire existed far before the count did in England and his enslaved were descendants. He used their knowledge of ancient magic in his quest for immortality."

Nora interrupted. "Isn't Mali the story about a city of gold in the heart of Africa somewhere?"

Emin beamed. "Not too late to change your course of study, miss. Yes, one of the most infamous rulers was Mansa Musa the first. He was said to be the richest man alive and would still be considered quite wealthy even by our standards. Supposedly, he built the fabled Timbuktu that I didn't believe in until colleagues of mine started sending emails with proof last year." He took a sip of water. "Their emails grew fewer and fewer. The video chats dwindled, and I saw erratic behavior on the screen—feverish eyes, gibberish, frantic gestures. That's when I went after them. You remember the sabbatical I took last summer to Gao? Well, I couldn't find them. It seemed like they'd disappeared. Until they reappeared as undead corpses wanting to kill me. Revenants."

Emin's hands shook, and he paused when the waitress arrived to take their order. They ordered plenty of burnt ends, pulled pork sandwiches, and fries. Wesley drank half of his water and waited while his brain tried to make sense of Emin's words. He also couldn't believe he was sitting next to the girl he'd gamed with for three years.

"They were exactly like what we see here—the dead

returning to life. Count Ulrich's curse, as I call it. He wanted to find eternal life by dabbling with ancient African magic. He found eternal life, but the price was what you see now; the undead walking violently upon the earth. In his achievement, he cursed the living for behaving irrationally and attacking each other, only to come back as walking corpses. In our research, we've also discovered that this might have been intentional—he wanted the world to decay in the undead while he built a new Timbuktu, a new city of gold. And then he'd rule over a chosen few—the new world. I know you don't want to believe this. No one does. But they attacked me." He rolled up his sleeve and showed a blackened patch of skin on his left forearm.

"It manifests differently in people when they're bitten, but they all die eventually and come back as animated corpses. I cauterized this after one of my friends nicked me with his teeth, and I didn't change by some miracle. Perhaps because it wasn't a full bite. I figured fire is the root of most cleansing rituals, and it appears to have worked. All this airborne nonsense is making people panic. The curse, the infection, followed me across the continent. I think the artifact is connected. Someone has resurrected the count's curse, but they can't complete it without the artifact being intact."

Wesley cocked his head. He bit his tongue to hear Emin out before calling it bullshit.

"In the fight ... uh ... taking care of my colleagues, they stole half of the artifact. I'm glad I sent you the other before this all started. I thought it was a nice gift." Emin took another sip of his water, and he shook his head. "They must have activated it."

Activate? Like a bomb? Wesley thought. This time he

couldn't help but interrupt. "You killed them?" It was said in a very low tone so no one would overhear.

Emin nodded, and tears filled his eyes. He blinked them away hastily. "Yes. They gave me no choice. Their attacks were vicious, and I accidentally started a fire trying to escape. They got locked in. The CDC had two FBI agents and a PHI pick me up because I inquired with a friend over here about ancient diseases to rationally explain what was happening. The African and UK governments have been hiding the trail for a few months now, but my colleagues must have attacked more people than only me, and I didn't know because of the spread. If one half of the artifact started this, maybe the other half could stop it. I know it sounds like the ravings of a madman."

Nora put her hand on her uncle's, and he sighed.

"You've noticed people get brave and violent, and then they meet some untimely end. I call them Revs, short for Revenants. I believe Ulrich's curse is passed by bites or deep scratches, which explains the irrational behavior—they get brave and bold and do things they normally wouldn't. I believe that was Ulrich's way of weeding out the strong, a way to choose who he wanted to survive. I could barely decipher the first piece of artifact, but he bound himself to a spirit form when he realized his body was mortal, but his soul wasn't. He's been waiting for someone to unleash him and his new order. It's begun."

Revs ... Mobs. Wesley recalled the chief saying that's what he called them.

Nora swallowed. "I have the second piece of artifact. Do you want to look at it now?"

"No, thank you. No need to bring it out. We need to get to my cabin in Pikes Bay. I have all the tools and equipment to translate it properly. But it's what's inside ..." Emin broke off as the door to the smokehouse opened. Wesley followed his gaze toward two men. One wore dark slacks with a faded beige long-sleeve shirt, the other brown pants with a plaid shirt. "You lost your tail, but I'm afraid I didn't shake mine. They must've seen me getting into your truck."

Emin gave Wesley an accusatory stare like he should have known they were being followed. Wesley stared right back.

"I let them follow us. I wanted to know who we were dealing with." Wesley didn't track the two men with his eyes but monitored their movements in his peripheral vision. They were seated at another table about thirty yards from theirs.

Emin's eyes widened, but he didn't argue. "All right, well, what's your take? Do we need to leave? They cannot be allowed to get the artifact."

Wesley bit into the pulled pork sandwich as his gaze swept around the place. Between bites, he said, "They look like professors, like you, but anyone can carry a weapon now. They don't look like they've trained in any combat situation. So, I bet I pull my piece and badge out, and they piss down their legs. On the other hand, maybe they're ready for a fight. Whatever you dug up is worth killing for."

Nora gulped audibly and nibbled on French fries.

"They used to work at the university with me. They're part of the Antiquarian Matrix Society, and we cannot underestimate them. A lot of their members are retired veterans with extensive military experience." Emin glanced subtly at the two men. "Ben and George, it looks like. They are not former military but lethal nonetheless." Emin sniffed and shook his head.

"They wanted me to join their society, but I'm not in the

business of shooting people who get in my way. The Antiquarians have a long history of betrayal and blood to get what they want —a priceless treasure. I knew they were sabotaging my colleagues in Gao; I just couldn't prove it. They know what happened there, but they don't want to make it right. They want bragging rights when they solve the crisis, or they want to raise the Count. The society is split into two factions—those that invite anarchy and those that want to save the world. I want the truth."

"Well, get ready for a big dose because I'm going to follow the first one who goes to the restroom. And I'm going to get some answers," Wesley said as he swallowed wonderful, soft, melt-in-his-mouth meat. He checked his phone and saw a missed call from Chief Gibson. He'd call him back later.

"Why wait? I'll draw them in if I go now," Emin said and stood up. Nora put a hand on his wrist and spoke up for the first time.

"No way. You let him handle this," she said and jerked him down into his seat. Emin rolled his eyes at her.

"You got kids or any family, Wesley? They're a pain in the ass." The love in his eyes didn't match the irritated tone.

"No kids. My dad lives in North Carolina, and I speak with him about twice a year." Wesley felt he owed them a bit of personal information, as it built trust. He didn't want Nora to think he helped her for disreputable reasons. He didn't want anything from her. In truth, he wasn't even quite sure why he was helping her so much. Perhaps in light of his probation at the marshals, he was searching for something else. Or he found a connection with Nora that he'd never had before, and it was something he wanted to explore before it was too late.

"I really do need to piss, Nora. Now, come on, let an old man up. I swear I'll come back—especially with Mr. Steel Eyes behind me." Emin winked at her, and she sighed.

"His gamer tag is Tango Strike," she said with a grin and tried to hide it behind a glass of water.

Emin glanced between them both, and Wesley waited. He waited for the uncle to say something like, "what's going on between you two?" But to his credit, Emin said nothing as he left for the bathroom.

It gave them a precious minute alone together before hell broke loose.

Chapter Eleven

"I never actually thanked you," Nora said in a rush as soon as Emin was out of earshot. She was still digesting the information her uncle had told them. It was a lot to wrap her mind around. She took a burnt end and shoved it in her mouth to avoid the awkward pause that never came. Wesley nodded, and his face lit up in a way that made her neck tingle.

"I volunteered. It took a lot of trust on your part."

Nora didn't say she had trusted him from pretty much the second month they'd started talking regularly online. It was incredibly lucky, though, that he was as good of a guy as she'd thought. His dark hair and soulful brown eyes were even more magnetic in person. He was quite a bit taller than she'd imagined, even when he'd said he was six feet. Maybe it was the way he carried himself. So often, reality wasn't what people portrayed online.

Wesley continued, "If it's not overstepping, and before I have to go knock some sense into heads, I wanted to tell you you're more beautiful in person than over a video chat."

Nora swallowed hard. She hadn't expected that. And on some level, he seemed like he hadn't either. Wesley stood quickly. He put several bills down on the table.

"Thanks. I ... I thought maybe you'd be disappointed for sure." Nora reached a hand out but pulled it back. "You look better than your picture too."

Wesley grinned and headed toward the men's bathrooms. "I'm not disappointed at all," he called over his shoulder.

Nora sat back for a second. She couldn't follow them to the men's bathroom. She was grateful to have his help, but how well did she know Wesley? Simply because she now knew he was a law enforcement figure didn't mean he was entirely honest. Was he helping her for some other reason? The thoughts didn't sit right with her, so she checked them. Her gut told her he was exactly what he said he was.

She smoothed her hair. She was sure she looked like a wreck. And her bladder informed her she needed a bathroom. She had to be ready for whatever came next. Nora flagged the waitress down for the check and paid with the money Wesley provided, intending to pay him back. She figured he and her uncle weren't returning to the table anytime soon.

Nora slipped into the bathroom, did her business, and while she washed her hands, she spotted something off on the floor. Was that blood trails? The lighting was dim, and the droplet trail was small. The crimson dots led to a stall with the door closed.

"Hey, are you okay?" she called. No one else was in the bathroom, and her voice echoed.

No response. Nora took out her phone and called Wesley.

Sounds of a scuffle and raised voices answered. Then a polite, calm, "Nora, can you meet us out front, now."

"I can, but you should know there's blood in this bathroom. I don't know if someone is hurt," she said and backed toward the exit. The bathroom door seemed to grow larger, and shadows crept under it.

"Get out and to my truck—silver Tundra."

Screams erupted inside the restaurant, and Nora sprinted out the door. She stood in the nook between the restrooms and the coat rack. The kitchens were to her left, the open dining room in front of her. People scattered as two girls with knives started hacking at anything that moved. Their eyes glowed a brilliant blue for a moment and then settled into a milky white. One of them with long blonde dreads hopped a table and ran at Nora.

Nora's breath froze as she ducked the knife swing. She didn't know if it was her mom's fighting spirit that helped her react, but instead of falling into a panic, Nora moved. Her mom had encouraged martial arts classes and self-defense courses. Dancing lessons early in her teens helped with her coordination, and Nora was grateful for all those lessons. The girl backed up on unsteady feet. Nora glanced around for a weapon; the closest thing was an umbrella on the coat rack. She held it up like a sword even as her hands shook.

"The end days have finally come," the girl said and threw her head back. She cut her wrist—not up and down, but horizontally—and blood dripped from the wound. "There's no escape. You can die now and escape the horrible fate the *Materlus* will bring."

"What the hell is that?" Nora stepped to her left to keep

the girl off balance. If Nora wasn't a believer in the curse, she was now.

Wesley threw open the door to the men's bathroom and shouts followed him. Nora used his distraction to lunge at the blonde girl and whack the knife from her hand. She pummeled her with the umbrella's metal handle. She'd never hit anyone in her life, and it was quite a bit harder to do than she imagined. The girl didn't go unconscious right away. She kept swinging bloody fists and slipping as she tried to attack.

Wesley picked up a chair and flung it. The chair didn't break, but the girl's skull took a good hit. She slumped to the ground.

"Your uncle may need assistance unless you want to deal with the second one," he said.

The second girl with two knives now ran at them, seeing her friend on the ground. Nora dashed into the men's bathroom. She was breaking so many of her rules that it was a miracle she was still on her feet.

She opened the door to find Uncle Emin holding two men at gunpoint. His graying hair was matted with sweat and wounds, a stark contrast of pale flesh covered in fresh blood in the fluorescent light.

"We need to get out front," Nora said in a low voice. She didn't want to startle him.

Emin's face was grim. "I know. These two were after me but also tracking the curse—it's here. Ulrich's curse."

The man with a bleeding lip glowered at them. "And you've known far too long, bastard. You could have stopped this in Gao."

"I went after the colleagues you murdered. You knew what they were after and thought it was just a golden city. When you found out it was much more, you let them fall.

You let them be the experiment! You were the ones who started this, weren't you?" Emin shouted, and his hand shook. The gun wavered in his grip. The two men didn't confirm, but the look on their faces raised her suspicions that this Antiquarian Matrix Society knew what they'd done.

Nora stepped toward him. "We all have to leave."

"You can feel the full weight of what you've done out that door. I didn't unlock Ulrich's tomb. I didn't sneak around government rules to dig at a site that should have never been disturbed."

"You're wrong, fucking idiot," the other man said as he spat blood on the floor. His gray hair and wrinkled skin spoke of hot days in the sun and hard work in the field. "We weren't unleashing anything; your friends did that. We were cleaning up all your messes."

"No, you knew what was going on and what you let them do. You've proved your point, and now you'll watch the world burn," Emin said. He shook his head. "You think you'll be one of Ulrich's chosen? He will destroy the world."

"You don't know that."

Loud thuds and more screams sounded in the dining area as Emin stepped toward the exit with Nora. She turned and opened the door to check that it was clear. A second later, her uncle gasped in pain.

Nora spun back around as the two men ran at them. Emin fired. The blast deafened Nora, and she clapped her hands to her ringing ears. Plaid-shirt grabbed her and shoved her into the wall. The other man with gray hair rushed Emin and took the gun from his hands.

Nora watched in stunned slow time as the man turned the pistol on Emin and fired. The second shot blinded her for a millisecond, and she went limp in the arms of the second man. He roughly grabbed a handful of her hair and yanked her head back. Nora fell into him, the pack still on her back. She lost the grip on the umbrella, and it fell at her feet. She heard rather than saw the door opening.

Wesley's dark frame whooshed in front of her. She barely registered his actions. Nora's eyes never left her uncle's fallen form, where a huge pool of dark blood flooded the white floor. He twitched, and his hand pointed toward her. He lay on his side. The bullet had entered his chest, and he'd been killed instantly at such short range.

Nora couldn't scream or cry or fight. She sank into a dead weight of shock but then felt the man trying to pry her pack off her shoulders. Emin's words reverberated in her mind. *Keep it safe.* She couldn't let them have the artifact, but her body rebelled; it wouldn't move, wouldn't fight. Wesley grappled with the older man in a short struggle. He didn't wait for the man to level the gun at him; he rushed him and, perhaps with a lot of luck, managed to get to him before he fired again. Wesley wrenched his gun arm down in an elbow lock, kicked his other ankle in, and shoved his head onto the sink rim. The porcelain cracked, and the man slumped.

Plaid-shirt still wrestled with Nora as she clung to the strap of her pack. He couldn't take it. She used every ounce of strength to hold on to it. The man's fist came at her head, and she ducked. His knuckles grazed her cheek and sent her reeling, but she still clutched the strap.

"Fuck!" he shouted and yanked the pack.

The strap went slack, and Nora tumbled backward as the man's head met Wesley's fist. His head bounced against the tiled wall, and he toppled over. Wesley took her arm and hauled her out the door.

"We can't leave him!" She pulled at the hands that dragged her out of the smokehouse and into cool air. Patrons stood in groups with shocked faces, and others jogged toward their cars. Tires squealed.

"We don't have time. If there were two after your uncle, you can bet there will be more. When they find his body, it might satisfy them long enough for us to get a head start." Wesley scanned the lot and shoved their path through and around people. He was clinical, so calm that it snapped her into action like a puppet. Her head reeled as she realized she was alone now. Her parents were gone, her uncle dead, and her roommate committed suicide.

Nora barely registered his hand over hers as she followed. She adjusted the pack with the weight of the artifact.

"I can't leave my car." She skidded to a stop by his enormous truck. Wesley paused in thought.

"Agreed. I don't want them to know you were here. Follow me." He unlocked the truck and motioned her to hurry to her car.

Nora sprinted to her car and slid into the driver's seat. Patrice's clean leather smell and soft seats cocooned her from the noise. She could run. What did Wesley have to gain now that her uncle was gone? She was alone with a man she'd met two hours ago.

Her phone pinged.

Nora glanced at the screen. It was from Wesley.

You have no reason to trust me, but please follow.

He was a US marshal, right? She checked the car locks three times. The engine roared as she sped after the silver

Tundra. *There are plenty of dirty cops.* Yet the words didn't match what she'd judged of him by now.

Tears blurred her vision as she kept up with Wesley. They sped on to the main road and pushed the speed limit. Cop cars flashed by them, heading toward the smokehouse. Nora and Wesley flew past the roadblock the police were attempting to set up.

Nora brushed the hot salt from her cheeks. She couldn't give in and shut down, not now. Her dad's deep voice reminded her of his favorite saying: *Go big or go home.* They would be ashamed if their only daughter died a pathetic death giving up because she was afraid.

She'd figure out the damn curse and fix it. Emin had all the clues ... she just had to find them. They needed to get to his cabin.

CHAPTER TWELVE

As she drove, Nora's phone went off several times in the next few hours. Wesley called once to ask how much gas she had. She had a full tank—she never let it get below half—and Wesley said he had over three-quarters. They would head toward the Wisconsin border unless she needed to return to her apartment. Nora said no. She was on autopilot driving now. She focused on what her parents and Emin would want her to do. She had no choice; she couldn't go back to her apartment, and what did she have to go back to? The only option was forward, and Nora was glad Wesley was leading that charge for the time being. She didn't think she had the capacity to at the moment.

The phone pinged again, and she glanced at the screen held in the hands-free mount. Rimfire and Cupcake had been texting her, both within the last few hours. She pictured their faces. Kyle had dirty blond hair and brown eyes, and Elena had short, spiky black hair with mahogany skin. She'd never video-chatted with them, but they'd gamed with her almost as long as Wesley had.

It seemed the world was going insane. The texts were frantic.

Are you okay? We're getting a lot of crazy shit here in Indiana. You're in Chicago, right? Has it spread there? Kyle.

This is like apocalypse times—people are bunking in their houses. Went to the grocery store, and all the toilet paper was gone already! A few rumors of undead walking around and people are shooting their neighbors by accident. Stay inside chica! Elena.

Nora pressed the speaker button to respond to them both.

I'm on the road—I had to leave my place. This is nuts. I'll be in touch later when I can. I hope you're safe.

She wanted to say more, but the less they knew, the better. Nora thought about all the people who'd died forty-eight hours ago, and those corpses were now infecting others. It wasn't a virus or something tangible for people to grasp, which made the chaos all the worse. They didn't know what to do with it or how to protect themselves.

Neither did she. How did one fend off the undead?

Nora kept her eyes on the road even as toxic thoughts invaded her mind. She should have moved faster. She shouldn't have taken her eyes off the two men to check the door. Uncle Emin would still be alive. She seemed destined to be surrounded by death. Even though she knew her parents' deaths weren't her fault, she couldn't help but feel everyone around her eventually left her. Fresh tears sprang to her eyes. She sniffed hard and shook her head. Her hands clutched the wheel until her knuckles turned white.

They took I-39 toward Wisconsin, and Nora knew the route well. Emin must've given Wesley the cabin address since he was taking the correct roads. His truck slowed and exited toward a rest stop and gas station. It was a Kwik Trip. Her parents and Emin had always made it a running joke that they only stopped at these gas stations. The stations were generally a tad cleaner, boasted a hot food bar, and some had car washes. Seeing the red-letter sign made Nora's throat close. Emin always brought her back the giant Krispy treats from a Kwik Trip as a kid. Nora pulled in behind Wesley at a pump and fished out her wallet. She got out and stretched her legs.

Wesley came around to her before even starting his pump. She wiped her eyes and finger-brushed her hair. It probably made no difference—she was a wreck, and he knew it. He didn't placate her with platitudes.

"We can fill up and rest over there for a few hours. It'll be dark soon, and I don't want you drowsy on the road at night," he said in a soft tone. It was as if he understood the depth of her grief but didn't know how to help.

Nora shook her head as she put the nozzle into the tank. "I don't drive at night if I don't have to. I don't like to be out when it's dark." Her fingers clenched the handle, and she mentally counted them. The admission made her feel inadequate and embarrassed. He'd probably leave if he knew the real her, but Nora was too strung out to care. She didn't have full-on nyctophobia, but her anxiety spiked when it got darker. Normally, she could handle it if she went slowly. But sometimes, like now, she had too many emotions to deal with it properly.

Wesley's brows rose. "Why not?"

The question was so blunt it startled her. Nora took a breath, and it threatened to shatter her. She couldn't talk about her parents' accident with Emin's death so recent. Tears filled her eyes.

Wesley backed off. "Hey, it's okay. We don't have to drive in the dark. Would you feel comfortable sleeping here for a while and then heading out? We may have to ditch one of our cars eventually."

Nora nodded numbly. She knew she might have to abandon Patrice, but tonight would not be that night. Besides, they might need two vehicles if one of them breaks down. But looking at old Patrice compared to the huge, shiny Tundra, Nora was pretty sure it would be her car breaking down first.

Wesley filled his truck, and they both pulled around to the rest station. Nora went inside to freshen up and took her pack with her. The bathrooms were large and mostly unoccupied. Her last bathroom experience had her nerves on edge. She checked every empty stall before selecting one and checking the lock three times. She attempted to remove the smudges of mascara and eyeliner from under her eyes. A quick wash under her arms and around her neck was all she could manage. Nora took out a toothbrush and paste since her teeth felt like they were growing mold on them.

Her stomach rumbled despite the BBQ they'd had only hours ago. Her mom used to joke that Nora could out-eat a horse. A few people milled around the brochures stand or sipped coffee. Some truck drivers walked outside with their dogs and ate hamburgers. The twilight cast a purple haze over the sky. Lamplights buzzed on. Nora walked back to their cars, and the smell of fries and sandwiches hit her. She reached for whatever Wesley handed her.

He looked like he'd washed his hair in the sink—it was slicked back wet. He smelled like pine and musky aftershave. Nora sat on a bench across from him as they ate in silence. Darkness loomed on the cloudy horizon, and a chilly March breeze made goosebumps stand up on her arms despite her jacket.

Nora was exhausted, but her mind whirred like a broken blender. She ate but didn't taste the food. She pulled her black jacket closer around her. "Thanks for the food. I can get the next one."

Wesley peered at her so long that she thought she'd insulted him.

"Or I can pay you now ..."

Wesley shook his head. "No need to pay me anything. I have a cooler and bought a few more sandwiches and drinks for the morning. The shop isn't open until eight, and I'd like to be long gone before then. I was wondering if anyone will be waiting for us at the cabin."

Nora shrugged. "I don't know, not likely. We used to vacation there a lot until ... until we didn't." She rubbed her face. "I haven't been up there in a few years, but I have good memories of that place."

Wesley stood and gathered their trash to throw in the bin. "Well, we'll be prepared regardless. Is four too early to get going?"

Nora didn't have the energy to argue. "No, I can set my alarm." It was early, but she doubted she'd get any sleep. She hated that she was such a coward. Her parents' accident had nothing to do with the darkness. There was no sane reason she should fear the dark. She rationalized it away, telling herself she shouldn't be drowsy while driving. Or had Wesley made that excuse for her? Sleepy drivers got a lot of people killed. She stood and headed toward Patrice.

She was slightly surprised Wesley hadn't said anything about her uncle or what had happened. It was nice to have the space but also upsetting because she had no one to talk to. *You've always been alone, Nor. This is no different. You can get through this just like you always do. Remember, mom and dad wouldn't want you to lie down now. Especially now.* Nora had been close with her parents in a way that some people didn't understand. She could talk to either one of them without fear of judgment and they'd always made it clear if she were in trouble, they'd be the ones to get her no matter what. Nora didn't know if it was her laid-back personality or their trust in her, but she'd never had to call them drunk or high. She'd enjoyed their company and the safety that came with knowing unconditional love. They'd taught her to be independent, but their absence was too abrupt, too cruel.

Nora tucked herself into the car's back seat and pulled a blanket over her. She heard Wesley shut his door. Truck drivers were sleeping on the other side of the lot too. They'd be relatively safe, considering the newest threat wasn't living humans but dead ones.

She couldn't help the tears that cascaded down her cheeks and leaked onto her shirt. She curled herself up and took deep breaths. She counted her fingers. *One, two, three, four, five.* Voices in her head wouldn't stop pestering her. *You should have done more. You could have saved him or Jess. You're truly alone now. How long before you revert to your old routine of hiding in fear? This bravery is not you.*

She put a corner of the blanket in her mouth to keep the sobs at bay. Her breath came in gasps, and she shuddered at the severity of her reality now. How was she supposed to go forward? Her crippling fear wouldn't let her go, and she had no home now.

A car door opened outside, and shortly after, Nora heard a tap on her window. She bolted up.

Wesley stood at the door and made an unlocking motion. Nora tapped the button on her key fob, and the car unlocked. He slid into the other side of the back seat; his weight shifted the car. She stifled her crying and wiped rapidly at her face.

"Was I too loud? I'm sorry, I'm fine," she said in a rush of words and hiccupped.

Wesley didn't respond but reached out to her. The instant his hand touched her forearm she let him pull her into his chest. He let her sob on him until she fell asleep.

Chapter Thirteen

Nora woke with crusted eyes and a sore back. She scrambled up to check the car locks as the previous night flooded back to her. The key fob was gone, but the doors were locked. The sky was pre-dawn dark, but her phone alarm had gone off. Wesley's scent lingered in the car. Her hand dipped into the divot in the blanket, still warm. He hadn't left long ago.

Embarrassment flooded her face with heat, and grief clung to her like a fungus. She didn't want Wesley to think of her as weak, even if that's how she felt all the time. She didn't want him to be the proverbial shoulder to cry on. Nora counted on her fingers as she peered out the window.

Wesley walked toward their cars with a black cowboy hat on his head. He still wore dark slacks and a light blue button-down shirt but had lost the tie. His tall form slid through shadows as if he belonged in them. He reached her window, saw she was up, and smiled. Wesley held up the key fob and unlocked the car.

"Morning. Tried to get coffee, but the machine is out,"

he said and tossed her the keys. Nora caught them and was glad the darkness hid most of her face as memories of the previous evening surfaced. She sat back to let him in. "Is it light enough that you think you can drive?"

He asked the question without judgment or impatience.

"Yeah. Sorry about ... me. I ..." Nora trailed off. She touched each finger, and Wesley's gaze fell on her hands. Nora tried to stop, but she couldn't. "I actually don't drink coffee. I don't like the taste."

Wesley half-smiled and didn't bring up her crying, literally, on his shoulder, to her relief. He seemed to be trying to reassure her as best he could.

"I'm no trauma counselor, but I know when to let people process. I know your uncle was like a father to you. The important thing is that you'll figure this out and use what he gave you to help find the solution." He took off the hat and played with it in his hands. "You don't like coffee?"

Nora giggled, and it broke the tears threatening to gush again at his words. "Nope. I'm a tea and pop kinda girl."

"Here, take these for the headache you probably have from the gun firing so close to you." He handed her some ibuprofen and a water bottle.

Nora swallowed the two pills with a nod of thanks. She hadn't wanted to complain, but her head was pounding, and her ears still rang.

She gestured to the hat. "You a cowboy in another life, too?"

Wesley shrugged. "I grew up in the backwoods of Texas, and this hat was my grandfather's. He sold his cattle ranch to pay for my grandma's leukemia treatments." He stopped as if he'd said too much. "I use it to sleep—block out light— you know."

Nora understood his reluctance to share. They weren't there yet, but she wanted to be.

"I'd like to live on a ranch, but my OCD probably wouldn't let me," she said. It felt like an admission of guilt. She continued to count each finger by tapping it.

"Maybe," was all he said, but it wasn't sarcastic or mean.

"Ever since my parents died, I don't like when it gets dark. It's stupid, but I feel safer if there's light." Nora stretched her neck and took deep breaths. Every time she thought about Emin her chest closed.

Wesley shifted uncomfortably, like he knew he shouldn't know such intimate details about her life yet. "I can understand that. Bad news comes at night, and unexplained things always seem to happen in the dark, eh?"

"Did I tell you that at some point?" Nora peered at him. He was more perceptive than she'd given him credit for.

"No, but reading people is part of my job."

The silence stretched as Nora thought about how much she wanted to trust him. But her life was already so upside down she wasn't sure she could take another surprise. It was better to think of him as someone who could turn on her at any moment, right? She looked into his dark eyes and second-guessed herself.

"Sometimes, I guess I need the push. It's not like I haven't driven at night; I choose not to if I can. Emin was good for making me face my tics." She played with her fingers and glanced down. "But that's enough of my sob story. You said your dad lives in North Carolina? Do you have any other family around?"

Wesley shook his head. "None that I know of. Dad moved to be near the psych facility my mom currently inhabits in Durham. He lives alone, and I have a sister who's in a treatment facility back home in Chalasaw, Texas." He didn't elaborate further, and Nora didn't want to pry. After a slight pause, he proceeded. "My mom was abusive to all of us. My sister, I guess, inherited her mental illness. I don't blame my mom for what she did, but that doesn't mean I want her in my life."

Nora nodded, relieved that the focus wasn't on her for a while. "That sounds rough. I'm sorry."

Wesley glanced at her, and his mouth opened, but no words came out. His jaw worked for a second while he tried to articulate himself. "Those are exactly the words I should say to you. I'm not good at this."

Nora touched his hand, and an unspoken comfort flitted between them. "I don't even know what 'this' is, but I appreciate you helping me. I have a hard time dealing with surprises. I like control, and this has been a chaotic ride I want to get off." She let out a halfhearted laugh. She didn't like admitting her OCD, but she wanted to stop feeling like Wesley was some stranger. They'd gamed for years and hadn't gotten sick of each other. He'd been there when Uncle Emin died and hadn't left her. Yet.

She continued, "I want you to be able to go, though. I don't want to keep you here. I can get to my uncle's cabin, and I'm sure I'll be safe there. He was even more prepared and paranoid than I am, so I'm sure the place is stocked for a few days at least. You probably want to check on friends or family, right?"

Wesley looked at her carefully. "My dad is very capable, but I'll give him a call. And as I mentioned before, my sister and mom are in mental health treatment facilities. They should be secure. The immediate problem is figuring out exactly what Emin was talking about. If more people keep turning or returning from the dead, then we're facing a global pandemic where no one will survive." He shifted in the seat as if he weren't used to talking so candidly with someone. "So, if it's all right with you, I'll stay."

Nora couldn't help the tingles that erupted. A burn of anticipation, something foreign, traveled up her arms and flushed her neck. It was like a haven, a solid patch of ground, in the middle of her grief, something she could cling to.

"I'm really glad we met up in real life," she said as an affirmative to his question. Wesley grinned and tilted his head.

"Also, your uncle would kill me if I abandoned you, now."

Nora jabbed his thigh with her toe and rolled her eyes. It was something Emin would say.

"You know the way better than me—are there shortcuts?" Wesley asked. He opened the door and cold air flooded in.

Nora shivered as she got out. She straightened the back seat and folded the blankets.

"Nope, we're on the most direct route."

"Mmm, okay, we'll make a few loops to be sure no one's following us. But we should be there by evening tonight." Wesley handed her a wrapped sandwich.

"Sounds good. I'll follow you." The words reminded her of a time in *Pirate Scourge* when they'd been on separate ships.

"Follow me!" she said, then sailed her ship toward the other battling ships on the horizon.

"Anywhere in the world," he replied.

He'd probably meant it as a joke, but she'd felt excitement at his words. It was flirty back then, and now too many serious events had happened for her to see if that spark was still there. She doubted he even remembered saying it.

Wesley turned before he opened his door. "Anywhere?" He cocked a brow up with a small grin.

Nora's breath caught, and she put out a hand to steady herself on the car frame. Perhaps that spark *was* there and not imagined. She nodded with a shy smile and slid into the driver's seat. They pulled out of the rest station lot and back onto the highway. The sun was barely peaking over the horizon with bruised, billowing clouds promising weather ahead.

The intensely warm feeling vanished about ten minutes down I-39. Several cars on the side of the road looked like a normal car accident. But people weren't calmly exchanging insurance information or talking on cell phones; they screamed into the phones and threw punches at each other.

Amidst their chaos, bodies walked out of the trees along the side of the road and started to run toward the fighting drivers.

CHAPTER FOURTEEN

WESLEY'S PHONE RANG, AND THE CHIEF'S NUMBER flashed across the screen. He eyed the commotion on the right side of the road and switched lanes to the far left.

"Soares."

"Where the hell have you been?" Chief Oliver Gibson's voice cracked over the phone speaker. "We need you in Wood Dale. The P.D. is overrun with emergency calls, and the National Guard is coming in, but not fast enough."

"I had to leave Chicago, sir. There was a family emergency." Wesley let the lie slip off his tongue easily. He was relieved not to be on duty and would much rather be driving with Nora behind him than facing this problem with his fellow marshals. Perhaps a career change was inevitable for him. He didn't want to think about it yet. The US marshal service was the only career he'd known; what else would he do?

"Becca?" Gibson knew about his sister's struggle with Bipolar and Schizophrenia. He was one of the few people who did.

"Friend of Becca's," Wesley said. It could be true. In any other circumstance, he was sure Nora would get along with his sister fine as long as she was prepared for everything that often came with it. Becca wasn't a monster. Thankfully medication had allowed her to get back to her old self, but there was always a risk she could take herself off them or forget to take them. "I'm heading to Pike's Bay for a bit. Hold on."

Hobbling figures started to emerge from the forest, just past the accident. Wesley slowed with the traffic. The figures became people—undead people—from the look of their sallow skin and dirty clothing. They weren't corpses decayed by months but also weren't alive.

"I've got about ten Mob sightings in Wood Dale and more coming from the city. The situation is becoming almost unmanageable," the chief said.

"I see three Revs on I-39 past the Wisconsin border, sir," Wesley interrupted him. Emin had called them Revs, short for Revenants. No matter what they called them, it was clear they were a growing danger to every living person.

"Revs? I thought we were all referring to them as Mobs," Gibson said. The background was filled with shouting, guns cocking, and clanking keys.

"Revenants. They're people returned from the dead, animated. Don't ask how I know, but the bite is infectious to the living. Use any term you want but be sure to use all the tactical gear you can and don't let them get close enough to break skin." Wesley slammed on his brakes.

The red Taurus in front of him braked hard and swerved. It hit the car in front—probably rubbernecking the accident. Wesley veered onto the shoulder and honked the horn to give a green Subaru time to pull up a little. The car didn't get the hint, and Wesley was forced onto the short grass over the shoulder. He stared at a Rev that groped its way around the truck. It had been a man once—short beard, beer belly, and milky white eyes. The pupils didn't focus like normal, but the Rev could see well enough that his fingernails scratched the truck's hood. Wesley cursed.

"Soares?"

Wesley forgot he was on a call. "Sir, I'm going to need to call you back. I've got Mobs in front of me." The call disconnected.

He put the truck in reverse and had about six feet to move. "Fuck this."

Two more Revs came ambling out of the trees in various states of decay. They didn't move particularly fast, but they were determined.

Fists pounded on windows so hard they cracked the glass. The Revs rocked the car's side to side as people screamed inside. Wesley grabbed his Glock and got out of his car. People scrambled to get away, but over a dozen cars crashed into each other and blocked all lanes of the highway. Horns blared, and it would only be a matter of time before someone fired a weapon.

Conceal and carry made it easy for a lot of people to have guns in their vehicles. Wesley pressed the speed dial for Nora's phone as he ran toward her black Hyundai Sonata. She was pulled over, blocked by a gray Ford, and had her phone to her ear.

"Revs are coming up by the dozen now. Where are they coming from?" She didn't bother with the preamble.

"I see them. We've got to get people back in their cars. Stay in yours; I'll see if I can get these assholes to move," he said and hung up.

Wesley shouted directions to panicked people in a loud, calm voice.

"Ma'am, I'm going to need you to reverse about fifty feet. The Jeep behind you will get out of your way as soon as I let him know how much space he has." Wesley had drivers roll their windows down even though it took some coaxing.

A Rev rushed up on his left, and the Jeep driver put his window back up with a shout. Wesley grabbed the Rev's arm and twisted it down, locking the elbow and wrist. The man writhed in his grasp, not in pain but in frustration. He thrashed like a gator and catapulted Wesley toward the Jeep. Wesley hit the side of the car with a thud. He pivoted and jammed his foot down into the Rev's right ankle. The bone snapped, and the guy dropped. His skin was clammy, and bits of flesh shed in Wesley's hand as he let go of the Rev's wrist.

Wesley grimaced. He shoved the Rev away from the Jeep and shouted for the driver to move. The Jeep sped out so fast smoke belched from beneath the tires. At least there was room for cars to move now. Wesley directed the woman to go next. He kept the Rev down with a booted heel to the guy's back. The body tried to maneuver, but he wasn't one of the stronger ones.

A shot was fired to his left.

Wesley spun and lost his footing on the Rev's back. The thing popped up and lunged. Wesley used the Rev's momentum to push him forward, slamming his head on the side door. The Rev's skull collapsed inward with an explosion of black viscera and brains. The family inside shrieked. The Rev slid down the car and lay on the road. Its limbs twitched as though it were still attempting to attack.

There were several more who charged at cars and banged on the windows.

They can be taken down but not killed. Interesting. Wesley surveyed the chaos before making his next decision.

The gunfire drew the Revs toward the yahoos who had fired the shots and were now running down the road to draw them away from the cars. Two men had handguns and ran out of bullets. Five Revs lay before them, but now they were in trouble. They were sixty yards down the road with no protection.

Wesley glanced toward Nora, who had pulled out with the rest of the unblocked cars. She met his gaze and gestured toward the runners. He nodded. He wasn't sure of her plan, but the determined tilt of her chin and narrowed eyes told him she was going to try something. The black Sonata raced out of the small gap and around still-gawking car drivers. Wesley sprinted back to his truck.

He kept an eye on Nora as she sped ahead of the six Revs, who stumbled after the men in a shuffling run. She swerved into the pack of them, and they lurched into each other like poorly organized dominos. Wesley followed in his truck and ran over a straggler at the back. The wet thump was disconcerting, but he reminded himself the Rev wasn't exactly alive.

Nora's car skidded to a stop, and the gun-toting guys flagged her down. Wesley's brow furrowed at their manic behavior. Instead of grateful profusions, they waved empty guns at her and stood in front of her car. They rapped on the window with the butts of the pistols. Nora's shoulders cringed inside as they yelled.

"Get out!"

"Get the fuck out!"

Two Revs still shuffled toward the men, having only minor injuries from Nora's car. They latched onto one of the guys, tearing at his throat. Wesley didn't bother to help as he braked hard. He jumped out of the truck, grabbed the other guy pounding on Nora's window, and threw him toward the Revs. The man flailed and fell. The second Rev left the first man and descended onto the second as his screams pierced the air.

"I'll meet you at the cabin, go!" Wesley shouted, and Nora nodded. She sped off as he leaped back into the truck.

He glanced back at the disarray of cars and bodies. Blood streaked the road. The Revs didn't "eat" their victims like zombies—once they killed them, they lost interest and left the body where it laid. It was as if they wanted everyone living to be dead like them. Wesley shook his head as he sped after Nora.

He hoped there were answers at Emin's cabin, but it was a long shot. The little voice that told him he was in over his head was drowned out by his need to see her safe. Maybe it was a sense of duty, but he knew his growing attachment was more than that.

CHAPTER FIFTEEN

THE WISCONSIN LANDSCAPE, FARM FIELDS, AND dense patches of forest stretched for miles before Nora's eyes. She glanced back every five minutes to see Wesley's silver Tundra following, and it reassured her that she didn't have to face this alone. She was torn between anger and disbelief. She thought she was helping the two men, but then they turned and wanted her car. To leave her for dead? Nora cursed people in general. Just when she thought the best of them, they proved humanity was nothing but selfish and loathsome. The men had no idea how much courage it had taken her to try to help.

And the Revs ... they had appeared more and more in the last seventy-two hours. Nora desperately hoped the cabin would be a good place to hole up for a while. Maybe it would blow over. Maybe the government would get a handle on the Revs. They had to be able to be killed somehow, right? Yet running them over with a car or shooting them hadn't done much except slow them down. How did one kill the undead?

Nora focused on driving as fast as possible. They didn't run into any more accidents as they headed into heavily wooded areas interspersed with farmland. The clouds that were once to the west now billowed across the sky in front of them. A few raindrops pelted the windshield, and Nora turned the wipers on.

Several cars raced past them. Sometimes cop cars with lights and sirens blaring flashed by. Other than that, it seemed like she was in her own world. The car's hum and the soft sounds of random jazz music on the radio calmed her nerves and brought forth happier thoughts. She'd often driven up to see Emin in those first years after the car accident. The cabin, affectionately known as Alfred, had been built by Emin and her mother's grandfather. They were big superhero fans who liked to debate Marvel versus DC. Emin's grandfather always said the name had nothing to do with Batman's trusted friend and confidant.

Rain pinged on the roof of the car, and Nora slowed a little in the onslaught. It was hard to see the lane markers, and the trees were blackened blurs on either side of the two-lane highway. They'd left the main highway and were now on the back-country roads. Soon the two-lane would turn into one dirt road. Nora tried not to reminisce as they passed through Pikes Bay's small "downtown" area. The town consisted of a few shops, quaint restaurants, and local establishments. She passed shops she and her parents would frequent on vacation. They'd gotten her candy or a toy of her choosing when she was a child. When she was older, her mom took her shopping.

Thunder cracked in the distance, and forks of lightning flashed down from the clouds. Nora blinked. She glanced at the black tactical bag on the seat next to her. The artifact sat inside, and she half expected it to start glowing. But the bag remained unobtrusive. She shook her head. She was letting her uncle's crazy theories get to her.

She loved Emin, and he'd taken care of her like a daughter when her parents died, but he was also interested in his own adventures. He'd disappeared for months at a time when she'd turned eighteen, and she was, in his words, "old enough to look after herself." Nora thought over the little he'd been able to tell them before he'd died ... was killed.

The pieces didn't fit together in any way that made sense to her.

Within thirty minutes, the cabin loomed ahead. It was located on a small gravel road with a few neighboring houses and backed onto Lake Michigan. The trees were bare for early spring, and she could see through them to the churning waters with frothing waves. Tall limestone cliffs stood to the north, and a few moored boats weathered the storm.

Nora circled the cabin once to be sure no one was waiting for her. *Perhaps Wesley's paranoia has rubbed off on me.* She nodded to herself—there could be worse things. The windows were dark, the curtains were drawn, there was no sign of smoke from the chimney, and no fresh tire tracks had disturbed the mud. Alfred stood as solemn yet welcoming as ever. The cabin was built from logs, and its high roof reached a peak. A staircase from the first-floor deck wound its way up to a wooden balcony on the roof. The cabin sat halfway built into a small cave—the back rooms she'd occupied as a kid were always cool and dark and perfect for reading.

The rain let up into a drizzle, and Nora got out with her umbrella to go to the secret key spot. Wesley parked his truck next to hers. With the engines cut, only the chirping of birds, dripping rain, and wash of the lake could be heard. Nora retrieved the key from the old stone with a crude X marked on it, carved by an old knife; you had to look for it to know it was there. It was their inside joke that X marked the spot. A twinge of sadness stole Nora's breath.

"You okay?" Wesley came up next to her, and she nodded.

"Yeah, got the key."

"You had good intentions, by the way, back there. Those guys were panicked assholes."

"Thanks. I appreciated the assist." Nora turned the key in the lock. It stuck slightly, and she jiggled it open. Musty but clean cabin air wafted out, and Nora flicked the switch near the door. Lights fluttered on and illuminated the plush couches, stone fireplace, armchairs, and pine board kitchen with an island. Stainless steel appliances accented the dark counters.

The woodsy bourbon cologne Emin wore drifted to Nora's nose, and she clutched the back of the couch with white knuckles. Wesley remained behind her, not barging in and taking up the space, which made Nora grateful. She needed a moment. Nora closed her eyes and could hear Emin's belly laugh as they played poker by the fire and her parents made dinner in the kitchen when she was little.

"Maybe this wasn't a good idea," Wesley said in a low voice. "Do you need to go somewhere else?"

Nora shook her head. She refused to let him see her cry again. "No, thanks, I'm fine; a lot of memories here. Please, make yourself at home. There are three bedrooms and two bathrooms. You can have whichever one you want."

Wesley cautiously moved into the space, and she noticed he wore his gun holster under a light jacket. The butt of the gun poked out. Nora had never been so close to so many guns before today. Emin and her dad weren't hunters. They had a few shotguns at the cabin, but more for defense against people than anything.

"Mind if I make a perimeter check? See how secure this place is," Wesley said as he moved around the cabin. He checked windows and doors, then slid like a shadow through the bedrooms. In the back one, she could hear him low whistle in appreciation for the beautiful rock walls and care that had been taken to carve the room.

Nora followed him and folded her hands together, counting her fingers.

"This was my favorite space. I melted one of my plastic horse's hooves on that lamp when I was seven," she said. The bedside lamp glowed in a pool of yellow. The hunter-green bedspread over a queen-sized bed was the same as when she was a child. As was the wooden floor with thick throw rugs. Nothing had changed in years.

"This is a great place. Only problem is there's only one way in and out of it." Wesley put his hand on the solid wall. It was made to look like stone from the cave but made from far lighter material.

"Ah, you'd think so, but Uncle Emin liked his secrets. There was nothing more he liked than ancient tombs with trap doors." Nora gestured for him to follow her into the large primary suite bathroom. The double sinks and waterfall shower glistened in white marble. Nora slid the rug over with her foot, and a latch in the floor appeared. She twisted, tugged, and lifted a small door. "This leads under the cabin and back to about where the cars are."

Wesley chuckled, and it echoed. "I like your uncle more and more."

Nora locked the door and swept the rug back over it. She let out a breath. She was aware that she was showing Wesley a childhood place close to her heart.

"Do you think more of Emin's associates, or whoever, will come looking here?" Nora led the way out of the primary bedroom and back into the living room space. She went to the black pack, chastising herself for leaving it, and ensured the artifact was still there. Ensuring it was still with her was now part of her checks. She moved to the front door lock, touched it quickly, and then checked her pack again.

If Wesley noticed, he didn't say anything.

"I would imagine it's a good bet. Let's keep the curtains closed and find what we can as fast as possible. We can't stay here long," Wesley said with a regretful expression. "This would be a good place to hole up if I weren't concerned about others tracking your uncle. I don't expect we'd get lucky that they'd ..." He stopped himself.

Nora cleared her throat. "It's okay. I thought about the same thing. If they find out he's dead already, why bother coming here?" She went to the bookshelves by the fireplace. A desk sat on the right side, facing the big picture windows overlooking the lake. "Except, there might be something here we can use to decipher that artifact. He usually sends backup to the computer here."

Wesley nodded. "We need to figure out what we're dealing with. Or what your uncle's colleagues unleashed." He went to the kitchen and opened the cupboards, freezer, and fridge. "Looks like he'd been here recently, which is both good and bad. We've got enough food for tonight, so I'll go out and get more supplies tomorrow."

Nora swallowed as she followed and took a bottle of water from the fridge. Her uncle's favorite beer,

Zombiedust, sat in a six-pack in the corner. The irony wasn't lost on her. "He said fire seemed to cleanse the wound, and he didn't turn."

"I'd say fire is a safe bet on killing the Revs." Wesley took the water and downed it.

"Everyone is treating this like a disease we've heard of, but we know it's not. We have to find a way to kill the curse," Nora said as she surveyed the pantry. Emin had stocked it with a lot of nonperishables like canned beans, potatoes, corn, fruit, and pasta sauces. Wesley came up behind her, and her back warmed. Nora tapped each finger repeatedly at the proximity to him. If she took a step backward, she'd run straight into him.

"I'm not going to lie and say I've ever cooked dinner for a girl, but I'm willing to try boiling some water for pasta," he said with a grunt.

Nora turned to face him and had to tilt her head up. She still wasn't used to how tall he was. Now that her adrenaline had worn off, she was starting to think more like herself. The old Nora would tell him to leave now. She was best left to her OCD ticks where she didn't feel judged. She could call him if she found anything. *You want him here. You don't like to think you need protection, but he's your best bet. And he hasn't judged you on anything yet.*

"I thought you dated pretty extensively," she said and slipped past him, so she didn't accidentally touch his arm. She grabbed a box of pasta on her way over to the other counter where the pots were. "I would imagine you'd have cooked something for those girls."

Wesley cocked his head, and those dark eyes twinkled even as he scanned everything over and over. She didn't miss that he kept checking the windows and door.

"You caught me—I once grilled some steak for a girl I met in college. It was a disaster since it rained, and I burned the crap out of them," he said. Wesley reached for a pot and started to fill it with water.

Nora rummaged through the other cupboards for plates and silverware and found an old Cabernet Sauvignon bottle.

"He never married?" Wesley asked when she told him what she found. Nora got out two glasses and found the corker.

"Nope. Said he was tired of dating women who pretended to understand he traveled a lot, but who in reality wanted to settle down with the white picket fence and two point five kids," she said. Emin's friends jokingly called him the "Asian Dr. Jones," but what Indiana lacked for in real archeology, Emin was nearly obsessed. He loved finding anything unusual or forgotten by time.

"I think he was smart. He understood he had a life no partner would want to settle with." Wesley set the pot on the stove, and the lights flickered. He went to the side window and peered out the curtain. Nora continued pouring the wine and setting the table when he didn't report anything.

"You sound like you agree with him." She was curious about this closed-off guy who was so flirty when they gamed.

Wesley returned to the kitchen and took a sip from the wine glass she offered him. He nodded agreeably with the taste. "I do. If you know you can't guarantee you can come back to your partner, why have one?"

"Is that common in your line of work?" Nora put the pasta in the water and stirred it. Then she moved on to heat the jar of sauce in another pot.

"It can be, but often not. The marshals take a lot of precautions, and it depends on the branch you work in. I chose fugitive apprehension, meaning I can be called at any time of the day or night." He pulled out his phone as if reminding himself. "But since this undead curse hit, there has been a hell of a lot fewer calls. And I already thought maybe the service isn't what I want in a career."

He seemed to want to say more but didn't. Nora wished they were in game—it was easy to chat behind a screen.

Wesley arranged their bowls, forks, napkins, and water glasses in line on the table, then came back to her wearing a boyish grin. The sauce continued to heat on the stove. "It's nice to meet you in a moment of calm."

Nora bobbed her head and held out her hand as if in proper first greeting. "Agreed."

As his hand met hers, it was the perfect time for both of their cell phones to ping.

CHAPTER SIXTEEN

WESLEY BROKE CONTACT AND HEADED INTO THE living room. "Chief."

"Bad connection, son." Chief Gibson's voice broke up as Wesley moved around the room to get better reception. Nora gave him an apologetic face as she plugged her phone into a charger. Her phone ring had been a text alert.

He gave her credit for being so put together after everything that had happened. He observed her closely and could see the OCD tics she worked hard to combat. They weren't unlike his own, except his were mainly internal, and he could hide them better. Wesley didn't blame her for having PTSD from her parent's accident and now her uncle's death. He wondered how she'd been able to cope. He also didn't know what to do because he wanted to be there for her. And he wouldn't admit it had been nice to give comfort to someone who wanted it.

"We're overrun in Wood Dale. Moving out toward the border of Wisconsin. The national ... need ... are you safe?"

"Safe, sir, but I can't get to the border. We're working on

a solution." Wesley paced around the coffee table strewn with hunting and fishing magazines. The cabin, Alfred, as Nora had informed him, was suitably set up for someone to live comfortably for quite a while. There was an extra freezer out in the garage and plenty of firewood.

"These Mobs are multiplying ... bullets don't kill them." The line cut off, and Wesley stared at the zero bars on his phone. He frowned and let out a breath. He shot an email to the chief explaining the only way he knew how to kill the undead was with fire.

Nora glanced up from where she'd plugged in her phone and laptop at her uncle's desk. "We have Wi-Fi but definitely spotty cell reception. I'm sorry. I didn't think about that. Is everything okay?"

"That was my chief, and he said they were in Wood Dale, but it's being overrun with Mobs, er, Revs. He calls them what everyone else is—Mobs. This thing is getting bigger by the day, but we're good here for now," Wesley assured her. He wanted her to get a good night's sleep, and hopefully, they could figure something out soon.

"Well, let me turn on my uncle's computer and start looking at his research. I know his email password."

"Why don't we finish eating first?" Wesley interrupted as his stomach rumbled. It had been a while since he'd had a meal cooked in a kitchen. Takeout and protein shakes were his usual go-to.

"Sure, sounds good. It's getting dark." Nora went to the front door to check the lock, and he noticed she tapped her fingers again, counting. He wasn't going to point it out and make her uncomfortable. Emin had told him that she was fragile, broken, and sensitive but also a survivor. She lived life in a way that made sense to her, which often blocked her from doing things other people did.

He didn't like getting secondhand knowledge, so he tried to read her for himself. He sat down at the table. Wesley rearranged the place setting again before she came. He aligned the plate with a straight set of silverware and the cup on the right side. The chair he picked faced the door and windows as usual.

"I'm sure you think I'm a pussy about the dark," Nora said as she flicked on a lamp in the corner. Light flooded the entire cabin space. "I think the curtains block a lot of the light, but I can turn this off. It's a habit." She chewed on her lip and sat down with a sigh.

"I think we all have fears we keep at bay with certain rituals or beliefs," he said. The spaghetti was wonderfully warm, and the Cabernet took the edge off slightly. There was no chance he was getting buzzed, though—he needed all his senses. "I mean, you've noticed my propensity for keeping my plate in line with my glass, the silverware pointed straight."

Nora ate her dinner quickly. She sipped on the wine. "I did, but it's not super unusual, really."

Wesley grunted, and she chuckled.

"I haven't been... after my parent's accident, I started to be afraid. Of everything. I know it's hard to believe, but I've come a long way."

"That's a pretty big event in someone's life so young. I can imagine there's a lot of post-traumatic stress involved."

Her eyes softened but she didn't say more. Wesley cleared their dishes and washed them in the sink while Nora took their wine glasses to the couch.

The fireplace was black and empty. He thought about

asking her to start a fire, but it might draw attention more than the lights in the windows. Thunder still rumbled in the distance over the crash of waves on a rocky shoreline.

"I definitely don't know how to deal with this. It's like I'm out of my body, and I see myself reacting, but I don't feel like me." Nora shivered and curled up in the corner of the couch. She shoved her hair away from her face.

Wesley sat on the opposite couch to give her space. Her large, almond eyes were framed with thick lashes and a heart-shaped mouth. He'd wanted to kiss her ever since he saw her. It was like being in game with her, except a thousand times better. It wasn't simply hearing her voice but sensing what she was feeling and being able to read her facial expressions.

"I think sleep will help. I'll watch tonight, and you go rest. I need to sort out my bag anyway," he said.

He finished his wine and went to the large black duffel he'd brought in from the truck. He always had an emergency bag with two changes of clothes, extra shoes, toiletries, a stash of a thousand dollars in cash, and a pistol. Some people called it paranoia, but he called it preparedness.

"Oh, I didn't realize you probably wanted to stop by your place too. Did you leave anything important there? We can go back," Nora said. The concern in her voice warmed him.

"Just a cactus named Ruth." He grinned. "I think she'll fare okay for a while. I don't have much at my apartment since I'm gone a lot. I always thought about getting a dog, but the poor thing probably wouldn't know I was his owner for all the time I'd be away."

Nora's lips curved up. "I've always wanted a dog too. I almost had my parents talked into getting a German Shepherd before their accident. But they had a point too:

that I was going to college and wouldn't be around to take care of it."

"Did you grow up with dogs?" Wesley asked. He wished he had, but his dad got rid of any animal his mom brought home. And when he grew older, he understood why. One day in the backyard, he'd found a freshly dug hole, and given his insatiable curiosity, he'd dug it up. The cat his mom had brought home five days previously was wrapped in a cloth, blood splotches all over. Wesley had vomited and covered the hole back up so fast that he threw dirt everywhere. His dad had noticed, and they'd chatted about his mom's lack of care for animals. His dad explained that some people thought animal life wasn't as valuable as human life and that they thought it was okay to take their anger out on them, which was wrong. Wesley agreed.

"Yeah, we had a Golden when I was a kid. She was the best. Did you?" Nora gazed at him as if they sat in a café instead of hiding from the undead. It was a nice break from the chaos.

"Nope. Mom didn't like animals," he said, and even though the words were on the tip of his tongue, he held back. She didn't need to deal with his mangled past on top of her loss. So, he did what he did best; he changed the subject. "Have you ever thought about finding your birth parents?"

Nora's brows rose at the change, but she went with it. "Sometimes, but it was a closed adoption. I can't find my birth mother unless she wants to find me." She shrugged. "So, it's a moot point. I know a lot of adopted kids feel this loss or like something's missing, but honestly, I didn't feel the need."

"I think that's great." Wesley was a little jealous of her

family background. He wished he could say his mother baked pies at Christmas, or his sister hadn't set the chemistry lab on fire on purpose in middle school.

"You have a sister, right? And you don't speak to your parents?" Nora pried, and for once, he didn't find it annoying. Most girls seemed to fish for information they could use against him later or liked to "fix" him, but Nora seemed sincere.

Wesley gave in and told a few details about his rough upbringing. He didn't sugarcoat it, but he also left out the truly violent outbursts his mom had. "She's in a psych facility, not the same as my sister Becca. I check in once in a while, but for the most part, it's still my dad who handles her affairs. They're married, but it isn't much of a marriage, really."

Nora shook her head. "I'm sorry, that sounds tough to deal with. I think, unlike many people, you've not let it derail your life."

He nodded at her in a sort of mock salute. "Thanks. I made it a point to cut myself off from all of them and start new. It kind of worked. I still feel obligated to check in."

"It's family." Nora shrugged. "My dad has a sister I've met once, and the one time I did, she threw juice at the wall and stormed out over an argument they had. I saw her at the funeral, and she didn't even acknowledge me. The things we put up with because they're 'family' is annoying."

"I'll second that." Wesley nodded.

Nora lay her head back on the couch cushion, and Wesley held up a finger.

"You're going to sleep in a bed. Not that couch." He rose at her protests.

"I'm not going to let you stay up all night alone. I can

read or something," she said. Her eyes were half-rimmed. "Plus, I don't know you still." There wasn't much conviction in her voice.

Wesley tried to put himself in her place, alone in a cabin with a guy she had just met and who'd gotten her uncle killed. *Emin did that part himself, but I shouldn't have left them.*

"I told you mental illness runs in my family. I get it," he teased. "Besides, you know me. You've talked with me for almost three years, nearly every night."

"I know a version of you." Nora tapped her fingers together, but it was slow and methodical, not rapid or anxious.

"What else do you want to know?" Wesley spread his hands and leaned back on the couch. He was good at reading body language and wanted to appear non-threatening.

"I don't know; you're right. I'm being paranoid. This is an unusual situation, to begin with. I mean, if we weren't here, we'd be gaming now, right?" Nora couldn't help the warm feeling that flooded through her at the thought and checked her phone for the time. 9:45 p.m.

"True. I bet some people are still on. The world will take a while to fall apart, so let's hope we can fix it before the kids in their parents' basements find out," Wesley said.

"Psh, yeah, what do you bet *Bigtool* is a huge tool in real life. He's probably a college dropout or so high that he can't function all the time." Nora lifted her hands. Wesley chuckled and didn't disagree. A few repeat gamers weren't friends but kept popping up on the servers they played on. *Bigtool* was amusing, but he sounded like he was in his teens and perpetually stoned.

"You're the only one I've ever video-chatted with," she continued and ducked her neck down.

Wesley hadn't chatted with many other gamers, male or female, via video chat. He didn't see the point because where would it lead? There were plenty of avenues for meeting people online that led to relationships, but gaming wasn't one of them.

"Well, I'm honored. I like no mic between us," he said. An unfamiliar uneasiness coated his throat, which he forced himself to swallow. "Even if we're not on a pirate ship, it's still pretty easy to talk to you."

Nora ducked her head and pulled her sleeves over her hands. She nestled further into the couch like a dog nesting.

"Oh, no, you don't. You're going to a bed," Wesley said and stood up. He expected her to react in alarm, but Nora didn't move. No fear in her eyes. It had a pleasant sensational effect on him for some reason. He stood over her, and she didn't seem to mind the nearness. He never wanted to come across like his mother—aggressive and unpredictable.

"I'll stay on the couch if that makes you more comfortable," he said, holding a hand to help her up.

Nora shook her head. "My head is pounding. You take the cave room, all right? I'll take my uncle's room." She took his hand, and the heat in their palms spread to his chest.

Wesley helped her stand. The top of her head was level with his chest, and she had to tilt her head back to look at him. The silken wave of her hair fell over her shoulder. He didn't let go of her hand because he didn't want the warmth to leave. Not yet. He'd be lying if he hadn't fantasized about meeting her one day and doing more than talking. But that was the charm of fantasies, anything could happen. In real life, there were awkward pauses, unsure body language, and electric heat that passed between them like a live wire.

Nora took a tiny step back, and he let go. He couldn't help but notice the way her sweater hugged her curves. She looked away from him as she started toward the bedroom hallway. "Night, Tango Strike. Maybe we can game again when the world's right."

"Night, Moonbeam." It wasn't her gamer tag, but Hypernova didn't suit her. Wesley couldn't remember when he'd given her that nickname. He remembered their conversation when she'd shyly told him she liked when he called her Moonbeam. He understood now that her fear of the dark had probably been a reason she'd liked it. As if he'd somehow known her fear and done something to dispel it— give it a name.

Wesley stared at the closed door to her room. Light blared under the slit of the door frame, and he didn't think she'd turn them off anytime soon. His cell rang again, and he moved into the cabin's front room to not disturb any sleep Nora might be getting.

"Soares."

"I know where you are." The voice was scratchy, feminine, and definitely on his short list of things that terrified him.

"How do you know that, Mom?"

CHAPTER SEVENTEEN

AFTER A NIGHT OF SLEEP WITH ALL THE LIGHTS ON, Nora felt as refreshed as she was going to get. She checked her phone and estimated she'd gotten at least four consecutive hours. Her head was much clearer and didn't pound like horses stampeded around in it. She threw back the covers, and a sense of curious dread settled in her stomach. In addition to the REM she needed, her brain had been all over the place. She'd started with a dream of Wesley on top of her, but soon a bullet wound appeared in his chest, leaving blood cascading down his body and weeping onto her. Her uncle's face flashed into her head. Nora shook her head. She wished being awake was less torture than her nightmares.

She hadn't been terribly concerned Wesley would hurt her. If he wanted to kill her, he'd have done it. If he wanted something more physical, he'd had ample opportunity. If he wanted a safe place to rest, that was about the only thing she could provide him with for now. Nora's throat closed when she thought about how close she wanted him by her.

She admitted she liked the idea of him staying with her until things calmed down and she could figure out her next move. The cell reception was spotty, but she'd gotten a few texts from classmates at Knox. It felt like a lifetime away. Even though Jess' death still haunted her, she was starting to understand her friend hadn't died from normal circumstances.

Nora didn't have time to worry about school payments or apartment rent. She'd take care of it if there was anything left to take care of. The world might soon be one giant population of undead people. She shuddered when she pictured students she knew being attacked, their throats ripped out, limbs bitten. It was ridiculous to think humans could start behaving like rabid dogs, yet she'd seen the proof herself. Bloody bodies, milky white eyes, fanged teeth, and scuttling, contorting movements.

She banished her dark thoughts with a quick shower, changed into clean leggings and a gray sweater, and applied minimal makeup. Her mother's infinity necklace and a pair of diamond stud earrings from her dad were the only pieces of jewelry she had or liked to wear. They reminded her of her resolve not to sit idly and to work on the problem. Nora peeked out the bedroom door and saw that the living room lights were all still on as she'd left them. She walked down the hall, following the smell of frying eggs and toast.

Wesley was in the kitchen with a smoking toaster and a frown on his handsome face. He was striking even in the artificial light with a day's worth of stubble. Her left hand tingled as she recalled how he'd held it for a moment too long to be considered just friends.

"Mornin'. I thought I'd try a foolproof meal like eggs,

but it turns out the toaster was set to nuclear before I realized it," he called to her.

"I'm sorry, Uncle Emin liked his toast burnt. If the eggs are still good, he must have been here not too long ago." She put two more slices of bread into the toaster and turned the setting down.

Wesley scoffed at the burnt toast. "Yeah, hopefully, he left some clue about what we're dealing with. Did you sleep okay?"

"Yes, thanks. Did you stay up all night? It seems like you never need sleep." Nora yawned as she waited for the toast. When Wesley scooped a mound on her plate, she used the bread to sop up the eggs. She'd never had anyone other than her mom make her breakfast before.

"I got enough. Insomnia, remember?"

Nora nodded, recalling many late-night conversations when she couldn't sleep. He'd been the only person awake. Given what she knew now about his job and his family background, it didn't surprise her. She thought it was great he even slept at all.

Wesley wore a white undershirt that clung to his arms and left little to imagine about the shape of his abdomen. He was still in black slacks, minus the belt. His dark hair was disheveled as if he'd slept on the couch. Nora gave him an accusatory stare as she took in the rumpled blanket on the longer couch.

"You could have turned off the lights. I don't demand everyone I room with leave them on because I do," she said, and to prove it, she went over to flip the fireplace lights off. Nora flinched at the shadows it created but turned with a flourish as if she'd done something amazing. For her, it kind of was. She did a silly jig, flipping her legs up like a cheerleader.

Wesley gave her a grin. Heat rushed to Nora's cheeks at his gaze that lingered over her legs, as if he wanted her to dance closer. "I did. But I turned them all back on at five this morning."

Nora's heart pulsed in her ears as she broke off their gaze. She tucked a strand of hair behind her ear. "I'm not, like, dysfunctional in the dark. I just don't like it."

"I don't like tailgaters or rude people, so we all have something." Wesley motioned for her to get the toast.

Nora took her breakfast to the desk in the corner. She peered out the curtained windows for a second. Both cars were in the same spot. Tall trees and overgrowth shaded the cabin, and the rush of waves on the shore soothed her. The cabin smelled of fried eggs, pine, and rain-scented wood. It took her back to childhood, idyllic days that Wesley probably hadn't experienced from what he'd told her. She didn't pity him, but she did have the urge to comfort him if she could. Helping other people soothed her and distracted her from her grief.

She glanced over at Wesley, and he was staring at his phone with a deep frown. She'd heard him speaking to someone last night but didn't want to eavesdrop. It must not have been a good conversation from the concerned tilt of his lips. She was too shy to ask about it, so she turned her attention to the problem.

Nora scanned through her uncle's computer and pulled her black pack close to her. The artifact sat in its box like an ordinary, regular rock. She brought it out and set it on the desk in the light. The rough face etched with runes and pictographs was a language she barely had the tools to decipher. She traced her finger over the ancient Malian carvings. Maybe it was created by the very people who Count Ulrich used to create his immortality curse.

Nora clicked through her uncle's files. Several were decoder keys but in the wrong language. She flipped through his notebook and found that Mandé was the language spoken in Mali. She cross-referenced the hieroglyphics with ancient Mandé and let out an excited gasp when it distinctly resembled the lines and pictographs on the tablet.

She was barely aware when Wesley announced he was going out for supplies. She half-waved, distracted by the files and old emails from Emin's colleagues. The mythology and facts about Timbuktu and the Mali dynasty were fascinating. Mansa Musa had created a city of gold but also protection for a chosen people. He was a ruthless leader who raided other countries and pillaged them. But there were conflicting sources citing he was simply one of many historical tyrants, and the fabled city was just that. She needed to sort through fact and fiction to shake out the truth.

The ancient Mandé had five sets of alphabets, so Nora picked the one closest to the artifact's symbols. She started to piece together a crude alphabet to use as a cipher. Hours passed, and Wesley startled Nora when he entered the cabin laden with bags. She stood, stretched, and went to help unload his truck.

"Any luck?" he asked as he hauled in a heavy black case that didn't look like it came from a grocery store.

"I think I've found something, but it'll take a little more time to be sure. There are dozens of emails between my uncle and his best friend, Norman. He led the team to Gao and uncovered the Mali tribal trail there. Emin suggested they travel to England and trace the connection to Count Ulrich—which he ended up doing himself, as we know."

"Have you turned on the TV?" Wesley flipped the remote on. The news showed various stages of chaos: gas stations burning, schools evacuating, people boarding up their homes and shops, and grocery stores overrun with panicked shoppers.

"The governors of all the states don't agree on much, but they're all issuing a mandate to stay inside for at least a week. Anything not mandatory is shut down for now," Wesley said.

That's why it took him so long to get supplies.

"I should have been paying closer attention. I've been buried in the past trying to figure out how this curse works," Nora said with a hand to her throat. She couldn't bear the sight of children crying as they were lost in stampeding crowds when Revs showed up.

"What were you saying before about the curse?" Wesley asked.

"Have you heard of the mythical Timbuktu?"

"Only from what your uncle mentioned."

"It's like the equivalent of El Dorado—you have heard of that, right?" Nora teased him with a side glance. The legends of cities of gold were universal, but Timbuktu wasn't as high on many people's radars.

"Yes." Wesley winked as he started to put the groceries away.

"In the thirteen hundreds, Mali was the center for West African trade. Emin told me many stories as a kid of Mali and the ruler Mansa Musa and how he was probably the richest ruler in history. But a lot of the factual evidence has been lost. Supposedly, he built a city of gold in the heart of

Africa somewhere. Gold and magic seem to go together. And where there's treasure, there are hunters." Nora stopped herself from getting caught up in the adventure that her uncle always incited in her. He'd spend hours talking to her about lost worlds and treasure, even when she was an adult.

"I believe this artifact is Malian and from Mansu Musa's era. Emin found it in England, but the slave trade was very big, even in the Middle Ages. I'm guessing some of this Count Ulrich's enslaved people were from Mali—maybe they practiced actual dark magic. I've coded an alphabet, and from the few lines I've read it, speaks about 'life after life' and 'unending blessing.' A curse that led to immortality."

Wesley, to his credit, didn't immediately push her ideas off as conjecture or crazy. It wasn't completely new to him, at least, since Emin had given them a brief but similar run down at the restaurant. Wesley paused in sorting the food items and regarded her curiously.

"You've done all that in three hours? I'm impressed."

Nora ducked her face due to burning cheeks. "Well, it's far from deciphered. But Emin was telling the truth. There's something about this tablet that holds the key." She gave it a little rap.

"So, this infection that makes people violent and ultimately kill themselves is a curse, like your uncle said?" He grimaced.

"Seems like it. I'm slow at translating." Nora sighed. "My uncle wanted me to follow his footsteps, and he's found a surefire way. But a little warning would have been nice." She joked, but it felt hollow. Nora desperately wished her uncle were here with them. He'd know what to do, and he'd certainly be a lot faster decoding the artifact. But at least they had leads; if this was a curse, there had to be a way to break it.

She peered into the bags Wesley had brought. "Are we staying here for a while?"

"Until we get a bearing. I still think the people tracking your uncle may come here, so we'll have to make it a little more secure. It's dangerous out on the roads right now. I drove to the next town over, and the stores are sold out of almost everything—if they aren't being looted." He moved to the black cases and opened them.

In one was a variety of knives and black vests. In another was a long rifle with a scope and several pistols. Boxes of ammunition sat in neat rows under the foam.

"I didn't think the marshals issued this kind of artillery," Nora said with raised brows. She'd never seen a sniper rifle up close, and the weapon drew her to it. She turned to the man she'd shot plenty of pirate zombies with, but not in real life. It occurred to her how dangerous he could be outside of a game. And, for a fleeting moment, how dangerous he might be to her. *Stop it. You've gone over this; trust him already. He literally threw a guy off your car for you.*

At the softening expression in his eyes, Nora felt even more guilty for the thought. He'd been nothing but kind to her. He probably had a million other things he could be doing, or he could have left. He'd come back—armed —for her.

"They don't. The rifle is from my personal collection that I keep in my truck. I like to think my preparedness has paid off now," he said with a wry smile. "I also may have stopped at a gun shop and flashed my badge. This *is* Wisconsin, and there are plenty of hunters in the area. Is it bothering you? You shoot pirates like they're whack-a-moles, but this is different. You ever shot before?"

Nora scratched her nose. "A few times with Emin's shotgun. As much as I'm awesome in a game, this is beyond my skill set. When you referenced stuff in the game, I had no idea you actually knew what you were talking about."

"I can show you how to use every weapon here. We need to first establish a clearing pattern for the cabin should we be attacked." Wesley pulled out a huge box of peanut M&M's, and Nora couldn't help but laugh.

"I'm sorry, but do you have enough M&M's?"

Wesley shook the box. "That depends on if you like them. If I'm sharing, then no, these aren't enough." He grinned, ripped open the package inside, and tossed her a few.

Nora fumbled to catch them. "If we're going to die in a Revenant apocalypse, this is the way to go." She savored the salty peanut and milk chocolate as she sighed. "The thing is, we're not only dealing with a Malian myth. All the email exchanges I've read confirm that my uncle's colleagues had also contacted this group called the Antiquarian Matrix."

"I'm going to assume these aren't the retired couch potatoes but the retired veterans?" Wesley stuffed a handful of M&M's into his mouth. He moved to the table and began to field strip his pistol in order to do a deep clean.

"Right. From what my uncle says in his emails, they're dangerous retired army guys and they like to dabble in experimental archeology. Meaning, they like replicating ancient sites by reproducing or using ancient technology to recreate life."

"So, by 'matrix' you don't mean like a Neo and Morpheus situation?" Wesley asked. Nora snorted.

"I thought you never watched popular movies. No, a matrix, in this sense, refers to dirt, like the place where artifacts are buried. This ties into what my uncle and his friends were up to in Gao if they found Mansa Musa and his famed city of gold. There must've been some ancient tribal magic that made its way to England and Count Ulrich from the enslaved people they traded in that region." Nora clucked her tongue and reached for more candy. Wesley pretended to be offended when she plucked only the red and green ones.

"The thing is, these guys like to 'recreate' sites which means they're going to be after the artifact. They must have started the curse, and now they need the second half to complete it. Or, as my uncle said, some of them may want it to stop the curse. It's a very divided society."

Wesley put down the pistol, and his hip cocked to the side. "How fast can you decipher what's on it?"

Nora went to the desk and picked up the stone. "I've bits and pieces, but so far, nothing good. I don't know how long it'll take.'" She glanced at Wesley, and his eyes crinkled with concern.

"I should secure this place while you read this thing," he said slowly, his head moving toward the window.

A scream shattered the still, the noise bouncing off the trees like a ghostly echo.

Chapter Eighteen

Nora clutched the artifact to her chest as she ducked under the desk. Wesley motioned for her to stay as he checked the window, his gun out. He moved from window to window but shook his head.

"Nothing." He paused, and Nora could tell he was thinking about going outside to survey the woods. She slid out from underneath the desk and sat in the chair. The faster she could decipher the artifact, the better. Wesley was right —they probably needed to find a safer place to lay low. But the cabin was so well-equipped that it would be hard to find someplace better.

"I don't think you should go out," she said as she scanned her uncle's emails and notes. She tapped her toes and mentally counted her fingers. The soothing number rhythm helped keep her focused.

"I won't say I disagree, but that scream was human. I couldn't find motion detectors, so I'm going to rig a few of my own. I won't be long—you should be able to see me from the window," he said and picked up a large plastic bag full of screwdrivers, wires, and other electronics Nora couldn't name.

Nora stopped her search and looked at him. She took a deep breath.

"Why are you helping me? You have a lot of other responsibilities, and I feel like I'm taking you away from them." The words rushed out like lightning, hoping she didn't offend him.

The bag crinkled in the silence. Wesley gave her a small grin. "Because I tend to run away from problems. Because I want to protect you and not in a 'women can't do shit' kind of way. I think I can be helpful *to* you. Would you rather be alone?"

"No." Nora brushed the hair from her face. She'd been alone too much. "I know we tried to keep it distant for three years gaming, but I admit I feel like I know you."

Wesley tilted his head, and the light hit his face so that he looked carved from marble. "I guess we're past the point where it would be awkward if I told you I often wondered what it would be like to meet." He turned away as if embarrassed.

Nora grinned and spread her hands wide. "Well, you've got 'live me' now. Didn't think I had OCD issues this bad, did you?" she teased, though her heart was in her throat.

"Like I said, we've all got our quirks. Let me make good use of mine, like setting traps, so we can defend this cabin if something ugly comes this way," Wesley said as he jangled the bag. "Even if we're only here another day."

"Like the battle of Rum Bay?" She chuckled softly. In *Pirate Scourge*, they'd had to set traps and bait the enemy instead of straight-up attacking. Patience was not Nora's strong suit. Wesley had forced her to sit in an abandoned cave while he searched the island and set traps.

"Exactly, except this time, keep your clothes on, eh?" He smirked, then turned and exited the front door. Nora was glad he couldn't see her blush. During the game, she'd been bored waiting and playing with her avatar's outfit to pass the time. When he'd returned, the female pirate was stark naked except for her boots.

Nora certainly wasn't disappointed in the real version of him. Wesley had always stood out compared to a lot of the guys she'd gamed with. She recalled when she, Wesley, Rimfire, and a guy named Pyro50 were in-game when a new gamer joined. The boy had been eleven.

The two guys had teased and cursed at him because he was slower to react, confused about where to go. Nora had tried to get him to follow her, but she was a girl, and the boy only wanted to follow the guys. She told Rimfire to lay off, but he kept cajoling the boy until he started to get upset.

Wesley had stepped in with humor and distraction. He had the boy follow him on the quest as if it were a military game. The boy loved military jargon, so Wesley would always say "over" or "copy," and the boy would start to giggle. He started to have fun gaming, which was the whole point. Rimfire and Pyro ended up raging and left to find a new game since Nora refused to kick the kid out. The three had a fun game and ended up raiding a bountiful pirate cache in an underwater cave.

That reminded Nora she wanted to log on to *Pirate Scourge*. She glanced at the time. She could spare a minute to check on her other friends. The game loaded, and her friends list popped up. Several boxes started to flash—messages.

Nora clicked on the first one from Elena. She was

curious if the gaming community was feeling any of the chaos.

Hey girl, you safe? I'm in some trouble I think ... my mom's missing and I'm alone. I told you she sometimes goes on benders, but this feels different. Are you seeing the news? That was March twenty-fifth.

Hi, sorry to keep messaging, but has Kyle talked to you recently? Or Tango Strike? No one's online anymore and it's freaking me out. Kyle keeps saying he's going to come find me and help. I don't know if that's creepy or hopeful. I'll try texting you. March twenty-seventh.

Nora glanced at her phone. No texts from Elena. She frowned and scrolled through a few other messages, invites to play, "hey there" messages, and one from a friend she didn't know well, saying the end of the world was coming. Some of the forums were exploding, with people speculating on what was happening and how they should meet to defend together.

She tried calling Elena's cell, but it went to voicemail. "Hey, Elena, sorry, I got your messages on the game. I hope you're okay and call me back, please. I'm safe for now. Let me know if I can help."

Nora sat back and rubbed her forehead. The urgency of her mission returned to full force. She needed to get reading the artifact so they could figure out some way to help. She went back to studying her uncle's notes and checking them against the artifact. The tablet's pictographs and hieroglyphs seemed to spell out some kind of disaster. She was able to piece together symbols and meaning, growing quicker at the task as she went. One image was of fire with a man burning to death. Another showed a spear-like weapon driven into the sternum of another. Was this how to kill the Revs?

The artifact warmed in her hands. It was only her body heat, right? Nora's head fogged and memories that she had no right to have, swirled in her brain. People, likely enslaved people given their dress, lay on slabs of stone, their insides dripping out but still alive in a state of shock, while a man in a long tunic spoke Ancient Malian over them, his hands glowing a soft gold. His fingers became claws, and he gasped as his spell began to work.

Nora was jolted out of the memories. She looked around, her eyes frantic, to ascertain she really was still in the cabin. She shivered. Her skin felt dirty, and she desperately wished she could wash her mind.

A new email popped up in her uncle's inbox. Nora's eyes narrowed as she read the short message.

Emin, we don't believe you're dead. Good fake, friend, but you have twenty-four hours to deliver the artifact to us. We will text you the location.

Nora swallowed hard. The Antiquarian Matrix logo was embedded at the bottom of the message, a quill sticking out of a stone with an ouroboros underneath.

Chapter Nineteen

Nora stood and raced to the front door to flag Wesley down. He was kneeling and fiddling with some electronics, likely a motion trigger trap.

"What's wrong?" Wesley immediately stopped his work and approached as she spoke.

"The Antiquarians sent my uncle an email. They don't believe he's dead. I didn't even think to take his cell phone."

Wesley followed her into the cabin, and as she slid into the desk chair again, he leaned over her shoulder. Nora was momentarily distracted by the amount of muscle so near her face. The scent of his light cologne mixed with the fresh air of the lake made her almost forget what she was doing.

"Is the g-chat live?" Wesley took the mouse, but before he could click to disable the chat, a popping sounded, and the g-chat box lit up.

Emin, you should respond.

Nora gasped. She realized the g-chat made it look like her uncle was online. She smacked her palm to her forehead. She clicked on "offline" and made the green dot by her uncle's name go grey. "Dammit, I'm so stupid!"

"Hold on." Wesley put a hand on her shoulder but took it off right away. Nora barely registered his contact. She could decipher the tablet on the run, but all of Emin's research and books were at the cabin. She was putting Wesley in so much danger now. Thoughts ambushed her sanity as more emails popped up.

I know you're there. Do you want your niece to suffer for your mistakes?

Nora checked the computer's security status and turned off any location or tracking on it, but she was sure that wasn't going to be enough.

"Good thinking, but they'll probably be able to track the IP address. However, that doesn't mean what people think. They can't locate us specifically from that. It depends on how much help they have. If they work with law enforcement, they can get around a subpoena and ask the internet provider for this address or hack into your uncle's emails. Just not sure how quickly," Wesley said as Nora stood up. She paced in front of the desk, counting her fingers and checking the window and door locks.

"I am such an idiot! We have to leave now. I can't bring all his shit with me, though!" Nora bit her lip and started going through some of the paper trail Uncle Emin left. He loved his ancient epigraph text with all the known codes for hieroglyphs. She'd need that.

"Hold on, Moonbeam. I can add a program to use a VPN that should hold them off for a bit. It'll give them a fake IP address. But you're right. We're running out of options, and sitting here is not going to be one of them." Wesley sat back and sighed, running his hands through his dark hair. "There's something I didn't tell you. I didn't want you to worry."

Nora didn't think she could take another piece of bad news. She stopped pacing and faced him, her heart pounding.

He cleared his throat. "My mother called me last night. She claims to know where I am, but I know she doesn't. She sounded weird. Like she was trying to make amends and get me to tell her where I was."

Nora didn't know if she was relieved that he was confiding in her or panicked that another person was looking for them. She swiped her hair back and tapped her fingers.

"She said she stopped by my condo, which is odd because she's never been there. I have a bad feeling something's wrong, like she was being forced to make the call by someone. How she was even allowed out of the psych facility is another question," he said. Wesley stood and headed for the front door but stopped when he was by her side. "Then again, I don't think she's a huge threat even if she were being held by someone. She doesn't know a damn thing about me."

"Okay, we can pack up and find her if she's waiting at your place."

Wesley shook his head. "You're a better person than me. Right now, we need to find a way to survive here while you figure out what the Antiquarian Matrix is after."

Nora nodded and went back to the desk. No more messages from whoever was out there. "How many do you think there are? How much time do we have?"

"Enough of them that we should get ready to leave," he replied. "I'll give you as much time as possible by setting an early alarm, but we'll probably have to find a new place to crash soon." Wesley went out front, his forehead creased in thought.

Nora tossed in bed. For the last two days, it had been mercifully silent at the cabin, and she'd gotten a lot deciphered. The words "fire" and "mineral" overlapped in her mind. There was something she wasn't seeing or translating correctly. And the more she understood, the more the disturbing images entered her head. It was as if the artifact were reading her too, seeing into her secrets, using her energy to spread its influence.

For days, the world was overwhelmed with waves of the undead, Mobs. The CDC no longer had answers or pretended to have answers. The President addressed the nation every evening, but his words were hollow promises, as there was no rational explanation for why people were returning from the dead.

More and more people started to act irrationally and violently. Their deaths led to more undead.

Keep it safe.

It's what's inside …

Emin's words ran through her mind like movie reels. He'd been cut off at the smokehouse. He'd been about to tell her something. Nora squeezed her eyes shut and tried to remember. Crickets sang outside her window, owls hooted, and the wash of waves was no longer soothing. She and Wesley were on borrowed time.

Shadows under her door made her sit up and clutch the pillow. She knew it was Wesley, but it didn't lessen the knot in her stomach. He'd tiptoed around her room for two days, and after two days, they'd fallen into old banter. She'd learned he loved oldies music because his dad used to take them away from their mother's tantrums in the car and that he wasn't a bad dancer. It was like fate tempted them with each glance or accidental bump. The thing between them kept her grounded as the violent images compounded and the artifact's effects burned into her head. Every night, while on watch, he'd paced by her door as if he wanted to speak with her but never knocked. *That's it!*

"You might as well come in, Tango," she called, her voice surprisingly calm. Nora got up and unlocked the door.

Wesley stood on the other side, bathed in shadow. His broad shoulders filled out a long-sleeved black shirt, and his dark pants were tucked into combat boots. Stubble coated his chin, and his eyes were hooded and restless.

He didn't say anything when she backed up to make room for him to enter. As his gaze met hers, a cork popped on the pressure that had been growing between them. Nora let him switch off two lights, and the room was plunged into semi-darkness. She didn't stop him when his hand reached down to caress her cheek.

Nora touched his hand and pressed closer to his warmth. She slid her hands over his chest and gripped the muscle in his biceps. He guided her toward the bed. She sat on the edge, his head level with hers, as he knelt between her legs. Her breathing increased as she anticipated him, wanting him to touch her. Wesley hung his head down and sighed.

"I should go. I came here with terrible intentions," he whispered and went to get up.

Nora caught his face between her palms. She'd waited for him to finally make a move on her, and she wasn't ashamed that she wanted it. She lifted his head. Wesley pushed up, and his lips caught hers. He tasted like chocolate mint. Nora held him close, and he unclasped his gun holster. It thudded as it hit the floor. He gently laid her back on the bed. She reveled in the weight on her and his hands that caressed her thighs. His palm moved slowly up her abdomen to cup her breast. Her hips ground up into his, and Wesley's mouth on hers stilled. He let out a soft breath and trailed kisses down her neck.

Nora moved under him, and his need for her was obvious. She grabbed the back of his shirt and pulled it up. Ridged muscle slid against her skin as he lifted her shirt as well. He pressed his lips on her breasts, and she moaned. Nothing else existed except Wesley's hard body and exploring hands for a few blissful minutes.

A scream erupted outside.

Wesley bolted off her and reached for his gun holster. With blinding speed, he had his shirt back on, and the holster buckled over it. Nora reached for her hoodie and zipped it up. She spied her boots by the nightstand and went to get them.

We've stayed too long. I should have listened and had him take us somewhere else. Nora's panic bubbled up inside her throat.

"Stay inside." He raced out the door and skidded back in for a moment. "Please."

Nora followed him into the living room, where all the lights were still on. She made sure her phone was in her hoodie's front pocket and picked up a Glock 22 from its case on the table. Wesley had shown her the basics. She knew there was a loaded magazine in it, but she made sure to check the chamber. Empty.

He disappeared into the darkness—they left the outside lights off. She stood and watched from a crack in the curtains for any sign of movement or light.

It's hard to see when there are so many lights on in here. Nora double-checked the front door lock and forced herself to flip the switch next to it. The front half of the cabin's lights went out. She shook her head and went toward the second switch that would kill all the lights except the desk lamp.

Shadows flooded around her. She pushed her anxiety into an imaginary box inside her. *Now is not the time to let it control you.* Nora shivered and ran back to the front door to make sure she could unlock it when Wesley came back. It was easier to see into the night now. The moon was about a quarter full, but the silver light didn't penetrate the thick trees well. She knew the land by heart, but it was disconcerting not being able to see.

She checked her phone. No text or call from Wesley. It was after midnight.

A gunshot shattered the quiet.

Nora closed her eyes and forced herself not to panic, to keep her breath steady. She put her hand on the door lock. She had to go after him.

CHAPTER TWENTY

WESLEY JOGGED BACK TO THE CABIN AND WAS
surprised to see all the lights off. The curtains blocked most
windows, but he could tell the inside lights were out. His
adrenaline spiked. Had someone cut the power to the cabin?
He ran around the perimeter as silently as possible. The trees
dripped with moisture from recent rain, and the ground was
uneven. He slowed to avoid a twisted ankle.

He'd made a large circle, hoping the scream would come
again, but instead, a gunshot sounded. He'd frozen and
waited. Nothing moved in the night. Animal sounds and
insects resumed their chatter. Wesley cautiously approached
the cabin when a dark shape burst from the front door,
facing away from him. A gun glinted in their hand. He
raised his gun but quickly dropped the line of sight when he
recognized her.

"Nora!"

She squeaked and turned toward him. Her arms
trembled as she hastily pointed the gun down.

"What's out there?" she asked, her voice cracking.

Wesley ushered her back inside, locked the door, and flicked the light switches on. Nora visibly calmed with the illumination. Her face was pale, and freckles stood out in stark relief.

"I don't know. I didn't want to follow the gunshot in the dark. I'll take a look around tomorrow. But I didn't find anything out of the ordinary. Were you going to come out there?" He half-scolded. He was more than touched she'd face her fear to come after him.

Nora shrugged as she put the Glock back in its case like a hot potato. He knew she was not comfortable yet with the firearms. "I couldn't see very well with all the light behind me inside. And then I heard the shot, and I thought ... I thought the worst, of course."

She put her arms around her waist like she was hugging herself. Wesley wanted to do that for her. He moved forward and drew her into his arms. Her body trembled, even as she tried hard not to show it.

"I'm the worst pirate queen," she said with a groan. "I can't even sleep with the lights off, and I check locks, and I compulsively count ... and I can't use guns in real life!"

Wesley sat her down on the couch and pulled a blanket over her legs. He removed her boots and then sat next to her.

"You don't have to be a pirate queen in real life. You're a lot—smarter, for one thing— and you don't take life for granted. Most people don't learn that lesson until right before they die." Wesley scanned the windows and door to be ready in case the scream came again. "We will find a more secure place, but we can't run off without direction or purpose. We stay for at least another twenty-four hours.

Maybe you can decipher something that will give us a heading or somewhere to go to fix this curse."

Nora rubbed her face. "All right, that's a solid plan. I can't sleep, so I'm going to go dig into the hieroglyphs again. Maybe we could ask for help from our friends online. Maybe Elena will be on."

Wesley wasn't as close to the other gamers as Nora.

"Hope she contacts you soon. I know you're worried."

"I feel like she's in trouble for some reason. But I'm sure a lot of people are. The news isn't getting better." Nora stood and took the blanket with her to the desk. Wesley turned the TV on low, and the news stories continued to show people looting stores, rioting in the streets, and Revs stampeding neighborhoods.

The cities suffered the worst as they had the densest populations. Wesley watched impassively as the news anchor tried to explain why the dead were returning to life. He encouraged people to remain inside and avoid places like hospitals, nursing homes, and morgues. Wesley rolled his neck, stretching tight muscles. Yes, because so many people liked to hang around those places usually. Doctors and nurses were planning to strike unless they got more military protection.

He thumbed through texts from the chief. The marshals were spread thin throughout the country, now assisting in the riots. Gibson said to stay where he was and pass on any information.

"Hey, I think I found something ..." Nora said, turning to face him. She turned the artifact over and touched the back.

Wesley rose, and the sight of the curve of her neck brought forth the interrupted moment he had tried to bury.

As soon as he was near her, his blood started to run hot. He forced the feel of her skin from his mind.

"It was something my uncle said at the smokehouse: 'it's inside.' I think there's something inside this thing because listen to this line in the middle here." She flipped it back over and traced her finger on a line of symbols. "It's speaking of fire and mineral. A weapon that's of the eye of the earth. I think that's the mineral part—fire is obvious. But it's showing the artifact in its entirety being split apart. And see, this weird star shape marks the spot?"

Her eyes lit up as she met his gaze. Wesley tapped the desk. "Great, how do we crack this open?" He held up the butt of the gun jokingly.

Nora chuckled and stood. She went to the bookshelves where a set of drawers sat under them. She pulled a tool kit out of one. Sharp metal knives, scalpel-looking tools, and brushes lay on a leather pouch. She took pictures of the artifact's face with her phone. If it cracked, they still needed to be able to read it.

She carefully selected a hammer with a fine tip and tapped at the back of the artifact in the star-shaped glyph. It took a few minutes of slow cracking, but a fissure erupted down the middle of the stone. Nora gulped as it crumbled a little and revealed a hollow chamber inside the tablet. The front remained intact.

Wesley peered over her shoulder. Inside the small chamber lay a substance of dagger-like silver and orange crystals. They piled together to form a spiky ball. No odor emitted from it to warn of poison. He backed up anyway.

"Is this what Emin and his colleagues were talking about? In the emails, they were excited by a substance that was never cataloged. It was all over Count Ulrich's tomb where the artifact was found." Nora looked through the computer files. "Here it is! Hutchinsonite, a rare mineral that's a hybrid of thallium, arsenic, and lead. Quite toxic. Back in ancient times, it was called Argen, according to my uncle's notes. The picture matches what's inside the artifact, don't you think?"

Wesley had to admit they appeared remarkably similar. "So, this deadly mineral is supposed to do what? Kill us?"

"I don't know yet. I don't think it'll kill us unless we somehow breathe it in or cut ourselves on it." Nora gasped. "A weapon. Maybe the old tribes made weapons out of it to fight the undead. This curse has been unleashed once before by Count Ulrich. There's little record of how it was stopped."

"That tiny thing does not look like it could make one weapon, let alone several." Wesley didn't want to be a downer, but facts were facts. And he was not touching that thing. "But it's obvious they must have stopped the outbreak, or we wouldn't be here today. I say we put duct tape or something over it until you know more."

Nora shrugged. "I can leave it facing down. I'll study the pictures I took. But if this is somehow the key to stopping the Revs, we've got to let the military know. It sounds insane, but I hope we're right."

"I hope *you're* right," he said with a grin. "I'm just the bodyguard."

Nora's lips parted slightly, and her eyes flashed in a way that made him shiver. But nothing more was happening tonight. The scream and gunshot were too hard to ignore. And he wasn't a one-night stand kind of guy, even if he wanted to be. He'd learned to accept and adapt his desires in exchange for his need to be alone. He looked at Nora, and all those ideas faded. Wesley turned his frustration into cleaning and checking over his weapons while listening for any triggers in his motion detection traps.

The night passed peacefully, and then came the telltale jingle of bells and the cursing of a man caught in his trap.

CHAPTER TWENTY-ONE

WESLEY DIDN'T WAKE NORA. HE'D GOTTEN FIVE hours sleep and that was good enough. He carried his Glocks in two holsters under his jacket and took the Mossberg 590 shotgun in his hands. The short twenty-inch barrel was perfect for tactical clearing, and the twelve-gauge shells provided more assurance he'd hit something should he need it for a running target.

The man in his trap was not outwardly armed. He struggled with the razor-thin wires and cut his hands trying to undo them.

"If you want to use your hands again, I'd suggest stop moving," Wesley said, and the man looked up.

He wore a camouflage vest and shirt with khaki pants. A beige ball cap sat on a mop of brown hair, and wrinkles spread around his eyes. Wesley estimated him to be in his late forties or early fifties. He had a short beard that hid a growing double chin.

"I'm a neighbor. I know the Moons. Who are you?

Haven't seen you before," the man said as he stilled and waited as Wesley approached with small snips. He slid the Mossberg around to his back and cut the wire that let the others loose.

"I'm a friend. What's your name, neighbor?" Wesley let him step out of the trap, and they stood face to face under tall, swaying trees. The waves crashing against the rocks made soft background noise.

"Rich Jefferds. My wife and I live up the road, about five minutes. I need some dimethyl sulfoxide for my horses, and Emin used to keep horses years ago. Figured he might have some lying around," Rich said and held up his hands in a show of innocence.

The front door opened, and Nora popped her head out. Wesley pivoted slightly but kept the other guy in his sight.

"Hey, Mara, right? Remember me?" Rich called out, and Nora cocked a brow.

"It's Nora, and yes, I remember you. He's okay," she said to Wesley and walked over. Wesley was happy to see she held a Glock in her hand.

Rich noted it too, and his hands remained up. Wesley motioned for him to put them down. This wasn't a Wild West hold-up.

"How are you two doing? Do you need anything?" Rich shifted foot-to-foot and scratched his head. "Is your uncle around?"

Nora shook her head. "He's on a trip. We're trying to stay away from people right now. Are you and your wife all right?"

"Julia and I are fine, thanks. I wanted to see who was up here and if they needed help."

Wesley eyed the man's muddy boots. *Why not use the main roads?* There was no car either, so the man must've been walking through the forest around people's houses.

"We're good too, thanks." Nora's tone booked no room for more small talk. Wesley was glad they agreed on that. He moved toward the man to escort him to the driveway and back down to the road.

"Well, stay safe y'all, and you know where we are, Nora. You need anything, use the landline," Rich said and lifted a hand in farewell. He headed down the drive and disappeared around the bend.

Wesley turned to Nora with a closed expression. "Where does he live?"

"Turn left at the road, and the house is about a five-minute drive north. He's the last house up here that far into the woods. Everyone else is below us. He and my uncle used to talk sometimes. Rich is a good neighbor. He never made noise or bothered us. Are you going to follow?" Nora walked with him back into the cabin and placed the gun back in its case. She checked that he had locked the front door.

"I think it's a good idea. I want to know who knows we're here."

Nora fidgeted with her hands, and he wanted to grab them to assure her she was safe. But that was a promise he couldn't guarantee.

"Can I go with you?" She folded her arms across her chest. Her long dark hair fell over her shoulders, and she stood in a determined stance.

Wesley stopped himself from saying no. She'd probably follow anyway. He knew she worried that he judged her for her OCD and fear of the dark, but he didn't think of her that way. She was dealing with her uncle's death extremely well. He supposed having research to do to save the world might be helping as a distraction. Wesley put his hands on his hips.

"If I say yes, what will you give me?"

Nora's gaze dropped as she tried to hide her grin. "What do you want?"

Wesley glanced around to make sure all the curtains were closed and the door locked. He stepped toward her and heard her small intake of breath.

"I want to finish what we started," he said in a low voice. He told himself it wouldn't count as a one-night stand with Nora. She wasn't some random girl; she hadn't ever been a random girl. He'd talked with her for months before realizing he missed their conversations when they didn't get to game for days or weeks. Wesley waited a beat to make sure she didn't hesitate. His body tensed when she came closer and put her hands on his chest.

Nora gently grabbed his cheek and pulled him down to her. He sank into the kiss as if he could vanish inside it. His arms circled her waist and picked her up. Wesley took her to the cave room and sat her on the bed. He took his time unzipping her hoodie, lifting her shirt and revealing every inch of skin.

She arched under him as his lips and tongue traced trails down her neck and to her breasts. Wesley let out a harsh breath as her fingers reached below to unzip his pants. He wanted to slow down, to savor the moment, but her movements were insistent. He buried himself inside her, and her moans were the only noise he could focus on.

Sometimes real life was better than fantasy. All the times

he'd thought about her paled in comparison to the sensual woman under him. Nothing could have prepared him for the softness of her lips or how right she fit with him.

The world might be going to hell, but he wasn't ready to give up. Not when they had a chance.

Chapter Twenty-Two

Nora slipped a knife into the sheath that belted around her leg and placed the Glock 22 into a holster at her side. The straps were long, but Wesley helped her adjust them. She no longer shied away from his touch. That dance was over—she now wanted him to be as close to her as possible. Nora had only been with one other guy, and Jeremy Colter was nothing compared to Wesley. Where Wesley was muscle and heat, Jeremy had been angles and weed. He was a distant memory ... that was suddenly on her phone.

Nora tapped her screen to find three missed calls from Jeremy. She blew out a breath. Wesley glanced up from preparing his own set of weapons and flashlights.

"You don't have to go out," he said. They'd spoken for a while lying in bed about her fear of the dark. Nora thought it was time to face it. They didn't want Rich Jefferds to see them coming, just as he hadn't wanted them to see him. It was also part of Wesley's nightly perimeter check. There were larger threats than Rich out there.

"It's not that. I mean, it is, but my ex is calling me. I'm torn between not caring and letting him get what he deserves," she said.

"Ended well, huh?" Wesley said.

"How many of your exes do you still talk to?" Nora didn't think this qualified as opening the "ex file," but she was curious.

"None."

"Really? Not one?" His frankness surprised her.

"No point, is there? I'm not one to dwell on what could have been or to keep ties." He shrugged.

Nora let her gaze wander to the artifact with the Argen inside it. Ever since she'd opened the artifact, the pull from it had grown stronger. She felt it whispering to her; the suggestion to break off a piece and carry it in a plastic bag in her pocket seemed to come from outside herself. Nora told herself it was to see what the mineral interacted with; they needed to understand it to use it. But the artifact's energy hummed through her, and she didn't want to admit her thoughts were not altogether her own.

They left through the front door. Nora checked the lock three times and headed out into the trees. She remembered a trail leading to the next property, but it wasn't imperative to use it because Wesley had done perimeter checks the past week and knew all the houses. He told her he hadn't bothered to introduce himself to the inhabitants because he didn't think they'd be staying long.

Nora kept her voice low as they walked. "So, you never wanted that white picket fence life?" She picked the path over rocks covered in moss and underbrush that were starting to bloom in the early spring.

"I didn't have the lifestyle for it. I'd be lucky to stay in one place for a few months or more." Wesley walked behind her so she couldn't see his face. "I don't want to pass on the bad genes in me, either."

Nora paused by a huge pine tree and looked at him. "You don't have bad genes. It's nature versus nurture, right?"

Wesley shook his head. "I like the idea of a dog and two kids, but it's not for me. Well, maybe the dog someday." He chuckled.

"You're great with the kids that game with us. You're patient and make it fun for them instead of kicking them out or being insulting," she said and started back up the trail. The path wasn't a real path. She followed her compass and moved to any opening between the trees wide enough for them to fit.

"Thanks." Wesley didn't ask follow-up questions like did she want kids? A family? Nora was glad, but it also made her think about it.

Did she want that life? Her parents had seemed quite happy together. She supposed at some point, she wouldn't mind marriage and a family. Or was that what the world told little girls they were supposed to want? She couldn't help but grin when she thought about Uncle Emin and his "words of wisdom" to her. He'd told her repeatedly that she could have a career and a family—she needed to find the right man to support her in both.

"I think we're getting close. I recognize that boulder," she said and pointed at a huge boulder shaped like a hunched gnome. They'd kept closer to the shoreline and now veered into the woods. Wesley had done an outer circle but not ventured closer in, so he wasn't entirely sure where the Jefferd's cabin was.

"Do you want the flashlight?"

"No, I'm okay." Nora swallowed and tapped her fingers, counting. The sun disappeared behind the horizon, and its dying rays barely broke through the thick tree branches. Their leaves were returning, which made the forest even more claustrophobic. Wesley had said she could turn on a dim light if she needed it but to shine it down at all times. Nora knew that would give them away.

"I still think we could knock on the door and ask," she said as she tripped over a rock. Wesley's firm hand grabbed her elbow and helped steady her.

"Listen." He stilled and scanned the growing darkness.

Grunts and shuffling, accompanied by metallic clinks, echoed in the semi-silence. Nora could barely see Wesley's face as the shadows swallowed it. He took another dozen steps, and a small shed's outline emerged in a clearing. It was a few yards off from the main log cabin. The Jefferd's cabin.

Wesley held up a hand, and Nora froze.

Two figures with flashlights walked down from the cabin toward the shed. Wesley and Nora moved behind a thick tree and waited for them to pass. As they drew closer, Nora recognized Rich and his wife. They were deep in conversation. Rich had a rifle strapped to his back, and his wife held a gasoline tank.

"Put this in either ear, doesn't matter which." Wesley handed her an ear plug, and he put one in his left ear.

"Why?" Nora put it in her left ear as well with unease.

"I don't want you to lose your hearing if we need to shoot."

"That's what you're thinking about right now?" she whisper-yelled.

Wesley gave her a slight smirk. "I had a senior mentor hand me ear protection in the middle of a shootout. It was stupid, I was annoyed with him for breaking my focus, but I also still have my hearing." He motioned for her not to respond as the couple moved in the direction of a shed.

Nora gripped the bark of the trunk with one hand and tried not to make a sound. The darkness coated her vision like a blindfold. She took deep breaths to stave off the panic. *Nothing good comes in the dark. Bad news always comes at night.* She willed her hands to stop shaking. She might be armed, but she knew it would be hard for her to use the weapons. She'd never aimed a pistol at a person in her life. *Stop thinking like a victim.*

Wesley didn't appear to have the same problems. He stood next to her like a living statue with a watchful gaze. He placed a hand on hers briefly to communicate that she should stay. She tapped his hand back to confirm yes. He moved forward as the couple opened the shed.

"Goddamn, it reeks!" Rich grumbled as he shoved the doors open. Julia stayed behind him with a frown on her face. Her lipstick made her lips look black in the moonlight.

Nora gasped as a Rev reached out a rotting hand toward the couple. The woman might have been in her forties when she'd been alive, but now she appeared to have aged a hundred years. She was pale with skin peeling from her face and made incoherent noises. Chains around her ankles and wrists rubbed the flesh raw as she tried to run at the Jefferds.

"You sure that's gonna hold her?" Julia swept up her pistol and aimed it at the Rev.

"It's done it for three days, hasn't it?" Rich swept his cap off and put it back on. He picked up the gas can.

Nora crept a little closer behind Wesley. He crouched behind a bush. The Rev had a giant hole in her chest, apparently from a rifle round, but she was still animated.

Her eyes were milky white, and she didn't appear to be cognizant of anything but getting to the living people in front of her. Her fingers stretched like claws, and her jaw snapped. Her teeth had morphed into long fangs. The stench of decay and something like sulfur blossomed the more she moved. Nora put a hand to her nose.

"Try lighting her up. The bullets put her down for about five hours last time," Julia said as she held up a lighter. The flame flickered, and the Rev's vacant eyes twitched toward the light. The undead woman stopped her efforts to grab them. She gazed straight at the fire. "Oh, you want this? You like fire?"

Julia waved the lighter in slow arcs, and the Rev's eyes followed it. She stepped back. Julia let out a shout of surprise. "Hey, I think fire is working. Come on, douse her foot, and let's see."

Rich tossed gasoline on the woman's foot, and Julia threw the flame on it. The gas took a second to light, and when it did, the Rev screamed so loud that Nora put her hands over her ears. The ear plug in her left ear helped, but it couldn't completely block the gut-wrenching sound.

"Shut her up!" Rich shouted. He looked around for something and found a shovel. He bashed her in the head several times, but the Rev stayed conscious. Her skull cracked repeatedly, but she kept flailing as the fire burned up her calf. Rich finally lodged the shovel's edge into her neck and severed her vocal cords.

The Rev's screams became gasping wet sounds as she clawed at the shovel. Rich pulled it out, and a gush of black blood rushed down her chest. Iron invaded Nora's nose with a foul, rotting smell. Nora shivered and put her face in her hands. No matter how dangerous a Rev was, she'd still been a person at one point in time. She'd been like Jess. Thank God Jess hadn't even gotten to that point. She fought the urge to vomit.

Wesley frowned as if he'd had enough too. He approached around the back of the couple, and Nora saw he was targeting the wife first, most likely to subdue her first and use her as a bargaining chip with her husband. Or a human shield. Nora couldn't move even if she wanted to. She had no idea what his plan was, but she didn't want to distract him. Moving at a stealthy pace, he waited while they were distracted.

He didn't have to wait long because the couple hadn't noticed the Rev had slipped off one of her chained cuffs. It must have been all the blood. Nora ran out of her hiding spot as the Rev's other ankle slid from the chain and twisted her arm to work at the wrist cuffs.

"Watch it!" Nora shouted.

"Nora? What the hell are you ..." Julia was cut short as the Rev rushed her. She fired her pistol into the Rev's mass.

Nora couldn't tell if she had hit anything since the undead woman grabbed Julia's arm and pulled her down. Rich rushed to help her and bashed at the Rev with the shovel. Blood flew in spurts, and Nora couldn't find a limb to grab; the corpse was so mangled.

Wesley's knife flashed in the moonlight and severed the Rev's limb at the wrist. The Rev fell to the side when Wesley's booted foot connected with her rib cage with a nauseating squish.

Rich threw another length of chain around her neck and yanked. The Rev gurgled, but she had Julia's wrist in her mouth and tore skin as she pulled back.

"Fuck!" Rich's shout echoed in the night.

Julia cradled her wrist as she ran back to where Nora stood. Nora backed up and held the Glock out in both hands. Her hands shook as if the gun were a fragile bird in them. *You have to shoot; she's been bitten. She'll turn soon.* But her finger refused to move on the trigger.

"Don't shoot, please," Julia said, tears streaming down her cheeks.

"Stay there." Nora made sure she was far enough away that if Julia rushed her, she could either dodge or fire. Wesley had stressed the importance of not letting someone get too close because she had no experience in close-quarters combat.

"She shoots Julia, and I'll shoot Nora," Rich said with his hands full of the chain. He wrapped it around a stake in the shed, and the Rev struggled. Her mouth dripped crimson.

Wesley flipped the shotgun up and around to his back. He put his hands out. He glanced at Nora, and she read the subtle message in his eyes. She lowered the Glock but didn't holster it.

"She's been bitten, Rich. You know what happens after that," Wesley said. His voice was low, calm, and steady.

Rich grabbed his hat and threw it with a curse. "What the hell is going on? What do you know about this shit?"

"I know she'll get violent, bold, and she might try to kill someone. Then when she dies, she'll come back, but not as herself." Wesley kept an eye on the Rev, who was moaning and trying to free herself.

"Stop talking about me like I'm not here!" Julia shouted. She turned her gun on herself. Rich raced a few steps toward her with a pleading face. She held up a hand. "If I come back, you need to burn me, Rich. We're not the bad guys."

"She was a person," Nora said, but at the same time, she understood what they were trying to do—find a way to kill a Rev.

Julia raised a brow. "She *was*. Revs? Is that what they're called? We shot her, cut her carotid, and starved her for three days. And she's the same. Rotting more and more, but violent. We weren't torturing her for our pleasure. We need to find a way to defend ourselves. We wanted to find a way to kill them."

Rich nodded and gestured to the lighter. "Fire seems to be the only thing they're afraid of. I've heard rumors of these things changing. No one is alike. My buddy up in Sagnot county said he was attacked by three undead with unusual strength. This one here seems to be a weaker version. Maybe she hasn't "matured." We don't know how this works." He stepped away from his wife and closer to the Rev.

"Put me down. I don't want to hurt anyone, and I don't want to wander like that. At least we've given you knowledge," Julia said and turned to her husband. "There's no way these two are going to let us walk. They can't. We wouldn't if we witnessed this."

Nora's body was taut, and she warred with what to do.

"Maybe you won't get super violent. Maybe that's some folks," Rich said, and his voice cracked. "I can keep her locked in our room and wait it out. Walk away, Nora."

Nora exchanged a glance at Wesley. His nearly imperceptible shake of the head was all she needed to solidify her decision. There was no story where a bitten person ended up alive and healthy. The curse didn't care who was bitten.

Wesley tensed, and Nora felt more than saw the explosion of action—he moved like lightning before a deafening crack of thunder. Rich flung his arm under the Rev's mouth, and she latched on to it like a shark. He screamed and dragged the chain off her. The Rev lurched toward Nora.

Nora fired into the mass of dead flesh that came at her. The gun's recoil made her stumble back a step. The Rev jolted as the bullet hit her shoulder. Julia's gun fired at almost the same time but into her own temple.

Wesley's shotgun was the bigger blast, and it took out Rich before he could aim his rifle. Brains scattered onto the trunks of the trees behind him. Wesley racked the shotgun and fired into the Rev. She toppled over, missing most of her head. He fired again into her sternum. Black goo splattered over the shed floor, but her body parts continued to twitch.

Nora stood with the Glock in her numb left hand and blinked rapidly.

Wesley turned to her, and as her ears were ringing, she only knew he was panting because his chest was moving rapidly. "Well, that did nothing to help your fear of the dark, huh?" he said, though she could barely make it out.

Chapter Twenty-Three

Wesley surveyed the dead and pursed his lips. He doused the body with gas and took out a lighter. The flames spread on the shed floor, illuminating the tools and making the dark seem impenetrable.

He went to Nora, where she remained rooted in place. He shook his head from the ringing in his ears, thankful for the one ear plug. He plucked it out. Her hand clenched the Glock as she scanned all the bodies. She glanced at him, and a harsh, high-pitched bark escaped her mouth. Nora inhaled deeply, then blew out a breath. Wesley carefully took the gun from her and placed it on the ground. He wasn't sure what he expected. In his experience, people reacted two ways: freezing or running.

Nora was between the two as she rubbed her arms and touched each finger. Counting, he knew now. She whispered something under her breath, but he couldn't make it out.

"Yeah, you're right; this has not helped," she said, and that weird, high-pitched sound came out again. Nora closed her mouth and gave him an apologetic glance.

"Hey, breathe. I'll get rid of the bodies, and you can wait here," he said with a soft hand on her shoulder.

Nora turned to him and took a deep breath. "We can confirm fire kills the Revs, now. I want to try something else too."

"What are you doing?" He didn't move to stop Nora but watched as she approached Julia's body. The body hadn't fully burned; her left arm and a quarter of her torso were unsinged by the flames as they died out. She'd pulled the knife out of her leg holster and knelt by the still body.

"I brought some of the mineral, Argen, with us. Don't ask why. There's a reason it's protected inside the artifact, and in the research my uncle and his friends did, they mention it frequently. They weren't sure of its purpose and why it was so important to the count." Nora held up the knife, and the blade was coated in a subtle white substance that glowed in the moonlight. "I poked it once with my pen and covered it in this substance. I couldn't get it off. It hardened almost like a coating."

"So, maybe it's meant to coat a weapon, not *be* the weapon." He certainly hoped so. Otherwise, they were dealing with what they thought was Hutchinsonite. It was something like that mineral, perhaps even deadlier than they knew. The circles under Nora's eyes concerned him. She'd told him not to ask why she'd even brought the mineral with her. He had a sneaking suspicion she wasn't telling him something.

"Maybe it kills them permanently. Gives them peace in death," she said, the latter almost as an afterthought. It was as if she needed to know she wasn't inflicting any more harm. Her hand dipped low and jabbed the point of the mineral-coated knife into Julia's forearm. "Remember the part I deciphered where it describes the mineral as the "eye of the earth" and the spear? I figure it might hurt the Revs."

The corpse shuddered and let out a sigh that sounded like a faint scream. From the point of contact with the weapon, Julia began to dissolve into gray ash. Nora stepped back with wide eyes, and Wesley let out a low whistle. They exchanged incredulous glances.

"You'd be correct. This changes some things. Shit, can we make more of this stuff?"

"I hope so. But I'm not sure." Nora held the knife like it was a lifeline.

Movement caught his eye, and Rich's hand twitched. Wesley stepped toward the man with a frown. "As he said, some people are changing faster. He's coming back."

Rich moaned, and his hands clenched into fists. His nails grew into talons, and he picked up his head.

"I suggest you stab him, now," Wesley said as he aimed the Mossberg at the man's head. He didn't want to waste the round.

Nora hurried and plunged the knife into Rich's back. The Rev's fanged mouth gaped. His milky white eyes turned black, and his skin dissolved into ash.

"We need to find out how to make more of that." Wesley exchanged glances with her.

Nora grinned back, but her limbs began to shake, likely from shock. This was a huge achievement, but how did they make more Argen? The substance was deadly to humans.

Chuffing and prancing hooves thudding in a paddock to their left alerted them to the presence of horses. Wesley hadn't even realized the animals were out. He recalled Rich saying he wanted DMSO from Emin. He hadn't been lying. Or perhaps it had been a good cover-up for sneaking around the cabin. Two horses sniffed the air and bobbed their heads. It was a black and white Pinto and a chestnut.

"I need a light ... please," Nora said, struggling to get her flashlight out. She trembled as the night's trauma caught up to her. She dropped the knife, and her breath came in gasps.

Wesley turned his light on and grabbed her hands. He thrust the solid metal into her fingers, and she shuddered but calmed down a little. There it was—the aftershocks of shock. He took her away from the piles of ash, picked up the knife, and brought her over to the horses at the fence. Nora clung to the wooden rails and kept the flashlight at her feet as if she were safe in the circle of light. Her chest heaved, and the horses chuffed at the dancing light.

He extracted another flashlight from his pack and brought it to her. The light illuminated another circle of ground, and the horses' irises glowed yellow. They shook their heads and extended their necks to sniff with long noses.

"Did you know wherever a horse's ear is pointing is where he's looking with the eye on the same side? If their eyes are pointing in different directions, then he's looking at two different things simultaneously," Wesley said to distract Nora's fear response.

He'd spent a dozen summers on a ranch to get away from home when school wasn't in session. His dad hadn't objected and had sent Becca with him when she was old enough. It kept them away from their mother long enough that the abuse faded like an old bruise. It was enough to delude himself that it would be better when he returned home. Wesley had always returned to his dad's same tired face and worn wrinkles around his mouth. There were often new repairs on the house, and his mother was either in a delirious state of happiness from prescription pills or in a drunken depression.

Wesley remembered asking for a horse one time and his mother laughing as if he'd told her a joke.

What for? She'd cackled. *It would kick and kill you, and then DCFS would take you away, and your father would leave and the money with him. But you're too young to understand, aren't you?*

Wesley turned his attention to Nora. She held the flashlight with white knuckles and tapped each finger rapidly. She took slower, deep breaths and kept her gaze on the two horses that were curiously sniffing them.

"They can't throw up, either. Did you know that?" Nora attempted to sound calm even if it was forced. "I spent a lot of summers with Emin on ranches in Colorado and Montana. I didn't know you knew about horses, too."

"I'm a cowboy at heart, I guess," Wesley said, equally surprised by what he didn't know about her. "Spent my summers on a ranch too."

"That explains the hat." Nora cocked her head and raised a brow.

Wesley grinned. "We should let them out so they have a shot. I think I'll go check in the Jefferd's house to see if there's anything that we can use. I doubt many people will pass by here soon."

"Or we could take them," Nora said with calm in her voice. She reached out to stroke the paint mare's nose.

"I suppose we could, but we'd have to feed them." Wesley glanced at their hooves and didn't see any nails. "At least they're not shod." He was tempted to take the horses, but they'd be more work than it was worth in the end. And they were liable to get hurt or killed if they came along.

These weren't the mustangs he'd helped train, who were hardy and used to long days of traveling for food. These were regular riding horses used to hacking in the woods for a few hours.

"I'm not a Ferrier, that's true. I suppose they'd be more work than necessary." Nora unlatched the gate and let it swing wide. The horses didn't move. She looped the chain around the post and left the gate open. "They'll leave when they need to." She shivered and let out a long breath. "Do you want help clearing the house?"

Wesley handed her the silver knife. "Nope. Stay here, and I'll be back in ten." He jogged up to the house with his pack. He hoped the Jefferds might have supplies they could use. He didn't want to risk going out to a store now.

The front door was open, and the lights were on. A fire glowed in the hearth, and he flicked the switch to turn the gas off. The flames died. He clicked the TV off, but not before he caught a glimpse of more rioting and looting. Panicked people had taken to hoarding essentials in their homes like bunkers. Police couldn't contain every outbreak of violence, and more Revs walked the streets with fanged teeth, open jaws, and clawing hands.

Wesley held the Glock out at a low angle as he cleared the house room by room. There was no one else in the small cabin. The kitchen was clean, the smell of a roasted chicken lingering in the air. He checked the pantry and put a few cans of fruits and vegetables in his pack. He found what he wanted most in the office: a gun safe.

"What are the odds you're open?" he muttered and tugged on the handle. The heavy metal door swung open, and he could have hugged Rich for his laziness.

Inside were two Remington 7600 rifles and three Smith

and Wesson M&P pistols. Ammunition was stacked neatly in rows under the weapons. Wesley took one of the Remingtons, most of the ammo, and one of the handguns. He didn't have room to carry more, and they already had his guns back at the cabin. Maybe some poor soul would find their way to the Jefferds and need a weapon.

Wesley headed back down the hill toward the paddock and Nora. The flashlights shone brightly in the dark and highlighted Nora's small figure. She patted the horse's neck and then pulled her phone out. His walk turned into a jog as she glanced up at him and beckoned for him to come. The pack bounced on his back as he leaped over a stone off the path.

"What's wrong?" he asked with his Glock out.

Nora waved the need for the gun away. "I got a text from Elena ... Cupcake, remember her? She said to check the game chats and that she needs help. Nothing else."

"Yes, I remember her. All right, let's go."

The mess they were in continued to spiral outward like ripples in a pond.

Chapter Twenty-Four

Nora waited in the dark, flashlights off, while Wesley did a perimeter check of Alfred. The cabin was the same as they'd left it, and he pointed out where the wire traps were. She clutched the flashlight tube with both hands to keep from shaking. The Argen-coated knife in the side holster on her leg was reassuring. The whispers stopped when she used it. The mineral was a counter to the curse but was it too late? They only had this small supply, and it wasn't just the Revs that scared her. People who were afraid tended to react violently instead of thinking ahead.

It was as if death were becoming a regular thing for her to see. She didn't know if she was getting desensitized to it or accepting that the world was forever changed. Even if they had found a way to kill the Revenants, people would find a way to kill each other. People would find something to be divided over.

"Looks good." Wesley motioned her through the front door, and Nora turned on the lights. Soft white light illuminated the familiar kitchen and living space.

Nora went to the desk and woke up her laptop. The *Pirate Scourge* gaming queue popped up, and her friends list populated. She clicked on Cupcake's chat, and messages appeared.

March 30, 4:35 a.m. *How are you? Safe? I'm trying to call my parents, but they aren't answering. The looting has gotten bad by me. All the stores are overrun, and police are being shady. Not sure who to trust anymore. Power has been off for two days, not sure when it's coming back on.*

April 6, 6:30 p.m. *I think Kyle is coming—I told him where I lived.*

April 8, 7:45 a.m. *I made a mistake, girl, you there? Shit, I don't know what his deal is, but I don't need his help. He's making things worse. Call me please!*

April 9, 5:45 p.m. *I'm at 4582 Clearwater court, Sagnot Bay, Michigan. I don't have anyone else to tell because no one is answering! What's going on out there? Maybe we can all meet up and do this together? I'm so scared—I know I said I live with a roommate, but I lied. It's just me, and I'm not close with anyone around here.*

Nora bit her lip and shook her head. "Dammit, I missed all these. I should have gotten the notifications on my phone from Serma." She checked her phone again, but Serma's app remained blank with no alerts. The universal gamer chat and video server allowed everyone from console to PC to board gamers to connect. She was also concerned that if Elena had tried to call or text, the cell signal wasn't letting her get through.

"Try re-installing it. Or maybe with the limited connectivity here, it's not getting a signal," Wesley said as he read the messages. "Or worse, the power grids are going in and out. Who knows when they'll get people to fix them, if ever."

Nora shuddered. If power grids were going out, it would be like a time warp into the Middle Ages. She couldn't imagine how people would survive without heat, electricity, or clean water. She recalled a book once that had addressed that very problem, and the results weren't good. It was estimated that ninety percent of the population would die over a year's time due to a lack of hygiene and shelter from the elements. In April, the weather was unpredictable and wet.

She tried re-installing the app and agreed it must be the signal around the cabin when no new notifications came up. She called Elena again but got her voicemail. She glanced down at her shoes and yelped when she spotted a blood spatter.

"She answer?" Wesley asked. He began undressing in the middle of the living room.

Nora stared. "What are you doing? And no, she didn't answer."

"I'm getting out of these clothes; I suggest you do the same. I don't know if a wash is going to help the blood stains. I've already tracked in enough dirt, sorry." He kept his boxers on while he gathered all his clothing up. He stuck his shoes in the sink and ran the tap. Nora added hers as she stripped.

She kept her head down even though he'd seen way more of her than underwear. The sight of him momentarily distracted her from worrying about Elena and power outages. Even with dirt and grime on his stubbled face, he presented a beautifully muscled body. He wasn't overly built, but he had bulk where she liked it. Nora couldn't shake the memory of those lips doing things to her she'd never experienced before. She held out her hand for his clothes.

"I can put these in the wash and see if they come out clean," she said, to stay focused.

Wesley came close and handed her the pile. His eyes traced the tops of her breasts and curve of her neck even as she tried to hide behind the clothes.

"Tomorrow, we can drive into town and see if the call goes through. Do you know where Elena lives? Why would Kyle be helping her?" Wesley asked.

"I don't know. I didn't think they were even that good of friends. She liked to flirt with everyone. Maybe she gave him the wrong idea, and she told him where she lived ..." Nora cursed. "She's stupid for doing that! But look at me; I met you."

Wesley cocked his head and raised a brow. "True. You said Kyle was with her?"

Nora walked to the laundry room and threw the clothes in the washer. She took out her phone and held it up. "I forgot; I have his number. He said he wanted to text me rather than chat on Serma. But I said I'd block it if he sent me dick pics or started asking for pics of me."

The phone rang and rang. No answer.

"I would've blocked him, anyway. I'll be in the shower if you need me." Wesley slanted his head down to throw her a look over his shoulder and chuckled as he walked away.

How can he be so calm? He shot a man tonight and killed a Rev, yet he's concerned that he tracked dirt into the house? She wished she had more of his confidence, but then again, he was probably used to being in situations of intense stress. And death. He'd hinted that someone close to him had died while on a fugitive hunt, that he'd shot traffickers, and was considering changing careers. From what she'd seen, the world needed people like him in careers with hard choices.

Nora let the phone hang up, went to check the front door lock, and followed him to the shower. She didn't want to be alone, even if it was hard to admit. She didn't like the idea of being dependent on anyone. But if there was one thing Wesley was, it was direct. He had told her the married family lifestyle wasn't for him. She could be certain there were no strings attached here.

Besides, they had to survive a changing world full of Revs first. Wesley would help her, and then they'd part. Nora understood that, and it helped assuage her guilt at using his company. If he'd wanted to go, he would have. She tried not to think past that. There was no point in making up a future she wasn't sure either had.

After a restless sleep filled with fire and gold lava, Nora stood in the kitchen eating peanut butter crackers and an apple, her mind jumbled with Elena's messages. The artifact sat on the desk. Even only looking at it sent chills up her arms. The more she decoded, the more her mind became a jungle of darkness. She couldn't help Elena right now, even with the address. How were they supposed to get to Michigan anyway?

She touched the surface of the tablet, and it purred. Nora jumped back. She focused instead on packing her bag. They'd both agreed time was almost up here. Nora carefully put the Argen into a plastic container with a lid. She set that into her black pack.

The TV news declared that more and more people with vacation homes in the rural areas of Wisconsin, Michigan, and Iowa were headed there, jamming up the roads. The CDC and government warned the population to stay put under the threat of tickets, jail time, and border violation fines. That didn't seem to be deterring anyone. Nora wondered how long they'd have to endure this. People couldn't hole up and avoid everyone forever.

"The National Guard and Army are having a terrible time keeping people in their respective states. Please, do not cross borders. Do not engage with anyone behaving strangely or violently. Care packages will be available at local Walmarts or town centers soon," the news anchor said. Her hair was frazzled, and her makeup was half done. "Power grids are being affected, so expect blackouts to continue across the country."

Wesley came in from the back cave room, holstered guns always on him, as they always were now, and he held up a remote control. "Look what I found." He pressed play, and the stereo lit up.

Nora flicked the TV off. "I haven't listened to a stereo in a long time." The oldies tunes filled her with comfort she now associated with him and being in the cabin. A comfort they didn't have the luxury of keeping. "I thought we were leaving."

"Emin has great taste. Remember CDs?" Wesley pressed play and waited. "And we *are* leaving, but let's pause for a moment."

As he spoke, the strains of Bobby Darin's *Dream Lover* started to blast from the speakers. He started to dance a version of the Twist. Nora suppressed a grin.

"You and your Oldies. You're in your twenties," she said as he slid up to her and grabbed her hands.

"Mid-twenties, and I'm an old soul."

Nora fell into his arms and let him lead her across the floor in a sloppy dance. *Be My Baby* came over the speakers. She giggled, and he twirled her. He bent to speak into her ear when she spun back into him.

"So, in the spirit of leaving, I have to tell you I saw something unusual on my checks this morning. No rush or need to panic, but I'm going to need you to grab your bag, get anything else you need, and get Patrice's keys." Wesley's eyes betrayed the light tone.

There was something wrong.

Nora gulped. She pointed to the counter bowl with keys in it. "They're there. Why do you need her? Have they found us?" She'd been dreading this moment. The Antiquarian Matrix wasn't going to let any corner go undiscovered.

"There's a boat moored off our shore about a half mile to the west. The guys around that boat are neither homeowners here nor regular guys. From what I saw, the five are armed. My guess is they want to hit this place when it gets dark," Wesley said in a light voice, and they stopped dancing. "You lead the watchers away in your car. I'll hide until I hear them come inside the cabin. Then I'll take Emin's trapdoor tunnel to get out. We can meet at the Shell station in Brooker. You know the one?"

Nora fidgeted with her fingers and swayed. "Yeah, I know it." They swayed for a minute, and then the song changed to *Runaround Sue*.

"I'd say we could switch, but I'm not going to leave many traces we were here, and I'm going to take out whoever comes into this cabin," he said with level calm.

Nora nodded and went to get her black tactical pack. "How long do I have to get ready?"

"Can you leave in half an hour to an hour? I want you to lead the watchers away so I can rig some things around here —split them up. And it's going to get dark in four hours." Wesley went to get his black Stetson from where it sat on the counter. "I don't know if this hat will survive what I need to do here, so hold on to it, yeah?"

Nora took the hat with reverent fingers. She didn't want to know what he would do to the men who showed up here. "Do you think they'll follow me?"

"I would if I were them. They think they have us outnumbered and can divide." Wesley's eyes narrowed. "You keep the knife. Can we coat anything else in the Argen?"

Nora went to Emin's gun safe and opened it. She hauled out a compound bow and pack of quivers.

"How about these suckers?"

CHAPTER TWENTY-FIVE

WESLEY ROLLED AN ARROW SHAFT IN HIS FINGERS. He wanted to try coating bullets in the mineral, but arrows would be just as deadly.

"Works for me. I can't say I'm any good with a bow, but it's better than nothing because we can't coat all the ammo. Let's try a few bullets, though. Does it lessen every time you use it?" He plucked an arrow from the quiver and brought it over to the plastic box Nora opened.

"It does look smaller since I put the pen and knife in it."

Wesley studied the silver Argen and agreed it appeared a little smaller. The mineral particles must adhere to metal and diminish the source. He touched the tip of twenty-five 9mm rounds on the crystal mound, fifteen rounds of .40 S&W40mm, and then five arrow tips. The crystals adhered themselves to the metal, and they glowed softly silver.

"Fire is always Plan B. When we meet up, we'll need to find some lighters or flares, anything flammable," Wesley said and scratched his chin. "You wouldn't know how to replicate Argen, would you? Anything in your uncle's notes?"

"I wish. I don't even think we should be inhaling near it, but I haven't felt any side effects. If we can get to the CDC and tell them, maybe they can help," Nora said with a shrug. "I don't like going to them. Emin was probably less than a cooperative candidate when they detained him."

"We'll work that out when we meet up. You drive like you're going to the store, a regular errand, giving them time to follow. I didn't see any vehicles along the shore, but I'd bet they have some stashed inland." Wesley pulled her in close and couldn't help resting his cheek on her head. Her hair smelled of vanilla orange shampoo. Her arms tightened around his waist, and his heart thudded faster.

"Do you think I should talk to them—the Antiquarians? Maybe they can help us," she said after a moment.

Wesley considered it. The threatening messages to Emin didn't help his belief that the Antiquarian Matrix society wanted to do anything but get their hands on the artifact for nefarious purposes. They could have approached Emin or Nora in a lot of ways that didn't include stealth and threats.

"I'll talk to anyone who wants to talk. But I imagine whoever's coming through that door doesn't want my lip service. They want the artifact and your uncle's research. They'll want you too. So, you need to leave, and we can regroup," he said.

Nora pursed her lips. "Okay, makes sense. But you get out. I don't care what you have to do—you better meet me at the gas station."

Wesley put her face in his hands, and her eyes met his. "I'll meet you there."

They stood in companionable silence that reminded Wesley of the lull before a storm. She pulled back and sighed. She gathered the last of the stuff she needed and went to the front door.

"We'll need to stage an argument for the benefit of whoever's watching and potentially listening. Think you can find something to hate me for?" He teased, and Nora smacked his arm.

"I'm sure I can."

Her response made his spirits lift.

You're letting emotion get you in trouble again. Wesley warred with his heart and mind. He had told Nora he expected nothing from her when things sorted themselves out. She hadn't been clingy or upset. She was levelheaded and smart. He hated that he loved that about her. He'd learned at an early age that people couldn't be counted on. Getting attached meant disappointment. Besides, it was only a matter of time before his suspicion and mistrust hurt her and pushed her away.

A small, nagging voice inside his head countered, *or you could see if this is a true chance to try something new and trust someone for a change.* He'd had no shortage of women interested in him over the years, but his past always seemed to linger between them like an invisible wall. Wesley could blame mother issues, but it was likely trust issues in general. It was far easier to look out for himself than worry about another person.

"You ready?" He stepped back and didn't like that he had to send her out alone. But they needed to divide the Antiquarians. There were five now that he'd counted, but who knew how many the society was made up of.

Nora grabbed her pack and let him check the holstered knife on her thigh. Her warm fingers caressed his cheek and slid down to his shoulder.

"What if I can't shake them when they follow? I don't want to lead them to the Shell," she said. Her almond eyes explored his like she might not see him again.

Wesley didn't want to tell her that that was a possibility. He didn't know how many would enter the cabin. He was going to prepare for five and hope it was only three or fewer.

"Call me and keep driving then. I'll catch up." He gestured to the front door. "Make it good, Moonbeam."

Nora opened the door. Her voice rose in fake anger as she said, "I don't need protection. I need answers, and I'm not sitting around here anymore."

Wesley stepped outside with her in the appearance of following the argument. "I'm not saying you need protection, but I can help. We should sit on this for a night."

Nora swung around, face pinched. "I don't need someone who only uses my resources until they're gone and won't be there after the world gets back to normal."

She was doing a damn good job because her words stung. Wesley assumed she was acting, but the best lies had truth in them.

"The world isn't going to be normal anymore. I was up-front with you that I work alone. If you can't handle that, maybe you're better off by yourself." He clenched his jaw. Nora's lips trembled, and she ducked her head as she made her way to her car. Were there tears in her eyes? Wesley didn't have time to send her a nonverbal signal and ask. She slammed the door to her car and sped out of the long drive.

Wesley glanced toward the shore, where the lapping

waves continuously eroded the rocks. The lake was visible through the trees and sparkled with faint light. The afternoon sun sank toward the horizon, and shafted light shone between tree trunks. Streaks of pink and yellow melted into the clouds, and the shush of the waves belied the peace that was about to be shattered.

Wesley moved inside and used binoculars to scan the forest for any movement. Almost the second the dust from Nora's car cleared, two shadows, dressed in black and camo, crept from their hiding spots. The men broke into a jog heading toward the main road. They tilted their heads to speak into radios. *Bingo.* Wesley hadn't been in a lot of hand-to-hand combat, and he wasn't a trained army soldier or marine, but he hoped he could ambush whoever was coming. He also wanted Nora out of the cabin when that happened. At least with their forces split, he'd have a chance to take out whoever was hiding in the trees.

He'd grown up setting traps outdoors and dreaming about ways to keep their home safe at night. Sometimes his dad would work late, and his mother would forget to lock the doors. Wesley had woken up to a stranger in his house one night when he was thirteen. He'd taken his baseball bat and charged at the man. Not the cleverest idea, but it had worked. The burglar had been so surprised he'd run off, but not before he'd taken their computer and had smashed jars looking for extra hidden cash. Wesley didn't like to think that event propelled him into the federal service but protecting others and hunting down criminals seemed like a career he was meant for.

He left the stereo on as the oldies continued to play. The sky faded into twilight as he wound thin barbed wire in front of the door. He didn't have grenades, so he would improvise with the gas from the generator. Wesley filled a few glass bottles with the liquid, stuffed rags into it, and stashed them in the bathroom where the trap door was.

He set to work rigging all the doors and windows. He didn't have enough shotguns to put on all the windows, so he put a Remington 870 there with a length of the fishing line connecting the trigger to the door handle. As soon as the door was opened, the trigger would pull back, and whoever was first through would get twelve-gauge buckshot to the chest.

Wesley raced the setting sun to rig buckets of gasoline over the windows. It took less than an hour, and the sunlight started to weaken as evening approached. He texted Nora to see where she was.

Heading south on Waterman Road. Can you get out of there yet?

Soon. He texted back.

Wesley hoped she'd find the well-lit Shell station to be a good place to wait after she'd shaken the tail. He hated asking her to operate in the dark again, but if he didn't make it, at least there might be someone at the station who could help her. She had the artifact and all the knowledge. She needed to survive more than he did. He'd give her that chance as long as he could.

The stereo's song started with *In the Still of the Night* by Fred Parris and the Satins. Wesley sighed at the crooning tune, as it reminded him of starlit summer nights driving with his dad and Becca when he was a kid. It was one of the rare, good memories he had of an otherwise too-short childhood. Moonlight had streamed over the black road, and it seemed like they were impossibly free. Becca would fall asleep in the back seat, and they'd jam to music for hours until the gas nearly ran out.

He heard a curse outside the window and the left side of his mouth quirked. The wire trap had caught another victim, and the wait was over.

Chapter Twenty-Six

THE SCENE BEFORE NORA WAS LIKE SOMETHING out of a movie. People ran over each other in their haste to get into the storefronts. She was fairly sure she'd lost the guys in the green truck ten minutes ago. She'd driven out of Pikes Bay and into the next town, Brooker. Not to the Shell station yet.

Nora picked a strip mall because of the lights and people, thinking she'd be safer in a crowd. There was a crowd all right, but it wasn't a friendly one. Store owners stood with bats and shotguns in front of their shops. They shouted at anyone who got too close. Other opportunists baited and cajoled them so that they ran after them; their friends swooped in to take on whoever was left inside the shop. There weren't many proprietors left.

It wasn't long before shots were fired. Nora remained in her car with the doors locked and the engine on. She was far enough away that she couldn't tell where the shots came from or who was shooting.

Screams rang out, and a group of girls fled past her car. Nora scrunched down in her seat and hoped to go unnoticed. She'd gotten the text from Wesley about half an hour ago. She didn't let her mind go to a place where he didn't make it out.

Her phone rang, and she jumped. Nora answered quickly.

"Nora?" The voice was distant and hard to hear, but it was unmistakably Elena.

"Oh my God, Elena! Are you okay?" Nora gripped the steering wheel and covered the other ear in a vain attempt to hear better.

"... I'm afraid. There are corpses walking ... insane! Kyle said ..."

The connection went in and out, and Nora swore.

"Is Kyle with you? Are you still at home?"

"I'm home. Can we ... need ..." The line cut off with a faint curse on the other end.

Nora called back, but the phone went to voicemail. Her gut instinct told her Elena was in trouble. She smacked the steering wheel and took deep breaths. *What am I supposed to do? Drive to Michigan? Text Wesley to meet me there?* She didn't move to put the address in her GPS, and the car remained in park. She needed to be sure he was okay before she left.

The fight might have been fake, but she meant some of it. Nora wasn't going to think she'd change Wesley's way of life—that kind of thing happened in romcoms, not real life. She was honest with herself; Wesley had always said he was a loner. Wasn't their fake fight proof of that? He'd said that his work was perfect, despite the issues he had with it currently because it took him away from getting close to anyone. Nora wanted to believe he'd at least keep in touch if or when they were able to fix Ulrich's curse. But she didn't delude herself into thinking that was a real possibility. It was more realistic that they would continue to game or have the occasional video chat.

Another volley of shots rang out. Nora's eyes widened when she saw the reason for the commotion. Two men had a Rev on a chain leash. They snickered and smoked cigars as they let the Rev chase after people. Every time the undead man tried to turn and get them instead, they took turns poking it with what looked like pool cues. The Rev looked newly turned—he was a middle-aged man with a beard and in relatively good shape. His eyes were chalky white, and his mouth hung open with pointed teeth.

The two guys let the Rev lead the way and looted anything they wanted. People scrambled to get clear of its reach. One teenage boy wasn't so lucky when he tripped, and the Rev reached for him. Nora honked the horn to distract it, but the Rev didn't care.

She got out of her car as the guys turned toward her and tugged the Rev back. The boy shrieked and ran off. At least it gave one more person a chance, but now Nora had bigger problems. She pulled out the knife coated in Argen and hated that she'd have to get close to kill it. She wished she were a professional knife thrower. The two men weren't going to make it a fair fight.

Idiot. Now what? You're going to fire at unarmed people? You going to kill them to get to the Rev? Nora gritted her teeth.

She took out the Glock and leveled it at the guys who had changed direction toward her. Well, at least they weren't terrorizing store owners for the moment. The two men looked to be in their mid-thirties. One wore a red ball cap, and the other had a black jersey with silver chains around his neck. They dragged the Rev toward her.

Nora aimed the Glock at them. One of the guys reached under his jacket, and she fired into the air. The shot startled the guy, and he paused. The Rev cocked his head at the noise, and his eyes tracked her.

"Back away from the ..." She hesitated. She and Wesley knew them as Revs, but most of the world was still calling them Mobs. "The Mob."

"Easy, baby, we've got control of this guy," the red cap guy said with his hands raised. A smirk adorned his face.

"Step away." Nora swallowed. This was no time to be civil or timid. She needed to overcome that right now. She could hear her mother's whisper of confidence in her ear. *Steady, remain calm, breathe.* Nora knew both her parents would have stood up for what was right.

"Sweetheart, you can come with us, and we'll protect ya." Black jersey smiled and showed a gold tooth. "Soon, everything's going to be overrun, and this is our insurance. We can get anything we need. What do you want?"

Nora stepped forward with narrowed eyes. "I'm not going to ask again. Keep holding the chains but don't come closer." She took one hand off the gun to reach for the knife on her thigh. The Rev reached out clawed hands for her.

As soon as the knife was out in front of her, the Rev hissed and shook its head. Nora ignored the sweat on her forehead despite the cool temperature. She struck fast so she could keep an eye on the two guys. The knife sliced the Rev's forearm, and it screamed. The Rev quickly turned into ash that floated away on the wind.

"What the fuck? What is it doing?"

"What did you do?"

Red cap let go of the chain and pulled out his silver pistol. Nora backed up into the door of her car. She took quick breaths and holstered the knife.

"Is that knife special or something? Come on. We can help each other." Black jersey didn't have a gun, but he looked like the faster of the two. Nora pictured him rushing her. She groped for the handle of the door behind her.

"Fire can kill them. Use it," she said and flipped the handle.

Red cap aimed his pistol at her, his eyes cold. "I'll shoot, baby, don't think I won't. I'm willing to make an exchange. You took away our currency, and we'll need compensation. You and your car seem like a fair trade. We'll drive you anywhere you want." The pistol wiggled in his grip, and Nora cringed.

She had seconds to decide if she would die in the parking lot or follow her instinct. There wasn't a good chance she would leave alive if she tried to get in her car. There wasn't a great chance she'd survive if she let them take her either.

Nora was sure her aim would suck, but she fired anyway. Red cap returned fire as Nora scrambled as fast as she could into her car. They were both bad shots. Her shot went wide, and black jersey jerked to the right and let out a scream of pain. Red cap's bullet hit her car's door with a ping. Nora didn't bother to close the door but shifted the car into drive and floored it.

More shots followed in her wake, and she instinctively ducked close to the steering wheel. But none of the bullets made it to the windshield. She hit a shopping cart and frantically steered around a group of girls who dove out of the way. People laden down with loot didn't even glance up at her as they loaded their vehicles.

Nora's breath came in gasps, and she didn't care what road she found. She'd take anything that looked open.

Chapter Twenty-Seven

WESLEY WAITED IN A CLOSET AFTER HAVING placed his pack in the trap door hole and dropped in the Remington from the Jefferd's safe and the compound bow. He had a vague idea of how to use it but hoped he wouldn't have to figure it out on the fly.

They cut the power first.

The cabin went dark, and the music stopped. The action further solidified that these guys weren't here to chat. Wesley gripped his Glock 22, and the other sat in his holster. The Mossberg shotgun lay on the ground where he could pick it up quickly.

For a few minutes, there was only silence, and then glass shattered. Something hard and metallic thumped along the ground. Smoke choked his nose. He wound a scarf around his face and cracked the door. Plumes filled the cabin in a blue-gray haze and his eyes watered. He wouldn't have long to make a move.

A shotgun blast made him wait. Cursing and footsteps pounded inside the cabin. So, they'd tried the side door, as he predicted. Wesley counted footfalls and estimated there were two men. There had been three, but he ventured that one was bleeding out with a hole in his chest.

More cursing as the buckets of gasoline fell on someone. A kick and the bucket hit the wall. Wesley grimaced at the damage he was about to do to Emin's cabin. But it was this or die. He crept from the closet and flicked the lighter on. It was like a beacon in the dark, and he had less than a second before gunfire came at him.

He tossed the lighter into the living room.

"Flame!" a man yelled. Boots trampled the floor in haste to find a new place to be.

The smoke in the room obscured his vision, but Wesley saw a shadow move in his periphery. The shadow wore night vision glasses. The lighter ignited the gasoline on the floor, and the flames went up in a torrent of heat. Wesley had seconds to get to the bathroom's hidden door before they adjusted their night vision. He fired a shot into the fire to further disorient the men and ran to the large bathroom.

Wesley dove into the room as the cabin caught fire. He slammed the door shut and kicked a laundry basket in front of it. He picked up a make-shift Molotov, lit it with a second lighter, and then threw it against the door. No going back. The trap door opened easily, and he jumped down, pulling the door shut over him. Screams of men burning to death became muted.

The cool, damp tunnel led him out to another door that he shoved open. Wesley cautiously poked his head up. The front of the cabin flickered with orange flame, and the forest surrounding it was dark in contrast. A sliver of a moon hung in the sky above the trees. He slipped from the tunnel and ran to his truck.

Wesley peeled out of the driveway and pulled out his phone. There were no texts from Nora. He spied movement behind him. A black Range Rover had pulled out onto the road and was racing after him.

"All right." He switched to prep for plan B.

CHAPTER TWENTY-EIGHT

NORA'S CAR LURCHED ONTO A WIDE TWO-LANE road without much traffic. She put the strip mall behind her and let out a sobbing breath. She slowed to the speed limit, put the safety back on the Glock, and placed it on the seat next to her. She tapped and counted her fingers on the steering wheel to keep calm. The black pack with the artifact sat on the floor.

Her uncle's words floated through her mind. *That guy wasn't worth the artifact, Nori; you have the only thing that can help. You need to protect yourself better.*

"I'm sorry." Nora sniffed and shook her head. "I'm not good in a crisis."

She thought back to her actions but didn't feel remorse. Maybe it was Wesley's influence, or maybe it was the artifact's humming energy through her, but her fear was able to be shoved back. She had seen a problem and hadn't shied away from it like a pussy. She'd done what her mom would have done, and that was more than she'd been able to do for a long time. She had potentially saved more people from being bitten, and it had been worth it. Nora wondered if black jersey was okay. She didn't think she'd hit anywhere vital; oddly enough, she wasn't terribly concerned. At least not worried enough to turn around to make sure he was okay. It was his fault if he wanted to go around trying to intimidate and rob people.

Her sweaty palms and a sudden chill made her slow even more. Nora's adrenaline dropped, and she tapped her phone in its car holder. The screen flashed, and the GPS showed her about six miles from the Shell station. As the streetlights were out, the only light was her headlights as she sped down the main road in Brooker.

Nora put the Glock in the glove compartment as she neared the Shell station. There were a few cars parked at the pumps under the bright fluorescent lights. She stopped at one and figured she might as well get gas since she was there. She cautiously slid from the car, put a credit card in the slot, and started the pump. Whispers filled her ears, and she peered into the black pack on the seat—it was as if the artifact didn't want her to go far. Nora ignored it even though it pained her.

Three cars were filling up, and four were parked by the store. The shadowed figure of one cashier talked with a customer and two other patrons milled inside, one of which was in a wheelchair. The pump clicked off, and Nora put it back. She moved Patrice into a parking spot in the back of the lot. Her bladder motivated her to go into the store, but her anxiety made her stay in her seat.

She drummed her hands on the steering wheel and checked her phone continuously. No texts or calls from Wesley. She didn't want to call him in case he was in a bad situation and his phone was a distraction or gave away his hiding spot. Nora drove herself crazy imagining what was happening at the cabin. She sat jiggling her keys and watching people come and go even at the late hour.

She tried to close her eyes, but sleep wouldn't come. Nora finally gave in and grabbed her pack as she headed toward the store. The cashier said a monotone "hello," and Nora half-smiled in acknowledgment. She headed for the bathrooms.

After trying to wash the sweat from her face and reapplying a little eyeliner, she browsed the store in search of food that wasn't in a can. The station's food buffet looked questionable, so she settled on a turkey and cheese sandwich, a bag of Doritos, and diet root beer. On impulse, she grabbed some peanut M&M's for Wesley. The cashier rang her up, and Nora tucked her card back into her wallet.

Sirens blared, and police car lights flooded the store's interior. Nora froze as the cop cars skidded to stops in front of the store. Each held two officers, and while one stayed behind an open door, the other came around with a gun drawn.

Nora slid the bag up her arm and held her palms up. Were they here because of the shooting at the mall? She trembled.

But the cops weren't interested in her. Their attention was riveted on a man in the back holding a shotgun. The long gun braced against his shoulder wobbled. Nora hadn't seen him enter, and he hadn't been in the store when she'd come out of the bathroom. *What the hell?* He wore dark clothing and had an open wound on his cheek that dripped blood.

As the young man in the wheelchair attempted to roll away from the altercation, the man with the shotgun grabbed the chair's handle. He yanked the wheelchair and its occupant toward him as a shield. The shotgun rested on the handlebar of the chair as the man tired of holding it up. The young man ducked his head but didn't fight. He remained calm even as police aimed their pistols at the man behind his chair. He wore a death metal band shirt, had piercings in his nose and ears, silver rings on his tattooed hands, and black lashes Nora would have been envious of if the situation had been different.

"Get down," a cop called. "Keep your hands out and up."

The armed man kept the wheelchair and a shelf of chips between him and the police. "You're chasing the wrong guy. Don't you have better things to do, like kill the undead? You have noticed that, right?"

"World's still standing, bud. We're doing what we can. That includes taking you in for the murder of George Fourt." The three officers fanned out with their pistols in front. Nora backed up toward the counter.

She recognized the concerned looks on the officers' faces. The mention of the undead unnerved them, and they all probably thought they should be out protecting others instead of tracking this douchebag down. Nora didn't like the expression on the man's face—he was eerily cheerful.

"You've all got about five minutes before my boys come, and trust me, you don't want these people's deaths on your hands." The man cracked up wickedly. The shotgun remained leveled at the cops without a tremble. "George tried to kill *me*, fuckers, got that? It was self-defense."

"And you can tell a lawyer your side of the story."

The cops didn't budge, and their radios squawked. Nora had never been so close to law enforcement with their weapons drawn—it was unsettling to be surrounded by so many people with the freedom to take life in an instant. Who would shoot first? Usually, the uniforms and guns intimidated her, but she didn't have the same attitude now. She slowed her breathing and thought about what Wesley told her to do—counting her fingers was fine, but better than that, try to assess. What was around that she could use? Where could she go for cover if it started to get ugly?

The bag crinkled as she moved her fingers together in an unconscious tic. The man with the shotgun glanced at her, and Nora's rational thoughts fled. His eyes were no longer a normal dark; they were clouding up. He didn't even have a good grip on the shotgun anymore.

The gash on his cheek ... she narrowed her eyes. Had he been bitten or scratched? The weight of her pack pulled at her. She'd left her knife in the car, but Argen's artifact and plastic container were in her bag.

He wasn't dead yet. He was displaying the behavior Jess had right before she died. Nora slid the pack onto the ground, and a cop noticed. He held up a finger to warn her not to move. Nora pointedly looked at the man's cheek and then back at the cop. He frowned and tried to decipher her message.

"You're all going insane. Walk out of here before I have to shoot," the man said. He didn't seem to care that he was outnumbered or about the hostage in the wheelchair. He'd put a hand around the guy's neck, and his fingers started to squeeze. The wheelchair guy gasped, and his hands came up to tug him off.

The man didn't let go, and the officers exchanged glances.

"Walk away before I choke him out!" the man shouted.

Nora sank low to her knees as the cops backed off.

"Okay, bud, let up." The cop she'd made eye contact with said. The man half-sobbed and wagged his head. He shook the young man in his grasp.

"This guy is toast anyway. You think the walking corpses will spare him because he's disabled? He'll be the first to get turned, and then he'll spread whatever the fuck this is to everyone else!" The man rapped the wheelchair guy on the head, who rolled disgruntled eyes.

A nervous sweep of long dark brown hair and blue eyes were the only part of the hostage that belied any concern. Nora noticed he had both hands on the gunman's forearm that had choked him, but he wasn't trying very hard to dislodge the arm. It was as if he were waiting for the right moment.

"I may not be able to run, dude, but you're making several crucial mistakes," the young man said.

The cops kept their weapons drawn but backed up to give them space. She was glad because if they shot and killed him; who knew how fast he'd turn? She'd thought it was forty-eight hours, but now it seemed like some people turned a lot faster. Her thoughts went to Rich, who had turned near-instantly.

Nora met the goth's gaze, and she tried to convey with her eyes how important it was for him not to get scratched or bitten. Her hand found a can of beans that had rolled under a shelf. She grabbed it and hurled it at the freezer doors next to the gunman.

He jumped, and the wheelchair guy hauled his forearm down, bringing his left arm up to hit the shotgun's muzzle. The blast hit the ceiling, and the cops rushed forward. They brought the gunman down and handcuffed him as Nora ran and shoved the wheelchair toward the door. The young man brushed her help away with a gruff, "I can do it, thanks."

She didn't have time to be embarrassed because the cops outside were being ambushed from behind. Revs clambered out of the darkness, moaning and snarling. Scattered gunshots rang out in the dark as a dozen Revs attacked the cops.

The cops inside rushed outside, with one officer holding the gunman. The man didn't struggle but constantly wheezed in a high-pitched, crazed manner. Nora unzipped her pack, put on a glove, grabbed a small chunk of the Argen, and put the pack over her shoulders. The mineral warmed in her palm, and particles started to coat the glove. She winced. She probably shouldn't be handling it so close to her skin.

"Ma'am, I need you to stay back," the cop called as she rushed toward them.

"He's different—he's changing before he's died. There must be some sort of mutation effect on certain people," Nora said as she raised her hand to show the Argen. "This will help him." No need to tell a cop that it would kill the guy.

The officer's brown eyes wavered as he glanced at his charge. The gunman was rolling his eyes and laughing like he was part of an inside joke. "I need you to stay back, please."

The man in the wheelchair had halted at the door when the Revs attacked, and he now wheeled back toward Nora. Sweat beaded on his brow.

"What the hell is in your hand?" he asked with a raised brow.

Screams punctured the air, and gunshots lessened as the Revs overtook the other cops. Nora held it out.

"It's Argen, an experimental compound. I need to get it into his system, and the change might stop," she lied. She stepped toward the cop and gunman. The cop was so distraught at his partners getting slaughtered that he didn't protest. He motioned with his gun for them to get back into the store.

Nora pressed her gloved hand on the man's wounded cheek, and he spasmed. He fell to his knees, a keening sound coming from deep in his throat. The other Revs shrieked back as if they were communicating. Nora backed up quickly, and the cop pointed to the back exit. The young man rolled that way without a word, shaking his head at the insanity.

The gunman choked and retched, but his eyes cleared, and he looked around in confusion. The Revs screeched and banged on the glass storefront windows and doors. They peered inside, and their squeals became more insistent. The glass cracked under their palms.

Nora was fascinated. Maybe because he hadn't died yet, the Argen didn't kill him. Not immediately, anyway. The gunman couldn't make coherent sounds as he struggled to get up. His hands writhed behind his back in the cuffs.

"I don't know what that is, but you need to get out of here. We don't stand a chance against six of them," the cop said with a hurried gesture to the back door. The goth was stuck on a couple of cinder blocks in the doorway. He rolled his eyes.

"I could use a push," he said to her.

Nora shoved the cinder block out of the way and pushed him out into the cold air. She jumped as a gunshot rang out. She whipped her head around.

The cop's gun smoked, and he shook his head as he

stood over the gunman. "He was going to get himself killed and turn eventually. We don't have time." He ran toward her as the front glass windows shattered under the pressure of the Rev's strength.

"He wasn't a Mob yet!" Nora shouted. She ran from the carnage, anger in each step. The cop didn't look back as he overtook the wheelchair and headed toward a squad car.

"Did he ..." she started to ask but stopped when it was obvious the cop was leaving them. Red and blue lights washed the parking lot and gas pumps in flashing lights. The Revs were running around in the store, searching. The police car's tires squealed as it zoomed away from the station.

"That he did," the young man said with a sigh. His rings clinked on the chair's wheels as he propelled forward. "Can you run faster than I can push these wheels?"

Nora ground her teeth. "We can try to get you into a car." She gazed at the two police cars left. There were keys in the ignition as the cars were running, but the doors were not accessibility friendly. Wesley's truck would be very useful right now. The darkness outside seemed blacker than normal against the bright store. For a second, she hesitated. Her fear reared its head, and she clutched the door frame.

"What's the hold-up?" the man asked as he sped away faster.

Shuffling and shrieks emanated from inside the store. Nothing like Revs to shock her into action. She plunged into the night.

Oh my God, Wesley, where are you? It was odd how worried she was for someone she'd met only a short time ago. She didn't have time to get her phone out. The Revs had found the back door and sniffed outside it with noses in the air like bloodhounds tracking. She couldn't use both hands to push the chair with the glove on. Nora stripped it off, thrust the clean glove into the man's hand, and then plopped the Argen-touched glove on top of it.

"Don't touch the Argen, the silver stuff, and if the Revs get near us, try to stab them with it." Nora grabbed the handles of the chair and erupted into a run. She had no idea where they were going, but anywhere was safer than their current place.

"Are these crystals? They don't seem stable," the goth said with a curious eye. He clutched the Argen glove like it was fragile. The tattoos down his forearms and rings on his fingers glowed in the soft silver gleam.

"I have no idea, except that they're deadly to both humans and the undead."

Nora shivered as the Rev's cries followed close behind them, as cloistering as the darkness.

CHAPTER TWENTY-NINE

WESLEY ACCELERATED DOWN THE ROAD, AND THE black Range Rover followed. They weren't making any effort to hide their pursuit. He headed toward Brooker with no intention of going to the Shell station. He didn't know how high-tech these guys were. If they were just retired army grunts with an interest in archeology, he could probably deal with them easily. But if they were CIA, or some other branch of the government, they probably had tech he couldn't compete with.

He peered in the rearview mirror and braked fast while turning into the other lane, letting the Rover shoot past him. He craned his neck and tried to see how many people were in the Rover. In the dim light, he counted one driver and one in the passenger seat. No one was in the back, or they were ducking. Or it was full of equipment or boxes. Lumpy shadows could be a person or things. The Rover slowed, its red brake lights illuminating the pavement.

Wesley sped up until they were side by side, even though it was a two-way highway. Why hadn't they fired a weapon at him or swerved to hit his truck off the road? He looked over at the driver.

It was a man in his late fifties, maybe, with silvered hair and stubble. He motioned for Wesley to pull over. No gun was pointed at his face, which was a good start. Wesley nodded but made a hand gesture for them to follow him. He wasn't going to let them dictate where they met. Wesley drove for a few miles. In the rural backwoods of northern Wisconsin, there wasn't much activity except the occasional deer eye flash in his brights.

Wesley took out his phone and called Nora. She didn't pick up. Wesley refused to lead the Antiquarians to her, so he'd have to hope she could wait for him. A large superstore parking lot loomed ahead, and he turned into it. A few lamps lit the space with yellow-orange light. According to his radio, power grids were going on and off. There weren't enough people able to run everyday things when everyone was being told to stay inside and lock their doors.

Wesley stopped the truck, and the Range Rover parked parallel to him, close enough that Wesley could see the driver's face. The older man lowered the window, then put both hands on the wheel and had his partner put his hands up.

"We're unarmed," he said and gestured for Wesley to show him the same.

Wesley flashed his teeth in a sarcastic grin as he opened his window, then lifted his hands and placed them on the top of the steering wheel.

"That doesn't reassure me," Wesley said. He had his Glock on the seat next to him, but the seconds it would take to reach and fire would put him at risk of getting shot. He had no doubt the two men had plenty of weapons where he couldn't see.

"You took out three of my colleagues, three of my friends." The man's voice caught, and he visibly composed himself.

"You came in hot and didn't give me much choice. Stealth boats, planted vehicles, cutting the power ..." Wesley said. Not a lot surprised him, but the emotion the other man conveyed did. "You could have approached me a dozen other ways that wouldn't have resulted in death."

The man nodded and rubbed his chin. "I underestimated who we were dealing with. We do not, however, underestimate *what* we are dealing with. Ms. Moon has half of an artifact that wants to piece itself back together. We want to get ahead of that."

At the sound of Nora's name, Wesley tensed. "So, you thought you'd sneak in and kill her?"

"We wanted surprise, yes, but we weren't going to kill anyone. My thoughts were to intimidate her; in my experience, fear is a fast motivator." The man shrugged. "Where is Ms. Moon?"

"Not here."

"And who are you?"

Wesley pursed his lips and cocked his head in a "come on, dude, you tell me first."

"I am Alazar Jelani, and this is my colleague, Anton Becker. We are retired Army vets and part of the Antiquarian Matrix society. We collect and find artifacts around the world."

"I know." Wesley didn't elaborate. He leveled them with a cold stare.

Alazar fixed him with an equally hard look. "We prevent

things like Ulrich's curse from being unleashed. Ah, I see you know more than we'd anticipated. Nora must be as smart as her uncle—she's started to read the artifact, no?"

Wesley was ready to play ball. "What do you know about the curse?"

"The artifact will complete it if it falls into the wrong hands, and the curse will spread indefinitely. We only have a finite amount of time to stop this. The Antiquarian Matrix split a century ago. Some wish to see Earth's destruction come at the hands of ancient magic rituals.

"You guys have been around that long? Are you all retired military?" Wesley shifted in the seat. He wanted to call Nora and make sure she was okay.

"Not all, no. And yes, our society has been around since the thirteenth century when Mali was the center of West African trade. You have heard of the fabled Timbuktu—not the real city—but the city made of gold?" Alazar smiled widely, and his white teeth shone in the dark.

"The old world El Dorado, so I've been told." Wesley couldn't count on one hand the things he'd learned since meeting Nora. It was like a new world opened itself up to him, and he found he didn't want to lose it.

"Exactly. If allowed to spread, this curse will wipe out all humanity, save for a few. They will follow the *Materlus*, and they will begin a new world. The new Timbuktu," Alazar said. His voice shook with excitement or anticipation; Wesley couldn't tell which.

"What the fuck is a *Materlus*?" The insane woman back at his apartment complex had used the same word. Wesley liked patterns. He started to piece together what he could understand.

"We don't know exactly. But it has been foretold 'they'

will come forth once the dead start to rise and cities fall. We surmise it might be the trapped spirit of the count himself, but we cannot know until the curse is complete. And we intend to stop that from happening. We are wasting precious time, Mr. ...?"

"Wesley Soares."

"Thank you. If you won't tell us Ms. Moon's location, let me warn you others will come for her too. The other Antiquarians are not as kind as we are. And they *will* find her because her half of the artifact is using her energy to connect itself to the other half," Alazar said, and there was haste in his tone that made the hairs stand up on Wesley's arms. "You seem like a man who understands action."

Wesley clenched his jaw. He had to contact Nora before he'd let these guys near her. He didn't care what sort of weird fucked up magic was using Nora; he wouldn't let it hurt her if he could help it.

"What can I do for you?"

"Do you know of the mineral inside the artifact, Mr. Soares?"

Wesley saw no point in lying since they already knew about the Argen. "Yeah. Kills the Revs indefinitely."

Alazar nodded. "We need some of it to reverse the curse. You wouldn't happen to have any?"

"If I did, would that make you go away?" Wesley countered.

"It could. We still would like to chat with Ms. Moon, but I can see with you around, she has enough protection for the moment. May I see the Argen?" Alazar's expression was sincere, but Wesley didn't trust it. However, if he could even buy a small window of time, it was worth a few arrows dipped in the mineral crystals.

He reached behind him in the back seat and withdrew two arrows with red and yellow feathers. "You want me to shoot them across to you?" He raised a brow.

"Anton will get them."

Wesley threw the arrows two feet from the truck, slid his hand to his Glock, and waited as Anton quickly scooped them up. He had the burly look of a guy not used to wearing a suit and a hitch in his gait that Wesley surmised was from a war wound.

Alazar inspected the tips of the arrows with wide eyes. "Thank you so very much. This is incredible. I've never seen Argen—only read about its existence."

"Great. Then we're settled, so you don't follow me, and I won't have to kill both of you," Wesley said with a polite smile. "And you could help the entire world by giving authorities this information. Is there a way to make more Argen quickly? Or a deposit they could mine somewhere?"

"We have already contacted the CDC and sent men to run it up to President Shoeman. Whether he'll listen and take it seriously is yet to be determined." Alazar licked his lips and ran a hand through his thick silvered hair. It contrasted with his darker complexion and clothing.

"One thing," Wesley said, foot on the gas, ready to go as soon as he had an explanation. "What did you mean the artifact is using Nora?"

"The artifacts are imbued with dark magic and are somewhat living entities themselves. Whoever has the artifact is used as a host for their energy and life force for the count's curse to complete itself. Nora is ground zero. If she's read and decoded some of the artifact, it will use her and those around her. Magic has a way of looking back at its possessor. The other Antiquarians know this and will not hesitate to kill the person closest to it, the person feeding it. You think you'll be able to stand in the way of ancient Malian magic?" Alazar lifted a hand in farewell.

Wesley shrugged. "I can try. And we don't have the artifact anyway—it can find a new damn host. We extracted the Argen and smashed it about thirty miles north in the forest." He didn't waver in his eye contact and hoped the lie would buy them even more time. He would have to distance Nora from all the people searching for her and the artifact.

Alazar rubbed his chin and sighed. "You have a lot of reason to lie to me, but you've been quite cooperative. We want similar things, Mr. Soares, so thank you for the information. Good luck in the changed world."

Wesley saluted him and drove for an hour to make sure he didn't have a tail. Nothing but darkness and dread followed him.

Chapter Thirty

Wesley drove down the dark road with Alazar's words in his mind.

Nora is ground zero. If she's read and decoded some of the artifact, it will use her. Magic has a way of looking back at its possessor.

Count Ulrich sounded more and more like an asshole to Wesley. Trees sped by, and road signs were blurred as he followed his GPS to the Shell station. His body was fried from all the adrenaline, and his mind wasn't as sharp as he needed it to be.

He wasn't prepared to see a woman running down the side of the road pushing a guy in a wheelchair. A familiar soft, silver glow emanated from something the man held in his lap.

"Shit. Nora!" He shouted out the window and slammed on the brakes, spinning the truck in a 180. As the truck stopped, he heard the screams.

Revs ran toward them with jolting gaits and open

mouths. Wesley jumped from the truck. Nora let out a half-sob, half-shout of exclamation.

"Oh my God!" She jumped into his arms and just as quickly backed out. Wesley held on to the warmth even as fear took its place.

"This is Damian Salas. Can you get him in the back?" Nora opened the second door of the truck, and Wesley nodded.

Damian was already lifting himself up out of the chair. "Gimme a sec." He hastily unhooked a catheter line connected to a bag hidden to the left side and under the wheelchair and screwed caps on both open ends of the line. Wesley bent forward so he could wrap an arm around his neck. He raised the young man into the truck and then secured the chair in the back bed. The Revs closed in as he slammed his door shut and gunned the engine.

"What happened?" Wesley and Nora both asked at the same time.

Nora exhaled and turned to check on Damian. Wesley glanced at him in the rear mirror. Was he wearing eyeliner? The silver, rings, and tattoos screamed goth. However, the other man carried it off well. He cradled a glove with a piece of Argen in it. Nora gingerly took it and put it back in the plastic container in her pack. Wesley was glad she had the pack and the artifact still with her.

"Damian, this is Wesley." She turned to him. "I didn't have time to tell him about what's going on, but I wasn't going to leave him," Nora said and explained quickly about the gas station disaster.

"Hey," Damian said and lifted a pale hand in the back. "Appreciate the lift. You're in law enforcement?"

Wesley was impressed the other man had picked up on

that so quickly, even if he was partially wrong. Nora must've said something. Or maybe it was his badge on the dashboard. "US marshal."

"Never met one." Damian glanced out the back window.

"Do we need to go back for your stuff and Patrice?" Wesley asked them both. Nora bit her lip. Damian shook his head.

"All my stuff is still at my house, I live fifteen minutes from the station, so I wheeled it there. Late night snack and all," Damian said with a huff of breath. "You can drop me back home anytime."

"You live alone or with someone?" Wesley asked.

"Friend, but he's on a month-long hunting trip up north." Damian shook long dark hair out of his eyes. He had that pop singer quality: smooth skin, soulful eyes, and a husky voice.

"I left the knife and Glock in Patrice. Can we go back?" Nora asked in a small voice. "Maybe when it gets light."

Wesley nodded.

"Who's Patrice?" Damian asked.

"My car." Nora smiled sheepishly. Her breath had returned to normal, and she sank back against the seat.

"You can crash at my place," Damian said. He gave Wesley directions, and they arrived at a large two-story house with a wraparound porch and ramp within fifteen minutes. The gray siding was illuminated with outside lights, and an attached garage sat to the left of the front door.

Wesley got the chair out of the truck bed and helped Damian back into it. He paused and motioned for Nora to move away with him for a second.

Damian looked up at them with a closed expression.

Wesley got the distinct impression the other guy wasn't a fan of him. Damian's eyes kept searching between him and Nora. *Ah, he's fallen under her charm too. And in such a short time. Not surprised.* Nora's silken black hair, freckled cheeks, and dark brown eyes would draw in the most hard-hearted. It wasn't her physical appearance, which Wesley had no complaints about, but she had a delicate fortitude. She exuded an aura of comfort to anyone who wanted it. And her quirky mannerisms grounded him.

"I wouldn't trust me either, I get it, but you look like you're about to fall over. I promise this house is safe for the night. You can check it, and I'll stay out here," Damian said, but he addressed Nora mostly.

She glanced at Wesley.

"I need to speak with Nora for a moment, thanks." Wesley moved her away from Damian and spoke in a low voice. "I think we should sleep in the truck somewhere else."

He scanned the surrounding. He wouldn't be surprised if a demon unicorn jumped out at them now. It reminded him that his mother was loose. She said she'd only wait for him for a few days and then come find him. Why now, of all times? Wesley would have to deal with that later.

"I don't know Damian well, but he doesn't seem like the type to ..." She trailed off at his stern look.

"I've got something to tell you, and it's not going to be easy to hear. But the Antiquarians aren't just after the artifact. They said it leeches power from you, and the longer you have it, the more the curse will spread."

Nora blew out a breath and folded her arms across her chest. "What does that mean? Did you talk to them?"

"I killed three, and the other two decided talking was a better course of action. They're apparently the "good guys" and said they can offer you protection. But I don't buy it quite yet—we need to sleep on this." Wesley put his hands on his hips and hoped he conveyed that no matter what, he wasn't going to leave her, he realized suddenly. Not if there was a slight chance she wanted him around.

"It latches on to me ..." Nora paced and tapped her fingers. She didn't seem as surprised as he'd thought she'd be. "I haven't been honest with you. I've started to hear whispers, and my dreams seem as if I'm looking at Ulrich's memories. Ever since I started deciphering the artifact, I can feel him looking inside me."

"All right, that's news to me. So, we find a way to keep you safe now. Can you distance yourself from the artifact?"

Nora ran a hand through her hair. She had been incredibly brave in the gas station, and Wesley couldn't imagine the stress she was coming down from. That reminded him that he should check in with his chief. Gibson needed to know what killed the Revs.

A ping went off, and Nora pulled out her phone. She sighed. "If I don't read everything on the tablet, we'll never know if there's a cure. I think we're already pretty fucked, so my proximity is the least of our worries. I'm not responsible for starting the curse, so it must be responding to my energy, my life force. It's not like Ulrich has spoken to me, or I'm losing track of time like he's controlling me."

"Fair enough. I'll trust your judgment on this." Wesley didn't know what it was like to see and hear images from the past in a head like Ulrich's. Nora was determined to fix this, and he didn't want to deter her.

She tapped her screen. "And I can't contact Elena anymore. But there are a lot of messages on Serma about gamers meeting up. Is there any way we can go to her house and check?"

Wesley sighed. "I don't know. The fastest way would be across lake Michigan, but as far as I know, we don't have access to a boat. And unlike a real pirate—I don't really know the first thing about them." His cheeks dimpled for a moment.

Damian's throat cleared, and he rolled up to them with a snarky smile. "I hate to interrupt but I don't want to sit out here. You know, Mobs on the loose and all. Or Revs, whatever you want to call them."

Wesley gritted his teeth. "I think we're going to leave. Good luck."

Damian pouted and cocked his head. "Is that what you both want? I've still got hot water and food. If the world's falling apart, like I suspect, you don't know when you'll get that again. Don't people band together in a zombie apocalypse?" He raised a brow. "Yeah, I'm calling this what it is. I don't care where they come from—they're dead attacking the living."

Nora nudged Wesley, and he knew he'd not be sleeping that night. Damian clicked his ringed fingers together.

"You may want to run yourself into the ground, but Nora deserves a rest. She saved my ass back there."

"And you want to repay her with a warm bed?" Wesley narrowed his eyes. "You've known her a total of two hours."

Nora looked between the two of them with an open mouth.

"And that's as long as I need to know she's awesome. I wouldn't have left her alone to 'meet me' somewhere." Damian clenched the sides of the wheelchair. "And go ahead and try to hit me. I'm not an invalid."

Wesley bit back an insult. He refused to hit another man when he knew his temper was already short and nerves frayed, even if the man hadn't been in a wheelchair.

"I know, I've got a big truck, a big gun, and I've even got a big hat. I must be compensating for something, right?" Wesley said in a last attempt at keeping the situation civil.

Damian paused for a second and then burst out with an amused laugh. "Well, I've got a huge boat."

Nora rolled her eyes and stood between them. "Wait, you've got a boat?" She looked at Wesley, and he could see the gears in her mind working fast.

Damian nodded. "It's a thirty-foot Catamaran fishing boat, but I may have an even better idea. I know the guy at the marina who drives a ferry part-time. That way, you can take a car if you need to."

Wesley was extra glad he hadn't punched Damian, but he wasn't ready to trust him either. "All right, if we can get a ferry, that would be faster than driving around the lake. I'm going to do a perimeter check, and we're out of here in six hours."

Nora put her pack on her back and stood by the truck with Damian while Wesley checked outside the house. Nothing out of the ordinary. He used Damian's key to unlock the front door.

One more step, and then you can maybe get a few hours of sleep. Wesley pushed his awareness to the next level. He needed to know Nora would be safe here. There were no surprises in the house. It was a regular two-story with wooden floors, a clean white kitchen, and an open floor plan with a wooden dining table and fireplace. There were wheelchair accommodations like ramps, lowered counters, and spaces designed specifically for Damian. An electric lift ran up the stairs to the upper level. He also noted what seemed like a recent renovation for a room on the first floor.

Wesley motioned for Nora to come in. Damian followed behind her and shared a private joke. It sent a red-hot streak of something foreign through Wesley. He checked himself harshly. He shouldn't be feeling anything like ... jealousy. He never had during gaming. But then again, he'd never seen her charm work in person. It was probably one of the many reasons she'd chosen psych/sociology as a major—she was good at studying people and learning how they worked. Despite her flaws, she wanted to break free of them and help others. He didn't want help, but it seemed he needed it.

He sighed to himself. "You need to get unfucked."

CHAPTER THIRTY-ONE

NORA SET HER PACK DOWN ON THE DARK WOODEN floor of the first-floor guest room. It had a quaint fireplace, yellow and blue floral curtains, and a queen-sized bed. Wesley was doing something outside, and she hoped he'd come to stay with her. They hadn't discussed him staying in the same room, but she had a lot she wanted to catch him up on.

Damian rolled in with a tray on his lap. "I can't cook for shit, so my friend pre-prepared me meals for a few weeks. It's microwaved, but I think it still tastes good."

Nora's stomach rumbled at the smell of fried chicken, green beans, a large biscuit, and a dish of applesauce. She happily reached for the plate and diet Coke.

"I left a plate out for Mr. Marshal, but he hasn't come back in yet."

"Thanks, I'm sure he'll appreciate it. He's probably doing a check or something," Nora said through mouthfuls of food. Chicken had never tasted so good.

Damian turned a knob on the fireplace and flicked a

lighter inside the corner. Flames erupted in pretty hues of orange and white. The gas fireplace emitted welcomed heat. "In the colder months, we don't even need the heat when we've got three fireplaces throughout the house. One in the living room, this room, and upstairs in the master."

Nora rubbed her arms. "Thanks. This must be a nice place to live—undead aside. I didn't think they'd reach here so quickly."

"Yeah, I love it up here. Since the car accident, I've taken time to really sort through my life. I'm a mechanic at the local shop, and the irony of being T-boned by a semi isn't wasted on me," Damian said with a lazy shrug. "Doctors say I may heal enough from the T7 injury, and with a lot of physical therapy, I could walk again with braces. That was going well until this broke out—my therapist left to take care of her family."

"I'm sorry." Nora wiped her mouth with a napkin.

"Not your fault." Damian fiddled with his catheter.

It kind of is, if this artifact is leeching onto my energy to keep the curse fueled. She sighed. *Uncle Emin, it would be nice if you were here. You'd know what to say to him.*

Damian ate his food slowly and methodically. He gazed at her from under dark lashes, and Nora was very aware of the silence in the house. The fireplace didn't crackle because it was gas-powered.

"So, how long have you known Wesley?"

"Um, it's hard to say. A few weeks in real-time and years in-game time," Nora said with a self-conscious tuck of hair behind her ear.

"Ah, gamer girl, I like that. I play *Form a Square* and any zombie game I can find. I also was into *Pirate Scourge* for a while," Damian said and finished his chicken. He sat back in the wheelchair and gazed at her with bright eyes.

"We totally are, were, into that. You're pretty calm for someone who got used as a hostage and ended up running from Revs." She grinned.

"I've seen a lot of shit in twenty-four years. I learn to roll with life's lows. I've been on Serma, and people are still gaming. Holing up in their houses and barricading them like bomb shelters. I think I'll do the same here." Damian took her plate, and she protested. He shushed away her help.

"So, you're going to stay here? I thought maybe you'd want to come with us to Michigan. I know it's not ideal, but I don't want you here alone," Nora said and thought better of it. How well did she really know Damian? And ...

Wesley appeared in the doorway, and when he saw Damian, a frown formed on his face. Nora winced. He had probably overheard her, and she hadn't thought about how he'd feel. She hadn't meant to invite Damian without asking, but she was also concerned about someone staying alone right now.

"I'll think about it." Damian wheeled closer so he could reach out to touch her arm. He took the tray with the empty plates to the kitchen.

Wesley walked into the room, holding a plate and eating as he stood. The dark scowl on his face annoyed her. She reminded herself she hadn't known him for years, so she wasn't sure how he reacted to this kind of situation. *And what situation is this? Is he jealous? Threatened? Does he sense something about Damian I don't?* Nora fiddled with the zippers on her pack as she tried to think what to say.

"I'll sleep out in the truck. We leave at seven since the marina isn't open until seven-thirty. I want to check out the area first," Wesley said. He sat on the chair by the fire, and the light flickered over his sharp features.

"I didn't mean to invite him without asking you," Nora said and stopped. She was in unfamiliar territory with him being upset at her. "I thought ..."

"That he was into you?" Wesley finished for her, like a slap in the face. She'd spent so much time facing her fears and doing what she thought was right that it didn't occur to her that he'd be jealous.

"Excuse me? Since when do you have concerns about that?" Nora crossed her arms and tried to keep her voice down. She shut the door even though it was so quiet that Damian could probably hear everything.

Wesley shrugged as he kept eating, and jammed sharp forkfuls into his mouth.

"I don't trust anyone. It worked out for you the first time, but I'd caution against it, is all," he said.

Nora scoffed. "You're seriously accusing me of having fewer trust issues than you? Oh, thank you. I'm glad my virtue was safe with you. I mean, you got what you wanted —what every gamer guy wants from me—I hope you aren't staying with me out of obligation." She swallowed away the prick of tears in her eyes. She knew he wasn't committed to her, yet he was acting as he had.

Wesley set the plate down—laid it out precisely with the fork and spoon on either side—and rubbed his face. He stood and checked the windows, staring out into the dark as if searching for something. He turned to face her, and Nora stepped back. His face fell.

"You know that's not the only thing I wanted." He stood so close she could feel the heat from his skin. She tilted her head to look at him. She did know that, but it gave her a thrill to hear him say it.

Nora blinked.

"I don't know what's making you upset. If I did something ..." There was a lot they needed to talk about, but the curse seemed far away at the moment. This wasn't about Revs or the Antiquarians. She wished she'd had more time in her classes before this chaos. Perhaps there would have been some nugget of truth she could have used from her sociology or psychology courses that would help her deal with this.

Wesley bent his head low. "I know that fight was fake, but it made me think. And talking with those Antiquarian idiots made me realize how much I'm *not* staying with you out of obligation."

His words were stunted as if he weren't used to admitting things like that. Nora took his face in her hands and brushed his lips with hers. He grabbed her shoulders; everything he couldn't say was in the kiss. She sat back on the bed as he straddled her, and his mouth burned against hers.

Nora pulled back for a second and pushed him back. "Jealousy is not a great look for you."

Wesley *hmphed*. "I haven't had any practice. I don't usually get to that point in any relationship." His hands caressed her arms and brushed her breasts. She groaned into him.

"We can't do that here."

Wesley cursed, but he pulled back and stood, half-bent over her. "I'm out of line. I'm sorry."

"Stay with me in here, okay? I'll protect you during the night," Nora said, and she went to open the door. "The bathroom is down the hall, and I need a shower. Alone." She winked. Wesley's jealousy made her feel so much more confident in his interest in her. To have him act like that meant she wasn't a nobody to him.

Wesley inclined his head.

Nora passed Damian sitting in the living room with a book on his lap. He glanced up with distance in his eyes.

"Are you sure you want to leave tomorrow? We could all hole up here and wait this out," he said.

Nora shook her head. "It would take too much time to explain, but this isn't going to blow over. And my friend needs help. I have to at least check on her and somehow let authorities know about the fire and Argen. It's the only thing that will kill the Revs."

"And how do you think you'll do that? Get past the president's security or find a way to contact the CIA, FBI, CDC, or any acronym of anyone in any position to get the word out and tell them, 'Hey, I have this mineral that kills the undead?'" The skepticism oozed from Damian's words.

Nora shrugged and lifted her hands. Her pack rested on her shoulders—she never wanted to be without it. "I don't know. But I have to try."

"With the marshal, eh? You think he'll stay with you after all this?" Damian held up a ringed hand. "I know, I haven't known you long, but I'm good at feeling people out. Their energies, if you will. There's something about you that I find very attractive."

Nora shifted and wavered between running to the bathroom or hugging him. The directness was nice, but she didn't reciprocate in the way he wanted. The loneliness radiating from Damian was palpable.

"Yes, I think he will." Nora hesitated. "I think under

different circumstances, maybe you and I could've gotten to know each other better."

Damian made a tsking noise. "When was the world ever normal?"

Nora couldn't argue with that. "Do you have weapons to defend yourself?"

"I grew up hunting with my dad and uncles. I have plenty of firepower, but sounds like that only stops humans," he said.

Nora nodded. At least she could leave him knowing he had a way to fight.

Chapter Thirty-Two

Nora sat in the passenger seat of Wesley's truck and stared at her car. Patrice still smoked from the fire that had been set in her. The paint had peeled away, and the steel was black. Damian sat in the back of the truck, whistling at the sight.

"Stay here," Wesley said.

"Can I get a gun?" Damian asked with a smirk. Wesley ignored him.

It had been a short night, and Nora was far from refreshed. She'd slept restlessly next to Wesley for a few hours. His alarm had woken her from dreams where she watched ritual sacrifices and men in armor etching the story on the tablet.

The sight of her damaged car distracted her from the black hole she felt tugging at her constantly. She was a little devastated about her car. Patrice had been a prize she'd worked hard for and was proud of.

Wesley approached the car with his 22 out at an angle in front of him. He circled the vehicle, but the parking lot was otherwise unoccupied. They'd driven around the pumps and store, but no sign of life. The store lights were out, and the glass was shattered all over the sidewalk. The cop cars were gone.

Wesley motioned for Nora to come if she wanted.

"I feel like that guy in *Jurassic Park* ... Okay, yeah, I'll keep an eye out," Damian called as she left the truck. He flailed around for the plethora of weapons Wesley had on the seat next to him. Nora normally would have laughed, but her throat was constricted with unshed tears.

"Don't touch the weapons," Wesley barked.

"Shouldn't have put them near me, then," Damian said. Nora heard him rummage around in the black bag of guns. Wesley glanced at the other man with annoyance.

"There's no room for accidents if you shoot yourself or one of us." The threat hung in the air like a sulfur poison."

"Duly noted." Damian sloppily saluted him.

Nora peered into Patrice's cloudy windows. Her heart sank at the damage. There was no repairing her. She recalled how proud Emin had been that she'd worked hard saving up for the car. Nora told herself the car wasn't a symbol for her parents—she could let it go. It was metal; all the memories were inside her. She gingerly touched the passenger door handle, and it half fell off. She hopped back. The glove compartment was blackened, but the Glock 22 was still in there with the knife. The silver Argen glowed subtly on the blade as she slid it into the leg holster. She spied Wesley's black hat on the backseat floor and picked it up. Surprisingly, the fire hadn't burned it, but it was singed around the edges.

"I'm sorry, Nora." Wesley held his Glock down at his side and watched the car smolder.

"I'm sorry about your hat." She handed it to him, and he swatted ash from it.

"It's survived worse."

"I just ... man, she's toast, huh." Nora swallowed back her grief. "We've got bigger problems anyway, and I don't know if we could have fit both on a ferry."

Wesley acknowledged the statement's truth. His voice was low and rough.

"Hey, guys, I remember the name of the guy in *Jurassic Park*. Ian Malcolm! And like Malcolm, I feel compelled to point out that we're drawing attention," Damian shouted out the open door.

They turned as Revs emerged from the wooded area behind the gas station. Before they could run, there was a loud *crack*. Nora spun against her car to take cover, but Wesley stood with arms crossed as he watched Damian.

The other man had the sniper rifle out and took out the three Revs. He took seven shots to get them down; *pop, pop,* Damian cursing, *pop, pop, pop, pop, pop.* The three bodies twitched on the ground, wounded but not dead. Wesley took out his Glock with the Argen-covered bullets and fired once into each one at a distance. They all vanished in a grey torrent of ash.

Nora ran to the truck, and Wesley beat her by a second.

"You could work on accuracy," Wesley said as he dug out earplugs for Damian. "And you should really wear ear protection."

Damian tilted his head as he put the rifle back in the back. "Nice piece. I have a Springfield M1A, too, or I wouldn't have touched it. And before you arrest me or kill me, I know I shouldn't touch law enforcement weapons.

But it kinda seemed like a dire situation there." He took the earplugs. "Thanks. I only have one pair at home."

Wesley inclined his head which Nora thought was about as much compliment Damian was going to get from him. It was pretty ballsy of Damian to have even touched a marshal's gun. Although, the situation was unusual, and she was both surprised and relieved Wesley wasn't making a big deal about it.

"How far to the marina?" Wesley asked as he revved the engine, and they sped away.

Damian gave them instructions to the marina, and they pulled into a large parking lot with moored boats along a dozen docks that stretched out into the lake like fingers. It was strangely quiet, with a slight fog over the water. Wesley helped Damian into the chair, and they followed him to the front of the shop.

Damian knocked and called, but no one was around. He frowned. "I don't know where Hank is. He's always here."

Nora glanced around and spied the ferry. A sign indicated it was mainly used for short tourist tours. Damian said his friend also made round trips to Sagnot Bay every month. She hadn't heard from Elena, but since they didn't have a cabin to return to, they might as well keep moving.

"Do you know how to drive a ferry?" Wesley asked Damian.

The other guy looked at him with a raised brow. "Yeah, but I see where this is going, and the answer is no. I don't have the keys."

Wesley unholstered his Glock and used the butt to smash the window of the front door. He reached in to unlock it, stepping back as it swung open. "Find them."

"Is this a hold-up? I think I've had my fill of being a hostage for a lifetime," Damian said with a frown.

Nora stepped between them. "Is that necessary? We could have waited for his friend."

"We can't. We need to get on the ferry soon, or there are going to be too many factors I can't protect you from," he said. She rubbed her arms at the chill.

"Damian, can you please find the keys? Give us a sec." She ushered Wesley toward the dock, where the water calmly lapped at the moorings. A stretch of sandy beach rolled around the inlet, and towering cliffs lined the water with trees sticking out of the rocks like awkward cake toppers.

Nora was pleasantly surprised when Damian disappeared into the store to find the keys to the ferry. She stared at Wesley with a question on her face.

"I'd like to get some distance from the Antiquarians," he said.

Nora gulped. "Right. Because the artifact is broadcasting where we are, I'm feeding it energy, but as long as they don't have both pieces, the curse can't be completed." She paced along the fence railing to keep people from falling into the water. Now she felt dirty, diseased. At least the strange whispers and dreams made sense now. She wanted to throw the pack into the lake and never think about it again.

"This guy, Alazar, said his ancestors or something saw this happen once before in the sixteenth century. He took the little Argen I gave him to help reverse it, so let's let them do the heavy lifting while we stay alive. And that means we keep moving." Wesley gazed at the dark blue expanse of water and low clouds on the horizon. Early birds winged across the surface, and insects hummed.

"If we need to keep moving, we can check on Elena

quickly, right? I don't know if Sagnot is safe, but we won't be there long." Nora shook her head and clucked her tongue. She tapped her fingers on the railing, counting. The pale morning light helped her to focus. If it had been dark, she would have melted down.

"Sure, we can make a stop." Wesley exhaled gently. "You want to help everyone."

Nora shrugged. She supposed she hadn't lost sight of what she wanted before the artifact and her uncle's death disrupted her routine life. She still wanted to work with adoptees and adopted children. She still wanted to help others if she could, whether that was as a guidance counselor or psychologist.

"I think it couldn't hurt since she sounded pretty upset."

"Like I said, I'll follow wherever you want to go as long as we're away from the Antiquarians. Alazar said they were the good guys, but my gut tells me there's a lot more to this than we understand ..." Wesley trailed off in thought.

"They didn't count on my having your help." Nora shrugged. "Do you think we should have listened to what they had to say first before running?"

"No, because they came in hot with intimidation—something is going on. And it was suspicious Alazar didn't try harder to convince me to hear him out. I told them we destroyed the artifact, but I know Alazar didn't buy it. He still left, though, so it bought us some time."

"You think they have a way of getting to us no matter where we go?" Nora chewed her lip. "But as long as we're moving, there's a chance we can avoid them until we find the answer."

"Exactly." Wesley glanced at her. "I promise they won't get to you until you want them to."

She knew it was an unwise promise, but Nora appreciated him for making it anyway.

Nora nodded and rubbed her face with raw hands. She didn't know how to solve any of this or save anyone. The helplessness threatened to overwhelm her. Run, stay, hide ... the options couldn't cycle forever. Eventually, someone or something would catch up, and either they'd have a cure for the curse, or it would destroy them too.

"Hey." Wesley grabbed her hand and turned her to look at him. "At least if Alazar was telling me the truth, then there's a chance he'll present us with proof on how to break the curse, and we give him the other half of the tablet. Until then, we keep our heads down. I also spoke with Oliver Gibson, the deputy marshal chief I report to. He's skeptical but looking into how to make Argen or Hutchinsonite. And he's armed with the knowledge that fire kills Revs, and he can help others. He'll try to run it up every chain he can."

Nora tapped his fingers as she counted over and over. It took her a moment to absorb his words and internalize them.

"Moonbeam, you're going to have to do one more thing for me," he said with a slight smirk.

Nora looked up at him.

"Convince Damian to ferry us to Sagnot Bay. I don't think my persuasion is gonna work on him."

Nora rested her forehead on his chest. Then she squared her shoulders and adjusted her pack.

Nora stood at the ferry's bow as it chugged into open water. Land melted away on either side, and the waves crashed against the huge hull. She glanced back at the helm pit where a sour-faced Damian sat at the wheel and control board. He gave her a tilt of the head and a sardonic thumbs up.

She grinned back. It had taken precious minutes of arguing and explaining in no small detail what was at stake for him to be swayed. She didn't know if he'd done it for her or because the Revs were a curse that was never going to be solved by simply killing them. There were too many, and the curse wasn't like a disease where isolation and a vaccine might work.

Wesley walked around the deck with a frown on his face. He inspected his truck as it sat on the flatbed, locked in with wheel boots and straps. He came to stand next to her at the railing.

"It isn't commandeering a ship, but sort of close," she said with a nervous wave of her hand.

"Remember when there was a Kraken that spat acid, and you refused to run?" He chuckled. "I had to work so fucking hard to make sure our team didn't die while you were plundering treasure."

"I like shiny things." Nora punched him on the arm. "Not my fault you're so good I knew I could count on you to keep us alive."

"I feel like I'm not doing such a great job at the moment. I'm concerned we can't reach anyone on the radio. And Hank's stuff was still in the store, but his body wasn't. I mean, why would he leave his wallet and keys?"

Nora shrugged and tossed her hair back. She had no idea, but all the possibilities weren't good ones. "I can try to decipher more before we get to Sagnot. I told Damian he could stay in Sagnot with us, but I don't think he wants to. I think Hank's disappearance has convinced him this is not going back to normal, ever."

"I'm inclined to say it was other things, but we'll agree to disagree." Wesley gave her a suggestive look, and Nora tried to ignore the flush of heat that went down her neck. Wouldn't her mother be proud that she finally had a real crush? Did they still call it that? Her mom had tried to talk to her about boys in high school, but Nora had been so shy she hadn't really dated. A few dinners and ice cream outings weren't real relationships. And Jeremy had been a blip of insanity.

Damian wheeled up behind them, and Wesley turned with a polite expression. The other man barely returned it.

"I hear bumping down in the pit, and I obviously can't walk down there. Any volunteers?" Damian looked at Wesley pointedly.

Wesley took off his Stetson to hand to Nora. "Try to take care of it this time."

Nora smirked and tied it to her pack. "What sort of bumping noise? Didn't we clear the ferry before we came on?"

Damian shrugged. "We did, but there are a lot of compartments down there. I think it sounds like a belt or something grinding on the wheel. Call me when you're down there, and I'll try to walk you through maintenance."

Wesley grabbed a flashlight and disappeared down into the ferry's engine pit. The space was sizeable, with a few lights that worked, but there were still dark corners. Nora stood at the edge with another flashlight and tried not to blind him. She shone it until she could no longer see the back of his black jacket.

Chapter Thirty-Three

Wesley grumbled to himself. *This is what I do, right?* He ran straight into problems to try to fix them. It was what drove him and had gotten him out of that dingy town in Texas. He didn't get out his phone right away to call Damian. He had a sinking feeling he knew what was making the banging noise. And it wasn't a stuck belt or sticky shaft.

He'd coated his knife in Argen before they left and now held it in his dominant right hand with the flashlight in the left. Their supply of Argen was diminishing, but it was a problem they'd have to deal with later. Wesley neither had fire nor did he want to set ablaze the bottom of a boat, even if it was made of steel.

Thunk, thunk, thunk. Clang.

Wesley approached the erratic noise with cautious steps. His boots gripped the semi-wet floor, and the dim emergency lights bathed the maintenance room in red light. The knife's hilt was solid in his grip, and there were only so many spaces he could maneuver into.

He hummed in his head the oldies song *Lovers who*

Wander to keep his nerves from overtaking his senses. The song bopped as he crept around a corner and closer to the noise. He adjusted his momentum with the rocking of the boat. Adrenaline spiked his awareness as he'd learned to channel it after years of training. He'd studied how to master the tremble in his muscles when fear reminded him of his mother's rages and the helplessness of being a child under the control of an angry adult. A child who didn't know it was abuse and thought having plates thrown at his head was normal.

The bangs became louder behind a steel door.

Wesley put the flashlight in his mouth and used his free hand to open the door. He grabbed the handle and whipped it open. A man with cloudy white eyes reached out but was stuck between pipes and conduits. He hissed and screeched as he tried to dislodge himself. His mouth opened to show fanged teeth and his hands groped with sharp, blackened nails.

"Hank, I'm guessing," Wesley said. The name tag confirmed it was Damian's friend.

The Rev, motivated now, began to distort his limbs and free himself. He'd been stuffed in the tiny closet by someone. Wesley couldn't even figure out how he fit until he saw the broken leg and dislocated shoulder. He winced. He guessed Hank had turned, and whoever was on the boat at the time had done what was needed to save themselves. Wesley swiped the knife on Hank's outstretched forearm, and the Rev screamed.

Wesley backed up as the Rev started to dissolve into ash. All that was left was the nametag. He pocketed it and headed back to the set of stairs. Muffled shouts met his ringing ears. He raced up the steps.

Nora's wide eyes found his. A Black man with tattoos spiraling up his arms held her as three other Caucasians boarded the ferry from the side. They gripped rifles, shotguns, and an AR-15. One of the men had a scar running down his right cheek, and he held an axe tinged with dried blood flaking on the blade.

Wesley remained hidden in the maintenance stairwell. Most likely, the three only knew Nora and Damian were on board. His chances of a surprise attack were high. It took all his willpower to remain hidden as Nora was wrenched around the boat out of his sight.

"Anyone else on board?" one of the men demanded.

"No," came Nora's reply before Damian could speak.

"Where are you headed?" the deep voice asked.

Damian answered, "Sagnot Bay."

"I like the look of this truck. Yours?"

They didn't realize Damian was a wheelchair user. Wesley frowned. On the one hand, the wheelchair tucked next to Damian in the wheelhouse was obvious. On the other, Damian didn't give the outward appearance of being unable to use his legs due to his wide-legged pants.

"Yeah." Damian's flat answer didn't matter to the men.

"We're in need of supply in Sagnot Bay, turns out." The guy exchanged glances with his friends, and Wesley heard Nora's muffled cry as she was shoved toward another guy.

"You can take the ferry, but we're not part of the deal," Damian said without a waver in his voice. "Coast guard has been notified of our arrival, and we requested help to dock."

"You are now. Coast guard is too busy to care about a stupid ferry—they've got other matters to deal with. People stealing boats, not knowing how to charter said boats, you know."

Wesley peeked out, and his stomach dropped. The tattooed guy had his hand in Nora's hair to hold her in place. Her eyes took on a focused distance, and Wesley could tell she'd withdrawn into her head. He'd bet she was counting her fingers as well.

"Fuck you." Damian threw a steel bolt at the Black guy, hitting him square in the forehead.

The guy staggered for a second before throwing Nora to the deck and charging at Damian.

"Stop!" Nora screamed.

The shorter, thin man wearing a blue windbreaker grabbed her before she could stop the tattooed guy. The third man, with short dark hair with even darker eyes, appeared bored as he waited to the side. He took out a cigarette and lit it with a gold lighter.

The tattooed guy grabbed Damian and thrust him out of the chair toward the railing. Damian grappled like a pro wrestler and twisted his upper body around his assailant. He jabbed his fists into the other man's throat and kidneys. But the angle was off, so his blows didn't hit enough to do damage. Tattooed guy was over six foot and even wearing a jacket his muscle was apparent when he lifted Damian and threw him.

Damian hit the metal railing with a cry of pain. He crumpled on legs that couldn't support him.

"Come on, that's all you got?" The tattooed guy sniggered and bent over him. He dodged Damian's punch.

"Afraid so. Now, I'd leave the girl alone, or the last thing you'll see is my ugly mug," Damian said, and Wesley realized he knew Wesley was hiding. He wished he had as much faith in his skills as Damian did.

Wesley had his Glock out, the fifteen-round clip full.

Wesley had plenty of bullets but only one chance at surprise. The four men were spread out, but the man in the blue windbreaker held Nora, and Wesley was not risking a shot in her direction. He could take out the first two, possibly getting a shot at the third, but that still left a fourth, who could kill Nora.

"He's a cripple," the tattooed guy shouted with a derisive sniffle as Damian struggled to pull himself up on the railing.

"I prefer a more politically correct term," Damian said, breathing heavily. Wesley peered through the crack in the door. Damian was army crawling toward Nora in a brave attempt to protect her. Tattooed guy's foot came down hard on his back, and Damian snarled.

"Throw that bitch over and see if he follows," Tattooed guy said with a roll of his shoulders.

"Get on with it, Torq. We don't have all day," the cigarette man said with a roll of his eyes. "I want to get to Sagnot before all the others do."

"What's in Sagnot?" Nora asked, and it diffused the situation by a degree.

The man dragged on the cigarette. "The best a world going to hell's got to offer. Law enforcement's down, overrun, and National Guard is calling it quits. Sagnot is where we can set up a formidable home base against the Mobs. Speaking of, we'll need to inspect you for any bites or scratches."

Windbreaker grinned, and his hand strayed close to Nora's breasts. She elbowed him in the ribs. It wasn't effective, but he did pause long enough for her to say, "Are any of *you* bitten? Is that why you're acting like this?"

Her eyes slightly slanted toward him. She was trying to

distract them on purpose. It was the opening Wesley wanted. He squirmed in the tight space and aimed the Glock carefully. The recoil from the .40 S&W caliber bullets boomed in his chest. Tattooed guy took one in the head, and cigarette guy took one to the chest. Tattooed guy fell over the railing while cigarette guy slumped to the deck. Given where he'd hit him, shy of the heart, it would take him a few minutes to bleed out. Wesley didn't care. Nor did he have time to double-tap him and make sure he'd stay dead.

Wesley jumped out of the hold even as Windbreaker was reacting. Windbreaker threw Nora in front of him as a shield. Damian grabbed the guy's legs and hauled him down. He slithered like a snake and threw his body weight into dragging windbreaker guy under the metal railing and over the side.

"Damian!" Nora grabbed the rail to look over and slipped on the blood.

Wesley rushed to the helm and pressed the red kill switch button. The engine stopped. The boat slowed, and the frothing wake settled into the deep blue water. Wesley grabbed a rope as he ran back to the railing, but Nora was ahead of him. She'd thrown a floatation ring out with a thick rope attached to the boat.

A splash followed, and Wesley cursed. Nora swam toward the floating ring in search of Damian. Wesley remained on the deck, knowing he'd have to help haul them back in. It didn't make sense for all three to be in the freezing water. With more patience than he felt, he waited.

Nora took a deep breath and dove.

Wesley found another ring and threw that overboard. Nora surfaced holding Damian, but she faltered under his weight. Damian tried to help by using his arms, and they slowly progressed toward the white and red ring.

Wesley pulled them toward the ferry. Nora clutched Damian under one arm and her other arm looped around the float. Wesley had never wanted to hold her so badly. She continued to amaze him. Her selflessness and drive to protect another life mirrored what he wished he could feel, could be. He tugged on the rope even as his hands burned.

He grabbed Damian by the shirt and hefted him over the side onto the deck. Damian spat out water and crawled to make room for Nora. She was a hell of a lot lighter, and Wesley accidentally tugged her so hard she rammed into his chest. He wrapped his arms around her shivering shoulders.

Wesley found spare blankets and tossed them around both Nora and Damian.

"Fuck, that's cold," Damian said and shook his head. His skin was pallid, and he rubbed his hands together. "You're a regular mermaid, Nora. Thanks."

Nora's teeth chattered. "You're welcome. You got thrown overboard for me."

"I don't really have a lot going on, so I thought it would be a noble way to die," Damian said without sarcasm.

Wesley glanced at him. "Your spinal injury isn't curable, is it?"

"No."

Nora's face fell, and she touched Damian's shoulder. "And you don't tell anyone that because you don't want people's sympathy. I get it."

Damian smiled grimly at her. "From the first time in the gas station, I knew you were interesting. Different."

Wesley crossed his arms over his chest. "And this friend you live with—he's not really coming back, is he? Let me guess? It was self-defense." His tone wasn't critical, but it was slightly impressed. He could piece it together—Damian didn't strike him as a killer for no reason. Something must have happened and for him to have defended himself was no small feat.

Damian cocked his head at them both, seemingly a bit relieved he wasn't going to have to spar verbally. "Yeah, self-defense. Who could foresee the dead body in my cellar and that my 'friend' was a wannabe serial killer?"

Nora shuddered. "I can't imagine what you went through before we met."

"There are worse situations."

"I'll get your pack from the truck, and you can change. I need to check cigarette guy," Wesley said and bent over the man. He wasn't breathing. Wesley nudged him with his boot and sent him sliding overboard. "No bite marks, so he should stay dead. And we don't need the Coast Guard asking questions."

Wesley used a few buckets of water to wash away the blood on the deck.

Damian cleared his throat and raised a brow. "I'm going to need help getting out of these pants."

Wesley pursed his lips and wasn't sure he believed that Damian actually needed help. He glanced at Nora.

"Seems like you do fine on your own at home," he said.

Damian shrugged. "They're wet and heavy, and I have a bar in my room and bathroom to help me lift myself."

"I'll do it, but only if you don't freak out," Nora said with a teasing taunt at him. Wesley nodded; fair enough. He'd reacted poorly before, and it wouldn't happen again.

Wesley got brief instructions from Damian on how to move the ferry in the right direction again. He and Nora disappeared below deck to get changed and use the bathrooms. A gray sky met the blue line of the water, and mist started to roll in. They were about an hour to Sagnot Bay, and Wesley hoped cigarette man was wrong about worse things waiting there. Because once they docked, there was no going back.

His cell phone pinged, and Wesley frowned. His mother again. Instead of calling, she'd simply left a cryptic text: *You won't even help your mother?*

Wesley hadn't spoken with Loretta in six months, and he wasn't about to change that. It was probably a ploy to get him to do something stupid like getting milk from the store. He'd flown out to North Carolina once because she'd asked for help, only to find she wanted him to fix her TV. The psych facility kept him updated and said that she was "getting better" with therapy and medication. But he didn't trust it. There wasn't anything she could do to erase years of childhood abuse.

All he wanted to do was escape his family and past. But it seemed it always found him. Then he thought about Nora and what it would be like to have most of her immediate family gone, never to be able to speak to them again. Perhaps he could call his mother ... when they got to a stable place.

Chapter Thirty-Four

"COAST GUARD, THIS IS THE *WINDWARD* HEADING toward Sagnot Bay, out of Brooker. We need you to know there are ways to kill the Mobs or Revenants. Fire and the mineral Hutchinsonite. Copy."

Nora sat back on a warm bench and listened as Wesley tried to spread the word. Damian sat out on the bow deck and watched the waves coming at them. He hadn't spoken much in the hour they'd been traveling. She didn't want to go sit and coddle him—he didn't need that—but she did want him to know that he shouldn't throw in the towel yet.

"That was a cold jump," Wesley said. It wasn't sarcastic or judgmental, curious.

Nora clasped her hands in her lap and shrugged. "I know, you think my anxiety and OCD should have prevented me from doing something so idiotic. I'm tired ... tired of letting it run my life."

Wesley came to sit next to her on the bench. "I think it's been a crash course in kicking bad habits for both of us."

Nora took a few settling, deep breaths. She leaned her

head against his shoulder, and it felt so right. This man she'd talked to for years was now her reality. Somehow, she'd known he wouldn't let her drown while trying to get to Damian, that he had her back. It was weird coming from someone who wasn't her family. She had figured if she ever did get married someday it would be to someone who tolerated her tics or wanted to fix them, not someone who fully accepted them. Because she, like most people, didn't want to die alone. Maybe it was genetic; maybe her birth parents had only been with each other because they had been lonely one night too. Maybe she was the result of a one-night stand. Nora didn't care about the details because they wouldn't change anything. She'd known a few kids who found their birth parents, and it had only complicated things rather than answering questions.

Nora didn't waste much time wondering if Wesley would go down that path with her—he'd been pretty firm that attachment wasn't his thing. Protection and sex were one thing, but a committed life was entirely another. Nora understood that and could respect it.

"Does shooting people get normal?" Nora asked in a soft voice.

"I'd say the normal response is no." Wesley's chest moved in a big intake of breath. He turned her to face him. His eyes were dark. "I wouldn't say I'm 'used to it' but I like the thrill. I've tried to hide it under a badge, but I want to control everything around me, including death."

He blew out a sigh and hung his head in shame. Nora touched his shoulder gently for a second. She didn't find his admission repulsive. If anything, it drew her toward him even more.

"So, the OCD reclusive gamer finds a sadistic control

freak," Nora said slowly. Wesley's mouth turned down, and he ran a hand through his short hair. She tenderly, briefly touched his forearm. "I don't think there's anyone who could help me more."

Wesley met her gaze, and his eyes were unusually soft. She realized he was struggling to accept himself, and maybe she could help. Or maybe by accepting his protection, she'd already helped him.

"I don't have serial killer tendencies, but I'd be lying if I told you the people I've killed keep me up at night. They don't," he said.

"I would imagine in your line of work that sort of stuff needs to be compartmentalized," Nora replied and flicked her wet hair over her shoulder. "I want to stop the counting, the checking locks, the fear of the dark, but I can't. It's like my brain won't let my body rest." Nora subconsciously had been tapping her fingers together, counting. "Do you think we can stop this curse?"

"Not us. The Antiquarian Matrix society is all over this, remember?" Wesley grinned. Nora loved the crease lines around his mouth. "I gave them Argen, so all we have to do is wait for the news announcement that the Revs are being taken out, and the world will go back to normal. No more undead walking around."

Nora chuckled at the absurdity of the whole situation. "I never thought I'd be in an actual pirate ship scenario. I did everything wrong!" She threw up her hands.

"Yeah, I think if this were *Scourge*, we'd be dead." Wesley tilted his head at her. "But joking aside, you didn't do anything wrong. You gave me time, and that was what saved us."

"'Saved' is a grand word for what I did. But thanks."

Nora glanced at the bow of the boat and the looming landmass.

Sagnot Bay was a lot more populated than Brooker and Pike's Bay. Boats glided in and out of the harbor, cries of people carried over the water, and sea birds cackled overhead. Damian rolled his wheelchair into the covered area in the middle of the ferry.

"We're about to pull in. Bay guard should radio in soon with confirmation and where we can moor," he said and took the radio receiver.

A burst of static, and then a male voice came over the radio. "How many passengers, Windward Ferry? Anyone injured or bitten?"

Damian glanced at them. "Three and no injuries, copy."

"There's a dock check in place. You'll have to wait a bit. Follow blue buoys, and you should be okay to pull into dock eleven, moor five. Over."

"Thank you." Damian set the handset down and throttled the engine down. The ferry inched toward the maze of docks and stayed out of the way of the flow of traffic. Nora gasped as a few speedboats nearly crashed into one another.

"Are they leaving or coming? Either makes me nervous," she said.

Damian frowned. "I think they're leaving. You sure you want to stay here? Is your friend worth this?"

"I've never met her, but we don't have anywhere else to go," Nora said with a tremor in her voice. She wasn't sure of anything. Sagnot wouldn't be any safer than Brooker or Pike's Bay, but they planned to keep on the move.

Damian turned to Wesley. "Maybe you're the right crazy to handle this. Good luck."

Wesley gave him a small smile.

Nora wasn't sure if Damian meant her or the situation, but she was too preoccupied with getting to Elena now. After an hour's wait, a physical check on the boat, and interrogation, they were allowed to get off the ferry. Wesley drove his truck onto dry land and waited while Nora hung back for a moment.

"Are you sure you won't come with?" she asked Damian.

Damian's dark eyes narrowed. "I'd crowd you guys, and I don't want to walk into something I know nothing about. No offense, but I think you're better off hunkering down with me. The offer is always open if you're ever back in Brooker." He held out his hand, and Nora took it. Damian gently pulled her into a semi-hug.

"Thanks for saving me," he whispered.

Nora hugged him tightly. "You saved yourself. I want you to have this and be safe. Maybe we'll see each other again." She gave him the Argen-coated knife from her thigh holster. Damian took it with careful hands and wrapped it in a cloth that he stuck in his bag.

"Maybe. Be sure that cowboy takes care of you."

Nora waved as she stepped away, and he rolled back onto the ferry. The far gray expanse looked like a wall of doom. Had they crossed one border into something far more dangerous on the other side? It was like walking up a dune in search of an oasis, only to see more ripples of sand.

It was time to find Elena and figure out what the hell else was on the tablet.

Chapter Thirty-Five

WESLEY DROVE THROUGH A THICK FOG WITH THE GPS pinging occasionally to give directions. The oldies CD in his truck played quietly in the background. He realized he was probably the only person under thirty-five who still had a CD player in their vehicle. But he didn't mind. He loved old things and had a certain nostalgia for vintage.

"I can't get her on the phone." Nora unplugged her fully charged cell phone and stared at it in frustration.

"We're about fifteen minutes out. We'll see what's there." Wesley wanted to put more distance between them and the Antiquarians.

His phone rang, and Wesley glanced at the screen before answering. It was the chief.

"Soares."

"Where are you?"

"Somewhere in Sagnot Bay, Michigan."

"I have something to tell you." There was a pause, and Wesley could imagine the shorter, stout man rubbing his head. "Your mother called a few days ago. She's adamant about tracking you down, and some idiot here couldn't get through to me but found your information and gave it to her."

Wesley frowned and tried not to let his stress show. Nora peered at him since the phone was on speaker.

"Thanks. I'll keep an eye out for her."

Gibson swore. "I have too much to do in Wood Dale right now. The Mobs are starting to multiply like rabbits. The phase between being bitten and returning from the dead seems shorter. Fire is working, though. I can't get a hold of anyone who knows what Argen or Hutchinsonite is. What are the chances of you coming back?"

As fog rolled across the black pavement, Wesley kept his eyes on the road. Trees crowded the sides of the road with twisting branches. Michigan looked an awful lot like northern Wisconsin. Elena lived in a deep, wooded area with a few inland lakes scattered between long patches of forests.

"Not high, sir. I apologize. I'm taking care of something I hope will be the solution," he said carefully.

Gibson cleared his throat. "No need; keep me updated. I can send a few marshals your way."

Nora looked at him, and Wesley raised a brow. On one hand, it would be nice to have backup, but he also didn't want to get more people killed or involved.

"I'm fine, thanks. I'll stay in touch." Wesley cut the call off, and they sat in silence for a few minutes.

"I feel like you should call your mom," Nora said.

"I don't think they let her out of the psych ward, so this could be another trick. Antiquarians? Are they that devious? I don't know, but we have to be smart. I have no idea why she wants to find me. I'll deal with her after we figure out Elena's situation." Wesley avoided any more questions by changing the subject. "Did you say there were other people with Elena?"

Nora nodded. "Her last message said Kyle was coming to her, but she didn't seem happy about it. Normally, it wouldn't bother me, but the message got cut off ..."

"Yeah, hopefully, we check it out for a few hours, and everything is okay. I think it's coming up. The white house with a porch. This is more of a neighborhood tucked back in here." Wesley drove out from the cover of trees into a sprawling complex with houses that ranged from fancy six-thousand square foot mansions with triple floors and white pillars to two-bedroom ranches.

"This is it." Nora tapped her fingers on her thigh as they pulled up the street to a two-story white house with a wraparound porch. The driveway was full of cars, and more were parked all along the street.

"Elena is throwing a party at a time like this?" Wesley joked as they got out.

Nora was already starting to feel relieved. Elena had so many people around her; perhaps she'd forgotten that she'd tried to get in touch with Nora. Still, her heart pounded as she knocked on the door.

A girl with blond dreads and bright blue eyes smudged with eyeliner answered. Bass-loaded trance music thrummed in the background, and two other people peered curiously behind her, including two young men; one with long braided hair and the other with a short dirty blond crew cut.

"Hi, is Elena here? I've been trying to get in touch with her—I'm Nora." Nora wasn't sure if she should extend her hand since the blonde girl wasn't smiling or moving to invite them in. She wore a crop top, a cardigan, and leather pants.

"What's her last name?" the girl asked, her tone suspicious.

"Um, I don't know. I only know her from gaming online," Nora said with a glance back at Wesley. He looked like he was ready to beat the door down so they could ascertain if Elena was okay and then leave.

The girl looked back at the dirty blond guy who came up behind her. He stood around five foot ten and had a beach boy vibe with soulful blue eyes.

"What was her gamer tag?" the guy asked with a slight defiant smirk.

"Cupcake. We played *Pirate Scourge* for years together, and she always took the cursed daggers, and that triggered an event, so we had to fight off a horde of undead," Nora said and tried to look into the house. She knew that Elena was dark-haired with brown eyes and tanned skin from the picture she'd sent her before. What she also knew about Elena was that despite her flirtatious behavior she wasn't a promiscuous girl in real life. They'd had that conversation before in a text chat, so Nora was suspicious of all these people in her house.

The guy cracked a wide grin and held out his hand. "Goddamn, are you Hypernova?" He laughed when Nora nodded with wide eyes.

"Kyle?" she guessed. She'd seen a picture of him, but it was not a good representation of the guy standing before her. He was at least a dozen pounds heavier, had a thick neck, and his hair was lighter blond than the profile pic on his gamer tag.

"Of course! Wow, this is amazing! What are you even doing here?" Kyle's enthusiasm was a little contagious, and Nora found she needed the optimism. He certainly sounded like his persona online. "I'm sorry, but we need to be sure you're not bitten or hiding wounds. It's a new world out there, eh?"

Nora took off her jacket, and Wesley did the same. They lifted their pant legs to Kyle's satisfaction. Kyle's eyes narrowed when he saw Wesley's shoulder holster gun.

"Whoa, dude, no need for that." Kyle put his hands up as if he were guilty. "No one here is going to jump you, and we've been holed up here for a while—no Mob bites."

Wesley held up the star badge. "I'm a US marshal, so it comes with me."

Kyle's joking manner dropped, and a fleeting dark expression crossed his face. Nora wasn't sure how to read it, but it made her pause.

"Okay, no problem; at least you know how to use it, then." Kyle turned to Nora as if he were shaking off a fly. "Did we game together, too, or is it only Nora? Wait, wait ... are you Tango Strike?"

Wesley inclined his head in confirmation and attempted a smile to be polite. "Wesley."

Kyle's brilliant white teeth showed themselves. "I mean, come on, fuck, dudes, this is amazing. What are the odds gamers from across states would meet up like this? How *are* you guys here?"

"We're here because Elena sent me all these messages. We're on the move anyway, so I thought I'd meet her and check in before we leave," Nora said as Kyle ushered them inside. The house was clean, with wood floors, an open floor plan, and a large family room boasting a brick fireplace. Tall bookshelves lined both sides of the fireplace, and dark furniture complimented the light wood laminate floor.

Nora could tell Wesley was checking out the house with

a critical eye. He was a few inches taller than both the guys. Kyle introduced Hailey and Josh. They weren't gamers, just friends of his who needed a place to crash in the chaos.

Hailey warmed slightly to them as she sat on the couch and picked up a drink from the table. Josh flopped back down as well and puffed on a joint. Nora ignored them both as she focused on Kyle. He was the more domineering personality, and something about him made her hesitant, despite his initial friendliness. She couldn't put her finger on it but thought it might be her nerves stretched so thin.

"I got several messages from Elena, and she seemed like she wasn't doing well," Nora said as she stood in the kitchen. It held stainless steel appliances, white cupboards, and a wine rack.

Kyle got a pitcher of water and proffered it if they wanted a drink. Nora waved her hand, and Wesley shook his head.

"Yeah, I got the same messages," Kyle said as he put back the water. "She's not here right now. She went to check on her aunt in the next town over but was so generous in letting us stay here for a while."

Nora didn't comment. Her fear for Elena was becoming annoyance that they'd come all this way and she was fine. Then again, it's not like they had anywhere else to go. It was akin to what her mom would sometimes tell her about students who claimed they needed "help," but really, it was an excuse to get out of class or avoid an assignment. Nora figured they could get out of there soon anyway. It wasn't like she'd come to counsel Elena; she only wanted to be sure her friend was all right.

"You're welcome to wait here for her. It's insane out there," Kyle said as he opened the fridge to take out chicken marinating in a plastic bag. "Do you like grilled chicken? Wesley, you look like you're good behind a fire."

Wesley's brows knit together, and he cleared his throat. "We're not staying. We wanted to make sure Elena was okay. Do you know when she'll be back?"

"Not sure." Kyle plucked the pieces out of the bag and put them onto a plate. "She sometimes stays a few days— gets her groceries and stuff. Her aunt suffers from paranoia or some shit and doesn't leave the house much." He rolled his eyes up to the ceiling.

Nora turned to Wesley and jerked her head to go into the other room. "Can you give us a minute? We're grateful for the offer."

Kyle grinned, and it made the crinkles around his eyes stand out. "Of course."

Nora stepped outside on the front porch, and Wesley followed. She noted his left hand was always close to the Glock he had strapped under his jacket. She sat on the swinging bench and would have found it quaint, but anxiety clouded her thoughts. A light mist threaded through skinny trees, and twilight started to creep the shadows closer to the house.

"So, what do we do now? Wait for Elena to show up? Trust that Kyle is telling us the truth, and she's letting them stay in her house?" Nora looked up at Wesley as if he had answers.

"Your call. I wanted distance from Wisconsin." Wesley remained standing, ever vigilant, and scanning the neighborhood. A few people walked their dogs like normal or stood conversing in hushed tones. Other than that, it was quiet. But eerily quiet, as if they were waiting for the storm to come.

Nora played with the zipper on her pack. It seemed a lifetime ago she had been with her uncle and seen him die in front of her when it had only been a few weeks.

"I need a place to decode the artifact. Wish we could destroy it, but I would bet it's not susceptible to much. I mean, I guess Elena's in good hands, right? We can move on, although I'd feel better if I saw her first." Nora had so many unanswered questions she couldn't stop them from vomiting out. She didn't know what to do, but her patience was wearing thin. The world couldn't continue like this. Or if it did, there soon wouldn't be a world to live in if everyone were undead corpses. The artifact whispered to her, and she tried not to listen. It burned in her pack like an addiction; it wanted her to look at it, to feel it.

Wesley shrugged. "We can try to reach people about the Argen. I wouldn't destroy the artifact yet just in case. And I'm not going to say I want to stick around, but if your gut is saying you want to wait for her, I'm game. I'm finding us a hotel, though."

"If there is one around here that's open." Nora jumped off the swing, and the front door opened.

Kyle poked his head out with a cheerful wave. "Hey, sorry to interrupt, but the chicken is almost done. And I didn't mean to overhear, but you're welcome to stay and then find a hotel."

Wesley glanced at her. "How about I go find us a place, and you can stay if you want to wait for Elena."

Nora nodded and was a little relieved he wasn't going to stay. He made everyone uncomfortable, and she didn't blame him. But she felt she could coax information out of Kyle without Wesley's shadow over them. She waved as he got into the Tundra and drove off.

Kyle ushered her back with an arm around her shoulders. "I want to tell you; you look way better than your pics. I didn't think Asian girls had asses like that."

Nora frowned as she extricated herself from his grasp, and for a moment, she thought about calling Wesley to come back.

Chapter Thirty-Six

THE CHICKEN WAS MOIST AND SEASONED TO perfection. Cooked sweet potatoes and broccoli completed a healthy meal. Nora ate everything on her plate and downed two glasses of water.

"You guys only know each other from a game online?" Hailey asked with a raised brow.

"It's not that unusual—people use so many online dating apps that gaming is another version of foreplay," Josh said as he drained his beer bottle. He sucked on another joint with cracked lips, got up, and sank back into the couch in relaxed bliss.

Kyle gave one of his wide grins, showing straight, white teeth. He'd been staring at her closely most of the dinner as if he couldn't believe she was there. Nora didn't find him flattering, had ignored his earlier comment about her ass, and she tried to keep a neutral face. She hoped Wesley found a nice, quiet hotel where she could try to decipher more of the artifact. As it was, she was thumbing through her uncle's emails and research on her phone to see if he mentioned a way to destroy it.

"Well, Hypernova is an excellent raider. We commandeered hundreds of ships. I still can't believe you're here," Kyle said with grand gestures and clapped his hands. "I swear, I didn't think that was a real picture of you."

Nora blinked serenely. "I suppose I could have lied, but that's not me."

"And may I say I'm glad. One of you on the beach with your friend—hot!" Kyle cleared the plates, and Hailey loaded them into the dishwasher.

Nora got up, but Kyle waved her back down. She supposed all the attention could be put down to Kyle's exuberant personality. But it felt pervy. She didn't mind being a girl in a game of mostly guys, but the invisible wall kept it safe—no last names, no information exchange, just fun and bantering. In reality, the attention wasn't as flattering as it was in-game, except from Wesley. She'd gotten lucky with him.

"Whatever you're doing seems like serious business."

"I'm trying to make sense of this crazy world. I mean, it's like something out of a movie or book," Nora explained.

Kyle pursed his lips. "Let's call them zombies, right? I mean, I don't know why the government is calling them Mobs. Some nerds online started that. I swear if it's online and in the right hands, it becomes hard truth. I like your Revs term better. I mean, this is every introvert's dream—lock yourself up and don't need to do unnecessary socializing."

"Until the info structure collapses and you don't have heat or electricity. We need people to do everything we're used to getting to keep society running," Nora said. She knew she wasn't one to talk since walking out her front door was sometimes hard for her. Her anxiety didn't make life easy, but she was also trying to overcome it so she could help others someday. She resisted the urge to get up and check that the doors were locked. Had Kyle locked the back door when he came in from the grill? She glanced at that door, and it was firmly shut; the lock turned to the left.

"True enough. We rely on people for many things, but I could use a break from forced social stuff. My family is split up, and they're holing up in North Dakota and Indiana." Kyle held out his hand. "I hope your boyfriend is okay out there. The hotels we passed weren't open due to 'contamination' issues, insurance, etcetera."

"He's ... he'll be fine." Nora gave him a tight-lipped smile. For one, she wasn't sure why Kyle hadn't offered that information until now. Had he wanted Wesley to leave? And two, she wasn't sure what to call Wesley but hearing him referred to as her boyfriend gave her pause. In some ways, it seemed right, but then again, they'd still only known each other in person for a short time.

Hailey had settled on the couch with Josh, and their lips and tongues were doing all the talking without a need for words. Nora shifted in her chair and tried not to look.

"Want to see the upstairs?" Kyle offered with a sympathetic gesture. He held his hand out. They were calloused, perhaps from hard labor? And he had a few shallow cuts on his wrists.

Nora didn't take his hand, but she did take the offer to leave the downstairs area. She grabbed her black pack. "How can they be so calm?"

"I'd like to blame the weed, but it's also denial. They don't want to believe this is happening, and rolling with me they don't have to. It's like I'm the camp director and father all in one," Kyle said with a shake of his head. "I like them, and they don't have any other family but each other. I figure it's better to travel with a group than solo anyway, so I came up here to find Elena."

"Yeah, I'm glad someone reached out to her." Nora recalled Elena's somewhat cryptic messages. "How long have you been here?"

"About four days then Elena said she should go to her aunt's." Kyle led her to a bedroom with a queen bed, a small desk, a lava lamp, and blue curtains. "This is her guest room, and we're all sleeping in here. Let me move the sleeping bags."

He shoved two sleeping bags into a closet and smoothed the queen bed's comforter. "It's clean, I promise. At least the water and electricity still work. I heard some towns are having issues because the undead are starting to outnumber the living."

Nora shuddered. She remained in the doorway. *Would it be rude to ask him to let me have this room alone to rest in for a bit?* She debated her manners. Kyle came up in front of her and took her upper arm gently to bring her in.

"You can relax here. You look like you need a lot of sleep —no offense, I mean you look beautiful," he said and moved to take the pack from her.

Nora sidestepped his reach. "I'm fine, thanks. I could use this room for a while, though, to nap." She glanced at him pointedly in hopes he got the message.

Kyle nodded. "All right. I'll let you rest and check on you later. Sound good?"

Nora smiled her thanks and slid the pack off when he shut the door. She got out the artifact and her phone to match the symbols. It was slow, tedious work, but after an hour, she'd made more headway through the glyphs. The artifact purred at her touch. She hated to think it was broadcasting her location to the other half, but she needed to know what it said. Nora translated as fast as she could.

The pictographs displayed the hatching of a "mother," a universal being. Other humanoid shapes surrounded it with outstretched arms as if they were feeding or worshipping it. Nora couldn't make sense of what this being was or why it existed. Was it being formed from the undead souls? Or was it like a chrysalis, and the infection fed it as it grew or rested? Some verses spoke of what she interpreted as a new world or plane of existence. But she wasn't her uncle, and her knowledge was so limited she had to stop. The fragments of Argen in the crevice glowed silver.

Nora peered closer and exhaled loudly. There was a smaller inscription by the Argen that was hard to read as the substance covered it. It was not in ancient Mandé, but Middle English. That was a dead language these days. Emin had taught her the basics, and being the geek she was, she'd actually liked learning it. Her Middle English was rusty, but it was far easier than hieroglyphs. The first few lines depicted this account by a knight who had been there at the first outbreak. So, had someone written an account and placed the very thing that would kill the infected in the tablet to prove their story? Nora didn't want to touch the Argen to move it to read the inscription better, so she settled for transcribing the little she could see. She took pictures on her phone to study it closer later.

Every ten minutes, she got up to check the lock on the door. And every two minutes. it seemed she subconsciously counted her fingers, touching them each as if they were prayer stones. After another half hour, Nora couldn't look at the artifact anymore without her eyes crossing.

She put the artifact back in the pack and sat on the edge of the bed. The mattress cushioned her so well. A soft thrum of exhaustion flowed through her like a lullaby. Maybe a few minutes of shut-eye until Wesley got back. Nora held the pack against her chest as she lay on her side with her head on the firm pillows. She sighed and closed her eyes. *Just until he comes back, my phone's volume is up, so I'll hear if he calls too.*

A warm hand slid up her arm, and lips caressed her neck. Nora moaned through her sleep haze as she turned to meet those lips. Wesley. His lips burned against hers, and hands roamed over her body. A heavy weight pushed her into the bed, and hips ground into hers in a demanding and violent way. Nora's eyes snapped open to see a familiar but unwanted face looming over hers.

The wide hips grinding into hers weren't Wesley's. She gasped. Kyle pinned both her arms above her head. She craned her head and saw the black pack on the floor next to the bed. A clock read eleven p.m. Where was Wesley? He should have been back by now.

She'd checked the door lock. So many times. It had been locked.

Nora swiveled to get Kyle off her. Had Elena been subjected to this maniac too? Had she fled her own house, and everyone here was lying?

Nora kicked out with both legs and unseated Kyle. He cursed.

Then he pitched forward, collapsing onto her.

Nora screamed as Kyle's eyes bulged and the knife tip stuck out of his throat. He gurgled, and she slid from under him and off the bed to escape the spurting blood. Nora landed on the black pack. She hastily pulled her shirt down.

The man wiped his blade on the comforter. In the dim light, she could see he was perhaps in his late thirties, with dark skin and black hair streaked with silver. He turned to her with hooded eyes.

It was not Wesley that had come to her aid.

Chapter Thirty-Seven

Nora was so surprised she sputtered to thank the man. She took a deep breath to calm her adrenaline.

"No thanks necessary, Ms. Moon. If you'll come with me, we have much to discuss," the dark-haired man said. His voice was raspy, as if he weren't used to being polite. Nora remained on the floor and nudged the black pack under the bed. The artifact's energy thrummed like a live wire as if calling to her not to leave it. She did a quick physical check over herself—all body parts were working, and there were a few bruises on her wrists, but nothing was broken.

She should have been shocked that Kyle was dead, but the immediate threat was more pressing.

"We can do this the hard way, but I very much doubt that would be fun for either of us." The man gave Kyle's corpse a disgusted glance. "He was not infected; he was simply one of humanity's abhorrent examples."

Nora stood on shaky legs and walked toward the man. Upon closer inspection, he had a tattoo on the right side of his neck. The Antiquarian Matrix society. Chills ran and up down her arms.

"I think the obvious question is, what do you want? But I also think I know what that is, and I don't have it," she said in a low voice.

The man turned to her with a sigh. "Don't try to tell me your partner has it since we have him in our custody. He clearly does not have the artifact. So, if neither of you has it, we may be forced to resort to some ugly consequences."

"Wesley is with you? Where?" She twisted her hands together and counted her fingers. Anxiety crippled her ability to think clearly. Nora wished she were better in crises —she'd been in enough lately—but all she could think of was Wesley being hurt for something she'd done.

"Come. You may wash the blood off your arm if you wish first," the man said and gestured to the hall bathroom.

Nora didn't bother to close the door. The window was small and a long drop from the second story. She might be alive after she fell but probably not in any condition to run. And where would she go? She had to make sure he wasn't lying about Wesley. The cold water splashed over her arms, and the lemon scent of soap washed her nose of the iron smell. Nora went first down the stairs and tripped when she saw Hailey and Josh on the couch.

Their bodies lay prone together, still and silent.

"Did you kill them?" Nora swung around, and the man shook his head. He held the knife at his side, and she glimpsed a holstered pistol under his jacket.

"They're tranquilized. We're not in the business of murdering everyone. Honestly, I had hoped for a little more gratitude," he said with a tsk.

"I had it handled." Nora stopped at the base of the stairs

and motioned for him to tell her where to go now. She was relieved two innocent people weren't dead on her account. She should have deciphered the damn thing faster. Who knew what side this man was on? Nora wished her uncle had had time to explain more about what they were dealing with.

The man scoffed.

"And who are you? Shouldn't I know your name since you know mine?" Nora fixed him with a glare.

"Salif Diallo. My ancestors came from the heart of Mali, but our blood has been mixed."

Salif motioned for her to go toward the basement. Nora hadn't been down there before, so she turned the knob slowly and peered into the dim light. Damp air wafted up the stairs. She stepped down, and it grew brighter. The basement was half finished. Naked beams and pipes ran along the ceiling, and white walls framed a set of couches with a TV.

Wesley was bound between two men in suits. He was on his knees with a slash of duct tape covering his mouth and his wrists zip-tied in front of him. His light blue button-down shirt was torn open, and the dirt that crusted his pants was evidence that he had put up a fight. A chain was wound around his neck, and the links were strung up around a beam, the end of the chain in one of the suited men's hands. Wesley's dark eyes found hers, and they narrowed with frustration.

Nora tried not to react. She'd always thought he was infallible, even if she knew in reality no one was indestructible. Wesley had confidence that inspired others. These were men looking for a prize. They were still human. They could be reasoned with. Everyone had their price, and

Nora intended to draw on all her communication skills to find out what theirs was.

Nora glanced over her shoulder at the sound of footsteps. A fourth and fifth man walked down the stairs. One was dark-skinned with long silvery gray hair, and the other looked of mixed race. The long-haired man sighed as he took in the sight and crossed his arms. He raised a brow at Nora's captor.

"Salif, this seems like overkill. Why don't you ask for the artifact?" He chuckled.

Wesley glared at them all, but he seemed to recognize the two new men. Salif shrugged and nudged Nora to the side. She glanced around the basement for a weapon. No broken wooden shards, bricks, or pieces of metal. It was a nice, half-finished basement. She doubted the laundry detergent would do any good.

"When I ask people what I want, they tend to lie. I don't have time for this," Salif said and motioned to this friend.

A man to the left of Wesley drove his fist into Wesley's abdomen. He crumpled with a grunt. His chest heaved as he struggled for air. He shook his head.

"All right, calm down. I'm sure we can all get what we want," Nora said and was proud her voice didn't shake. She tried to assume her mother's stern and confident tone when doling out punishment.

Salif turned to Nora, and she kept her face as neutral as possible even though inside she was boiling.

Nora continued. "I think you all should make a case for which side of the Antiquarians you're on and why you deserve to find the artifact."

The man with silver hair made a half-bow gesture. "I am Alazar, and this is my partner, Anton. We spoke with Wesley some time ago." He glanced at Wesley, who had recovered and was waiting, listening. "I'm sorry, my friend, that some of our brethren have found you first. We are on the right side. I was coming after your uncle, my dear, and you had the unfortunate timing to be in the way with half of the tablet. Time is of the essence now—the creature grows as his curse spreads."

Salif grumbled. "You don't need to tell them anything."

Nora cocked her head at him. "What creature? The mother?" Her thoughts went back to the little she'd deciphered. *Materlus*. The word had come up, and she also recalled Wesley mentioning having heard the woman in his building saying the name.

Salif cut her a glance, and his eyes were bright with curiosity. "So, you have a little Emin in you after all. Busy deciphering the artifact? Yes, the *Materlus*. The *all-mother*. She is all-powerful and all genders, though you can refer to her as 'she' if you prefer. Count Ulrich is one of the names she goes by." A smile crested his face in his rapture.

Nora raised her brows. "And you all believe this? You're okay with a curse wiping out all of humanity—you can't be immune. Are you willing to die for this?"

Salif sighed. "The *Materlus* has blessed us, yes; we are chosen. It is a matter of faith—we do not know what new world she will create—but we are the vessels to bring her forth. She's drawn on your energy and used you, but she calls to us. It is our birthright, our heritage."

Nora let the chills run up and down her arms. She couldn't see a way out of this. One of her favorite mantras was "you can't reason with crazy." So much for talking their way out of this.

"Now, where is the artifact?" Salif asked.

Alazar and Anton didn't move, but Nora sensed their apprehension at the situation. Were they not part of Salif's group? Nora really wished she were psychic and could read minds.

She met Wesley's gaze, and his eyes told her not to give it up.

"Why do you need it?" she countered.

"To locate the *Materlus* and complete her mission." Salif fixed her with a hard stare. "Don't make one of my men finish what your boy started upstairs."

Nora's brows rose. "You're threatening me with rape? You must be desperate." She eyed the two men that held Wesley. Neither of them seemed eager at the prospect. They gave her a once over, but their attention was on their leader.

Wesley's expression darkened at the implied threat and allusion to what had happened upstairs. Nora shook her head slightly to let him know she was fine. He blew out a breath through his nose.

"We don't have time for this. Jamie," Salif barked and motioned to the man on Wesley's right.

Jamie took out a rubber baton and slammed it into Wesley's gut. The hollow thud dropped him so that his forehead touched the ground. Wesley heaved breaths and shuddered as the blows kept coming.

Nora swallowed, and tears stung her eyes. She didn't know how much longer she could do what Wesley wanted.

Chapter Thirty-Eight

Wesley's muscles screamed through the pain. The Antiquarians were no strangers to warfare and torture. They knew how to hit him without causing major damage, and they avoided his head—for now. Every once in a while, they'd lift him to a seated position, and a slap to the face sent him careening back. Blood pooled in his mouth.

The chain around his neck tightened as they yanked on it, and his body weight was used against him. Wesley gagged behind the duct tape as air became scarce. He prayed Nora would remain strong. They couldn't get the artifact. He didn't know where she'd put it, but it might take longer than they had to find it. They needed her.

The duct tape was loosening due to sweat and saliva. Wesley spat it off and a glob of blood with it. Air came into his lungs, but not the amount he wanted.

"Watching someone strangle to death can take five minutes or more, Ms. Moon," Salif said in a bored voice. "There are greater things at stake here—we can save some of the population if we help the *Materlus* achieve her true form. Where is the artifact?"

Wesley was lowered to his knees again, and he took a moment to breathe. The chain chafed his neck, and the plastic zip ties bound his hands and cut off circulation. But that was the good news. Most people assumed being zip-tied was a problem. It wasn't. He needed to wait for the right time, though.

"If you tell me how to kill the *Materlus*, I'll give it to you. We can race and see who wins," Nora said, her voice shrill but uncompromising.

Good, keep them talking, he thought with a proud grin. Maybe they'd tell the truth, but even if they didn't, it gave him time to make a plan. Jamie, on his right, had a pistol in his holster on his left side. The other man had a pistol tucked into the back of his waistband.

Alazar and Anton would surely be packing as well, but they winced each time he was hit. Wesley wasn't sure they would impede his progress should he get free. However, he wasn't sure they'd help either. They seemed reasonable, and perhaps Alazar told the truth that he was on the "right side," but Wesley trusted no one. It could all be for show. Therefore, it was five on two.

"Hush, wait a moment. What is that?" Alazar asked as they all paused.

A soft whine and scratching carried throughout the basement. Nora's gaze landed on a small door that perhaps led to more storage space under the house's foundation. Wesley followed her line of sight and his pain subsided for a moment as apprehension took its place.

Nora's face went pale as Anton went over to the small door and tugged on it. Wesley recognized the Argen-coated arrow tip, now attached to a knife he'd given them. Anton had the same suspicion they all did. He pulled on the door and stepped back quickly.

Three rats squeaked shrilly and vanished into the darkness; their meal interrupted.

The murky space revealed a dead girl. Black hair knotted around a bloated face with bruising around her neck. The rope loosely bound her wrists and ankles. Her left arm jutted out at an awkward angle, clearly broken, and her torn clothes revealed a decaying body. The smell hit them after a few seconds, kept well masked by the closed door.

"Elena," Nora said with a sickening gasp. She stepped to the side and held on to a post to keep her balance. "Motherfuckers." It was no longer Elena but a Rev. She was tied to a cement block that rasped along the ground as she tried to move.

Wesley blinked, and, in the space it took for them all to react to Elena, he responded faster. He whipped his bound hands in a hard slash down the zip tie. He exploded to the right and knocked Jamie's knees out so the man tumbled. Wesley kicked hard, and Jamie's left knee crunched, disabling him for the moment. Wesley grabbed Jamie's gun, thumbed the safety off, and pulled back the slide.

Wesley shot out the left man's right knee. He put another bullet in the side of the man's head when he was down. Brain matter and blood spattered all over. He pulled the chain from around his neck and used it on Jamie like a body shield.

Salif, Alazar, and Anton stared at him with various expressions rolling across their faces like from a cartoon sketch: shock, amusement, and irritation. Anton threw the Argen-coated knife into Elena's abdomen. She hissed, and only a pile of ash remained in a few seconds. Nora gasped. Anton retrieved the knife, sheathed it, and brought out a second, normal knife.

Wesley wrapped his right arm around Jamie's neck and pulled him to a stand as he rose. At least the Rev wasn't an issue anymore. Jamie didn't struggle, his disabled knee making it impossible to do much of anything.

Wesley panted with the effort of restraining a man as large as himself, and his bruised ribs ached. One or two were likely fractured. He pointed the gun at Salif.

"Don't make ..." Wesley began as Salif decided him. Salif charged toward Nora, but before he could make it, Wesley fired.

Salif's body stumbled when the shot hit his gut. Wesley shot him again as Nora jumped out of the way, and Salif tumbled to the floor. The older man struggled to crawl but then collapsed. Jamie cursed and thrashed in Wesley's hold.

Wesley let him go and pushed him forward. Jamie fell but caught himself with his hands. He twisted around and faced Wesley's pistol in his face.

"We have to leave. Kill him and be done with it," Anton said in a gruff voice.

"That means you're not going to throw that knife at me?" Wesley asked. His sarcasm was a little lost on the other guy.

"No, this is for my own protection. Salif made sure we didn't have pistols on us, but I can hide knives in a lot of places." Anton inclined his head at his own cleverness. Wesley rolled his eyes.

"I told you we are on the right side," Alazar said with outstretched hands in a gesture of goodwill.

Nora wiped her eyes as Wesley debated on whether he

wanted to kill Jamie just for being a dick. He had no problem defending himself, but killing when his target was incapacitated was a line he didn't cross. If he killed the man now, he might as well hand in his badge, and the career change would be made for him. Jamie was clearly out of the fight. The man was trembling and in the fetal position.

Wesley turned to Nora instead. From the look in her eyes, he wasn't sure she was nearly as okay as he was. A haunted hollowness to her expression told him to keep vigilant.

"I'm sorry I didn't get here in time," she whispered as tears slid down her cheeks. She let out a frustrated cry.

"I'm fine, Moonbeam."

Wesley turned at Alazar's throat clearing. "I don't mean to be indelicate, Ms. Moon, and I'm sorry for the loss of your friend. But we do need the artifact before more Antiquarians show up. More like *him*, I mean." He gestured at Salif.

Nora's eyes blazed with anger. "First, what about him?" she asked with a glance at Jamie.

Alazar exchanged looks with Anton. The younger man strode forward and, before Jamie could protest, slid a knife into the base of Jamie's skull. The Antiquarian shuddered and fell back, his eyes open but devoid of life. Nora sniffed and clenched Wesley's forearm.

"Okay, you made your point. Now, if you'll excuse me, I'm going to kill those two upstairs," she said, and her hands formed fists. "May I borrow that gun?"

"Um, no." Wesley didn't know what had happened in his absence, but he surmised Kyle had tried to assault her and that his "friends" probably knew about it.

"Fine." Nora marched up the stairs.

Wesley motioned for Alazar and Anton to go in front of him. They reached the landing of the first floor. Nora clattered around the kitchen. She came up with a long BBQ poker, scissors, and a butcher knife. She held all three as she walked toward the sleeping figures on the couch. Wesley intercepted her. He held the Smith and Wesson down at his side.

"Hey, talk to me. Don't do something you'll regret," he said in a low voice.

Nora didn't even seem to hear him. Her face was cold. The emotion in her eyes was beyond rage. It was born of regret that she couldn't ever change. She and Wesley hadn't gotten to Elena in time, and she blamed herself for that. Wesley recognized guilt all too well.

"They knew what a piece of shit Kyle was, and they didn't care." Nora's voice was not her own. She choked on tears. "I could tell there was something wrong with them the second we met them. I ignored my instinct. They must have known he likely raped and killed Elena too. And they did *nothing*."

She raised the fist with the scissors above Josh's eye.

Wesley made "stay back" motions to Alazar and Anton. They observed with wide eyes but did not seem alarmed.

"Maybe they did, maybe they didn't. Do you want to kill someone in cold blood while they have no chance to defend themselves?" Wesley reached out and touched her forearm. Nora shivered at his touch, but she lowered the scissors.

She jerked her arm out of his grip and threw the scissors, knife, and poker at the wall. They dented the white walls and clanged to the ground. Nora screamed in the silence and wiped furiously at her eyes. She took heaving breaths and moved her fingers together rapidly. Counting, counting.

Wesley grabbed her hands and held them to his chest. He bent his head toward hers and let her rage at him. His aching abdomen and bruises protested, but he didn't care.

"Did Kyle hurt you?" he asked.

"No. Not really." Nora took shuddering breaths and visibly calmed herself. The warmth flooded back into her face, and she stepped back. "Sorry. How are you? Are you hurt?" She looked him over and ran a gentle hand over his chest and arms.

"I am afraid I need to interrupt again," Alazar said with an impatient gesture. "But we did help you both, remember."

"You're a regular white knight, eh," Wesley said. He pursed his lips. It meant little to him that Alazar had helped or that Anton had killed Jamie. They were strangers still. Their actions didn't prove much yet because both were done to get what they wanted. They needed Nora as much as Salif had.

Nora sighed and brushed back her dark hair. She put her hands on her hips. "Fine, you want the artifact? You win. You've got a better understanding of stopping this anyway."

Wesley didn't argue with her. Every muscle ached, and his head was pounding. He had the feeling the shit was only starting.

His cell rang—in Alazar's pocket.

CHAPTER THIRTY-NINE

NORA WAS CONCERNED ABOUT WESLEY'S INJURIES, but the ringing phone seemed to concern him more than getting first aid. Wesley looked at Alazar with a "don't fuck with me" stare, and the other man held his hands up.

"I kept it for Salif." Alazar took it out and glanced at the screen. "Your mother."

Wesley grabbed the phone and answered.

Nora couldn't hear the woman on the other end, but Wesley was less than pleased to hear from her. He winced as he held the phone up to his ear and kept the pistol by his side.

"I can meet you there, sure," he said and hung up. Wesley pocketed his phone and glanced at her.

Nora held on to the upstairs railing for support. All her energy was sapped, and she wanted to find a safe place to take care of Wesley. She had a lot of questions but would not ask them in front of Alazar and Anton.

"We will use the artifact to stop the curse and let you

take care of your mother." Alazar spread his hands innocently as if it were that easy.

Wesley nodded at Nora, and she climbed the steps to retrieve her pack. The low voices of conversation faded as she stepped into the guest room. The stink of iron and death threatened to overwhelm her. Kyle's dark lump of a body lay on the other side of the bed, and she avoided looking in that direction.

She sank to her knees and slid the pack from under the bed. The artifact was still inside. Nora took it downstairs and held it out to Alazar.

The man's eyes lit up, and he exhaled. "At last." He took the stone tablet and ran his hands over the etched pictographs and runes.

Anton stepped closer to peer over his shoulder and his face beamed. "It is exquisite. These carvings are thousands of years old. Malian magic," he whispered reverently.

"Thank you." Alazar half bowed to Nora and cradled the artifact.

Wesley limped to her and pulled her aside. Nora wasn't sure if the two men would disappear with the artifact or wait for them. Anton went out the front door, but Alazar seated himself at the kitchen table, his expression still in awe. His eyes roamed over the artifact, and he took out his phone.

"How did they get you?" she asked in a whisper.

Wesley cursed. "Truck pulled up next to mine at a light. Two guys got out and bashed in the windows. We had a dramatic fight that ended up with them telling me they had you. So, I stopped resisting, and here we are. Are you okay?"

He looked her over as Nora nodded. "I'm better than you." For once, she didn't fidget or count her fingers because his hand held hers. "I wasn't sure how much longer I could watch that." She looked away at the thought of what might have happened.

"Opportunity struck, and I'm sorry it was at Elena's expense," he said with a shake of his head.

"I didn't know her, but I feel like I failed her." Nora pressed her knuckles into her thighs. "I mean, we gamed with her for years. It felt like we were friends, at least in some capacity."

"I understand what you mean." Wesley lowered his voice even more. "I have a favor to ask. My mother seems to be in trouble and wants me to meet her near Maple, Minnesota in the Superior National Forest. I have no idea why or how she got there."

He paused and rubbed his stubbled chin. "Would you go with me? It would mean hoping dumbfuck and asswipe will deal with the Revs and curse."

Nora chuckled despite the situation. "You don't have to ask. I'm going wherever you are. But how are we getting there? Driving seems like it'll take a long time, and who knows what roadblocks they have now between states."

"It's the only option we've got—the truck is still drivable. And if we run into barriers, we'll deal with them," he said with a small shrug. "I think a police barricade is the least of our worries."

Alazar walked over to them with an apologetic face. "I couldn't help but overhear that you need to get to Lake Superior? I have a pilot with a Piper M350 a few hours away I can utilize.

Nora was beyond caring who they could trust at this point. She'd given them the artifact, so the curse was out of her hands now. Alazar had proved himself to her, as he hadn't stopped Wesley from killing the other Antiquarians and now he was offering help. They had no other options. Driving to Minnesota would take too much time given the situation—Nora felt that Wesley wanted to see his mother and settle whatever business was between them. Yet Wesley was more hesitant.

"Why would you want to fly us anywhere? Don't you have a curse to break?" He fixed Alazar with a glare.

"I do. But I can drop you both off and continue without much interruption. My colleague has the other half of the artifact and will meet me wherever I choose. You're on the way up to my destination." Alazar turned as Anton came in with a black box. He placed the artifact in the box, and the lid latched.

Nora shared a look with Wesley. "If we can sleep on the plane, I'm all for it."

Wesley's mouth tightened, but he nodded. "Fine. Is there a bathroom facility at this place too?"

Alazar waved his hands excitedly. "The airstrip has a large washroom facility you may use. Follow us."

Nora slung the pack on her back, significantly lighter than before, and walked out to the silver Tundra. As Wesley had told her, she saw that the passenger and driver windows were indeed smashed in. Most of the glass had been cleared from the seats, but she accepted a towel to place over the seat.

"It's going to be a cold ride." Wesley started the truck with a wince as he bent to get in.

"Are you sure we shouldn't take you to a hospital? They've got to be still functioning," Nora frowned.

"I'm sure they are, but this is more important. I think it's bruised ribs and some cuts. I'll be fine if I can sleep for a bit somewhere and get a first aid kit." His tone was hollow.

Nora agreed. She hoped they could rest for a while.

CHAPTER FORTY

NORA WAS SLIGHTLY SURPRISED WHEN ALAZAR was true to his word. She'd had a fleeting thought he might turn and hand them over to the other Antiquarians, though without the artifact in her possession, what would be the point? Wesley followed Alazar and Anton's vehicle to a small airport with open fields. It was a breath of fresh air to leave Elena's house. Nora hoped Hailey and Josh would be scarred for life when they found all the dead bodies in the house. She hoped they were dumb enough to think they'd come alive as Mobs and eat them too, even though that wasn't a possibility since the person had to be bitten or scratched deeply to turn.

The bathrooms at the quiet airport were clean and well-lit. Nora used Alazar's friend's private suite with a shower. Mike Johnson, the pilot, had one of the commonest names she'd ever heard. He had a beer belly, an easy demeanor, and his brown eyes held a deep intelligence.

Nora offered to let Wesley use the facilities first, but he'd refused. He stood watch while she showered and changed into the last outfit she had in her pack: dark wash jeans, a long sleeve V-neck hunter oversized green sweater, and black boots. She threw her hair into a messy bun as no dryer was in sight.

Wesley sat on a bench outside the shower picking shards of who-knew-what out of his skin. He turned at her entrance, and the hard lines on his face softened. His eyes lit with a glow she couldn't miss as they traced her curves.

Nora swatted him on the shoulder and checked first that the door was locked, then took the first aid kit. She supposed they should be relieved. The responsibility was gone, and it was up to the Antiquarians to fix this now. Alazar had assured them they could.

Wesley sat shirtless on a metal bench, and she went over every inch of his muscled torso and arms, smoothing antibacterial ointment over the open wounds. He flinched a few times but was silent in contemplation. He caught her hand as it slid over his chest and pulled her into him. His hands cupped her face, and his lips brushed hers.

"I love you," he said in a brusque voice.

Nora straddled him and pressed her lips against his. She pulled back to gaze at him. "I love you, too."

"I can't promise you ..." he started, but Nora put a finger to his lips.

"I'm not thinking about the future like that." She lifted her finger and pushed a stray piece of hair behind his ear. "Yet."

Wesley didn't regret his words. If there was anyone there could be a "yet" for, it was her. His lips parted at her closeness, and his chest tightened at the thought of not being around her.

Wesley kissed her nose and then nodded toward the

door. "How long can I keep you here before you check that lock?"

Nora laughed and found that she didn't feel the urge to check it for once. She was safe and warm in his lap, which was enough for the moment. Wesley held her for a few minutes and rested his head on her shoulder.

"You want to meet my mother?" he asked with a grunt. It was a rhetorical question, and Nora knew it.

She cocked her head as if thinking. "Will she insult me, kill my character, hurt my feelings?"

"Yes."

"Then I'd be delighted to meet her," Nora said. She didn't think his mother could be much worse than she'd already survived. She hated that Wesley had to deal with an adult figure who should have been more to him than an emotional battering ram. She'd never get to that point where, as an adult, she saw her parent's mortality and limitations. They were still strong, young, and confident role models to her. She knew it wouldn't last forever, but it was the way she wanted to remember them.

Wesley sighed as he stood to head toward the shower. "I don't know what I did to have been so lucky to have met you, but I wouldn't change it." He turned on the water and half-shut the door.

Nora stood to check the door lock and then stopped herself. *No, you don't need to. OCD can be helped. You control it.* She forced herself to sit on the bench and watch the door. Wesley's Glock lay on the bench next to her in its holster.

The plane ride was uneventful, but it shed light on what was happening outside their bubble. Nora pressed her forehead against the small window and clung to the flimsy seatbelt. The small luxury aircraft only sat six with interior lighting and a mini fridge. Mike didn't seem concerned as he talked Alazar's ear off in the front cockpit.

Anton sat diagonally across from Wesley, and the two men took turns avoiding each other's gazes and staring at one other in silence. Anton held the artifact box in his hands as gingerly as if it was a bomb.

Lights of police cars flashed beneath them. The wilderness of northern Michigan turned to crop fields and then to dense forests split up around lakes as they entered Minnesota. The strips of roads were being blocked off as local police set up barriers. National Guard helicopters and trucks raced to get into position below the Piper.

"We're fine," Mike called as a helicopter got dangerously close. "World's gone crazy. Soon no aircraft will be allowed to fly. They're trying to contain the infection but don't know what it is. They've figured out fire kills the Mobs, though."

Nora watched as the borders were set aflame. Some other towns had erected torches on the perimeter, glowing like tiny sparks from her vantage point. The sun started to set, and the glow of fires became more prominent. All across the landscape, bonfires raged to keep people safe.

"The fire must be hot enough, though," Alazar said over the hum of the plane. "If any part of the Rev remains, it will animate and try to reunite its body."

"Was this Ulrich's big plan?" Nora scoffed. "I think it backfired, and it's not doing so well now. Why live in a world of the undead?"

Alazar side-eyed her and shook his head. "You've not deciphered it all. Ulrich wanted immortality, yes, but he also wanted a new race of humans. I'm sure you noticed by now the Revenants have begun to change their human form, grow claws, and have keener senses. He wanted to resurrect a new city of gold for his chosen to reside in and take over nations, other worlds even. Having Revs was a defense system as well, should anything else try to inhabit the new world he'd built. He believed there were portals to other realms and who's to say he was wrong?"

None of them answered.

Nora shuddered. A small part of her was glad she got to journey almost to the end—to remain within arm's distance of the artifact. It still whispered to her, but the further they flew, the less it pulled at her. It was like oil dripping off her body, letting go of her skin.

Wesley leaned his head back against the cushioned seat. He'd slept for a few hours. The bruises on his tanned skin had darkened, and he was sore from the beating. She didn't regret her words from earlier. Perhaps it was too soon to say "love," but she didn't know if they'd make it through this new world. And he'd said it first. Nora's body flushed at the thought. He hadn't followed up with "I shouldn't have said that" or "I don't usually move this fast." He was honest, and she respected that.

She'd probably started to more than like him, even before they met in person. They used to talk all night a few times a week when gaming. In her opinion, it wasn't entirely possible to fall in love online, but it was possible to form a bond. She'd had gamer friends come and go. Wesley had stayed constant for three years.

She gripped the plane's armrests as Mike descended

toward the airfield near Superior National Forest. Red and white strip lights guided him down. Nora wondered what Wesley's mother would be like. From the little he'd told her, she had left the family several times, and when she was home, she was verbally and physically abusive.

Nora was glad to be doing something to help Wesley. She knew he didn't expect her to return any favors, but she expected it of herself. Not everything could be black and white, but this was something she could do for him.

The plane's wheels touched down, and the craft jolted. Nora took deep breaths and thanked God they landed safely. Tall torches flickered along the outside of the airfield and in the distance. Air traffic control towers glittered with light, and police cars lined a parking lot to the left. Nora unbuckled her seatbelt as the plane rolled to a stop. Alazar and Anton stood to disembark as well.

"What's going on? You have friends here too? I thought you were moving on." Nora glared at Alazar as she hefted her pack over her shoulders.

Alazar's hands fidgeted as he took the black box from Anton. "I might have been hazy with the details. We are coming with you, my dear."

Wesley frowned as he followed Nora down the stairs and onto the tarmac. Police and a dozen other men and women in black suits swarmed them. "This is not a re-fuel stop for you, is it?" he asked Alazar.

The older man shook his head.

Nora was confused. "You meant to come here all along? Why?"

Alazar shook hands with an officer with a badge. He gave her a sidelong glance. "Because we need the final piece. Only Wesley could provide that."

Nora's mouth opened. She felt stupid for trusting him.

"What does my mother have to do with your insanity?" Wesley ground his teeth.

Nora took a protective step toward him. Did they already have his mother? She scanned the crowd, but no one was bound or captive. Officers mingled with the suits, and they all shot glances at Alazar.

"She is the *Materlus'* host. She will free them. As I said before, a new race of humans will emerge, and we will be better, stronger, and less overpopulated." Alazar didn't explain further as six giant SUVs with blacked-out windows pulled up beside them. He got in one with Anton and motioned for Wesley and Nora to get in the back.

"Come, please." It wasn't a request.

Wesley rolled his shoulders, but they were outnumbered and outgunned. There was no way out. He let an officer take his Glock as he climbed in the back. Nora followed after being lightly frisked. She didn't have any weapons except the knife buried in her pack. The plastic box of Argen sat inside as well. The officers took a cursory look inside the pack but didn't seem overly concerned.

She sat next to Wesley and buckled in. "Is this going to be long? I have to pee."

Alazar glanced at her from the driver's seat with a frown. "There's a restroom where we're going. Not far."

"You don't need her. Let her stay. I'll contact my mother for you," Wesley said, but his face expressed that he thought it was a long shot.

"She may stay if she wishes." Alazar shrugged. "But I can see in her eyes that she will not leave you, so I didn't bother to ask."

Nora glared at Wesley. Alazar was correct. She wouldn't

leave Wesley to face his mother alone; this whole thing had just gotten bigger. She kicked herself for being so trusting and naïve. So far, her psychoanalyzing skills were failing, and she could almost hear her mom's disappointed tone.

They drove for forty-five minutes until they crossed under a huge wooden arch welcoming them into the Superior National Forest. Tall fir, pine, and maple trees spread as far as she could see. The air was crisp, hinting at spring.

Tents and a few cabins dotted the open area. Huge bonfires flickered orange and yellow light into the shadows. More people emerged as the convoy of vehicles circled and halted. Nora got out and wrapped her arms around herself.

Alazar raised a hand, and the people quieted. He motioned, and a man brought forth a second black case.

Nora's skin prickled. The other half of the artifact was in there. She knew it.

"Why my mother?" Wesley asked in a low voice. It mirrored her question.

Alazar turned to them.

"I did tell you the artifact used Nora, and through that connection, we learned who was with her. We staked your house out and figured out what family you had. It wasn't hard to grab her from the psychiatric facility and try to lure you to us. The *Materlus* chose your mother because her mind was pliable, open." Alazar beamed and set the two boxes down, side by side. They released a charged energy that stood all Nora's hair on end. "Shall we begin?"

Chapter Forty-One

Wesley scanned everyone present, mostly Antiquarians with tattoos on the right side of their necks and some police and bystanders dressed in business casual attire. His lips thinned as his mother, Loretta Soares, walked from the back of the crowd. He wasn't thrilled at seeing her, but he was even less thrilled when she emerged with a swollen belly. *What the fuck?*

Even more abhorrent were the bite marks on her exposed forearms. She was a Rev. But her eyes were not entirely milky. Her skin had not started to decay.

Loretta wore a three-quarter sleeve, floral-patterned white dress that showed off her bump. She didn't seem to feel the cold, as she was not shivering or rubbing her hands together. She looked as if she belonged in the desert with a pale sun rising behind her and the dry wind billowing her skirts. Her face was haggard, and her hair hung limply in dark ringlets down her shoulders. Her eyes, the same deep brown as his, stared at him with a menace he remembered all too well from his childhood.

How is she undead but not entirely changed? Wesley narrowed his eyes at Alazar. He should be furious the man used Nora to use him. But the more pressing concern was his mother's state. The other man inclined his head and had the decency to appear apologetic. Alazar kept a close eye on a woman next to Loretta. She held a medical bag and was withdrawing a syringe filled with a silver substance.

"What did you do?" Loretta spat and cursed at him.

Wesley couldn't help the flinch. It was brought on by years of her insults and learning to keep quiet.

"You let them take me! They took me to your fancy condo in the city, but you never came!" Loretta's voice pierced the night air. She clawed at her belly, and an Antiquarian woman hurried forward. She was tall, broad-shouldered, and had a neck that would rival a linebacker. She grabbed Loretta's hand to keep her from harming herself. Loretta's eyes glowed white, and her voice magnified, not quite her own. The other woman with the medical bag grabbed her arm and inserted the needle. She depressed the plunger, and Loretta calmed. Her eyes returned to a normal brown, and she gasped for air.

Wesley tilted his head down. He took deep breaths, and Nora wanted more than anything to grab his hand. But she felt that would embarrass him even more. She turned to Alazar.

"You injected her with Argen? How many have you killed to determine the correct dose?" she asked with an accusatory stare.

Alazar shrugged. "I'm not in charge of the medical team. We only need her until the curse is complete and a touch of Argen keeps her from changing completely into a Revenant."

"This is torture," Wesley said with a curse. "She's half alive, half dead."

Alazar again had the decency to apologize. "It is for the greater sum, don't you see? I'm surprised you care. I've heard of the tumultuous growing up you had."

Wesley ground his teeth. Nora could tell he was restraining himself from attacking Alazar.

"I still need the ladies' room," she said to interrupt the moment.

Wesley turned away from his mother, poised to follow Nora. Alazar pointed at the public restroom structure, and Nora nodded as if she were grateful. She walked toward the structure while Antiquarians gathered around Loretta and Alazar, talking excitedly about the Revenants and Count Ulrich.

"So, congratulations? You're going to be a big brother? Again?" Nora asked with a smirk as she stopped at the toilet door.

"Thank you for joking." Wesley shook his head derisively, and they stood and laughed together for a minute. It was all they could do to keep themselves from losing it.

Nora was sure they appeared insane, but her patience and tolerance were zero. "Alazar said she's the host ... for what? Is this how the 'new race' is born?" She grimaced. "Gross."

"I am inclined to agree with your last statement. I don't want to know what's going on with this. Take as long as you want in the bathroom." He wiggled his eyebrows as Nora opened the door. She stuck her tongue out.

Nora took her time, but after five minutes, she had to leave the brightly lit facility. The darkness enveloped her like a shroud when she walked out. Wesley's dark figure emerged from the shadows, and the firelight flickered over his face. She took his hand. It was warm and dry, but a fine tremor ran through him.

A low murmur started beyond the forest line. Nora craned her head around to look for the source. White eyes blinked between the trees, and Revenants walked toward the ring of torches. Tree shadows dappled their decaying skin, and they stopped like obedient dogs outside the line of fire. Nora estimated about three dozen made a semi-circle in the back of the camp.

Alazar and the other Antiquarians were not alarmed. Instead, they welcomed the Revs—at a safe distance. They held glimmering objects in their palms. Nora peered closer and realized they had carried gold items. Coins, candle sticks, bars, necklaces, rings, and watches.

Alazar grinned at the audience, and he lifted his hands once again. He glanced behind him to make sure Nora and Wesley had returned. Two men in black suits moved to stand behind them.

Loretta stood with two men by her side, who held ropes leading to her bound hands in front of her. The ropes were loose, the knots tight. Wesley's sharp intake of breath was inaudible to anyone but Nora. She understood no matter how much his mother had hurt him, she was still his mother. His innate sense to protect people overrode that painful past.

"Come to the new Timbuktu," Alazar said to the crowd, and applause broke out. He carried the two black boxes and led the way into a torch-lit pathway into the forest. Anton shoved Wesley and Nora in behind Alazar. Nora looked at him to see if she could reason with him, but his eyes glazed with excitement and the torch in his hand trembled.

The artifacts in the two separate boxes spoke to each other. Buzzing like a distant chainsaw in her head but it was nothing like it had been before. The artifact didn't need her anymore ... it had its other half.

"So much for stopping the curse," Nora muttered.

Wesley heard her and pursed his lips.

Revs huffed and shuffled alongside them in the dark. Nora couldn't tell how many there were now. People carried torches, and the light glinted off the gold in their hands. The torch-lit path ended, but firelight surged forward with the contingent of Antiquarians behind them. No animal sounds in the night, a full moon glowing down through the branches of trees. The newly budding leaves rustled softly, and the path started getting trickier to navigate.

Alazar slowed as he picked his way through the over-grown brush, rocks, and tree roots. Somewhere nearby, a waterfall rushed, and the resulting stream trickled through the trees. The hush and bubble covered their muted footfalls. The journey seemed to take a long time and no time. They trekked miles from the entrance and deep into the forest.

Nora slipped and reached for Wesley's arm. He steadied her as they neared the source of the waterfall. A huge cave mouth opened on a rocky side, and trees jutted out of it like spikes. Moonlight streamed in silvery slants in the open space. It illuminated the walls of stone as if the cave had exploded up from under the earth, and its mouth yawned open to swallow them. She couldn't see the waterfall, but the roar meant it was close. They all waded through ankle-deep, freezing water and rocks covered in moss. A tiny run-off stream flowed over the cave entrance and probably to a pool inside. Nora shivered as they stopped at the huge entrance of the cave.

Anton raised his torch higher, and the crevices of the rocks glowed a familiar silver sheen.

"Argen," Nora said with a deep breath. "We need masks or something. Alazar, we shouldn't breathe this in."

Alazar waved his hand. "It's only deadly in liquid and powder form."

"You've canvassed and tested every inch of these caves?" Nora glared at him.

"It doesn't matter. The only thing that does is it keeps the Revenants from harming us until we can complete the curse—give the count his new body."

Wesley interrupted. "And then you'll be one of Ulrich's chosen ones? What makes you think he will honor that? You want to live in a world full of the undead?"

Alazar did a slight dance in place and shook his head as if he were dealing with a two-year-old. "No, the count will give us new bodies. We will exist beyond the physical scope of 'now.'"

"And how did this count become an all-powerful god to give you these new bodies?" Wesley asked with a glare.

"The short answer is Malian magic. We don't have accurate records of what transpired hundreds of years ago. But from what we do know, old god power will be unleashed through Count Ulrich, what he intended all those years ago. He is creating something vastly peaceful and unique. Instead of dense populations fighting for resources or hating each other for the color of their skin, we will simply be vastly superior beings and take over worlds. He will only need a few hundred in his army to rule. Everyone else unworthy will walk the earth as the undead until he decides he has no more use for them."

Nora raised a brow and shook her head. This went far beyond even what Uncle Emin had understood. She glanced behind at the Antiquarians that flooded into the cave. The Revs halted beyond the small stream of water as if they sensed fire and Argen. Their soft groans and white eyes glowed in the darkness. The Antiquarians started to throw pieces of gold into the cave.

Wesley ducked as a gold cup dinged against the rock next to him. The cup quivered and then melted into the stone. His eyes went wide. The gold items all began to melt and affix themselves to the rocks. The stone underfoot turned to gold. Wesley grabbed Anton's torch. The other man protested, but Wesley held out a hand that warned he'd punch him if he got closer.

Nora stepped toward him to see into the firelight. The gold on the floor spread to the walls like blood seeping upwards. Wesley moved the light into the dark back of the cave. The space was huge—there was no end—more rock covered in gold. Or was it Argen coated in gold? The cave was a veritable bomb of death.

They followed Alazar a little further into the cave; the sight took her breath away. Buried in the cave was a city—towers with parapets and tall gilded buildings. Archways stood sentry in shadowed alcoves, and fountains glittered in the city's center. The streets were paved with gold bricks around the fountains, and winding paths to the buildings were etched into the cave walls.

A city of gold.

Chapter Forty-Two

WESLEY TOOK THE OPPORTUNITY WHEN EVERYONE was distracted to take out his cell phone. To his surprise, he still had reception. But it was only one bar. Any further, and he was going to lose reception. He stopped, as if in awe, like everyone around him. It wasn't that he wasn't impressed, but he viewed each moment as a chance to get out or call for help. Low, reverent murmurs echoed in the cave city. He tapped the Serma app, and it generated all the gamers on his friends list.

He took a picture of the city of gold and posted it in the forum with the message if anyone saw this to come with weapons, any and all firepower they had—the threat of humanity's survival depended on it. It was dramatic, it was dire, and it was what gamer nerds lived for. Wesley wasn't sure if that would help, but he also thought, at the very least, some gamers showing up and distracting Alazar and the Antiquarians wasn't a bad idea. The longer they could delay the inevitable, the more possibility of some solution would present itself. He tapped the "show location" button and hoped it would save before the signal cut off. Wesley also opened a text to Oliver Gibson and sent a quick GPS text. The message was implied. *This is where I died* or *Get here now*—either one.

Wesley didn't have a plan, but he kept his eyes open for an opportunity. The insurmountable odds put pressure in his chest like he'd never felt before. He couldn't save Nora and his mother and stop the curse. Wesley sagged, and his shoulders bent under that reality. Maybe it was for the better. Humans destroyed their planet, and their time had always been limited. He hadn't even recycled for years, and he didn't care if lights were left on in the apartment. Wesley fought the hysteria bubbling in his stomach.

"How long does the Argen in her system last?" Nora asked Anton as they were shuffled along further inside the city of gold. In addition to other worshippers and waiting Revs there were two lines of what appeared to be soldiers—Revenant soldiers. They wore thirteenth-century armor, and their faces were all but decaying bone. Fangs glinted, black eye sockets with sparks of white stared out at the pavilion.

Loretta's breath was ragged, and she fought her restraints as they led her to the middle of a walkway. There were no actual roads, just smoother paths of rock. The two women, the hulking giant and the medic, held her ropes easily. The medical woman brought out another syringe as if to answer Nora's question. They weren't entirely necessary because standing in the shadows were Revenants like her. Except no one injected them with Argen—they stood like stone statues except for their feverish white eyes.

"So far, I think about twenty-four hours, but soon she

won't need it. The curse is nearly complete," Anton answered with grand gestures and bobbing his head. "He will rise again."

The cave trembled as Alazar brought out the two tablets.

"Are those Revs down there or people in transition?" Wesley asked as he stared at the anomalies. The people stood in a line like soldiers. Their chests rose and fell in small movements that led him to believe they were still alive, yet they were clearly half-dead, like his mother.

"Ulrich's army waits for his return." Anton shushed them.

Wesley took a few steps away from him and motioned for Nora to follow. They stood in a pocket where people didn't pay them any attention. Loretta's roar of pain echoed in the chamber, and a wave of excitement went through the crowd. Wesley tensed. Alazar started to chant and brought the two pieces of the artifact together.

"We don't have a lot of time, so any ideas?" he asked Nora. He'd hoped she knew something about this city of gold that he didn't. When she lifted her hands, he nodded.

"I wish I did, but even the craziest ones all end up with us getting killed. I mean, we're dead anyway, right? But I don't know enough about the Timbuktu myth, and I didn't have time to study my uncle's notes. I'm sorry I dragged you into this! I ..." Nora stopped when he grabbed her hands as she manically counted her fingers.

"I've got an idea, okay? But you'll have to be ready with that Argen left in your bag. You still have it, right?"

Nora nodded and took a deep breath. "What will I need it for?"

"To hit me with. Cut me, stab me, whatever, but I think

even a nick of it should slow the change. Or I may be able to snag some off of the medic."

"Are you ... no, I mean, come on." Nora clung to his hands, and the fear in her eyes almost made him back down.

"You remember the old, 'if you can't beat them, join them?' Ulrich has a new army and will need a general. If that's me, maybe better than one of his servants. And if you can find a way to blow up this cave when they release him, that would be great." Wesley's lips drew back in a grim "I have no other plan" expression, and she stared in disbelief.

"You think you can handle the change enough to turn his army against him? How am I supposed to blow up a cave made of gold? Do I look like a demolition expert? I barely know how to fire a gun!" Nora's voice was strained as she whispered.

"I know it's a long shot, but I'll give you as much time as possible when I change. Or half-change, I hope."

Nora's tilted her head. "Wait, in our half of the artifact, there was a hidden compartment of Argen. It's the other old adage of 'every light has a shadow.'"

"I don't think that's an actual adage," Wesley interrupted.

Nora glared at him. "My uncle used to say it. An added story was written in Middle English by a knight who witnessed Ulrich's attempts. It looked like he'd placed the Argen in the tablet for a reason. I didn't get to finish deciphering it, but I took pictures." She whipped out her phone and flicked through pictures until she stopped on one with the artifact in full detail.

Alazar's chant grew faster. The hum of energy in the cave exploded like the blast of an open oven door. Wesley grimaced as the ancient magic pulsed through him. He had tripped on LSD once in his misspent teen years, which was not dissimilar to this. Nora swept a hand to her head as if she thought she was bleeding. Wesley would do anything to have that beautiful face free of fear.

"Read fast," he urged and then ran out of their small space toward his mother.

Chapter Forty-Three

ALAZAR TURNED AT THE INTERRUPTION BUT DIDN'T stop his ritual. The tablets were aligned, and the crack between them was gone now. Wesley halted at the rush of power that rose a wall around Alazar and Loretta. The older man stood next to her, chanting.

"I will speak with my mother before you destroy her," Wesley said in a low voice. He felt naked without his Glock, but now the only weapon he needed was Loretta.

Alazar sighed. "The ritual is complete. You have perhaps five minutes." He grinned and lifted the stone tablet high. People cheered, and some shed tears. The Revenant soldiers' eyes flickered to life as they gazed upon it. They grasped swords, axes, and polearms. The crowd grew restless and chanted.

Wesley ignored all the chaos as he got closer to his mother. The force of the curse subsided when he entered their circle. Loretta groaned and clutched at her belly as if she were in the throes of labor. But her eyes were clear and fierce. She was in the over-confident stage of the change, where she wanted someone to kill her. The first stage of his plan was going to be easy.

He kept an eye on the medical woman outside the circle but was keeping watch. The other Amazonian woman chanted with Alazar when he started up again.

"Don't tell me you're waiting for words of love and affirmation," Loretta spat. She grinned, and her teeth elongated to fangs. Her skin paled and she spasmed.

"Mama, I never told you how much I hate you." Wesley choked on his words. He found they were harder to say out loud than he anticipated.

"You were always alone. Always outside doing something perverted, and your slut sister was always showing her goods to any boy who looked at her." Loretta cackled, and her spine cracked. She gasped with the pain, but a feral jeer crested her bloody lips as sharp teeth tore them. "No matter how often I told you what a pathetic shit stain you are, you always came back."

Wesley wiped his brow with his sleeve. He took several breaths to steady his nerves. He stepped close to her, and she gnashed her teeth at him.

"I never wanted children, but your father did. He thought it would make me stay. I thought at least if I had a girl, I could make her into what I wasn't—but I had you. A stupid useless boy," Loretta said. Her words were slurred, and she twitched violently. No one was paying her much attention since they were focused on the purple smoke from the artifact. The walls of gold shimmered and trembled as if thunder had crashed overhead.

Wesley told himself it was the curse, Ulrich, or the demon echo of his mother's spirit. He wasn't naïve to think the words weren't hers, but they were laced with such poison that it still wounded him.

"You didn't exactly do good by your daughter, did you? She's in a psychiatric facility probably for life now," Wesley said. His eyes narrowed, and he braced himself for the attack. "You chose this."

"I am sacred. He sees my value like none of you ever did."

Loretta launched at him, and her teeth sank into the forearm he proffered. He grimaced at the pain as she tore flesh and her clawed hands grabbed for his face.

His fist collided with the side of her face, and she screamed, letting go of his arm. Wesley shoved her back as the walls of gold started to run like molten lava. A thunderclap resounded in the cave, and the city's turrets cracked. Debris fell toward the crowd in knife-like shards.

Wesley ran to the Antiquarian medic, who stood open-mouthed. He grabbed her bag and ran into the crowd. The change started quickly. His blood raced like it was on fire as he shoved people out of the way. His joints cracked, and his brain grew foggy. Wesley staggered to his knees and ripped open the bag. He didn't have time to check in with Nora. The curse was taking over his body so fast his hands shook as he took out a syringe with Argen.

He grunted at the pain that ran up and down his limbs. The vicious part of him that enjoyed it, the urge to kill something, emerged like a second skin. Wesley slid the needle into the crook of his arm, not sure if it mattered where he injected the Argen, and depressed the plunger. The liquid cooled his fevered skin. Wesley jerked as the curse's change took hold of him like a bear gnawing on his head.

Wesley's muscles hardened, his breath nearly stopped,

and his eyesight improved with laser focus. He picked up a rock and crushed it in his hand. The Argen kept him from turning, but barely. He was still human and still alive.

He let out a roar that shattered the chanting, and the Revs' heads snapped toward him.

Chapter Forty-Four

Nora flipped between the photo of the artifact and the symbol key Emin had created. She squinted at the pictographs. Her head shot up at the monstrous howl.

She swallowed a fearful breath as Wesley emerged from the shadows. The golden torch light illuminated his tattered shirt and gleaming eyes. Veins pulsed under bronzed skin, and his hands grew talons. He was halfway between Rev and human.

Nora blinked back tears as she deciphered the knight's account, a possible way to capture Ulrich's spirit again. Perhaps destroy him forever. The knight had written in Middle English that he'd witnessed the first "revival" and that Ulrich had tried to resurrect his mistress or his goat— Nora was rusty on the slang from seven hundred years ago. She'd never been happier than now that Emin had insisted she learn it to impress someone someday.

"That's got to be 'destroyed,' I think," she muttered. The inscription was faded, but she had a semblance of a plan. The timing might be a problem, though. If she read it correctly, there was a finite amount of time when Ulrich was released that he could be killed. A spear, sword, or arrow weapon would be effective if coated in sacrificial blood and Argen. Then doused in sacred fire. Nora sighed at the vague instructions. She hoped the regular plain fire would suffice. But that would be too easy.

If only she had a way to communicate with Wesley or what was left of him. The monster stalking toward the line of Revs was not the man she knew. An Antiquarian brushed past her with a pistol out. He grabbed Alazar and pointed to the entrance of the cave. Nora followed them as Alazar appointed a dozen men and women to leave. She glanced back at Wesley, who was fighting for rank with the Revs, and his mother lay on the ground and writhed as Ulrich's curse completed. Her skin split and she exploded into an iridescent light.

Nora shielded her eyes and ducked as a blast of wind tore through the cave. A deep chortle resonated and chilled her bones. It was not a newborn mutant but Ulrich himself, born from his chosen host. The new race Alazar had spoken of would begin with Ulrich. In place of Loretta stood a black-shrouded figure of a man, wreathed in a gold flame that draped like skin over him. He had dark spindle-like needles that spiked from the back of his head down his spine and his arms were outstretched like spider legs. The same vibrating hum she'd felt from the artifact increased a hundred-fold. Nora shivered as the Malian magic shot out like missiles.

She didn't think anything could distract her from the sight, but the chatter of gunfire did.

Nora slid behind a pillar of stone as the Antiquarians clashed with three US marshals and two civilians dressed in black with rifles out. *Is this the cavalry?* she thought with irony. Perhaps Wesley had gotten a message out to his boss.

"You don't have jurisdiction here!" an Antiquarian man shouted and fired at a marshal. The marshal held a riot shield, and the bullets dented it, knocking him back a few feet.

"Get down on the ground. Now!" the marshal shouted, but the man fired again.

This time, a civilian woman opened fire, and her bullets caught the man in the chest. He dropped, and the other Antiquarians drew their guns. The marshals' irritated faces made the woman stand down and get behind their shields. The Antiquarians fired into the small group, and empty shells pinged off the rocks. Nora clapped her hands over her ears as the gunfire echoed in the cave. The marshals put down all except two of the Antiquarians; they lay on the ground wounded and out of the fight.

Another roar shook the cave. Everyone paused and looked for the source.

"What the fuck is that?" A marshal shouted, and no one had an answer for him.

"Oliver Gibson?" Nora called and added a "Sir?" for good measure. Everyone froze as her voice rang out over the thunderous roars and shouts.

A man dressed in combat gear, with the marshal badge on his left arm, stepped forward cautiously. He held a shield in front of him, and his helmet only allowed her to see his eyes as he searched for the voice.

Nora stepped around the pillar with her hands up in case she appeared threatening. The man removed his helmet and lowered the shield a fraction.

"Yes, ma'am. Please be Nora and not another psycho." His deep voice echoed in the cave.

"Yes. I'm Nora." She attempted a friendly smile but knew it was strained. They didn't have a lot of time. "You didn't bring anything besides guns with you, huh?"

Oliver blew out a breath and lowered the shield completely. "Wesley didn't explain much, so no. We have a few pounds of explosives. Which, before you ask, marshals are not in the business of carrying. But apparently, this guy Mac is always prepared." He had nodded his head to a tall, thin civilian man on his left with a goatee.

Mac nodded. "What's going on in here?"

Nora bit her lip. "Too much to explain. Suffice it to say we're out of time and somehow need to blow the entrance to this cave. Nothing can get out." She leveled them all with a stare, and they whispered among themselves.

"Will something eventually get out?" Oliver asked with a knowing tilt of his head.

"It'll buy us time unless Wesley's plan goes accordingly. I have to construct a spear of some sort—now. Argen, the silver stuff on the walls, kills the Revs. Knives and other weapons that can be coated in it are more effective than bullets." Nora gave them a quick rundown on how to protect themselves more effectively. To their credit, the marshals and two civilians listened without interruption or dispute.

Nora glimpsed the woman's black T-shirt under her jacket, and it read *Call of Duty*. "Are you gamers? Are you with the marshals?"

The woman barked a laugh. "I'm Wynona. We ran into them on our way here, and they didn't believe someone named Tango Strike put out a worldwide message on Serma.

We live a town over and figured we had nowhere else to go. If the world's ending, we want to see it." She punched Mac on the shoulder. The way they stood together, Nora assumed they were a couple. No rings on their fingers, but that didn't mean much.

Mac grinned wolfishly. "Why not, eh?"

Oliver introduced his two marshals, Todd and Jonathan, who were in their late thirties. "We didn't have the resources to bring more guys. This is an unusual circumstance at best. Took us breaking our necks to get here." He ran a hand through his thinning hair.

"Wesley will appreciate the support." Nora's voice cracked. She realized she hadn't been counting her fingers. She wanted to survive and find a cure for Wesley. Maybe if she could stop the curse, he'd be human enough to change back. She couldn't hope for that yet. He'd sealed his death when he'd chosen to be bitten.

"Is he in there? *What's* in there?" Todd asked. His brows knit together in concern. The roaring had lowered to a rumble of rolling thunder. It was as if something was breathing, waiting to gather strength.

"Yes ... he's been bitten. But don't attack him; the change is affecting him differently. He's attempting to keep his mind, but I wouldn't test his resolve," she said with a shake of her head.

Nora turned at the sound of footsteps. Antiquarians were coming to check on their comrades, no doubt. They all whispered their agreed course of action, and the marshals, Wynona, and Mac went to hide. Nora jumped behind a rock pillar and scouted for her potential spear. A tree branch half calcified in the rocks caught her eye.

Antiquarians shouted to one other that someone had

breached the cave. Nora quickly snapped off the branch into a five-foot-long makeshift spear. It was sturdier than plain wood, and she rubbed the end on rocks to sharpen it. Nora felt like a Neanderthal as she sharpened the spear to a point, or as best a point as she could get. She dreaded what she had to do with it. The knight's words rang in her mind. *Sacrifice of blood before the Argen.*

She'd have to kill someone to save the world—no big deal.

CHAPTER FORTY-FIVE

NORA RACKED THE SPEAR IN THE GOLD-COVERED Argen on the cave walls. The gold flaked off, and the silver substance coated the branch's tip and length. She took steadying breaths and crept behind the rock pillars.

A low moaning sounded from outside the entrance. Nora adjusted her position and gasped. Hundreds of Revs emerged from the darkness outside the cave and headed toward them. If they didn't blow the entrance, they'd be trapped with the undead regardless. Nora prayed for Oliver and the others to hurry. Trapped with Ulrich was one thing, but being trapped with Ulrich and hundreds of Revs and Antiquarians was more than a death sentence. It was the mouth of hell. They couldn't let Ulrich get out, not before she had a little more time.

Nora raced back from the entrance toward the inner part of the cave where the city of gold glittered. Antiquarians took turns standing before Ulrich with awe and fear in their eyes.

Ulrich had taken a more physical human-like form, and his eyes shimmered sky blue. He stood like a newly emerged butterfly: unable to fly until his wings dried. He surveyed the bowing Antiquarians and the Revenants that stood in a line before him. Wesley stood among them with shoulders back and eyes devoid of emotion. Nora noted the wounds on his arms and torso and half a dozen dead Revs on the ground behind him. He'd won the battle for supremacy. But now, he stood in front of Ulrich like an obedient general. Antiquarians and Revs whispered his name: *Materlus.*

Nora hoped Wesley was putting on an act. She had no way of knowing what had gone on in the twenty minutes she'd been talking with Oliver. Had the Argen injection not worked? She put aside fear to vow that Wesley's sacrifice would count. There was no time to mourn his decision.

Alazar shouted at some of his lackeys, and she assumed he was wondering where she was. Alazar pointed and scanned the cave looking for her. She scrambled into shadow as torch flames lit up the city's crevices. She waited for Oliver and his team.

Ulrich touched a few "worthy" people, and they contorted with power. Their spines elongated, eyes glowed white, and they transformed into undead soldiers. These were not normal Revs, but bigger and faster. They fought each other, tore rocks from the wall, and careened around the gold floor like crazed monkeys. Ulrich's deep voice echoed all around like fuel on a fire.

A blast deafened her.

Nora instinctively ducked low and covered her head, holding the spear. She was grateful for the black pack on her back that protected her from falling debris. Gold shimmered in the air as the cave shuddered like a waking giant. Nora hoped it was enough to seal the entrance from the Revs careening toward them.

She steeled her nerves, took a deep breath, and shot out from her hiding spot.

CHAPTER FORTY-SIX

THE ONLY WAY WESLEY COULD KEEP HIS MIND from aligning with Ulrich's will was to sing oldies songs in his head. *Be My Baby* and *Don't Worry Baby* crooned, and he saw each word in his mind like a banner. He imagined the glittering ambiance like a dance floor and twirled Nora in his arms. She wore a short, flared red dress that revealed her elegant legs. Ulrich couldn't get in.

The blast shook him.

Wesley wanted to run and find Nora, but his body was almost not his own. The sinew and muscle and bone were enslaved to the curse's power. The Revs had understood he was alpha—he'd won the general's respect—but Ulrich was the king. Even if he could get the image of his mother birthing Ulrich out of his head, it would haunt him until he died, which might not be long now.

Gather, chosen, to the Materlus. To me. Ulrich's voice commanded their attention. The unturned people held out pleading hands. Ulrich had merely scratched them with his clawed hand, and they shuddered into Revs. The change was instant, with no waiting period.

This is the great plan? Wesley thought with a sneer. *To turn everyone into Revs like some sort of rabid army? This isn't immortality—it's enslavement.*

Ulrich's head twisted to look at him. Wesley cursed. The black shadow wreathed in flame moved like a snake toward him. Giant wings flowed behind him like a shroud.

"I have been waiting for hundreds of years, and here I stand. A new era shall begin. The earth will no longer suffer under human rule, for they will not be human," Ulrich said aloud. His voice rasped like winter wind through dead branches. "The cities of gold will be paradises. No wars over resources. We shall explore the entire cosmos and make it ours."

"You're a real environmentalist," Wesley said with a snicker. He didn't know what the blast signified, but his instinct told him it was time to act. He hoped Nora was putting some sort of plan into action.

He charged forward, and Ulrich met him with a rush of black magic. The count's fist turned into a flaming sword that slashed above Wesley's head. Wesley ducked and slid on his knees. He picked up a handful of rocks and threw them at Ulrich's face. The *Materlus* roared as the pebbles pelted his eyes. He wasn't strong enough yet to block them.

Wesley grabbed a Rev's axe. He chopped and hacked at any part of him he could reach, but the blade went through smoke and flame. Ulrich was not yet fully formed.

A flash of movement caught his eye. Nora ran with a spear, ducking Revs and people in her path, toward the *Materlus*. Sweat marred her brow and the black pack bounced on her back. She flanked them to get behind the count. Wesley heard Ulrich's voice in his head, but he blocked it out. He doubled his effort to hurt the count, but it was like swatting at a fly which kept flying out of reach.

Wesley swore and took hold of the only solid parts of Ulrich—the spikes and his head. He put him in a chokehold as Revs dashed toward them to help their master. His clawed talons dug deep into whatever solid flesh they could find.

Wesley ground his teeth at the pain of knives and spears piercing his sides and back. But he was half-dead, and his body didn't respond like normal. His strength didn't give out. He bled, but it wasn't life-threatening. That was both good and bad. The good news was he would be able to hold the *Materlus* long enough for Nora to spear him, and the bad news was that the Argen was fading in his system, and soon he'd change for good.

Wesley clung to the count as his vision started to spot. The city of gold shimmered before him. This was how it ended. All the years of trauma and abuse from a mother who couldn't control the impulses in her brain, all the therapy that gave him false hope he could be "cured." This was what he was meant for—to protect. His father had done his best. Wesley could see that now. Those late-night drives to distract him and Becca were the best he could do.

And now it's time for me to do better than he did. He gazed at the city of gold with wide eyes. *It is remarkable and terrible at the same time.*

CHAPTER FORTY-SEVEN

NORA WISHED HER UNCLE COULD SEE HER NOW. She wished he could see the city of gold and know it was real. Her parents would have been amazed and thrilled too. It probably paled in comparison to ancient Timbuktu. She ran faster and faster toward the struggling *Materlus*.

Alazar got in her way, and he was the one she'd been hoping would.

Nora skidded to a stop as Alazar pointed a gun at her. His eyes burned with fire, and he leveled the pistol at her head. She didn't waste time trying to reason with him. The spear was a good five feet out in front, so she charged like a knight without a horse. He didn't get a chance to fire as the tip caught him on the inner left thigh. He screamed as he dropped. The gun flew from his grip and fell over a rock cliff.

Nora shoved the spear into the thigh as deep as she could, then wrenched it out. Alazar grasped his leg and stumbled, trying to get up. He roared in frustration as the femoral artery bled profusely. Nora gasped as the spear shivered in her hand. The blood soaked into the silver and started to glow like an ember, but it wasn't hot.

"My leg? You're as stupid as you are clumsy," he said in a pained rasp. Alazar tried to tear off a shirt sleeve to use as a tourniquet, but his hands were shaking.

Nora sneered and jabbed the arm that was ripping the fabric. "I was aiming for your dick." She left him bleeding out on the golden floor of his tomb.

She didn't care if he survived or not, but chances were, he wouldn't. Nora paused for a millisecond, realizing what she'd done. But Wesley's cry woke her from the old self-doubt and fear. Nora plunged ahead through shocked Antiquarians. The spatter of gunfire told her Oliver had left at least a couple of people inside.

Antiquarians fell in front of her as they tried to stop her flight. She glanced back and saw the husband-wife gamer team opening fire on the enemy. The Antiquarians weren't mostly civilians. They were retired military men and women. They easily found cover, and Nora knew it was a matter of minutes before Mac and Wynona would be surrounded. She sprinted faster.

Anton's fist came at her so fast she didn't have time to duck. Nora reeled at the impact. She fell to a knee and let the spear help prop her up. Anton cursed at her as he attacked like a man possessed. Nora clumsily pivoted and tried to keep him at a distance by jabbing at him with the spear. He tried to grab it, but she was prepared for that and yanked it out of his reach.

A shot rang out, and Anton jerked from the impact. Nora couldn't find the source, but she didn't have to when Wynona came barreling down the rocky path. The red-haired woman took a shot as she ran, and it found its mark on Anton's chest. He collapsed with blood spattered all over. Nora cringed, but she nodded at her in thanks.

Nora continued in her crazy flight toward the source of the curse as Wynona engaged in hand-to-hand combat with an Antiquarian twice her size. Nora wished she could turn back, but if they didn't stop Ulrich now, it wouldn't matter.

Ulrich and Wesley wrestled in the middle of the city's streets.

Nora tried to get a good angle from the back, but the count pivoted, and flames shot from his hands. As it neared its mark, the spear quivered as if guided by an invisible force.

Ulrich's eyes glowed wide as he realized the weapon was not merely a foolish tool. He let out a piercing scream, and the city of gold began to crumble. Nora jammed the spear into the *Materlus'* chest, but she was afraid to push harder because Wesley was behind him with his arms wrapped around the count's neck.

Wesley slammed his feet down and forced Ulrich down an inch by grabbing the black spike on the side of his head. He grasped the spear and leaned forward. Gunfire blasted in the background as the fight raged.

"No!" Nora shouted as the spear impaled them both.

Wesley's lips thinned in pain as he slumped onto Ulrich. The *Materlus* shuddered, and his eyes dimmed. The Revenants froze. The Antiquarians, not engaged in fighting, stopped their chanting and kneeling. Golden rocks fell as the cave rumbled and started to collapse. Gold dust filled the air with corrosive particles that burned in Nora's lungs. She drew her shirt up over her nose and let go of the spear. But not before a spark of power from the spear jolted her right forearm, and Nora cried out in agony as the bone splintered.

She sank to the ground, holding her right arm, blood coating the bone fragments jutting out.

Ulrich contorted and raged at the shock. His black flames extinguished, and he sank into shadow upon the rubble. The artifact beside him burst into fire, and the runes and pictographs melted into gibberish. The stone cracked and shriveled into dust.

People screamed as the debris fell on them. They rushed for the exit, and Nora didn't bother to tell them there wasn't one.

Nora ran to Wesley as he staggered back, the spear impaled in his left side. She cradled her arm and tried to ignore the excruciating pain. She didn't care that there was no way out or about binding the arm—this was the end for them. She wasn't going to leave him. She touched his shoulder as he lay on his back with the spear pointing up. The shaft disappeared in a torrent of black flame.

She glanced over her shoulder. Ulrich's form disintegrated into ash, and all the Revs around him did the same. The still-alive humans wailed or scrabbled like rats for a way to get out. They no longer cared about a new world order or becoming immortal. Nora didn't see Mac or Wynona, and her chest tightened. If they were alive, they'd have come down by now.

Stalactites dropped from the cave ceiling, impaling people, and fire licked the golden walls and spread a glittering smoke throughout the space. Nora hunkered over Wesley and opened her pack. She took out a foldable parka and opened it one-handed, cursing as shocks of agony ran up her right arm at every movement. The plastic wasn't a shield but covered them from the dust and small rocks.

"Let me bind that arm." Wesley weakly grabbed her

hand. He struggled to breathe, and his skin was sickly pale. He was no longer changing into a Rev but dying as a human. "Get out."

Nora shook her head and lay next to him. She put pressure on his wound with her left hand but the warm blood seeping through her fingers wasn't a good sign. She had a first aid kit in the bag, but she didn't think gauze and antiseptic ointment would help. She wasn't ready to give up despite the truth of the reality. Her mom's soothing voice in her head instructed her to stay calm and work slowly to avoid mistakes. Nora sprained her ankle when she was nine from a soccer injury and limped home. She'd expected her mom to make a big fuss and panic, but she'd surprised her by asking when and where the injury occurred. Then she tended to it calmly and said they would go to the ER if Nora felt like it was broken.

Nora took deep breaths even as her brain understood it was futile. She sprinkled rubbing alcohol all over the arm and wound a bandage over it. She nearly blacked out from the pain as the light fabric jarred the bones. Nora had no idea if binding it would help, but it was better than staring at the shattered mess of flesh.

"Get out," Wesley repeated.

"I can't get out even if I wanted to. The entrance was blown to shit in hopes if we didn't stop Ulrich here, we could delay him by trapping him," she said and fought to keep her voice from breaking. He didn't need to see how upset she was. She couldn't even climb now. There was no way out.

"We?" Wesley whispered weakly as the cave collapsed around them. Screams echoed as the torches were extinguished by falling debris; only a few dozen remained.

Fire scalded the walls and melted the city's buildings into pools of lava.

Nora briefly wondered if they'd burn to death before suffocating as the smoke grew thicker and thicker. A cold wind swept through the cave, and the flames died with shrieks as if they were souls. Nora spotted a falling piece of stalactite and used her left forearm to block it. She let out a yelp as it cut through the plastic parka and her jacket. But the piece of lava mineral wasn't big enough to break her other arm. It bounced off and clicked down the rock ledge they were on. Somehow that pain distracted her from the pulsing ache in her right arm, if only for a few minutes.

It was silent.

The magnificent city was reduced to cave rock, and the semi-glowing lichen illuminated the remnants. Their light diffused the gold, and a few torches remained lit. It didn't appear that anyone had survived; if they did, they were unconscious.

"Oliver Gibson and his team. He's here, and he's going to get us out," she said gently. If only they could both believe that.

"You deserve the life I never wanted." Wesley coughed and closed his eyes. "You find a way out of here ... Oliver is on the outside?"

"I think so. Hang on." Nora wiped tears from her cheeks to hide them. Wesley brushed a knuckle over the salty wetness.

"He'll get you out." Wesley was so still for a moment Nora thought he'd left her. His breath was shallow. "Tell my dad and sister that my mom and I died in a caving accident, please. They won't be able to handle the truth."

Nora nodded in an attempt to keep her hands from shaking. "That's a lame death."

Wesley smiled, blood cracking on his lips.

"It is, but that's all I can come up with now. I'm ... I'm glad you're here with me. I don't want to be alone." The admission of vulnerability took all the strength he had left. Nora wiped tears from her cheeks. Wesley closed his eyes, and he didn't open them again this time.

"Neither do I," she whispered.

Nora kept her hand on his chest to assure herself that he was breathing. She'd let him rest for a few minutes but then keep him awake. Maybe she could give him the painkillers, or maybe she should take them for herself. Maybe she could patch the wound. Her mind spun out with the impossible possibilities.

Finally, she lay her head on her forearm next to Wesley's head. Oldies tunes strummed through her thoughts, and she closed her eyes. Just for a minute.

Chapter Forty-Eight

Scratching in the darkness. Pebbles falling like rain.

Nora opened her eyes, and every muscle in her body was stiff. Her right arm lay useless at her side, and it hurt to even think about moving it. Slowly, she scrabbled up to find Wesley's body in the dim light. The torches started fading, and a damp cold invaded the air. The crashing of rocks continued to her left, and Nora swore when she saw Wesley's haggard form shifting rocks. He couldn't stand, so he clumsily threw rocks from a semi-seated position.

Nora could barely stand, and doing so made her nauseous. She swayed and then moved toward him.

"What the hell are you doing?" she asked and grabbed his hand. The rock fell from his weak fingers. The black claws were chipped but still sharp.

Wesley's face was pale even in the dark, and sweat marred his brow.

"Getting you out of here. I'm no survival expert, but the longer we stay quiet, the less likely they'll find us. I heard running water over here, so I'm hoping that means there's an opening somewhere," he said, but his words slurred together. And then he vomited. His hands clutched his abdomen as he wheezed in pain.

"Shit." Nora rushed and eased him back down with her pack as a pillow under his head. Taking care of him distracted her from her wounds, and she was grateful to have something to focus on. She winced at the amount of blood that coated his tattered clothing. He trembled and groaned. His forehead burned when she pressed it with the back of her hand. She sat back with a curse, realizing that whatever Argen had been in him to fend off the curse's change was probably now poisoning him. Besides his gaping wound, he was fighting arsenic, thallium, and lead toxicity. It might not be unlike her situation if they were trapped here much longer. Infection was a real possibility for her as well, with her ravaged arm.

"Okay, let's not give up," she said and took a deep breath to convey a calmness she didn't have. "I'll try for a while." Nora peered up at the darkness and wasn't sure she heard water at all. He was probably hallucinating. Wesley didn't answer as he lay like he was already dead. A faint pulse gave her hope he was hanging on.

The steady dripping of water amidst the otherwise silent cave threatened to make her crazy after ten minutes. She didn't know what time it was. Her phone was broken. The cynical part of her whispered that Wesley would be the lucky one if he died soon. She'd be stuck in the cave for days before dehydration and starvation killed her. Nora bit her lip and refused to give in. It had only been a few hours—there was still time for some hope. When she felt stronger, she'd try to dig and shift rocks again.

She didn't know how long she lay there, but there were voices. She tilted her head to be sure she wasn't imagining them. Nora jolted up and shouted. She threw rocks in the direction of the muffled voices. Groaning and crashing filled the silence. A sliver of light broke through about fifty feet above their heads, and Nora craned to see who was at the top.

"Nora? Wesley?" Oliver's shout echoed in the space.

"Here! We're here, and he needs help immediately!" Nora hoped they could hear her. Ropes snaked down, and within minutes, two men rappelled through the small opening.

She had never been so relieved to see humans. They introduced themselves as park rangers, and one was a paramedic. She explained the Argen or Hutchinsonite poisoning, and the medic's eyes widened. He bent low over Wesley with brows knitted together and snapped orders so fast that Nora had trouble following them.

Luckily, his partner didn't. A stretcher was lowered, and Wesley loaded on it. The paramedic did take a cursory look at her arm and told her to stay still. Nora waited an agonizing fifteen minutes before they repelled down and took her up. She grabbed her pack as they secured her in a harness. The lift took a precarious ten minutes, and Nora barely had the strength to cling to the ranger. It seemed like her body was numb to more pain, but a jolt at the top had her crying out.

She was helped up and out by Oliver's hand. The US marshal's face seemed to have aged fifteen years. He pulled her into a light hug despite her injuries and then roughly let go as if he weren't used to physical affection. Nora shook his hand.

"Thank you. Are they getting Wesley to a hospital? Is there one nearby still standing?" She fired out questions as quickly as lightning.

Oliver raised a hand. "You're going to the hospital as well, and he's on his way in a chopper. I'd love to ask you what happened, but I can wait. I'm ... glad you're alive." His tone said what Nora suspected—no one thought they'd make it out. "Is it over?"

Nora nodded as reassuringly as she could. "Ulrich was destroyed, and I assume his curse with it. Are there Revs still walking around?"

She answered her own question when she looked around the hole. The cave had sunk in the explosion. Hundreds of dead bodies lay around it: the Revs who hadn't been able to get in when Oliver and his guys blew up the entrance. Nora's head pounded, and she swayed on her feet. So many dead. They hadn't vanished into ash—they were human again.

Oliver motioned to a paramedic, and they took her to sit in an ambulance. Police were moving the bodies and trying to identify them. There was so much work to do.

"One step at a time. I'll be in touch, I promise. I suspect most of what happened will be covered up or misrepresented, but you stick to whatever story you want to tell." Oliver did a good job keeping police and detectives away from her. Nora heard mumbles of bringing in the FBI and CIA as well. She cringed. Would they believe her? It would seem like all the intelligence and military forces of the United States would want a version of the truth. She didn't know if any of them would agree with it.

Nora spied Oliver holding a familiar black Stetson hat. Her lips turned up, and her throat bobbed. She prayed she'd see it on Wesley's head again.

CHAPTER FORTY-NINE

IN THE WEEKS AFTER THE CURSE WAS BROKEN, THE digital world snapped back to important business; like Instagram and TikTok influencers, how much loot people had gotten, political debates on whether the President should be impeached for his response to the crisis, and puppies spilling their food in adorable ways. Nora tapped her new phone's screen and avoided social media. The news app flashed, but she ignored that too.

She sat in a cushioned chair next to Wesley's bed and waited for the nurse to come with his medication. Her right arm, bound in a cast, itched. Nora rubbed it as if that would help the dry skin.

Wesley was awake after forty-eight hours, having been in a medically induced coma where he'd undergone surgery for the spear wound and drastic flushing of his system. Most of the Argen was out. The doctor said he'd have residual effects, but no one was sure what they would be. His intense dark brown eyes looked at her in a way she never tired of. He'd lost some weight being on a liquid diet, but the hollows in his cheeks would fill in over time. The razor-sharp cheekbones framing his square jaw now sported scars.

"Do you think I'll Hulk-out someday?" Wesley asked with a hoarse laugh. He moved his fingers, which bore scars, as did most of his body. No more black claws, though, only bruised fingers and missing nails.

Nora grinned. "I hope not because I don't think I can handle that." She tried to keep his attitude positive as he'd woken up in immense pain and unable to move his legs. That had subsided, but he'd have to undergo months of physiotherapy. She was thankful beyond measure that he was alive. The surgeons had been impressed.

"You can handle anything." Wesley pushed hair off his cheek, and the bruises on his face shadowed his skin. "I noticed you're not counting your fingers or watching the door."

Nora blew out a relieved breath. Her OCD had calmed way down to practically nothing. Fear had taken a back seat to simply living with the uncontrollable. Nora accepted that bad things happened but it was how she dealt with them mattered. She knew her parents and Emin would be proud of her survival, and it was time to move forward again. Nora would be in therapy for a while after this, but she would also use that to further her interest in being a counselor or psychologist.

"Yeah, all it took was an ancient curse and Revenants to bump me over the edge into being semi-normal," she said with a shake of her head. "I want to finish college and get my doctorate in psych eventually."

"I think you should. How's the arm?"

"Eight weeks to heal, eh," Nora said and lifted her

injured arm slightly. "Nothing compared to what you're going through."

Wesley waved his hand dismissively and then winced at the movement.

"I want to take you out on a real date when I get out." Wesley leaned back on two pillows. IVs and catheter lines ran from his bed to machines like veins. Nora didn't like looking at them, but she made herself. She was not going to live in fear any longer. She couldn't have controlled or been prepared when her parents or her uncle died. But she could control how she lived and possibly help others who couldn't see a way out.

"I'd like that."

Nora was about to ask if he liked Italian or Mexican food better when two men in black suits passed the window. They were middle-aged and appeared to be in good shape with slim physiques and short haircuts. The older man had silver-streaked hair at his temples and dark tanned skin. He reminded her of someone. He wore glasses and took them off as the US marshal on duty—appointed by Oliver—stopped them. There was muffled arguing through the glass, and Nora exchanged glances with Wesley.

"Tell Dan to let them in," Wesley said with a sigh. "What else could happen, right?"

Nora shot him a look but got up and opened the door. Dan cocked his head as she told him Wesley permitted the visitors.

"Pardon the interruption. May we have a word, Ms. Moon and Mr. Soares?" The man's British accent lilted pleasantly, and his tone was friendly. He wore a crisp navy suit with a beige shirt and boots. For some reason, his presence reminded her of sand-swept dunes, palm trees, and exotic cuisine. He radiated an African desert vibe, a treasure hunter's confidence. There was something familiar about him. It couldn't be … Nora frowned. He looked remarkably like Alazar, but he'd died in the cave-in, right? She glanced at Wesley, but his face remained neutral.

The other man had dimples on his cheeks and lines around his eyes and mouth. He was darker skinned with curly hair and wore silver rings on his fingers. They stood like ancient pillars of authority. They also had the Antiquarian tattoo on the right side of their necks, the tell-tale rune with a dagger in the infinity snake with a skull for a head. He'd noticed their tattoos as well, and his face darkened. "Never mind, Dan, get them out."

The British man half-bowed and held his hands out innocently. "May I please have two minutes? I fear there's been a huge miscommunication, and we're doing all we can to unravel this."

Nora crossed her arms and thought better of it as the cast got in the way. She settled for putting one hand on her hip and glaring.

Wesley managed to sit straighter. He ran a hand through disheveled dark hair. "If Nora wants to hear you out, fine."

Nora stepped back protectively at the foot of Wesley's bed and looked for a weapon. She spied a pen and grabbed it. It wasn't great, but even the metal chair could do some damage if she used it correctly. The man seemed to follow her train of thought and kept his distance.

"Let me introduce myself. I am Alazar Jelani, and this is my colleague, Peter Wright. We are the head of the Antiquarian Matrix society." Alazar stopped at their dual intake of breath. He cocked his head with a sigh. "Your reaction has been similar to the others we've interviewed."

Wesley grunted. "Then you either have a brother with the same name, or someone was impersonating you. Or there's another bizarre ancient secret we don't know about." He looked at Nora. "He died in the cave, right?"

Nora swallowed. The other Alazar had done a good job impersonating the man before her. They weren't exact twins, but they had the same hair, eye color, and build. All things easy to alter. "He bled out. I read the official list, and that name was on it."

Alazar reached into his jacket pocket slowly. "I'm going to take my phone and show you a picture."

Nora did not relax. She and Wesley peered at a clear image of Alazar. The supposed Alazar they'd traveled with, had been kidnapped by, and to whom they'd willingly given up the artifact. Nora wrapped her arms around her stomach. She was already guilty of her role in the betrayal, but this hurt worse. The picture showed a man similar in appearance to the Alazar standing before them, but upon close inspection, the nose was bigger and less pointed, the cheekbones not quite as angular, and the skin tone not quite as tanned. Nora glanced up and down several times, and then Alazar moved to show Wesley.

"So, you're saying this Alazar was fake? He pretended to be you? Or are *you* pretending to be him?" Nora accused. She couldn't wrap her head around how a man could have fooled so many people in the Antiquarian Matrix society.

Alazar nodded with pursed lips. "He sent me on a wild goose chase to the Mali desert, and by the time I figured it out, all air travel was banned. The curse spread for a few months, but in that time, it certainly brought out every flaw in the system and every evil in humanity." He seemed to get caught up in his philosophical musings.

Peter spoke. "This man, Aaron Yattara, was indoctrinated into the society ten years ago, and he'd been planning this for quite some time. His partner, Anton Becker, was who he said he was. He was instrumental in staging the coup." He fidgeted with a watch on his right wrist. "Alazar's assassination was supposed to have happened in the desert."

Alazar unbuttoned his jacket and opened his shirt.

"I don't need a candy striper, dude," Wesley said but with a twinkle in his eye.

Alazar took it with the intended humor. "I want to prove our story as much as I can." He tugged his shirt over his right shoulder, and an angry wound puckered his skin. It was so close to his heart that Nora was surprised he was alive.

"The sniper couldn't predict to the milli-second the desert winds, and they saved my life."

"Or he was a crap sniper," Wesley said, and both men chuckled.

Alazar fixed his shirt. Nora couldn't help but notice other scars across his chest and abdomen. Clearly, he'd seen some action.

"I knew your uncle, Nora. I'm sorry for his murder. We want to pay for the funeral costs and a headstone or whatever you need." Alazar bowed his head.

Nora still didn't trust him or the Antiquarian Society, but it was a nice offer.

"I remember he liked so much cream and sugar in his coffee, I told him he should heat up ice cream," Alazar said with soft amusement. "He told me he'd found something amazing overseas and wanted to take the credit for it. I would never have begrudged him because he was the hardest worker I knew. And he always made you a priority, even if it didn't feel like it sometimes, I'm sure."

Nora blinked at the burn in her eyes and nodded. All those details were so Emin that her instincts told her to believe this man. This Alazar.

"We shall let you rest, but please contact us if you need anything." Alazar handed them each a card. "Or if you want to know about the real Antiquarian Matrix. I promise we're not all out to destroy the world. The world is doing a fine job on its own."

"I can't argue with that." Nora shook his hand awkwardly since her dominant hand was in a cast.

"There's going to be a lot of confusion in the coming years, and this isn't over. Timbuktu, Musa's empire, spans so much land that many artifacts are lost. There are also moles in our society that need to be found." Alazar smiled confidently. "And we will find them, but it will take time."

Nora sat on the edge of Wesley's bed as the two men left. Dan checked in to make sure things were good, and she thanked him. Wesley closed his eyes and sighed.

"Do you want me to go so you can rest?" She gathered her purse, but he reached out for her. Nora stroked his arm and sat in the chair next to him.

"No." Wesley played with the buttons on the remote and tilted his head at her.

Nora's face warmed, and her heart thudded loudly. He'd meant what he'd said in the cave. He didn't want to be alone anymore. She didn't know if that meant he'd changed his mind about the white picket fence with two-point-five kids, but it was something she had to think about too. All she knew for certain was that she'd found someone she trusted implicitly. How many people were that lucky?

"So, did we save the world, only to find out it's pretty much all for nothing?" Nora asked with a sigh. "Should I even bother going back to school?" Wesley joined her in laughter until he was in too much pain.

"I got halfway turned into an undead freak and pumped full of poison, and there's a possibility more Alazars are out there unearthing artifacts that will bring about another apocalypse. So, you might as well finish school. You never know when you'll need to psychoanalyze the undead again." Wesley snorted, and they both attempted to stop laughing again.

"You said the family life wasn't the life for you. Maybe chasing dangerous artifacts is." Nora wiped tears from her eyes, and it felt good to smile so much. "We can contact Alazar when you're out of here and find out what's going on. We can be the anti-Antiquarians."

Wesley grinned and looked at her. "I'd be open to revising my life plan. I think I'll stay with the marshal service if you understand the hazards of the job."

"Of course."

Nora ducked her head under the heat of his gaze. His answer assuaged any doubt in her mind as to whether they'd have a life together. Nora tried to imagine miniatures of them running around someday, and that both terrified and thrilled her. She was happy that he'd finally chosen the path she always knew he was right for, even if it scared him. That's where she came in, and she wouldn't change that for the world.

She was glad of another interruption because speaking of intimate feelings wasn't her strong suit either. Oliver Gibson knocked on the window, and they motioned him in. The older man held Wesley's black Stetson in his hands.

"Like every good movie ending, I'm here with the hat," Oliver said, placing the hat with a soft thunk on the table beside Wesley.

Nora couldn't wait to see it on him again. Perhaps wearing less. She shared a look with Wesley that said he thought the same thing about her.

"Some damn protestor egged my car in the parking lot," Oliver grumbled as he took a seat, oblivious to the pair's exchange. "Now that there's no threat of the undead, people are back to their usual bat-shit crazy."

Nora sat back in the chair. The world was almost back to where it had begun. As long as humans populated the space, they would find ways to kill and hate each other. Ulrich's curse and the Revenant destruction only masked the real problem. She held her hands steady in her lap. There was a slight urge to count her fingers. She was confident now she wanted to finish school and go into counseling.

The system might take a bit to get back on track, but Nora bet most people would try to ignore what had happened. They'd want to get back to "normal" as fast as possible. The old Nora was banished, and her routine blown to shreds. She wanted to explore new possibilities without constraints.

Wesley spoke with Oliver, and she turned her attention back to them.

"You said something about quitting the marshals," Oliver said, squinting. "You still stand by that?"

Wesley shook his head. Nora understood he needed to be needed, as odd as it sounded for such a loner.

"No, sir. But I am taking some time off. Maybe see my dad and Becca," Wesley said with a glance at her. Nora nodded. She couldn't say she was excited to meet what was left of his family, but she would support him if he wanted to try a different approach. They didn't speak of Loretta, and Nora would let him decide what to tell his family.

"Good. I'll expect to hear from you within a month, then." Oliver winked. "Now, I'm hearing the name Alazar a lot, and I feel like you two can explain that to me."

Wesley handed Oliver the business card Alazar left. "When you call him, tell him we want two new gaming laptops, yes, laptops because we've got to be able to move, with top-of-the-line mice and headsets."

The marshal took it with a raised brow. "What sort of request is that? I will be hitting him hard with a lot of red tape and questions."

"He will do whatever we want because he wants us to give him what he needs. Information," Wesley said with a nod. Nora grinned. She was glad he'd requested something mobile because she'd had the same thought. PC rigs were better, but laptops had their place for her.

"Good thing the internet didn't completely die during the crisis. I mean, undead on top of no internet would have ruined the world for certain," she said.

"We have some marauding to do." Wesley put his hat on, and Nora adjusted it to a jaunty angle.

"That's not a pirate hat, mate."

"Where's your imagination, Moonbeam?"

Nora ignored Oliver's thoroughly confused look as she leaned over to kiss him. His lips were rough, calloused, and dry, but they'd never felt better. There were seas to sail and deserts to cross. She'd found someone to keep the ghosts from making her crazy, and she was sure her dad would approve. Her mom would have liked Wesley's no-nonsense attitude, and in the short time Emin was with him, there was at least some trust between them. Emin would have loved Wesley the more he got to know him; Nora was certain of that. If she could survive the undead, she could survive committing to a man who loved her. She touched her mom's infinity necklace that survived along with her. It was time to stop living in fear. *Unchained Melody* softly crooned in the back of her head as she thought about the future.

ACKNOWLEDGMENTS

To you, the readers, who keep writers' dreams alive, and the storytellers who spread magic. I hope this story gives you an escape for just a moment!

Thank you to Rising Action Publishing Collective, Tina and Alex, who took a chance and made this book a reality. Their amazing eye for details, incredible hard work, and passion for books inspires me and makes me work even harder.

To my critique partners and circle of writers who are always there for me and storyboard hypothetical scenarios anytime: Grace Prince, Joy Thomas, K.C. Aegis.

Thank you to the endless number of people who have given me shout-outs, read ARC's, and supported me even if they hadn't met me in real life: Valorie, Daniel, Don Bentley, Heather Cavill. What a wonderful community to be part of.

Thank you to my mom friends who keep me sane: Sara, Shelby, Andrea, and Donna T. for reading even though it's not her genre of choice and for getting me back to horses!

A huge thank you to my parents who have always believed that whatever I wanted to do would be successful. The writing wouldn't have happened without you taking me on adventures and dad for having Indiana Jones, Star Wars, and Lord of the Rings marathons. Thank you for taking on the kids as well so I could write/edit!

And of course, a special thank you to my family; my kiddos who inspire me with their curiosity and enthusiasm for life. But mostly to Greg, who enables me to fly around chasing dragons and dreams! You not only embrace the words (and jokes) but make them come to life in crazy pictures. Thank you.

ABOUT THE AUTHOR

E.A. Field lives in Chicago, and before deciding to write full-time, she tried to make her creative brain conform to a career in veterinary medicine. She directs the goat rodeo that is her home with her husband and a zoo of animals and children, which always includes rescue dogs. When she's not writing, she's painting, thinking up Cosplay ideas, reading, gaming, horseback riding, and honing apocalyptic life skills. She has been previously published, under the pen name Anne Bourne, with the fantasy romance *Blue Moon*, and her short story—featuring a character from *IRL*—is included in the post- apocalyptic anthology *Through the Aftermath*.